# Saga Six Pack 7

# Saga Six Pack 7

By

Emilie Kip Baker

Benjamin Franklin DeCosta

Thomas Wentworth Higginson

Florence Holbrook

Jean Lang

Snorri Sturluson

Enhanced Media
2016

*Saga Six Pack 7*

*Tales of the Enchanted Islands of the Atlantic* by Thomas Wentworth Higginson. First published in 1899.

*Saga of King Harald Grafeld and of Earl Hakon Son of Sigurd* by Snorri Sturluson. From *The Heimskringla: or, Chronicle of the kings of Norway*. Translated by Samuel Laing. First published in 1844.

*The Death of Baldur* by Jean Song. From *A Book of Myths* by Jean Lang. First published in 1914.

*The Story of the Magic Mead* by Emilie Kip Baker. From *Stories from Northern Myths* by Emilie Kip Baker. First published in 1914.

*The Viking's Code* by Florence Holbrook. From *Northland Heroes* by Florence Holbrook. First published in 1909.

*The Pre-Columbian Discovery of America by the Northmen* by Benjamin Franklin DeCosta. First published in 1890.

*The Sagas* by Andrew Lang. From *Essays in Little* by Andrew Lang. First published in 1891.

*Saga Six Pack 7*. Published 2016 by Enhanced Media.

Enhanced Media Publishing
Los Angeles, CA.

First Printing: 2016.

ISBN-13: 978-1532707629

ISBN-10: 1532707622

# Contents

Tales of the Enchanted Islands of the Atlantic by Thomas Wentworth Higginson ................................................................. 7

NOTES ................................................................................ 90

Saga of King Harald Grafeld and of Earl Hakon Son of Sigurd by Snorri Sturluson ........................................... 110

The Death of Baldur by Jean Song ........................................ 125

The Story of the Magic Mead by Emilie Kip Baker ......... 132

The Viking's Code by Florence Holbrook ......................... 137

The Pre-Columbian Discovery of America by the Northmen by Benjamin Franklin DeCosta ............................. 138

Major Narratives (Pre-Columbian Discovery) ............... 162

Minor Narratives ................................................................. 196

# Tales of the Enchanted Islands of the Atlantic by Thomas Wentworth Higginson

THE STORY OF ATLANTIS

The Greek sage Socrates, when he was but a boy minding his father's goats, used to lie on the grass under the myrtle trees; and, while the goats grazed around him, he loved to read over and over the story which Solon, the law-giver and poet, wrote down for the great-grandfather of Socrates, and which Solon had always meant to make into a poem, though he died without doing it. But this was briefly what he wrote in prose:—

"I, Solon, was never in my life so surprised as when I went to Egypt for instruction in my youth, and there, in the temple of Sais, saw an aged priest who told me of the island of Atlantis, which was sunk in the sea thousands of years ago. He said that in the division of the earth the gods agreed that the god Poseidon, or Neptune, should have, as his share, this great island which then lay in the ocean west of the Mediterranean Sea, and was larger than all Asia. There was a mortal maiden there whom Poseidon wished to marry, and to secure her he surrounded the valley where she dwelt with three rings of sea and two of land so that no one could enter; and he made underground springs, with water hot or cold, and supplied all things needful to the life of man. Here he lived with her for many years, and they had ten sons; and these sons divided the island among them and had many children, who dwelt there for more than a thousand years. They had mines of gold and silver, and pastures for elephants, and many fragrant plants. They erected palaces and dug canals; and they built their temples of white, red, and black stone, and covered them with gold and silver. In these were statues of gold, especially one of the god Poseidon driving six winged horses. He was so large as to touch the roof with his head, and had a hundred water-nymphs around him, riding on dolphins. The islanders had also baths and gardens and sea-walls, and they had twelve hundred ships and ten thousand chariots. All this was in the royal city alone, and the people were friendly and good and well-affectioned towards all. But as time went on they grew less so, and they did not obey the laws, so that they offended heaven. In a single day and night the island disappeared and sank beneath the sea; and this is why the sea in that region grew so impassable and impenetrable, because there is a quantity of shallow mud in the way, and this was caused by the sinking of a single vast island."

"This is the tale," said Solon, "which the old Egyptian priest told to me." And Solon's tale was read by Socrates, the boy, as he lay in the grass; and he told it to his friends after he grew up, as is written in his dialogues recorded by his disciple, Plato. And though this great island of Atlantis has never been seen again, yet a great many smaller islands have been found in the Atlantic Ocean, and they have sometimes been lost to sight and found again.

There is, also, in this ocean a vast tract of floating seaweed, called by sailors the Sargasso Sea,—covering a region as large as France,—and this has been thought by many to mark the place of a sunken island. There are also many islands, such as the Azores, which have been supposed at different times to be fragments of Atlantis; and besides all this, the remains of the vanished island have been looked for in all parts of the world. Some writers have thought it was in Sweden, others in Spitzbergen, others in Africa, in Palestine, in America. Since the depth of the Atlantic has been more thoroughly sounded, a few writers have maintained that the inequalities of its floor show some traces of the submerged Atlantis, but the general opinion of men of science is quite the other way. The visible Atlantic islands are all, or almost all, they say, of volcanic origin; and though there are ridges in the bottom of the ocean, they do not connect the continents.

At any rate, this was the original story of Atlantis, and the legends which follow in these pages have doubtless all grown, more or less, out of this first tale which Socrates told.

## TALIESSIN OF THE RADIANT BROW

In times past there were enchanted islands in the Atlantic Ocean, off the coast of Wales, and even now the fishermen sometimes think they see them. On one of these there lived a man named Tegid Voel and his wife called Cardiwen. They had a son, the ugliest boy in the world, and Cardiwen formed a plan to make him more attractive by teaching him all possible wisdom. She was a great magician and resolved to boil a large caldron full of knowledge for her son, so that he might know all things and be able to predict all that was to happen. Then she thought people would value him in spite of his ugliness. But she knew that the caldron must burn a year and a day without ceasing, until three blessed drops of the water of knowledge were obtained from it; and those three drops would give all the wisdom she wanted.

So she put a boy named Gwion to stir the caldron and a blind man named Morda to feed the fire; and made them promise never to let it cease boiling for a year and a day. She herself kept gathering magic herbs and putting them into it. One day when the year was nearly over, it chanced that three drops of the liquor flew out of the caldron and fell on the finger of Gwion. They were fiery hot, and he put his finger to his mouth, and the instant he tasted them he knew that they were the enchanted drops for which so much trouble had been taken. By their magic he at once foresaw all that was to come, and especially that Cardiwen the enchantress would never forgive him.

Then Gwion fled. The caldron burst in two, and all the liquor flowed forth, poisoning some horses which drank it. These horses belonged to a king named Gwyddno. Cardiwen came in and saw all the toil of the whole year lost. Seizing a stick of wood, she struck the blind man Morda fiercely on the head, but he said, "I am innocent. It was not I who did it." "True," said Cardiwen; "it was the boy Gwion who robbed me;" and she rushed to pursue him. He saw her and fled, changing into a hare; but she became a greyhound and followed him. Running to the water, he became a fish; but she became another and chased him below the waves. He turned himself into a bird, when she became a hawk and gave him no rest in the sky. Just as she swooped on him, he espied a pile of winnowed wheat on the floor of a barn, and dropping upon it, he became one of the wheat-grains. Changing herself into a high-crested black hen, Cardiwen scratched him up and swallowed him, when he changed at last into a boy again and was so beautiful that she could not kill him outright, but wrapped him in a leathern bag and cast him into the sea, committing him to the mercy of God. This was on the twenty-ninth of April.

Now Gwyddno had a weir for catching fish on the sea-strand near his castle, and every day in May he was wont to take a hundred pounds' worth of fish. He had a son named Elphin, who was always poor and unsuccessful, but that year the father had given the son leave to draw all the fish from the weir, to see if good luck would ever befall him and give him something with which to begin the world.

When Elphin went next to draw the weir, the man who had charge of it said in pity, "Thou art always unlucky; there is nothing in the weir but a leathern bag, which is caught on one of the poles." "How do we know," said Elphin, "that it may not contain the value of a hundred pounds?" Taking up the bag and opening it, the man saw the forehead of the boy and said to Elphin, "Behold, what a radiant brow" (Taliessin). "Let him be called Taliessin," said Elphin. Then he lifted the boy and placed him sorrowfully behind him; and made his horse amble gently, that before had been trotting, and carried him as softly as if he had been sitting in the easiest chair in the world, and the boy of the radiant brow made a song to Elphin as they went along.

> "Never in Gwyddno's weir
> Was there such good luck as this night.
> Fair Elphin, dry thy cheeks!
> Being too sad will not avail,
> Although thou thinkest thou hast no gain.
> Too much grief will bring thee no good;
> Nor doubt the miracles of the Almighty:
> Although I am but little, I am highly gifted.
> From seas, and from mountains,
> And from the depths of rivers,
> God brings wealth to the fortunate man.
> Elphin of lively qualities,
> Thy resolution is unmanly:
> Thou must not be over sorrowful:
> Better to trust in God than to forebode ill.
> Weak and small as I am,
> On the foaming beach of the ocean,
> In the day of trouble I shall be
> Of more service to thee than three hundred salmon.
> Elphin of notable qualities,
> Be not displeased at thy misfortune:
> Although reclined thus weak in my bag,
> There lies a virtue in my tongue.
> While I continue thy protector
> Thou hast not much to fear."

Then Elphin asked him, "Art thou man or spirit?" And in answer the boy sang to him this tale of his flight from the woman:—

> "I have fled with vigor, I have fled as a frog,
> I have fled in the semblance of a crow scarcely finding rest;
> I have fled vehemently, I have fled as a chain of lightning,
> I have fled as a roe into an entangled thicket;
> I have fled as a wolf-cub, I have fled as a wolf in the wilderness,
> I have fled as a fox used to many swift bounds and quirks;
> I have fled as a martin, which did not avail;
> I have fled as a squirrel that vainly hides,

I have fled as a stag's antler, of ruddy course,
I have fled as an iron in a glowing fire,
I have fled as a spear-head, of woe to such as have a wish for it;
I have fled as a fierce bull bitterly fighting,
I have fled as a bristly boar seen in a ravine,
I have fled as a white grain of pure wheat;
Into a dark leathern bag I was thrown,
And on a boundless sea I was sent adrift;
Which was to me an omen of being tenderly nursed,
And the Lord God then set me at liberty."

Then Elphin came with Taliessin to the house of his father, and Gwyddno asked him if he had a good haul at the fish-weir. "I have something better than fish." "What is that?" asked the father. "I have a bard," said Elphin. "Alas, what will he profit thee?" said Gwyddno, to which Taliessin replied, "He will profit him more than the weir ever profited thee." Said Gwyddno, "Art thou able to speak, and thou so little?" Then Taliessin said, "I am better able to speak than thou to question me."

From this time Elphin always prospered, and he and his wife cared for Taliessin tenderly and lovingly, and the boy dwelt with him until he was thirteen years old, when Elphin went to make a Christmas visit to his uncle Maelgwyn, who was a great king and held open court. There were four and twenty bards there, and all proclaimed that no king had a wife so beautiful as the queen, or a bard so wise as the twenty-four, who all agreed upon this decision. Elphin said, on the contrary, that it was he himself who had the most beautiful wife and the wisest bard, and for this he was thrown into prison. Taliessin learning this, set forth from home to visit the palace and free his adoptive father, Elphin.

In those days it was the custom of kings to sit in the hall and dine in royal state with lords and bards about them who should keep proclaiming the greatness and glory of the king and his knights. Taliessin placed himself in a quiet corner, waiting for the four and twenty bards to pass, and as each one passed by, Taliessin made an ugly face, and gave a sound with his finger on his lips, thus, "Blerwm, Blerwm." Each bard went by and bowed himself before the king, but instead of beginning to chant his praises, could only play "Blerwm, Blerwm" on the lips, as the boy had done. The king was amazed and thought they must be intoxicated, so he sent one of his lords to them, telling them to behave themselves and remember where they were. Twice and thrice he told them, but they could only repeat the same foolishness, until at last the king ordered one of his squires to give a blow to the chief bard, and the squire struck him a blow with a broom, so that he fell back on his seat. Then he arose and knelt before the king, and said, "Oh, honorable king, be it known unto your grace that it is not from too much drinking that we are dumb, but through the influence of a spirit which sits in the corner yonder in the form of a child." Then the king bade a squire to bring Taliessin before him, and he asked the boy who he was. He answered:—

"Primary chief bard I am to Elphin,
And my original country is the region of the summer stars;
I am a wonder whose origin is not known;
I have been fostered in the land of the Deity,
I have been teacher to all intelligences,
I am able to instruct the whole universe.
I was originally little Gwion,
And at length I am Taliessin."

Then the king and his nobles wondered much, for they had never heard the like from a boy so young. The king then called his wisest bard to answer Taliessin, but he could only play "Blerwm" on his lips as before, and each of the king's four and twenty bards tried in the same way and could do nothing more. Then the king bade Taliessin sing again, and he began:—

"Discover thou what is
The strong creature from before the flood,
Without flesh, without bone,
Without vein, without blood,
Without head, without feet;
It will neither be older nor younger
Than at the beginning;
Great God! how the sea whitens
When first it comes!
Great are its gusts
When it comes from the south;
Great are its evaporations
When it strikes on coasts.
It is in the field, it is in the wood,
Without hand and without foot,
Without signs of old age,
It is also so wide,
As the surface of the earth;
And it was not born,

Nor was it seen.
It will cause consternation
Wherever God willeth.
On sea and on land

It neither sees, nor is seen.
Its course is devious,
And will not come when desired.
On land and on sea
It is indispensable.
It is without equal,
It is many-sided;
It is not confined,
It is incomparable;
It comes from four quarters;
It is noxious, it is beneficial;
It is yonder, it is here;
It will decompose,
But it will not repair the injury;
It will not suffer for its doings,
Seeing it is blameless.
One Being has prepared it,
Out of all creatures,
By a tremendous blast,
To wreak vengeance
On Maelgwyn Gwynedd."

And while he was thus singing his verse near the door, there came suddenly a mighty storm of wind, so that the king and all his nobles thought the castle would fall on their heads. They saw that Taliessin had not merely been singing the song of the wind, but seemed to have power to command it. Then the king hastily ordered that Elphin should be brought from his dungeon and placed before Taliessin, and the chains came loose from his feet, and he was set free.

As they rode away from the court, the king and his courtiers rode with them, and Taliessin bade Elphin propose a race with the king's horses. Four and twenty horses were chosen, and Taliessin got four and twenty twigs of holly which he had burnt black, and he ordered the youth who was to ride Elphin's horse to let all the others set off before him, and bade him as he overtook each horse to strike him with a holly twig and throw it down. Then he had him watch where his own horse should stumble and throw down his cap at the place. The race being won, Taliessin brought his master to the spot where the cap lay; and put workmen to dig a hole there. When they had dug deeply enough they found a caldron full of gold, and Taliessin said, "Elphin, this is my payment to thee for having taken me from the water and reared me until now." And on this spot stands a pool of water until this day.

## THE SWAN-CHILDREN OF LIR

King Lir of Erin had four young children who were cared for tenderly at first by their stepmother, the new queen; but there came a time when she grew jealous of the love their father bore them, and resolved that she would endure it no longer. Sometimes there was murder in her heart, but she could not bear the thought of that wickedness, and she resolved at last to choose another way to rid herself of them. One day she took them to drive in her chariot:—Finola, who was eight years old, with her three younger brothers,—Aodh, Fiacre, and little Conn, still a baby. They were beautiful children, the legend says, with skins white and soft as swans' feathers, and with large blue eyes and very sweet voices. Reaching a lake, she told them that they might bathe in the clear water; but so soon as they were in it she struck them with a fairy wand,—for she was of the race of the Druids, who had magical power,—and she turned them into four beautiful snow-white swans. But they still had human voices, and Finola said to her, "This wicked deed of thine shall be punished, for the doom that awaits thee will surely be worse than ours." Then Finola asked, "How long shall we be in the shape of swans?" "For three hundred years," said the woman, "on smooth Lake Darvra; then three hundred years on the sea of Moyle" (this being the sea between Ireland and Scotland); "and then three hundred years at Inis Glora, in the Great Western Sea" (this was a rocky island in the Atlantic). "Until the Tailkenn (St. Patrick) shall come to Ireland and bring the Christian faith, and until you hear the Christian bell, you shall not be freed. Neither your power nor mine can now bring you back to human shape; but you shall keep your human reason and your Gaelic speech, and you shall sing music so sweet that all who hear it shall gladly listen."

She left them, and ere long their father, King Lir, came to the shore and heard their singing. He asked how they came to have human voices. "We are thy four children," said Finola, "changed into swans by our stepmother's jealousy." "Then come and live with me," said her sorrowing father. "We are not permitted to leave the lake," she said, "or live with our people any more. But we are allowed to dwell together and to keep our reason and our speech, and to sing sweet music to you." Then they sang, and the king and all his followers were at first amazed and then lulled to sleep.

Then King Lir returned and met the cruel stepmother at her father's palace. When her father, King Bove, was told what she had done, he was hot with anger. "This wicked deed," he said, "shall bring severer punishment on thee than on the innocent children, for their suffering shall end, but thine never shall." Then King Bove asked her what form of existence would be most terrible to her. She replied, "That of a demon of the air." "Be it so," said her father, who had also Druidical power. He struck her with his wand, and she became a bat, and flew away with a scream, and the legend says, "She is still a demon of the air and shall be a demon of the air until the end of time."

After this, the people of all the races that were in Erin used to come and encamp by the lake and listen to the swans. The happy were made happier by the song, and those who were in grief or illness or pain forgot their sorrows and were lulled to rest. There was peace in all that region, while war and tumult filled other lands. Vast changes took place in three centuries—towers and castles rose and fell, villages were built and destroyed, generations were born and died;—and still the swan-children lived and sang, until at the end of three hundred years they flew away, as was decreed, to the stormy sea of Moyle; and from that time it was made a law that no one should kill a swan in Erin.

Beside the sea of Moyle they found no longer the peaceful and wooded shores they had known, but only steep and rocky coasts and a wild, wild sea. There came a great storm one night, and the swans knew that they could not keep together, so they resolved that if separated they would meet at a rock called Carricknarone. Finola reached there first, and took her brothers under her wings, all wet, shivering, and exhausted. Many such nights followed, and in one terrible winter storm, when they nestled together on Carricknarone, the water froze into solid ice around them, and their feet and wings were so frozen to the rock that when they moved they left the skin of their feet, the quills of their wings, and the feathers of their breasts clinging there. When the ice melted, and they swam out into the sea, their bodies smarted with pain until the feathers grew once more.

One day they saw a glittering troop of horsemen approaching along the shore and knew that they were their own kindred, though from far generations back, the Dedannen or Fairy Host. They greeted each other with joy, for the Fairy Host had been sent to seek for the swans; and on returning to their chiefs they narrated what had passed, and the chiefs said, "We cannot help them, but we are glad they are living; and we know that at last the enchantment will be broken and that they will be freed from their sorrows." So passed their lives until Finola sang, one day, "The Second Woe has passed—the second period of three hundred years," when they flew out on the broad ocean, as was decreed, and went to the island of Inis Glora. There they spent the next three hundred years, amid yet wilder storms and yet colder winds. No more the peaceful shepherds and living neighbors were around them; but often the sailor and fisherman, in his little coracle, saw the white gleam of their wings or heard the sweet notes of their song and knew that the children of Lir were near.

But the time came when the nine hundred years of banishment were ended, and they might fly back to their father's old home, Finnahà. Flying for days above the sea, they alighted at the palace once so well known, but everything was changed by time—even the walls of their father's palace were crumbled and rain-washed. So sad was the sight that they remained one day only, and flew back to Inis Glora, thinking that if they must be forever solitary, they would live where they had lived last, not where they had been reared.

One May morning, as the children of Lir floated in the air around the island of Inis Glora, they heard a faint bell sounding across the eastern sea. The mist lifted, and they saw afar off, beyond the waves, a vision of a stately white-robed priest, with attendants around him on the Irish shore. They knew that it must be St. Patrick, the Tailkenn, or Tonsured One, who was bringing, as had been so long promised, Christianity to Ireland. Sailing through the air, above the blue sea, towards their native coast, they heard the bell once more, now near and distinct, and they knew that all evil spirits were fleeing away, and that their own hopes were to be fulfilled. As they approached the land, St. Patrick stretched his hand and said, "Children of Lir, you may tread your native land again." And the sweet swan-sister, Finola, said, "If we tread our native land, it can only be to die, after our life of nine centuries. Baptize us while we are yet living." When they touched the shore, the weight of all those centuries fell upon them; they resumed their human bodies, but they appeared old and pale and wrinkled. Then St. Patrick baptized them, and they died; but, even as he did so, a change swiftly came over them; and they lay side by side, once more children, in their white night-clothes, as when their father Lir, long centuries ago, had kissed them at evening and seen their blue eyes close in sleep and had touched with gentle hand their white foreheads and their golden hair. Their time of sorrow was ended and their last swan-song was sung; but the cruel stepmother seems yet to survive in her bat-like shape, and a single glance at her weird and malicious little face will lead us to doubt whether she has yet fully atoned for her sin.

## USHEEN IN THE ISLAND OF YOUTH

The old Celtic hero and poet Usheen or Oisin, whose supposed songs are known in English as those of Ossian, lived to a great old age, surviving all others of the race of the Feni, to which he belonged; and he was asked in his last years what had given him such length of life. This is the tale he told:—

After the fatal battle of Gavra, in which most of the Feni were killed, Usheen and his father, the king, and some of the survivors of the battle were hunting the deer with their dogs, when they met a maiden riding on a slender white horse with hoofs of gold, and with a golden crescent between his ears. The maiden's hair was of the color of citron and was gathered in a silver band; and she was clad in a white garment embroidered with strange devices. She asked them why they rode slowly and seemed sad, and not like other hunters; and they replied that it was because of the death of their friends and the ruin of their race. When they asked her in turn whence she came, and why, and whether she was married, she replied that she had never had a lover or a husband, but that she had crossed the sea for the love of the great hero and bard Usheen, whom she had never seen. Then Usheen was overcome with love for her, but she said that to wed her he must follow her across the sea to the Island of Perpetual Youth. There he would have a hundred horses and a hundred sheep and a hundred silken robes, a hundred swords, a hundred bows, and a hundred youths to follow him; while she would have a hundred maidens to wait on her. But how, he asked, was he to reach this island? He was to mount her horse and ride behind her. So he did this, and the slender white horse, not feeling his weight, dashed across the waves of the ocean, which did not yield beneath his tread. They galloped across the very sea, and the maiden, whose name was Niam, sang to him as they rode, and this so enchantingly that he scarcely knew whether hours passed or days. Sometimes deer ran by them over the water, followed by red-eared hounds in full chase; sometimes a maiden holding up an apple of gold; sometimes a beautiful youth; but they themselves rode on always westward.

At last they drew near an island which was not, Niam said, the island they were seeking; but it was one where a beautiful princess was kept under a spell until some defender should slay a cruel giant who held her under enchantment until she should either wed him or furnish a defender. The youth Usheen, being an Irishman and not easily frightened, naturally offered his services as defender, and they waited three days and nights to carry on the conflict. He had fought at home—so the legend says—with wild boars, with foreign invaders, and with enchanters, but he never had quite so severe a contest as with this giant; but after he had cut off his opponent's head and had been healed with precious balm by the beautiful princess, he buried the giant's body in a deep grave and placed above it a great stone engraved in the Ogham alphabet—in which all the letters are given in straight lines.

After this he and Niam again mounted the white steed and galloped away over the waves. Niam was again singing, when soft music began to be heard in the distance, as if in the centre of the setting sun. They drew nearer and nearer to a shore where the very trees trembled with the multitude of birds that sang upon them; and when they reached the shore, Niam gave one note of song, and a band of youths and maidens came rushing towards them and embraced them with eagerness. Then they too sang, and as they did it, one brought to Usheen a harp of silver and bade him sing of earthly joys. He found himself chanting, as he thought, with peculiar spirit and melody, but as he told them of human joys they kept still and began to weep, till at last one of them seized the silver harp and flung it away into a pool of water, saying, "It is the saddest harp in all the world."

Then he forgot all the human joys which seemed to those happy people only as sorrows compared with their own; and he dwelt with them thenceforward in perpetual youth. For a hundred years he chased the deer and went fishing in strangely carved boats and joined in the athletic sports of the young men; for a hundred years the gentle Niam was his wife.

But one day, when Usheen was by the beach, there floated to his feet what seemed a wooden staff, and he drew it from the waves. It was the battered fragment of a warrior's lance. The blood stains of war were still on it, and as he looked at it he recalled the old days of the Feni, the wars and tumult of his youth; and how he had outlived his tribe and all had passed away. Niam came softly to him and rested against his shoulder, but it did not soothe his pain, and he heard one of the young men watching him say to another, "The human sadness has come back into his eyes." The people around stood watching him, all sharing his sorrow, and knowing that his time of happiness was over and that he would go back among men. So indeed it was; Niam and Usheen mounted the white steed again and galloped away over the sea, but she had warned him when they mounted that he must never dismount for an instant, for that if he once touched the earth, she and the steed would vanish forever, that his youth too would disappear, and that he would be left alone on earth—an old man whose whole generation had vanished.

They passed, as before, over the sea; the same visions hovered around them, youths and maidens and animals of the chase; they passed by many islands, and at last reached the shore of Erin again. As they travelled over its plains and among its hills, Oisin looked in vain for his old companions. A little people had taken their place,—small men and women, mounted on horses as small;—and these people gazed in wonder at the mighty Usheen. "We have heard," they said, "of the hero Finn, and the poets have written many tales of him and of his people, the Feni. We have read in old books that he had a son Usheen who went away with a fairy maiden; but he was never seen again, and there is no race of the Feni left." Yet refusing to believe this, and always looking round for the people whom he had known and loved of old, he thought within himself that perhaps the Feni were not to be seen because they were hunting fierce wolves by night, as they used to do in his boyhood, and that they were therefore sleeping in the daytime; but again an old man said to him, "The Feni are dead." Then he remembered that it was a hundred years, and that his very race had perished, and he turned with contempt on the little men and their little horses. Three hundred of them as he rode by were trying to lift a vast stone, but they staggered under its weight, and at last fell and lay beneath it; then leaning from his saddle Usheen lifted the stone with one hand and flung it five yards. But with the strain the saddle girth broke, and Usheen came to the ground; the white steed shook himself and neighed, then galloped away, bearing Niam with him, and Usheen lay with all his strength gone from him—a feeble old man. The Island of Youth could only be known by those who dwelt always within it, and those mortals who had once left it could dwell there no more.

BRAN THE BLESSED

The mighty king Bran, a being of gigantic size, sat one day on the cliffs of his island in the Atlantic Ocean, near to Hades and the Gates of Night, when he saw ships sailing towards him and sent men to ask what they were. They were a fleet sent by Matholweh, the king of Ireland, who had sent to ask for Branwen, Bran's sister, as his wife. Without moving from his rock Bran bid the monarch land, and sent Branwen back with him as queen.

But there came a time when Branwen was ill-treated at the palace; they sent her into the kitchen and made her cook for the court, and they caused the butcher to come every day (after he had cut up the meat) and give her a blow on the ear. They also drew up all their boats on the shore for three years, that she might not send for her brother. But she reared a starling in the cover of the kneading-trough, taught it to speak, and told it how to find her brother; and then she wrote a letter describing her sorrows and bound it to the bird's wing, and it flew to the island and alighted on Bran's shoulder, "ruffling its feathers" (says the Welsh legend) "so that the letter was seen, and they knew that the bird had been reared in a domestic manner." Then Bran resolved to cross the sea, but he had to wade through the water, as no ship had yet been built large enough to hold him; and he carried all his musicians (pipers) on his shoulders. As he approached the Irish shore, men ran to the king, saying that they had seen a forest on the sea, where there never before had been a tree, and that they had also seen a mountain which moved. Then the king asked Branwen, the queen, what it could be. She answered, "These are the men of the Island of the Mighty, who have come hither to protect me." "What is the forest?" they asked. "The yards and masts of ships." "What mountain is that by the side of the ships?" "It is Bran my brother, coming to the shoal water and rising." "What is the lofty ridge with the lake on each side?" "That is his nose," she said, "and the two lakes are his fierce eyes."

Then the people were terrified: there was yet a river for Bran to pass, and they broke down the bridge which crossed it, but Bran laid himself down and said, "Who will be a chief, let him be a bridge." Then his men laid hurdles on his back, and the whole army crossed over; and that saying of his became afterwards a proverb. Then the Irish resolved, in order to appease the mighty visitor, to build him a house, because he had never before had one that would hold him; and they decided to make the house large enough to contain the two armies, one on each side. They accordingly built this house, and there were a hundred pillars, and the builders treacherously hung a leathern bag on each side of each pillar and put an armed man inside of each, so that they could all rise by night and kill the sleepers. But Bran's brother, who was a suspicious man, asked the builders what was in the first bag. "Meal, good soul," they answered; and he, putting his hand in, felt a man's head and crushed it with his mighty fingers, and so with the next and the next and with the whole two hundred. After this it did not take long to bring on a quarrel between the two armies, and they fought all day.

After this great fight between the men of Ireland and the men of the Isles of the Mighty there were but seven of these last who escaped, besides their king Bran, who was wounded in the foot with a poisoned dart. Then he knew that he should soon die, but he bade the seven men to cut off his head and told them that they must always carry it with them—that it would never decay and would always be able to speak and be pleasant company for them. "A long time will you be on the road," he said. "In Harlech you will feast seven years, the birds of Rhiannon singing to you all the while. And at the Island of Gwales you will dwell for fourscore years, and you may remain there, bearing the head with you uncorrupted, until you open the door that looks towards the mainland; and after you have once opened that door you can stay no longer, but must set forth to London to bury the head, leaving it there to look toward France."

So they went on to Harlech and there stopped to rest, and sat down to eat and drink. And there came three birds, which began singing a certain song, and all the songs they had ever heard were unpleasant compared with it; and the songs seemed to them to be at a great distance from them, over the sea, yet the notes were heard as distinctly as if they were close by; and it is said that at this repast they continued seven years. At the close of this time they went forth to an island in the sea called Gwales. There they found a fair and regal spot overlooking the ocean and a spacious hall built for them. They went into it and found two of its doors open, but the third door, looking toward Cornwall, was closed. "See yonder," said their leader Manawydan; "that is the door we may not open." And that night they regaled themselves and were joyful. And of all they had seen of food laid before them, and of all they had heard said, they remembered nothing; neither of that, nor of any sorrow whatsoever. There they remained fourscore years, unconscious of having ever spent a time more joyous and mirthful. And they were not more weary than when first they came, neither did they, any of them, know the time they had been there. It was not more irksome for them to have the head with them, than if Bran the Blessed had been with them himself. And because of these fourscore years, it was called "The Entertaining of the Noble Head."

One day said Heilwyn the son of Gwyn, "Evil betide me, if I do not open the door to know if that is true which is said concerning it." So he opened the door and looked towards Cornwall. And when they had looked they were as conscious of all the evils they had ever sustained, and of all the friends and companions they had ever lost, and of all the misery that had befallen them, as if all had happened in that very spot; and especially of the fate of their lord. And because of their perturbation they could not rest, but journeyed forth with the head towards London. And they buried the head in the White Mount.

The island called Gwales is supposed to be that now named Gresholm, eight or ten miles off the coast of Pembrokeshire; and to this day the Welsh sailors on that coast talk of the Green Meadows of Enchantment lying out at sea west of them, and of men who had either landed on them or seen them suddenly vanishing. Some of the people of Milford used to declare that they could sometimes see the Green Islands of the fairies quite distinctly; and they believed that the fairies went to and fro between their islands and the shore through a subterranean gallery under the sea. They used, indeed, to make purchases in the markets of Milford or Langhorne, and this they did sometimes without being seen and always without speaking, for they seemed to know the prices of the things they wished to buy and always laid down the exact sum of money needed. And indeed, how could the seven

21

companions of the Enchanted Head have spent eighty years of incessant feasting on an island of the sea, without sometimes purchasing supplies from the mainland?

## THE CASTLE OF THE ACTIVE DOOR

Perfect is my chair in Caer Sidi;
Plague and age hurt not who's in it—
They know, Manawydan and Pryderi.
Three organs round a fire sing before it,
And about its points are ocean's streams
And the abundant well above it—
Sweeter than white wine the drink in it.

Peredur, the knight, rode through the wild woods of the Enchanted Island until he arrived on clear ground outside the forest. Then he beheld a castle on level ground in the middle of a meadow; and round the castle flowed a stream, and inside the castle there were large and spacious halls with great windows. Drawing nearer the castle, he saw it to be turning more rapidly than any wind blows. On the ramparts he saw archers shooting so vigorously that no armor would protect against them; there were also men blowing horns so loud that the earth appeared to tremble; and at the gates were lions, in iron chains, roaring so violently that one might fancy that the castle and the woods were ready to be uprooted. Neither the lions nor the warriors resisted Peredur, but he found a woman sitting by the gate, who offered to carry him on her back to the hall. This was the queen Rhiannon, who, having been accused of having caused the death of her child, was sentenced to remain seven years sitting by the gate, to tell her story to every one, and to offer to carry all strangers on her back into the castle.

But so soon as Peredur had entered it, the castle vanished away, and he found himself standing on the bare ground. The queen Rhiannon was left beside him, and she remained on the island with her son Pryderi and his wife. Queen Rhiannon married for her second husband a person named Manawydan. One day they ascended a mound called Arberth which was well known for its wonders, and as they sat there they heard a clap of thunder, followed by mist so thick that they could not see one another. When it grew light again, they looked around them and found that all dwellings and animals had vanished; there was no smoke or fire anywhere or work of human hands; all their household had disappeared, and there were left only Pryderi and Manawydan with their wives. Wandering from place to place, they found no human beings; but they lived by hunting, fishing, and gathering wild honey. After visiting foreign lands, they returned to their island home. One day when they were out hunting, a wild boar of pure white color sprang from a bush, and as they saw him they retreated, and they saw also the Turning Castle. The boar, watching his opportunity, sprang into it, and the dogs followed, and Pryderi said, "I will go into this castle and get tidings of the dogs." "Go not," said Manawydan; "whoever has cast a spell over this land and deprived us of our dwelling has placed this castle here." But Pryderi replied, "Of a truth I cannot give up my dogs." So he watched for the opportunity and went in. He saw neither boar nor dogs, neither man nor beast; but on the centre of the castle floor he saw a fountain with marble work around it, and on the margin of the fountain a golden bowl upon a marble slab, and in the air hung chains, of which he could see no end. He was much delighted with the beauty of the gold and the rich workmanship of the bowl and went up to lay hold of it. The moment he touched it, his fingers clung to the bowl, and his feet to the slab; and all his joyousness forsook him so that he could not utter a word. And thus he stood.

Manawydan waited for him until evening, but hearing nothing either of him or of the dogs, he returned home. When he entered, Rhiannon, who was his wife and who was also Pryderi's mother, looked at him. "Where," she said, "are Pryderi and the dogs?" "This is what has happened to me," he said; and he told her. "An evil companion hast thou been," she said, "and a good companion hast thou lost." With these words she went out and proceeded towards the Castle of the Active Door. Getting in, she saw Pryderi taking hold of the bowl, and she went towards him. "What dost thou here?" she said, and she took hold of the bowl for herself; and then her hands became fast to it, and her feet to the slab, and she could not speak a word. Then came thunder and a fall of mist; thereupon the Castle of the Active Door vanished and never was seen again. Rhiannon and Pryderi also vanished.

When Kigva, the wife of Pryderi, saw this, she sorrowed so that she cared not if she lived or died. No one was left on the island but Manawydan and herself. They wandered away to other lands and sought to earn their living; then they came back to their island, bringing with them one bag of wheat which they planted. It throve and grew, and when the time of harvest came it was most promising, so that Manawydan resolved to reap it on the morrow. At break of day he came back to begin; but found nothing left but straw. Every stalk had been cut close to the ground and carried away.

Going to another field, he found it ripe, but on coming in the morning he found but the straw. "Some one has contrived my ruin," he said; "I will watch the third field to see what happens. He who stole the first will come to steal this."

He remained through the evening to watch the grain, and at midnight he heard loud thunder. He looked and saw coming a host of mice such as no man could number; each mouse took a stalk of the wheat and climbed it, so that it bent to the ground; then each mouse cut off the ear and ran away with it. They all did this, leaving the stalk bare, and there was not a single straw for which there was not a mouse. He struck among them, but could no more fix his sight on any of them, the legend says, than on flies and birds in the air, except one which seemed heavier than the rest, and moved slowly. This one he pursued and caught, put it in his glove and tied it with a string. Taking it home, he showed it to Kigva, and told her that he was going to hang the mouse next day. She advised against it, but he persisted, and on the next morning took the animal to the top of the Mound of Arberth, where he placed two wooden forks in the ground, and set up a small gallows.

While doing this, he saw a clerk coming to him in old, threadbare clothes. It was now seven years since he had seen a human being there, except the friends he had lost and Kigva who survived them. The clerk bade him good day and said he was going back to his country from England, where he had been singing. Then the clerk asked Manawydan what he was doing. "Hanging a thief," said he; and when the clerk saw that it was a mouse, he offered a pound to release it, but Manawydan refused. Then a priest came riding up and offered him three pounds to release the mouse; but this offer was declined. Then he made a noose round the mouse's neck, and while he did this, a bishop's whole retinue came riding towards him. The bishop seemed, like everybody else, to be very desirous of rescuing the mouse; he offered first seven pounds, and then twenty-four, and then added all his horses and equipages; but Manawydan still refused. The bishop finally asked him to name any price he pleased. "The liberation of Rhiannon and Pryderi," he said. "Thou shalt have it," said the bishop. "And the removal of the enchantment," said Manawydan. "That also," said the bishop, "if you will only restore the mouse." "Why?" said the other. "Because," said the bishop, "she is my wife." "Why did she come to me?" asked Manawydan. "To steal," was the reply. "When it was known that you were inhabiting the island, my household came to me, begging me to transform them into mice. The first and second nights they came alone, but the third night my wife and the ladies of the court wished also to accompany them, and I transformed them also; and now you have promised to let her go." "Not so," said the other, "except with a promise that there shall be no more such enchantment practised, and no vengeance on Pryderi and Rhiannon, or on me." This being promised, the bishop said, "Now wilt thou release my wife?" "No, by my faith," said Manawydan, "not till I see Pryderi and Rhiannon free before my eyes." "Here they are coming," said the bishop; and when they had been embraced by Manawydan, he let go the mouse; the bishop touched it with a wand, and it became the most beautiful young woman that ever was seen. "Now look round upon the country," said the bishop, "and see the dwellings and the crops returned," and the enchantment was removed.

"The Land of Illusion and the Realm of Glamour" is the name given by the old romancers to the south-west part of Wales, and to all the islands off the coast. Indeed, it was believed, ever since the days of the Greek writer, Plutarch, that some peculiar magic belonged to these islands; and every great storm that happened among them was supposed to be caused by the death of one of the wondrous enchanters who dwelt in that region. When it was over, the islanders said, "Some one of the mighty has passed away."

MERLIN THE ENCHANTER

In one of the old books called Welsh Triads, in which all things are classed by threes, there is a description of three men called "The Three Generous Heroes of the Isle of Britain." One of these—named Nud or Nodens, and later called Merlin—was first brought from the sea, it is stated, with a herd of cattle consisting of 21,000 milch cows, which are supposed to mean those waves of the sea that the poets often describe as White Horses. He grew up to be a king and warrior, a magician and prophet, and on the whole the most important figure in the Celtic traditions. He came from the sea and at last returned to it, but meanwhile he did great works on land, one of which is said to have been the building of Stonehenge.

This is the way, as the old legends tell, in which the vast stones of Stonehenge came to be placed on Salisbury Plain. It is a thing which has always been a puzzle to every one, inasmuch as their size and weight are enormous, and there is no stone of the same description to be found within hundreds of miles of Salisbury Plain, where they now stand.

The legend is that Pendragon, king of England, was led to fight a great battle by seeing a dragon in the air. The battle was won, but Pendragon was killed and was buried on Salisbury Plain, where the fight had taken place. When his brother Uther took his place, Merlin the enchanter advised him to paint a dragon on a flag and bear it always before him to bring good fortune, and this he always did. Then Merlin said to him, "Wilt thou do nothing more on the Plain of Salisbury, to honor thy brother?" The King said, "What shall be done?" Then Merlin said, "I will cause a thing to be done that will endure to the world's end." Then he bade Utherpendragon, as he called the new king, to send many ships and men to Ireland, and he showed him stones such as seemed far too large and heavy to bring, but he placed them by his magic art upon the boats and bore them to England; and he devised means to transport them and to set them on end, "for they shall seem fairer so than if they were lying." And there they are to this day.

This was the way in which Merlin would sometimes obtain the favor and admiration of young ladies. There was a maiden of twelve named Nimiane or Vivian, the daughter of King Dionas, and Merlin changed himself into the appearance of "a fair young squire," that he might talk with her beside a fountain, described in the legends as "a well, whereof the springs were fair and the water clear and the gravel so fair that it seemed of fine silver." By degrees he made acquaintance with the child, who told him who she was, adding, "And what are you, fair, sweet friend?" "Damsel," said Merlin, "I am a travelling squire, seeking for my master, who has taught me wonderful things." "And what master is that?" she asked. "It is one," he said, "who has taught me so much that I could here erect for you a castle, and I could make many people outside to attack it and inside to defend it; nay, I could go upon this water and not wet my feet, and I could make a river where water had never been."

"These are strange feats," said the maiden, "and I wish that I could thus disport myself." "I can do yet greater things," said Merlin, "and no one can devise anything which I cannot do, and I can also make it to endure forever." "Indeed," said the girl, "I would always love you if you could show me some such wonders." "For your love," he answered, "I will show you some of these wondrous plays, and I will ask no more of you." Then Merlin turned and described a circle with a wand and then came and sat by her again at the fountain. At noon she saw coming out of the forest many ladies and knights and squires, holding each other by the hand and singing in the greatest joy; then came men with timbrels and tabours and dancing, so that one could not tell one-fourth part of the sports that went on. Then Merlin caused an orchard to grow, with all manner of fruit and flowers; and the maiden cared for nothing but to listen to their singing, "Truly love begins in joy, but ends in grief." The festival continued from mid-day to even-song; and King Dionas and his courtiers came out to see it, and marvelled whence these strange people came. Then when the carols were ended, the ladies and maidens sat down on the green grass and fresh flowers, and the squires set up a game of tilting called quintain upon the meadows and played till even-song; and then Merlin came to the damsel and asked if he had done what he promised for her. "Fair, sweet friend," said she, "you have done so much that I am all yours." "Let me teach you," he answered, "and I will show you many wonders that no woman ever learned so many."

Merlin and this young damsel always remained friends, and he taught her many wonderful arts, one of which was (this we must regret) a spell by which she might put her parents to sleep whenever he visited her; while another lesson was (this being more unexceptionable) in the use of three words, by saying which she might at any time keep at a distance any men who tried to molest her. He stayed eight days near her, and in those days taught her many of the most "wonderful things that any mortal heart could think of, things past and things that were done and said, and a part of what was to come; and she put them in writing, and then Merlin departed from her and came to Benoyk, where the king, Arthur, rested, so that glad were they when they saw Merlin."

The relations between Merlin and Arthur are unlike those ever held towards a king even by an enchanter in any legend. Even in Homer there is no one described, except the gods, as having such authority over a ruler. Merlin came and went as he pleased and under any form he might please. He foretold the result of a battle, ordered up troops, brought aid from a distance. He rebuked the bravest knights for cowardice; as when Ban, Bors, and Gawain had concealed themselves behind some bushes during a fight. "Is this," he said to King Arthur and Sir Bors, "the war and the help that you do to your friends who have put themselves in adventure of death in many a need, and ye come hither to hide for cowardice." Then the legend says, "When the king understood the words of Merlin, he bowed his head for shame," and the other knights acknowledged their fault. Then Merlin took the dragon banner which he had given them and said that he would bear it himself; "for the banner of a king," he said, "should not be hid in battle,—but borne in the foremost front." Then Merlin rode forth and cried with a loud voice, "Now shall be shown who is a knight." And the knights, seeing Merlin, exclaimed that he was "a full noble man"; and "without fail," says the legend, "he was full of marvellous powers and strength of body and great and long stature; but brown he was and lean and rough of hair." Then he rode in among the enemy on a great black horse; and the golden dragon which he had made and had attached to the banner gave out from its throat such a flaming fire that the air was black with its smoke; and all King Arthur's men began to fight again more stoutly, and Arthur himself held the bridle reins in his left hand, and so wielded his sword with his right as to slay two hundred men.

There was no end to Merlin's disguises—sometimes as an old man, sometimes as a boy or a dwarf, then as a woman, then as an ignorant clown; —but the legends always give him some object to accomplish, some work to do, and there was always a certain dignity about him, even when helping King Arthur, as he sometimes did, to do wrong things. His fame extended over all Britain, and also through Brittany, now a part of France, where the same poetic legends extended. This, for instance, is a very old Breton song about him:—

MERLIN THE DIVINER

Merlin! Merlin! where art thou going
So early in the day, with thy black dog?
Oi! oi! oi! oi! oi! oi! oi! oi! oi! oi!
Oi! oi! oi! oi! oi!

I have come here to search the way,
To find the red egg;
The red egg of the marine serpent,
By the seaside, in the hollow of the stone.

I am going to seek in the valley
The green water-cress, and the golden grass,
And the top branch of the oak,
In the wood by the side of the fountain.

Merlin! Merlin! retrace your steps;
Leave the branch on the oak,
And the green water-cress in the valley,
As well as the golden grass;

And leave the red egg of the marine serpent
In the foam by the hollow of the stone.
Merlin! Merlin! retrace thy steps;
There is no diviner but God.

Merlin was supposed to know the past, the present, and the future, and to be able to assume the form of any animal, and even that of a menhir, or huge standing stone. Before history began he ruled in Britain, then a delightful island of flowery meadows. His subjects were "small people" (fairies), and their lives were a continued festival of singing, playing, and enjoyment. The sage ruled them as a father, his familiar servant being a tame wolf. He also possessed a kingdom, beneath the waves, where everything was beautiful, the inhabitants being charming little beings, with waves of long, fair hair falling on their shoulders in curls. Fruits and milk composed the food of all, meat and fish being held in abhorrence. The only want felt was of the full light of the sun, which, coming to them through the water, was but faint, and cast no shadow.

Here was the famous workshop where Merlin forged the enchanted sword so celebrated by the bards, and where the stones were found by which alone the sword could be sharpened. Three British heroes were fated to wield this blade in turn; viz., Lemenisk the leaper (Leim, meaning leap), Utherpendragon, and his son King Arthur. By orders of this last hero, when mortally wounded, it was flung into the sea, where it will remain till he returns to restore the rule of his country to the faithful British race.

The bard once amused and puzzled the court by entering the hall as a blind boy led by a greyhound, playing on his harp, and demanding as recompense to be allowed to carry the king's banner in an approaching battle. Being refused on account of his blindness he vanished, and the king of Brittany mentioned his suspicions that this was one of Merlin's elfin tricks. Arthur was disturbed, for he had promised to give the child anything except his honor, his kingdom, his wife, and his sword. However, while he continued to fret, there entered the hall a poor child about eight years old, with shaved head, features of livid tint, eyes of light gray, barefooted, barelegged, and a whip knotted over his shoulders in the manner affected by horseboys. Speaking and looking like an idiot, he asked the king's permission to bear the royal ensign in the approaching battle with the giant Rion. The courtiers laughed, but Arthur, suspecting a new joke on Merlin's part, granted the demand, and then Merlin stood in his own proper person before the company.

He also seems to have taught people many things in real science, especially the women, who were in those days more studious than the men, or at least had less leisure. For instance, the legend says of Morgan le fay (or la fée), King Arthur's sister, "she was a noble clergesse (meaning that she could read and write, like the clergy), and of astronomy could she enough, for Merlin had her taught, and she learned much of egromancy (magic or necromancy); and the best work-woman she was with her hands that any man knew in any land, and she had the fairest head and the fairest hands under heaven, and shoulders well-shapen; and she had fair eloquence and full debonair she was, as long as she was in her right wit; and when she was wroth with any man, she was evil to meet." This lady was one of Merlin's pupils, but the one whom he loved most and instructed the most was Nimiane or Vivian, already mentioned, who seems to have been to him rather a beloved younger sister than anything else, and he taught her so much that "at last he might hold himself a fool," the legend says, "and ever she inquired of his cunning and his mysteries, each thing by itself, and he let her know all, and she wrote all that he said, as she was well learned in clergie (reading and writing), and learned lightly all that Merlin taught her; and when they parted, each of them commended the other to God full tenderly."

The form of the enchanter Merlin disappeared from view, at last—for the legends do not admit that his life ever ended—across the sea whence he came.

The poet Tennyson, to be sure, describes Nimiane or Vivian—the Lady of the Lake—as a wicked enchantress who persuaded Merlin to betray his secrets to her, and then shut him up in an oak tree forever. But other legends seem to show that Tennyson does great injustice to the Lady of the Lake, that she really loved Merlin even in his age, and therefore persuaded him to show her how to make a tower without walls,—that they might dwell there together in peace, and address each other only as Brother and Sister. When he had told her, he fell asleep with his head in her lap, and she wove a spell nine times around his head, and the tower became the strongest in the world. Some of the many legends place this tower in the forest of Broceliande; while others transport it afar to a magic island, where Merlin dwells with his nine bards, and where Vivian alone can come or go through the magic walls. Some legends describe it as an enclosure "neither of iron nor steel nor timber nor of stone, but of the air, without any other thing but enchantment, so strong that it may never be undone while the world endureth." Here dwells Merlin, it is said, with nine favorite bards who took with them the thirteen treasures of England. These treasures are said to have been:—

1. A sword; if any man drew it except the owner, it burst into a flame from the cross to the point. All who asked it received it; but because of this peculiarity all shunned it.

2. A basket; if food for one man were put into it, when opened it would be found to contain food for one hundred.

3. A horn; what liquor soever was desired was found therein.

4. A chariot; whoever sat in it would be immediately wheresoever he wished.

5. A halter, which was in a staple below the feet of a bed; and whatever horse one wished for in it, he would find it there.

6. A knife, which would serve four-and twenty men at meat all at once.

7. A caldron; if meat were put into it to boil for a coward, it would never be boiled; but if meat were put in it for a brave man, it would be boiled forthwith.

8. A whetstone; if the sword of a brave man were sharpened thereon, and any one were wounded therewith, he would be sure to die; but if it were that of a coward that was sharpened on it, he would be none the worse.

9. A garment; if a man of gentle birth put it on, it suited him well; but if a churl, it would not fit him.

10, 11. A pan and a platter; whatever food was required was found therein.

12. A chessboard; when the men were placed upon it, they would play of themselves. The chessboard was of gold, and the men of silver.

13. The mantle of Arthur; whosoever was beneath it could see everything, while no one could see him.

It is towards this tower, some legends say, that Merlin was last seen by some Irish monks, sailing away westward, with a maiden, in a boat of crystal, beneath a sunset sky.

## SIR LANCELOT OF THE LAKE

Sir Lancelot, the famous knight, was the son of a king and queen against whom their subjects rebelled; the king was killed, the queen taken captive, when a fairy rose in a cloud of mist and carried away the infant Lancelot from where he had been left beneath a tree. The queen, after weeping on the body of her husband, looked round and saw a lady standing by the water-side, holding the queen's child in her arms. "Fair, sweet friend," said the queen, "give me back my child." The fairy made no reply, but dived into the water; and the queen was taken to an abbey, where she was known as the Queen of Great Griefs. The Lady of the Lake took the child to her own home, which was an island in the middle of the sea and surrounded by impassable walls. From this the lady had her name of Dame du Lac, or the Lady of the Lake (or Sea), and her foster son was called Lancelot du Lac, while the realm was called Meidelant, or the Land of Maidens.

Lancelot dwelt thenceforward in the castle, on the island. When he was eight years old he received a tutor who was to instruct him in all knightly knowledge; he learned to use bow and spear and to ride on horseback, and some cousins of his were also brought thither by the Lady of the Lake to be his comrades. When he was eighteen he wished to go to King Arthur's court that he might be a knight.

On the eve of St. John, as King Arthur returned from the chase, and by the high road approached Camelot, he met a fair company. In the van went two youths, leading two white mules, one freighted with a silken pavilion, the other with robes proper for a newly made knight; the mules bore two chests, holding the hauberk and the iron boots. Next came two squires, clad in white robes and mounted on white horses, carrying a silver shield and a shining helmet; after these, two others, with a sword in a white sheath and a white charger. Behind followed squires and servants in white coats, three damsels dressed in white, the two sons of King Bors; and, last of all, the fairy with the youth she loved. Her robe was of white samite lined with ermine; her white palfrey had a silver bit, while her breastplate, stirrups, and saddle were of ivory, carved with figures of ladies and knights, and her white housings trailed on the ground.

When she perceived the king, she responded to his salutation, and said, after she had lowered her wimple and displayed her face: "Sir, may God bless the best of kings! I come to implore a boon, which it shall cost you nothing to grant." "Damsel, even it should cost me dear, you should not be refused; what is it you would have me do?" "Sir, dub this varlet a knight, and array him in the arms he bringeth, whenever he desireth." "Your mercy, damsel! to bring me such a youth! Assuredly, I will dub him whenever he will; but it shameth me to abandon my custom, for 'tis my wont to furnish with garments and arms such as come thither to receive chivalry." The lady replied that she desired the youth to carry the arms she had intended him to wear, and if she were refused, she would address herself elsewhere. Sir Ewain said that so fair a youth ought not to be denied, and the king yielded to her entreaty. She returned thanks, and bade the varlet retain the mules and the charger, with the two squires; and after that, she prepared to return as she had come, in spite of the urgency of the king, who had begged her to remain in his court. "At least," he cried, "tell us by what name are you known?" "Sir," she answered, "I am called the Lady of the Lake."

For a long way, Lancelot escorted the fairy, who said to him as she took leave: "King's son, you are derived from lineage the most noble on earth; see to it that your worth be as great as your beauty. To-morrow you will ask the king to bestow on you knighthood; when you are armed, you will not tarry in his house a single night. Abide in one place no longer than you can help, and refrain from declaring your name until others proclaim it. Be prepared to accomplish every adventure, and never let another man complete a task which you yourself have undertaken." With that, she gave him a ring that had the property of dissolving enchantment, and commended him to God.

On the morrow, Lancelot arrayed himself in his fairest robes, and sued for knighthood, as he had been commanded to do. Sir Ewain attended him to court, where they dismounted in front of the palace; the king and queen advanced to meet them; each took Sir Ewain by a hand, and seated him on a couch, while the varlet stood in their presence on the rushes that strewed the floor. All gazed with pleasure, and the queen prayed that God might make him noble, for he possessed as much beauty as was possible for man to have.

After this he had many perilous adventures; he fought with giants and lions; he entered an enchanted castle and escaped; he went to a well in the forest, and, striking three times on a cymbal with a hammer hung there for the purpose, called forth a great giant, whom he slew, afterwards marrying his daughter. Then he went to rescue the queen of the realm, Gwenivere, from captivity. In order to reach the fortress where she was prisoner, he had to ride in a cart with a dwarf; to follow a wheel that rolled before him to show him the way, or a ball that took the place of the wheel; he had to walk on his hands and knees across a bridge made of a drawn sword; he suffered greatly. At last he rescued the queen, and later than this he married Elaine, the daughter of King Pelles, and her father gave to them the castle of Blyaunt in the Joyous Island, enclosed in iron, and with a deep water all around it. There Lancelot challenged all knights to come and contend with him, and he jousted with more than five hundred, overcoming them all, yet killing none, and at last he returned to Camelot, the place of King Arthur's court.

One day he was called from the court to an abbey, where three nuns brought to him a beautiful boy of fifteen, asking that he might be made a knight. This was Sir Lancelot's own son, Galahad, whom he had never seen, and did not yet know. That evening Sir Lancelot remained at the abbey with the boy, that he might keep his vigil there, and on the morrow's dawn he was made a knight. Sir Lancelot put on one of his spurs, and Bors, Lancelot's cousin, the other, and then Sir Lancelot said to the boy, "Fair son, attend me to the court of the king;" but the abbess said, "Sir, not now, but we will send him when it shall be time."

On Whitsunday, at the time called "underne," which was nine in the morning, King Arthur and his knights sat at the Round Table, where on every seat there was written, in letters of gold, the name of a knight with "here ought to sit he," or "he ought to sit here;" and thus went the inscriptions until they came to one seat (or siège in French) called the "Siege Perilous," where they found newly written letters of gold, saying that this seat could not be occupied until four hundred and fifty years after the death of Christ; and that was this very day. Then there came news of a marvellous stone which had been seen above the water, with a sword sticking in it bearing the letters, "Never shall man take me hence, but only he by whose side I ought to hang, and he shall be the best knight of the world." Then two of the knights tried to draw the sword and failed to draw it, and Sir Lancelot, who was thought the best knight in all the world, refused to attempt it. Then they went back to their seats around the table.

Then when all the seats but the "Siege Perilous" were full, the hall was suddenly darkened; and an old man clad in white, whom nobody knew, came in, with a young knight in red armor, wearing an empty scabbard at his side, who said, "Peace be with you, fair knights." The old man said, "I bring you here a young knight that is of kings' lineage," and the king said, "Sir, ye are right heartily welcome." Then the old man bade the young knight to remove his armor, and he wore a red garment, while the old man placed on his shoulders a mantle of fine ermine, and said, "Sir, follow after." Then the old man led him to the "Siege Perilous," next to Sir Lancelot, and lifted the cloth and read, "Here sits Sir Galahad," and the youth sat down. Upon this, all the knights of the Round Table marvelled greatly at Sir Galahad, that he dared to sit in that seat, and he so tender of age. Then King Arthur took him by the hand and led him down to the river to see the adventure of the stone. "Sir," said the king to Sir Galahad, "here is a great marvel, where right good knights have tried and failed." "Sir," said Sir Galahad, "that is no marvel, for the adventure was not theirs, but mine; I have brought no sword with me, for here by my side hangs the scabbard," and he laid his hand on the sword and lightly drew it from the stone.

It was not until long after, and when they both had had many adventures, that Sir Lancelot discovered Galahad to be his son. Sir Lancelot once came to the sea-strand and found a ship without sails or oars, and sailed away upon it. Once, when he touched at an island, a young knight came on board to whom Lancelot said, "Sir, you are welcome," and when the young knight asked his name, told him, "My name is Sir Lancelot du Lac." "Sir," he said, "then you are welcome, for you are my father." "Ah," said Lancelot, "are you Sir Galahad?" Then the young knight kneeled down and asked his blessing, and they embraced each other, and there was great joy between them, and they told each other all their deeds. So dwelt Sir Lancelot and Sir Galahad together within that ship for half a year, and often they arrived at islands far from men where there were but wild beasts, and they found many adventures strange and perilous which they brought to an end.

When Sir Lancelot at last died, his body was taken to Joyous-Gard, his home, and there it lay in state in the choir, with a hundred torches blazing above it; and while it was there, came his brother Sir Ector de Maris, who had long been seeking Lancelot. When he heard such noise and saw such lights in the choir, he alighted and came in; and Sir Bors went towards him and told him that his brother Lancelot was lying dead. Then Sir Ector threw his shield and sword and helm from him, and when he looked on Sir Lancelot's face he fell down in a swoon, and when he rose he spoke thus: "Ah, Sir Lancelot," said he, "thou wert dead of all Christen knights! And now I dare say, that, Sir Lancelot, there thou liest, thou wert never matched of none earthly knight's hands; and thou wert the curtiest knight that ever beare shield; and thou wert the truest friend to thy lover that ever bestrood horse, and thou wert the truest lover of a sinful man that ever loved woman; and thou wert the kindest man that ever strooke with sword; and thou wert the goodliest person that ever came among presse of knights; and thou wert the meekest man and the gentlest that ever eate in hall among ladies; and thou wert the sternest knight to thy mortall foe that ever put speare in the rest."

THE HALF-MAN

King Arthur in his youth was fond of all manly exercises, especially of wrestling, an art in which he found few equals. The old men who had been the champions of earlier days, and who still sat, in summer evenings, watching the youths who tried their skill before them, at last told him that he had no rival in Cornwall, and that his only remaining competitor elsewhere was one who had tired out all others.

"Where is he?" said Arthur.

"He dwells," an old man said, "on an island whither you will have to go and find him. He is of all wrestlers the most formidable. You will think him at first so insignificant as to be hardly worth a contest; you will easily throw him at the first trial; but after a while you will find him growing stronger; he seeks out all your weak points as by magic; he never gives up; you may throw him again and again, but he will conquer you at last."

"His name! his name!" said Arthur.

"His name," they answered, "is Hanner Dyn; his home is everywhere, but on his own island you will be likely to find him sooner or later. Keep clear of him, or he will get the best of you in the end, and make you his slave as he makes slaves of others whom he has conquered."

Far and wide over the ocean the young Arthur sought; he touched at island after island; he saw many weak men who did not dare to wrestle with him, and many strong ones whom he could always throw, until at last when he was far out under the western sky, he came one day to an island which he had never before seen and which seemed uninhabited. Presently there came out from beneath an arbor of flowers a little miniature man, graceful and quick-moving as an elf. Arthur, eager in his quest, said to him, "In what island dwells Hanner Dyn?" "In this island," was the answer. "Where is he?" said Arthur. "I am he," said the laughing boy, taking hold of his hand.

"What did they mean by calling you a wrestler?" said Arthur.

"Oh," said the child coaxingly, "I am a wrestler. Try me."

The king took him and tossed him in the air with his strong arms, till the boy shouted with delight. He then took Arthur by the hand and led him about the island—showed him his house and where the gardens and fields were. He showed him the rows of men toiling in the meadows or felling trees. "They all work for me," he said carelessly. The king thought he had never seen a more stalwart set of laborers. Then the boy led him to the house, asked him what his favorite fruits were, or his favorite beverages, and seemed to have all at hand. He was an unaccountable little creature; in size and years he seemed a child; but in his activity and agility he seemed almost a man. When the king told him so, he smiled, as winningly as ever, and said, "That is what they call me—Hanner Dyn, The Half-Man." Laughing merrily, he helped Arthur into his boat and bade him farewell, urging him to come again. The King sailed away, looking back with something like affection on his winsome little playmate.

It was months before Arthur came that way again. Again the merry child met him, having grown a good deal since their earlier meeting. "How is my little wrestler?" said Arthur. "Try me," said the boy; and the king tossed him again in his arms, finding the delicate limbs firmer, and the slender body heavier than before, though easily manageable. The island was as green and more cultivated, there were more men working in the fields, and Arthur noticed that their look was not cheerful, but rather as of those who had been discouraged and oppressed.

It was, however, a charming sail to the island, and, as it became more familiar, the king often bade his steersman guide the pinnace that way. He was often startled with the rapid growth and increased strength of the laughing boy, Hanner Dyn, while at other times he seemed much as before and appeared to have made but little progress. The youth seemed never tired of wrestling; he always begged the king for a trial of skill, and the king rejoiced to see how readily the young wrestler caught at the tricks of the art; so that the time had long passed when even Arthur's strength could toss him lightly in the air, as at first. Hanner Dyn was growing with incredible rapidity into a tall young fellow, and instead of the weakness that often comes with rapid growth, his muscles grew ever harder and harder. Still merry and smiling, he began to wrestle in earnest, and one day, in a moment of carelessness, Arthur received a back fall, perhaps on moist ground, and measured his length. Rising with a quick motion, he laughed at the angry faces of his attendants and bade the boy farewell. The men at work in the fields glanced up, attracted by the sound of voices, and he saw them exchange looks with one another.

Yet he felt his kingly dignity a little impaired, and hastened ere long to revisit the island and teach the saucy boy another lesson. Months had passed, and the youth had expanded into a man of princely promise, but with the same sunny look. His shoulders were now broad, his limbs of the firmest mould, his eye clear, keen, penetrating. "Of all the wrestlers I have ever yet met," said the king, "this younker promises to be the most formidable. I can easily throw him now, but what will he be a few years hence?" The youth greeted him joyously, and they began their usual match. The sullen serfs in the fields stopped to watch them, and an aged Druid priest, whom Arthur had brought with him, to give the old man air and exercise in the boat, opened his weak eyes and closed them again.

As they began to wrestle, the king felt, by the very grasp of the youth's arms, by the firm set of his foot upon the turf, that this was to be unlike any previous effort. The wrestlers stood after the old Cornish fashion, breast to breast, each resting his chin on the other's shoulder. They grasped each other round the body, each setting his left hand above the other's right. Each tried to force the other to touch the ground with both shoulders and one hip, or with both hips and one shoulder; or else to compel the other to relinquish his hold for an instant—either of these successes giving the victory. Often as Arthur had tried the art, he never had been so matched before. The competitors swayed this way and that, writhed, struggled, half lost their footing and regained it, yet neither yielded. All the boatmen gathered breathlessly around, King Arthur's men refusing to believe their eyes, even when they knew their king was in danger. A stranger group was that of the sullen farm-laborers, who left their ploughs and spades, and, congregating on a rising ground, watched without any expression of sympathy the contest that was going on. An old wrestler from Cornwall, whom Arthur had brought with him, was the judge; and according to the habit of the time, the contest was for the best two bouts in three. By the utmost skill and strength, Arthur compelled Hanner Dyn to lose his hold for one instant in the first trial, and the King was pronounced the victor.

The second test was far more difficult; the boy, now grown to a man, and seeming to grow older and stronger before their very eyes, twice forced Arthur to the ground either with hip or shoulder, but never with both, while the crowd closed in breathlessly around; and the half-blind old Druid, who had himself been a wrestler in his youth, and who had been brought ashore to witness the contest, called warningly aloud, "Save thyself, O king!" At this Arthur roused his failing strength to one final effort, and, griping his rival round the waist with a mighty grasp, raised him bodily from the ground and threw him backward till he fell flat, like a log, on both shoulders and both hips; while Arthur himself fell fainting a moment later. Nor did he recover until he found himself in the boat, his head resting on the knees of the aged Druid, who said to him, "Never again, O king! must you encounter the danger you have barely escaped. Had you failed, you would have become subject to your opponent, whose strength has been maturing for years to overpower you. Had you yielded, you would, although a king, have become but as are those dark-browed men who till his fields and do his bidding. For know you not what the name Hanner Dyn means? It means—Habit; and the force of habit, at first weak, then growing constantly stronger, ends in conquering even kings!"

## KING ARTHUR AT AVALON

In the ruined castle at Winchester, England, built by William the Conqueror, there is a hall called "The Great Hall," where Richard Coeur de Lion was received by his nobles when rescued from captivity; where Henry III. was born; where all the Edwards held court; where Henry VIII. entertained the emperor Charles V.; where Queen Mary was married to Philip II.; where Parliament met for many years. It is now a public hall for the county; and at one end of it the visitor sees against the wall a vast wooden tablet on which the names of King Arthur's knights of the Round Table are inscribed in a circle. No one knows its date or origin, though it is known to be more than four hundred years old, but there appear upon it the names most familiar to those who have read the legends of King Arthur, whether in Tennyson's poems or elsewhere. There are Lancelot and Bedivere, Gawaine and Dagonet, Modred and Gareth, and the rest. Many books have been written of their deeds; but a time came when almost all those knights were to fall, according to the legend, in one great battle. Modred, the king's nephew, had been left in charge of the kingdom during Arthur's absence, and had betrayed him and tried to dethrone him, meaning to crown himself king. Many people joined with him, saying that under Arthur they had had only war and fighting, but under Modred they would have peace and bliss. Yet nothing was farther from Modred's purpose than bliss or peace, and it was agreed at last that a great battle should be fought for the kingdom.

On the night of Trinity Sunday, King Arthur had a dream. He thought he sat in a chair, upon a scaffold, and the chair was fastened to a wheel. He was dressed in the richest cloth of gold that could be made, but far beneath him he saw a pit, full of black water, in which were all manner of serpents and floating beasts. Then the wheel began to turn, and he went down, down among the floating things, and they wreathed themselves about him till he cried, "Help! help!"

Then his knights and squires and yeomen aroused him, but he slumbered again, not sleeping nor thoroughly waking. Then he thought he saw his nephew, Sir Gawaine, with a number of fair ladies, and when King Arthur saw him, he said, "O fair nephew, what are these ladies who come with you?" "Sir," said Sir Gawaine, "these are the ladies for whose protection I fought while I was a living man, and God has given them grace that they should bring me thither to you, to warn you of your death. If you fight with Sir Modred to-morrow, you must be slain, and most of your people on both sides." So Sir Gawaine and all the ladies vanished, and then the king called upon his knights and squires and yeomen, and summoned his lords and bishops. They agreed to propose to Sir Modred that they should have a month's delay, and meanwhile agreed to meet him with fourteen persons on each side, besides Arthur and Modred.

Each of these leaders warned his army, when they met, to watch the other, and not to draw their swords until they saw a drawn sword on the other side. In that case they were to come on fiercely. So the small party of chosen men on each side met and drank wine together, and agreed upon a month's delay before fighting; but while this was going on an adder came out of a bush and stung a knight on the foot, and he drew his sword to slay it and thought of nothing farther. At the sight of that sword the two armies were in motion, trumpets were blown instantly, and the men of each army thought that the other army had begun the fray. "Alas, this unhappy day!" cried King Arthur; and, as the old chronicle says, "nothing there was but rushing and riding, fencing and striking, and many a grim word was there spoken either to other, and many a deadly stroke."

The following is the oldest account of the battle, translated into quaint and literal English by Madden from the book called "Layamon's Brut"; "Innumerable folk it came toward the host, riding and on foot, as the rain down falleth! Arthur marched to Cornwall, with an immense army. Modred heard that, and advanced against him with innumerable folk,—there were many fated! Upon the Tambre they came together; the place hight Camelford, evermore lasted the same word. And at Camelford was assembled sixty thousand, and more thousands thereto; Modred was their chief. Then thitherward 'gan ride Arthur the mighty, with innumerable folk,—fated though it were! Upon the Tambre they encountered together; elevated their standards; advanced together; drew their long swords; smote on the helms; fire outsprang; spears splintered; shields 'gan shiver; shafts brake in pieces. There fought all together innumerable folk! Tambre was in flood with blood to excess; there might no man in the fight know any warrior, nor who did worse, nor who better, so was the conflict mingled! For each slew downright, were he swain, were he knight.

"There was Modred slain, and deprived of life-day, and all his knights slain in the fight. There were slain all the brave, Arthur's warriors, high and low, and all the Britons of Arthur's board, and all his dependents, of many kingdoms. And Arthur wounded with broad slaughter-spear; fifteen dreadful wounds he had; in the least one might thrust two gloves! Then was there no more remained in the fight, of two hundred thousand men that there lay hewed in pieces, except Arthur the king alone, and two of his knights. Arthur was wounded wondrously much. There came to him a lad, who was of his kindred; he was Cador's son, the earl of Cornwall; Constantine the lad hight, he was dear to the king. Arthur looked on him, where he lay on the ground, and said these words, with sorrowful heart: 'Constantine, thou art welcome; thou wert Cador's son. I give thee here my kingdom, and defend thou my Britons ever in thy life, and maintain them all the laws that have stood in my days, and all the good laws that in Uther's days stood. And I will fare to Avalon, to the fairest of all maidens, to Argante the queen, an elf most fair, and she shall make my wounds all sound, make me all whole with healing draughts. And afterwards I will come to my kingdom, and dwell with the Britons with mickle joy.' Even with the words there approached from the sea that was a short boat, floating with the waves; and two women therein, wondrously formed; and they took Arthur anon, and bare him quickly, and laid him softly down, and forth they 'gan depart. Then was it accomplished that Merlin whilom said, that mickle care should be of Arthur's departure. The Britons believe yet that he is alive, and dwelleth in Avalon with the fairest of all elves; and the Britons ever yet expect when Arthur shall return. Was never the man born, of any lady chosen, that knoweth, of the sooth, to say more of Arthur. But whilom was a sage hight Merlin; he said with words,—his sayings were sooth,—that an Arthur should yet come to help the English."

Another traditional account which Tennyson has mainly followed in a poem, is this: The king bade Sir Bedivere take his good sword Excalibur and go with it to the water-side and throw it into the water and return to tell what he saw. Then Sir Bedivere took the sword, and it was so richly and preciously adorned that he would not throw it, and came back without it. When the king asked what had happened, Sir Bedivere said, "I saw nothing but waves and wind," and when Arthur did not believe him, and sent him again, he made the same answer, and then, when sent a third time, he threw the sword into the water, as far as he could. Then an arm and a hand rose above the water and caught it, and shook and brandished it three times and vanished.

Then Sir Bedivere came back to the king; he told what he had seen. "Alas," said Arthur, "help me from hence, for I fear I have tarried over long." Then Sir Bedivere took King Arthur upon his back, and went with him to the water's side. And when they had reached there, a barge with many fair ladies was lying there, with many ladies in it, and among them three queens, and they all had black hoods, and they wept and shrieked when they saw King Arthur.

"Now put me in the barge," said Arthur, and the three queens received him with great tenderness, and King Arthur laid his head in the lap of one, and she said, "Ah, dear brother, why have ye tarried so long, until your wound was cold?" And then they rowed away, and King Arthur said to Sir

Bedivere, "I will go unto the valley of Avalon to heal my grievous wound, and if I never return, pray for my soul." He was rowed away by the weeping queens, and one of them was Arthur's sister Morgan le Fay; another was the queen of Northgalis, and the third was the queen of Waste Lands; and it was the belief for years in many parts of England that Arthur was not dead, but would come again to reign in England, when he had been nursed long enough by Morgan le Fay in the island of Avalon.

The tradition was that King Arthur lived upon this island in an enchanted castle which had the power of a magnet, so that every one who came near it was drawn thither and could not get away. Morgan le Fay was its ruler (called more correctly Morgan la fée, or the fairy), and her name Morgan meant sea-born. By one tradition, the queens who bore away Arthur were accompanied in the boat by the bard and enchanter, Merlin, who had long been the king's adviser, and this is the description of the island said to have been given by Merlin to another bard, Taliessin:—

"'We came to that green and fertile island which each year is blessed with two autumns, two springs, two summers, two gatherings of fruit,—the land where pearls are found, where the flowers spring as you gather them—that isle of orchards called the "Isle of the Blessed." No tillage there, no coulter to tear the bosom of the earth. Without labor it affords wheat and the grape. There the lives extend beyond a century. There nine sisters, whose will is the only law, rule over those who go from us to them. The eldest excels in the art of healing, and exceeds her sisters in beauty. She is called Morgana, and knows the virtues of all the herbs of the meadow. She can change her form, and soar in the air like a bird; she can be where she pleases in a moment, and in a moment descend on our coasts from the clouds. Her sister Thiten is renowned for her skill on the harp.'

"'With the prince we arrived, and Morgana received us with fitting honour. And in her own chamber she placed the king on a bed of gold, and with delicate touch, she uncovered the wound. Long she considered it, and at length said to him that she could heal it if he stayed long with her, and willed her to attempt her cure. Rejoiced at this news, we intrusted the king to her care, and soon after set sail.'"

Sir Thomas Malory, who wrote the book called the "Historie of King Arthur," or more commonly the "Morte d'Arthur," utters these high thoughts concerning the memory of the great king:—

"Oh, yee mightie and pompeous lords, shining in the glory transitory of this unstable life, as in raigning over great realmes and mightie great countries, fortified with strong castles and toures, edified with many a rich citie; yee also, yee fierce and mightie knights, so valiant in adventurous deeds of armes; behold, behold, see how this mightie conquerour king Arthur, whom in his humaine life all the world doubted, see also the noble queene Guenever, which sometime sat in her chaire adorned with gold, pearles, and precious stones, now lye full low in obscure fosse or pit, covered with clods of earth and clay; behold also this mightie champion Sir Launcelot, pearelesse of all knighthood, see now how hee lyeth groveling upon the cold mould, now being so feeble and faint that sometime was so terrible. How and in what manner ought yee to bee so desirous of worldly honour so dangerous! Therefore mee thinketh this present booke is right necessary often to be read, for in it shall yee finde the most gracious, knightly, and vertuous war of the most noble knights of the world, whereby they gat praysing continually. Also mee seemeth, by the oft reading thereof, yee shall greatly desire to accustome your selfe in following of those gracious knightly deedes, that is to say, to dread God, and to love righteousnesse, faithfully and couragiously to serve your soveraigne prince; and the more that God hath given you the triumphall honour, the meeker yee ought to bee, ever feareing the unstablenesse of this deceitfull world."

## MAELDUIN'S VOYAGE

An Irish knight named Maelduin set forth early in the eighth century to seek round the seas for his father's murderers. By the advice of a wizard, he was to take with him seventeen companions, neither less nor more; but at the last moment his three foster brothers, whom he had not included, begged to go with him. He refused, and they cast themselves into the sea to swim after his vessel. Maelduin had pity on them and took them in, but his disregard of the wizard's advice brought punishment; and it was only after long wanderings, after visiting multitudes of unknown and often enchanted islands, and after the death or loss of the three foster brothers, that Maelduin was able to return to his native land.

One island which they visited was divided into four parts by four fences, one of gold, one of silver, one of brass, one of crystal. In the first division there dwelt kings, in the second queens, in the third warriors, and in the fourth maidens. The voyagers landed in the maidens' realm; one of these came out in a boat and gave them food, such that every one found in it the taste he liked best; then followed an enchanted drink, which made them sleep for three days and three nights. When they awakened they were in their boat on the sea, and nothing was to be seen either of island or maidens.

The next island had in it a fortress with a brazen door and a bridge of glass, on which every one who ascended it slipped and fell. A woman came from the fortress, pail in hand, drew water from the sea and returned, not answering them when they spoke. When they reached at last the brazen door and struck upon it, it made a sweet and soothing sound, and they went to sleep, for three days and nights, as before. On the fourth day a maiden came who was most beautiful; she wore garments of white silk, a white mantle with a brooch of silver with studs of gold, and a gold band round her hair. She greeted each man by his name, and said, "It is long that we have expected you." She took them into the castle and gave them every kind of food they had ever desired. Maelduin was filled with love for her and asked her for her love; but she told him that love was sin and she had no knowledge of sin; so she left him. On the morrow they found their boat, stranded on a crag, while lady and fortress and island had all vanished.

Another island on which they landed was large and bare, with another fortress and a palace. There they met a lady who was kinder. She wore an embroidered purple mantle, gold embroidered gloves, and ornamented sandals, and was just riding up to the palace door. Seventeen maidens waited there for her. She offered to keep the strangers as guests, and that each of them should have a wife, she herself wedding Maelduin. She was, it seems, the widow of the king of the island, and these were her seventeen daughters. She ruled the island and went every day to judge the people and direct their lives. If the strangers would stay, she said that they should never more know sorrow, or hardships, or old age; she herself, in spite of her large family, being young and beautiful as ever. They stayed three months, and it seemed to all but Maelduin that the three months were three years. When the queen was absent, one day, the men took the boat and compelled Maelduin to leave the island with them; but the queen rode after them and flung a rope, which Maelduin caught and which clung to his hand. She drew them back to the shore; this happened thrice, and the men accused Maelduin of catching the rope on purpose; he bade another man catch it, and his companions cut off his hand, and they escaped at last.

On one island the seafarers found three magic apples, and each apple gave sufficient food for forty nights; again, on another island, they found the same apples. In another place still, a great bird like a cloud arrived, with a tree larger than an oak in its claws. After a while two eagles came and cleaned the feathers of the larger bird. They also stripped off the red berries from the tree and threw them into the ocean until its foam grew red. The great bird then flew into the ocean and cleaned itself. This happened daily for three days, when the great bird flew away with stronger wings, its youth being thus renewed.

They came to another island where many people stood by the shore talking and joking. They were all looking at Maelduin and his comrades, and kept gaping and laughing, but would not exchange a word with them. Then Maelduin sent one of his foster brothers on the island; but he ranged himself with the others and did as they did. Maelduin and his men rowed round and round the island, and whenever they passed the point where this comrade was, they addressed him, but he never answered, and only gaped and laughed. They waited for him a long time and left him. This island they found to be called The Island of Joy.

On another island they found sheep grazing, of enormous size; on another, birds, whose eggs when eaten caused feathers to sprout all over the bodies of those who eat them. On another they found crimson flowers, whose mere perfume sufficed for food, and they encountered women whose only food was apples. Through the window flew three birds: a blue one with a crimson head; a crimson one with a green head; a green one with a golden head. These sang heavenly music, and were sent to accompany the wanderers on their departing; the queen of the island gave them an emerald cup, such that water poured into it became wine. She asked if they knew how long they had been there, and when they said "a day," she told them that it was a year, during which they had had no food. As they sailed away, the birds sang to them until both birds and island disappeared in the mist.

They saw another island standing on a single pedestal, as if on one foot, projecting from the water. Rowing round it to seek a way into it they found no passage, but they saw in the base of the pedestal, under water, a closed door with a lock—this being the only way in which the island could be entered. Around another island there was a fiery rampart, which constantly moved in a circle. In the side of that rampart was an open door, and as it came opposite them in its turning course, they beheld through it the island and all therein; and its occupants, even human beings, were many and beautiful, wearing rich garments, and feasting with gold vessels in their hands. The voyagers lingered long to gaze upon this marvel.

On another island they found many human beings, black in color and raiment, and always bewailing. Lots were cast, and another of Maelduin's foster brothers was sent on shore. He at once joined the weeping crowd, and did as they did. Two others were sent to bring him back, and both shared his fate, falling under some strange spell. Then Maelduin sent four others, and bade them look neither at the land nor at the sky; to wrap their mouths and noses with their garments, and not breathe the island air; and not to take off their eyes from their comrades. In this way the two who followed the foster brother on shore were rescued, but he remained behind.

Of another island they could see nothing but a fort, protected by a great white rampart, on which nothing living was to be seen but a small cat, leaping from one to another of four stone pillars. They found brooches and ornaments of gold and silver, they found white quilts and embroidered garments hanging up, flitches of bacon were suspended, a whole ox was roasting, and vessels stood filled with intoxicating drinks. Maelduin asked the cat if all this was for them; but the cat merely looked at him and went on playing. The seafarers dined and drank, then went to sleep. As they were about to depart, Maelduin's third foster brother proposed to carry off a tempting necklace, and in spite of his leader's warnings grasped it. Instantly the cat leaped through him like a fiery arrow, burned him so that he became ashes, and went back to its pillar. Thus all three of the foster brothers who had disregarded the wizard's warning, and forced themselves upon the party, were either killed or left behind upon the enchanted islands.

Around another island there was a demon horse-race going on; the riders were just riding in over the sea, and then the race began; the voyagers could only dimly perceive the forms of the horses, but could hear the cries of their riders, the strokes of the whips, and the words of the spectators, "See the gray horse!" "Watch the chestnut horse!" and the voyagers were so alarmed that they rowed away. The next island was covered with trees laden with golden apples, but these were being rapidly eaten by small, scarlet animals which they found, on coming nearer, to be all made of fire and thus brightened in hue. Then the animals vanished, and Maelduin with his men landed, and though the ground was still hot from the fiery creatures, they brought away a boat load of the apples. Another island was divided into two parts by a brass wall across the middle. There were two flocks of sheep, and those on one side of the wall were white, while the others were black. A large man was dividing and arranging the sheep, and threw them easily over the wall. When he threw a white sheep among the black ones it became black, and when he threw a black sheep among the white ones, it became white instantly. The voyagers thought of landing, but when Maelduin saw this, he said, "Let us throw something on shore to see if it will change color. If it does, we will avoid the island." So they took a black branch and threw it toward the white sheep. When it fell, it grew white; and the same with a white branch on the black side. "It is lucky for us," said Maelduin, "that we did not land on this island."

They came next to an island where there was but one man visible, very aged, and with long, white hair. Above him were trees, covered with great numbers of birds. The old man told them that he like them had come in a curragh, or coracle, and had placed many green sods beneath his feet, to steady the boat. Reaching this spot, the green sods had joined together and formed an island which at first gave him hardly room to stand; but every year one foot was added to its size, and one tree grew up. He had lived there for centuries, and those birds were the souls of his children and descendants, each of whom was sent there after death, and they were all fed from heaven each day. On the next island there was a great roaring as of bellows and a sound of smiths' hammers, as if striking all together on an anvil, every sound seeming to come from the strokes of a dozen men. "Are they near?" asked one big voice. "Silence!" said another; and they were evidently watching for the boat. When it rowed away, one of the smiths flung after them a vast mass of red-hot iron, which he had grasped with the tongs from the furnace. It fell just short, but made the whole sea to hiss and boil around them as they rowed away.

Another island had a wall of water round it, and Maelduin and his men saw multitudes of people driving away herds of cattle and sheep, and shouting, "There they are, they have come again;" and a woman pelted them from below with great nuts, which the crew gathered for eating. Then as they rowed away they heard one man say, "Where are they now?" and another cried, "They are going away." Still again they visited an island where a great stream of water shot up into the air and made an arch like a rainbow that spanned the land.

They walked below it without getting wet, and hooked down from it many large salmon; besides that, many fell out above their heads, so that they had more than they could carry away with them. These are by no means all of the strange adventures of Maelduin and his men.

The last island to which they came was called Raven's Stream, and there one of the men, who had been very homesick, leaped out upon shore. As soon as he touched the land he became a heap of ashes, as if his body had lain in the earth a thousand years. This showed them for the first time during how vast a period they had been absent, and what a space they must have traversed. Instead of thirty enchanted islands they had visited thrice fifty, many of them twice or thrice as large as Ireland, whence the voyagers first came. In the wonderful experiences of their long lives they had apparently lost sight of the search which they had undertaken, for the murderers of Maelduin's father, since of them we hear no more. The island enchantment seems to have banished all other thoughts.

THE VOYAGE OF ST. BRANDAN

The young student Brandan was awakened in the morning by the crowing of the cock in the great Irish abbey where he dwelt; he rose, washed his face and hands and dressed himself, then passed into the chapel, where he prayed and sang until the dawn of the day. "With song comes courage" was the motto of the abbey. It was one of those institutions like great colonies,— church, library, farm, workshop, college, all in one,—of which Ireland in the sixth century was full, and which existed also elsewhere. Their extent is best seen by the modern traveller in the remains of the vast buildings at Tintern in England, scattered over a wide extent of country, where you keep coming upon walls and fragments of buildings which once formed a part of a single great institution, in which all the life of the community was organized, as was the case in the Spanish missions of California. At the abbey of Bangor in Wales, for instance, there were two thousand four hundred men,—all under the direction of a comparatively small body of monks, who were trained to an amount of organizing skill like that now needed for a great railway system. Some of these men were occupied, in various mechanic arts, some in mining, but most of them in agriculture, which they carried on with their own hands, without the aid of animals, and in total silence.

Having thus labored in the fields until noonday, Brandan then returned that he might work in the library, transcribing ancient manuscripts or illustrating books of prayer. Having to observe silence, he wrote the name of the book to give to the librarian, and if it were a Christian work, he stretched out his hand, making motions with his fingers as if turning over the leaves; but if it were by a pagan author, the monk who asked for it was required to scratch his ear as a dog does, to show his contempt, because, the regulations said, an unbeliever might well be compared to that animal[1]. Taking the book, he copied it in the Scriptorium or library, or took it to his cell, where he wrote all winter without a fire. It is to such monks that we owe all our knowledge of the earliest history of England and Ireland; though doubtless the hand that wrote the histories of Gildas and Bede grew as tired as that of Brandan, or as that of the monk who wrote in the corner of a beautiful manuscript: "He who does not know how to write imagines it to be no labor; but though only three fingers hold the pen, the whole body grows weary." In the same way Brandan may have learned music and have had an organ in his monastery, or have had a school of art, painting beautiful miniatures for the holy missals. This was his early life in the convent.

[Footnote 1: Adde ut aurem tangas digito sicut canis cum pede pruriens solet, quia nec immerito infideles tali animati comparantur. —MARTÈNE, De Antiq. Monach. ritibus, p. 289, qu. by Montalembert, Monks of the West (tr.) VI. 190.]

Once a day they were called to food; this consisting for them of bread and vegetables with no seasoning but salt, although better fare was furnished for the sick and the aged, for travellers and the poor. These last numbered, at Easter time, some three or four hundred, who constantly came and went, and upon whom the monks and young disciples waited. After the meal the monks spent three hours in the chapel, on their knees, still silent; then they confessed in turn to the abbot and then sought their hard-earned rest. They held all things in common; no one even received a gift for himself. War never reached them; it was the rarest thing for an armed party to molest their composure; their domains were regarded as a haven for the stormy world. Because there were so many such places in Ireland, it was known as The Isle of Saints.

Brandan was sent after a time to other abbeys, where he could pursue especial studies, for they had six branches of learning,—grammar, rhetoric, dialectics, geometry, astronomy, and music. Thus he passed three years, and was then advised to go to an especial teacher in the mountains, who had particular modes of teaching certain branches. But this priest—he was an Italian—was suffering from poverty, and could receive his guest but for a few weeks. One day as Brandan sat studying, he saw, the legend says, a white mouse come from a crack in the wall, a visitor which climbed upon his table and left there a grain of wheat. Then the mouse paused, looked at the student, then ran about the table, went away and reappeared with another grain, and another, up to five. Brandan, who had at the very instant learned his lesson, rose from his seat, followed the mouse, and looking through a hole in the wall, saw a great pile of wheat, stored in a concealed apartment. On his showing this to the head of the convent, it was pronounced a miracle; the food was distributed to the poor, and "the people blessed his charity while the Lord blessed his studies."

In the course of years, Brandan became himself the head of one of the great abbeys, that of Clonfert, of the order of St. Benedict, where he had under him nearly three thousand monks. In this abbey, having one day given hospitality to a monk named Berinthus, who had just returned from an ocean voyage, Brandan learned from him the existence, far off in the ocean, of an island called The Delicious Isle, to which a priest named Mernoc had retired, with many companions of his order. Berinthus found Mernoc and the other monks living apart from one another for purposes of prayer, but when they came together, Mernoc said, they were like bees from different beehives. They met for their food and for church; their food included only apples, nuts, and various herbs. One day Mernoc said to Berinthus, "I will conduct you to the Promised Isle of the Saints." So they went on board a little ship and sailed westward through a thick fog until a great light shone and they found themselves near an island which was large and fruitful and bore many apples. There were no herbs without blossoms, he said, nor trees without fruits, and there were precious stones, and the island was traversed by a great river. Then they met a man of shining aspect who told them that they had without knowing it passed a year already in the island; that they had needed neither food nor sleep. Then they returned to the Delicious Island, and every one knew where they had been by the perfume of their garments. This was the story of Berinthus, and from this time forward nothing could keep Brandan from the purpose of beholding for himself these blessed islands.

Before carrying out his plans, however, he went, about the year 560, to visit an abbot named Enda, who lived at Arran, then called Isle of the Saints, a priest who was supposed to know more than any one concerning the farther lands of the western sea. He knew, for instance, of the enchanted island named Hy-Brasail, which could be seen from the coast of Ireland only once in seven years, and which the priests had vainly tried to disenchant. Some islands, it was believed, had been already disenchanted by throwing on them a few sparks of lighted turf; but as Hy-Brasail was too far for this, there were repeated efforts to disenchant it by shooting fiery arrows towards it, though this had not yet been successful. Then Enda could tell of wonderful ways to cross the sea without a boat, how his sister Fanchea had done it by spreading her own cloak upon the waves, and how she and three other nuns were borne upon it. She found, however, that one hem of the cloak sank below the water, because one of her companions had brought with her, against orders, a brazen vessel from the convent; but on her throwing it away, the sinking hem rose to the level of the rest and bore them safely. St. Enda himself had first crossed to Arran on a large stone which he had ordered his followers to place on the water and which floated before the wind; and he told of another priest who had walked on the sea as on a meadow and plucked flowers as he went. Hearing such tales, how could St. Brandan fear to enter on his voyage?

He caused a boat to be built of a fashion which one may still see in Welsh and Irish rivers, and known as a curragh or coracle; made of an osier frame covered with tanned and oiled skins. He took with him seventeen priests, among whom was St. Malo, then a mere boy, but afterwards celebrated. They sailed to the southwest, and after being forty days at sea they reached a rocky island furrowed with streams, where they received the kindest hospitality, and took in fresh provisions. They sailed again the next day, and found themselves entangled in contrary currents and perplexing winds, so that they were long in reaching another island, green and fertile, watered by rivers which were full of fish, and covered with vast herds of sheep as large as heifers. Here they renewed their stock of provisions, and chose a spotless lamb with which to celebrate Easter Sunday on another island, which they saw at a short distance.

This island was wholly bare, without sandy shores or wooded slopes, and they all landed upon it to cook their lamb; but when they had arranged their cooking-apparatus, and when their fire began to blaze, the island seemed to move beneath their feet, and they ran in terror to their boat, from which Brandan had not yet landed. Their supposed island was a whale, and they rowed hastily away from it toward the island they had left, while the whale glided away, still showing, at a distance of two miles, the fire blazing on his back.

The next island they visited was wooded and fertile, where they found a multitude of birds, which chanted with them the praises of the Lord, so that they called this the Paradise of Birds.

This was the description given of this island by an old writer named Wynkyn de Worde, in "The Golden Legend":—

"Soon after, as God would, they saw a fair island, full of flowers, herbs, and trees, whereof they thanked God of his good grace; and anon they went on land, and when they had gone long in this, they found a full fayre well, and thereby stood a fair tree full of boughs, and on every bough sat a fayre bird, and they sat so thick on the tree that uneath [scarcely] any leaf of the tree might be seen. The number of them was so great, and they sang so merrilie, that it was an heavenlie noise to hear. Whereupon St. Brandan kneeled down on his knees and wept for joy, and made his praise devoutlie to our Lord God, to know what these birds meant. And then anon one of the birds flew from the tree to St. Brandan, and he with the flickering of his wings made a full merrie noise like a fiddle, that him seemed he never heard so joyful a melodie. And then St. Brandan commanded the foule to tell him the cause why they sat so thick on the tree and sang so merrilie. And then the foule said, some time we were angels in heaven, but when our master, Lucifer, fell down into hell for his high pride, and we fell with him for our offences, some higher and some lower, after the quality of the trespasse. And because our trespasse is so little, therefore our Lord hath sent us here, out of all paine, in full great joy and mirthe, after his pleasing, here to serve him on this tree in the best manner we can. The Sundaie is a daie of rest from all worldly occupation, and therefore that day all we be made as white as any snow, for to praise our Lorde in the best wise we may. And then all the birds began to sing evensong so merrilie that it was an heavenlie noise to hear; and after supper St. Brandan and his fellows went to bed and slept well. And in the morn they arose by times, and then those foules began mattyns, prime, and hours, and all such service as Christian men used to sing; and St. Brandan, with his fellows, abode there seven weeks, until Trinity Sunday was passed."

Having then embarked, they wandered for months on the ocean, before reaching another island. That on which they finally landed was inhabited by monks who had as their patrons St. Patrick and St. Ailbée, and they spent Christmas there. A year passed in these voyages, and the tradition is that for six other years they made just the same circuit, always spending Holy Week at the island where they found the sheep, alighting for Easter on the back of the same patient whale, visiting the Isle of Birds at Pentecost, and reaching the island of St. Patrick and St. Ailbée in time for Christmas.

But in the seventh year they met with wholly new perils. They were attacked, the legend says, first by a whale, then by a griffin, and then by a race of cyclops, or one-eyed giants. Then they came to an island where the whale which had attacked them was thrown on shore, so that they could cut him to pieces; then another island which had great fruits, and was called The Island of the Strong Man; and lastly one where the grapes filled the air with perfume. After this they saw an island, all cinders and flames, where the cyclops had their forges, and they sailed away in the light of an immense fire. The next day they saw, looking northward, a great and high mountain sending out flames at the top. Turning hastily from this dreadful sight, they saw a little round island, at the top of which a hermit dwelt, who gave them his benediction. Then they sailed southward once more, and stopped at their usual places of resort for Holy Week, Easter, and Whitsuntide.

It was on this trip that they had, so the legend says, that strange interview with Judas Iscariot, out of which Matthew Arnold has made a ballad. Sailing in the wintry northern seas at Christmas time, St. Brandan saw an iceberg floating by, on which a human form rested motionless; and when it moved at last, he saw by its resemblance to the painted pictures he had seen that it must be Judas Iscariot, who had died five centuries before. Then as the boat floated near the iceberg, Judas spoke and told him his tale. After he had betrayed Jesus Christ, after he had died, and had been consigned to the flames of hell,—which were believed in very literally in those days,—an angel came to him on Christmas night and said that he might go thence and cool himself for an hour. "Why this mercy?" asked Judas Iscariot. Then the angel said to him, "Remember the leper in Joppa," and poor Judas recalled how once when the hot wind, called the sirocco, swept through the streets of Joppa, and he saw a naked leper by the wayside, sitting in agony from the heat and the drifting sand, Judas had thrown his cloak over him for a shelter and received his thanks. In reward for this, the angel now told him, he was to have, once a year, an hour's respite from his pain; he was allowed in that hour to fling himself on an iceberg and cool his burning heat as he drifted through the northern seas. Then St. Brandan bent his head in prayer; and when he looked up, the hour was passed, and Judas had been hurried back into his torments.

It seems to have been only after seven years of this wandering that they at last penetrated within the obscure fogs which surrounded the Isle of the Saints, and came upon a shore which lay all bathed in sunny light. It was a vast island, sprinkled with precious stones, and covered with ripe fruits; they traversed it for forty days without arriving at the end, though they reached a great river which flowed through the midst of it from east to west. There an angel appeared to them, and told them that they could go no farther, but could return to their own abode, carrying from the island some of those fruits and precious stones which were reserved to be distributed among the saints when all the world should be brought to the true faith. In order to hasten that time, it appears that St. Malo, the youngest of the sea-faring monks, had wished, in his zeal, to baptize some one, and had therefore dug up a heathen giant who had been, for some reason, buried on the blessed isle. Not only had he dug the giant's body up, but St. Malo had brought him to life again sufficiently for the purpose of baptism and instruction in the true faith; after which he gave him the name of Mildus, and let him die once more and be reburied. Then, facing homeward and sailing beyond the fog, they touched once more at The Island of Delights, received the benediction of the abbot of the monastery, and sailed for Ireland to tell their brethren of the wonders they had seen.

He used to tell them especially to his nurse Ita, under whose care he had been placed until his fifth year. His monastery at Clonfert grew, as has been said, to include three thousand monks; and he spent his remaining years in peace and sanctity. The supposed islands which he visited are still believed by many to have formed a part of the American continent, and he is still thought by some Irish scholars to have been the first to discover this hemisphere, nearly a thousand years before Columbus, although this view has not yet made much impression on historians. The Paradise of Birds, in particular, has been placed by these scholars in Mexico, and an Irish poet has written a long poem describing the delights to be found there:—

> "Oft, in the sunny mornings, have I seen
> Bright yellow birds, of a rich lemon hue,
> Meeting in crowds upon the branches green,
> And sweetly singing all the morning through;
> And others, with their heads grayish and dark,
> Pressing their cinnamon cheeks to the old trees,
> And striking on the hard, rough, shrivelled bark,
> Like conscience on a bosom ill at ease.
>
> "And diamond-birds chirping their single notes,
> Now 'mid the trumpet-flower's deep blossoms seen,
> Now floating brightly on with fiery throats—
> Small winged emeralds of golden green;
> And other larger birds with orange cheeks,
> A many-color-painted, chattering crowd,

Prattling forever with their curved beaks,
And through the silent woods screaming aloud."

## KIRWAN'S SEARCH FOR HY-BRASAIL

The boy Kirwan lay on one of the steep cliffs of the Island of Innismane— one of the islands of Arran, formerly called Isles of the Saints. He was looking across the Atlantic for a glimpse of Hy-Brasail. This was what they called it; it was a mysterious island which Kirwan's grandfather had seen, or thought he had seen—and Kirwan's father also;—indeed, there was not one of the old people on the island who did not think he had seen it, and the older they were, the oftener it had been seen by them, and the larger it looked. But Kirwan had never seen it, and whenever he came to the top of the highest cliff, where he often went bird-nesting, he climbed the great mass of granite called The Gregory, and peered out into the west, especially at sunset, in hopes that he would at least catch a glimpse, some happy evening, of the cliffs and meadows of Hy-Brasail. But as yet he had never espied them. All this was more than two hundred years ago.

He naturally went up to The Gregory at this hour, because it was then that he met the other boys, and caught puffins by being lowered over the cliff. The agent of the island employed the boys, and paid them a sixpence for every dozen birds, that he might sell the feathers. The boys had a rope three hundred feet long, which could reach the bottom of the cliff. One of them tied this rope around his waist, and then held it fast with both hands, the rope being held above by four or five strong boys, who lowered the cragman, or "clifter," as he was called, over the precipice. Kirwan was thus lowered to the rocks near the sea, where the puffins bred; and, loosening the rope, he prepared to spend the night in catching them. He had a pole with a snare on the end, which he easily clapped on the heads of the heavy and stupid birds; then tied each on a string as he caught it, and so kept it to be hauled up in the morning. He took in this way twenty or thirty score of the birds, besides quantities of their large eggs, which were found in deep clefts in the rock; and these he carried with him when his friends came in the morning to haul him up. It was a good school of courage, for sometimes boys missed their footing and were dashed to pieces. At other times he fished in his father's boat, or drove calves for sale on the mainland, or cured salt after high tide in the caverns, or collected kelp for the farmers. But he was always looking forward to a time when he might get a glimpse of the island of Hy-Brasail, and make his way to it.

One day when all the fleet of fishing-boats was out for the herring fishery, and Kirwan among them, the fog came in closer and closer, and he was shut apart from all others. His companion in the boat—or dory-mate, as it would be called in New England—had gone to cut bait on board another boat, but Kirwan could manage the boat well enough alone. Long he toiled with his oars toward the west, where he fancied the rest of the fleet to be; and sometimes he spread his little sprit-sail, steering with an oar—a thing which was, in a heavy sea, almost as hard as rowing. At last the fog lifted, and he found himself alone upon the ocean. He had lost his bearings and could not tell the points of the compass. Presently out of a heavy bank of fog which rose against the horizon he saw what seemed land. It gave him new strength, and he worked hard to reach it; but it was long since he had eaten, his head was dizzy, and he lay down on the thwart of the boat, rather heedless of what might come. Growing weaker and weaker, he did not clearly know what he was doing. Suddenly he started up, for a voice hailed him from above his head. He saw above him the high stern of a small vessel, and with the aid of a sailor he was helped on board.

He found himself on the deck of a sloop of about seventy tons, John Nisbet, master, with a crew of seven men. They had sailed from Killebegs (County Donegal), in Ireland, for the coast of France, laden with butter, tallow, and hides, and were now returning from France with French wines, and were befogged as Kirwan had been. The boy was at once taken on board and rated as a seaman; and the later adventures of the trip are here given as he reported them on his return with the ship some months later.

The mist continued thicker and thicker for a time, and when it suddenly furled itself away, they found themselves on an unknown coast, with the wind driving them shoreward. There were men on board who were familiar with the whole coast of Ireland and Scotland, but they remembered nothing like this. Finding less than three fathoms of water, they came to anchor and sent four men ashore to find where they were; these being James Ross the carpenter and two sailors, with the boy Kirwan. They took swords and pistols. Landing at the edge of a little wood, they walked for a mile within a pleasant valley where cattle, horses, and sheep were feeding, and then came in sight of a castle, small but strong, where they went to the door and knocked. No one answered, and they walked on, up a green hill, where there were multitudes of black rabbits; but when they had reached the top and looked around they could see no inhabitants, nor any house; on which they returned to the sloop and told their tale. After this the whole ship's company went ashore, except one left in charge, and they wandered about for hours, yet saw nothing more. As night came on they made a fire at the base of a fallen oak, near the shore, and lay around it, talking, and smoking the lately discovered weed, tobacco; when suddenly they heard loud noises from the direction of the castle and then all over the island, which frightened them so that they went on board the sloop and stayed all night.

The next morning they saw a dignified, elderly gentleman with ten unarmed followers coming down towards the shore. Hailing the sloop, the older gentleman, speaking Gaelic, asked who and whence they were, and being told, invited them ashore as his guests. They went on shore, well-armed; and he embraced them one by one, telling them that they were the happiest sight that island had seen for hundreds of years; that it was called Hy-Brasail or O-Brazile; that his ancestors had been princes of it, but For many years it had been taken possession of by enchanters, who kept it almost always invisible, so that no ship came there; and that for the same reason he and his friends were rendered unable to answer the sailors, even when they knocked at the door; and that the enchantment must remain until a fire was kindled on the island by good Christians. This had been done the night before, and the terrible noises which they had heard were from the powers of darkness, which had now left the island forever.

And indeed when the sailors were led to the castle, they saw that the chief tower had just been demolished by the powers of darkness, as they retreated; but there were sitting within the halls men and women of dignified appearance, who thanked them for the good service they had done. Then they were taken over the island, which proved to be some sixty miles long and thirty wide, abounding with horses, cattle, sheep, deer, rabbits, and birds, but without any swine; it had also rich mines of silver and gold, but few people, although there were ruins of old towns and cities. The sailors, after being richly rewarded, were sent on board their vessel and furnished with sailing directions to their port. On reaching home, they showed to the minister of their town the pieces of gold and silver that were given them at the island, these being of an ancient stamp, somewhat rusty yet of pure gold; and there was at once an eager desire on the part of certain of the townsmen to go with them. Within a week an expedition was fitted out, containing several godly ministers, who wished to visit and discover the inhabitants of the island; but through some mishap of the seas this expedition was never heard of again.

Partly for this reason and partly because none of Captain Nesbit's crew wished to return to the island, there came to be in time a feeling of distrust about all this rediscovery of Hy-Brasail or O-Brazile. There were not wanting those who held that the ancient gold pieces might have been gained by piracy, such as was beginning to be known upon the Spanish main; and as for the boy Kirwan, some of his playmates did not hesitate to express the opinion that he had always been, as they phrased it, the greatest liar that ever spoke. What is certain is that the island of Brazil or Hy-Brasail had appeared on maps ever since 1367 as being near the coast of Ireland; that many voyages were made from Bristol to find it, a hundred years later; that it was mentioned about 1636 as often seen from the shore; and that it appeared as Brazil Rock on the London Admiralty Charts until after 1850. If many people tried to find it and failed, why should not Kirwan have tried and succeeded? And as to his stretching his story a little by throwing in a few enchanters and magic castles, there was not a voyager of his period who was not tempted to do the same.

THE ISLE OF SATAN'S HAND

The prosperous farmer Conall Ua Corra in the province of Connaught had everything to make him happy except that he and his wife had no children to cheer their old age and inherit their estate. Conall had prayed for children, and one day said in his impatience that he would rather have them sent by Satan than not have them at all. A year or two later his wife had three sons at a birth, and when these sons came to maturity, they were so ridiculed by other young men, as being the sons of Satan, that they said, "If such is really our parentage, we will do Satan's work." So they collected around them a few villains and began plundering and destroying the churches in the neighborhood and thus injuring half the church buildings in the country. At last they resolved to visit also the church of Clothar, to destroy it, and to kill if necessary their mother's father, who was the leading layman of the parish. When they came to the church, they found the old man on the green in front of it, distributing meat and drink to his tenants and the people of the parish. Seeing this, they postponed their plans until after dark and in the meantime went home with their grandfather, to spend the night at his house. They went to rest, and the eldest, Lochan, had a terrible dream in which he saw first the joys of heaven and then the terrors of future punishment, and then he awoke in dismay. Waking his brothers, he told them his dream, and that he now saw that they had been serving evil masters and making war upon a good one. Such was his bitterness of remorse that he converted them to his views, and they agreed to go to their grandfather in the morning, renounce their sinful ways and ask his pardon.

This they did, and he advised them to go to a celebrated saint, Finnen of Clonard, and take him as their spiritual guide. Laying aside their armor and weapons, they went to Clonard, where all the people, dreading them and knowing their wickedness, fled for their lives, except the saint himself, who came forward to meet them. With him the three brothers undertook the most austere religious exercises, and after a year they came to St. Finnen and asked his punishment for their former crimes. "You cannot," he said, "restore to life those you have slain, but you can at least restore the buildings you have devastated and ruined." So they went and repaired many churches, after which they resolved to go on a pilgrimage upon the great Atlantic Ocean. They built for themselves therefore a curragh or coracle, covered with hides three deep. It was capable of carrying nine persons, and they selected five out of the many who wished to join the party. There were a bishop, a priest, a deacon, a musician, and the man who had modelled the boat; and with these they pushed out to sea.

It had happened some years before that in a quarrel about a deer hunt, the men of Ross had killed the king. It had been decided that, by way of punishment, sixty couples of the people of Ross should be sent out to sea, two and two, in small boats, to meet what fate they might upon the deeps. They were watched that they might not land again, and for many years nothing more had been heard from them. The most pious task which these repenting pilgrims could undertake, it was thought, would be to seek these banished people. They resolved to spread their sail and let Providence direct their course. They went, therefore, northwest on the Atlantic, where they visited several wonderful islands, on one of which there was a great bird which related to them, the legend says, the whole history of the world, and gave them a great leaf from a tree—the leaf being as large as an ox-hide, and being preserved for many years in one of the churches after their return. At the next island they heard sweet human voices, and found that the sixty banished couples had established their homes there.

The pilgrims then went onward in their hidebound boat until they reached the coast of Spain, and there they landed and dwelt for a time. The bishop built a church, and the priest officiated in it, and the organist took charge of the music. All prospered; yet the boat-builder and the three brothers were never quite contented, for they had roamed the seas too long; and they longed for a new enterprise for their idle valor. They thought they had found this when one day they found on the sea-coast a group of women tearing their hair, and when they asked the explanation, "Señor," said an old woman, "our sons and our husbands have again fallen into the hand of Satan." At this the three brothers were startled, for they remembered well how they used, in youth, to rank themselves as Satan's children. Asking farther, they learned that a shattered boat they saw on the beach was one of a pair of boats which had been carried too far out to sea, and had come near an islet which the sailors called Isla de la Man Satanaxio, or The Island of Satan's Hand. It appeared that in that region there was an islet so called, always surrounded by chilly mists and water of a deadly cold; that no one had ever reached it, as it constantly changed place; but that a demon hand sometimes uprose from it, and plucked away men and even whole boats, which, when once grasped, usually by night, were never seen again, but perished helplessly, victims of Satan's Hand.

When the voyagers laughed at this legend, the priest of the village showed them, on the early chart of Bianco, the name of "De la Man Satanagio," and on that of Beccaria the name "Satanagio" alone, both these being the titles of islands. Not alarmed at the name of Satan, as being that of one whom they had supposed, in their days of darkness, to be their patron, they pushed boldly out to sea and steered westward, a boat-load of Spanish fishermen following in their wake. Passing island after island of green and fertile look, they found themselves at last in what seemed a less favored zone—as windy as the "roaring forties," and growing chillier every hour. Fogs gathered quickly, so that they could scarcely see the companion boat, and the Spanish fishermen called out to them, "Garda da la Man do Satanaxio!" ("Look out for Satan's hand!")

As they cried, the fog became denser yet, and when it once parted for a moment, something that lifted itself high above them, like a gigantic hand, showed itself an instant, and then descended with a crushing grasp upon the boat of the Spanish fishermen, breaking it to pieces, and dragging some of the men below the water, while others, escaping, swam through the ice-cold waves, and were with difficulty taken on board the coracle; this being all the harder because the whole surface of the water was boiling and seething furiously. Rowing away as they could from this perilous neighborhood, they lay on their oars when the night came on, not knowing which way to go. Gradually the fog cleared away, the sun rose clearly at last, and wherever they looked on the deep they saw no traces of any island, still less of the demon hand. But for the presence among them of the fishermen they had picked up, there was nothing to show that any casualty had happened.

That day they steered still farther to the west with some repining from the crew, and at night the same fog gathered, the same deadly chill came on. Finding themselves in shoal water, and apparently near some island, they decided to anchor the boat; and as the man in the bow bent over to clear away the anchor, something came down upon him with the same awful force, and knocked him overboard. His body could not be recovered, and as the wind came up, they drove before it until noon of the next day, seeing nothing of any land and the ocean deepening again. By noon the fog cleared, and they saw nothing, but cried with one voice that the boat should be put about, and they should return to Spain. For two days they rowed in peace over a summer sea; then came the fog again and they laid on their oars that night. All around them dim islands seemed to float, scarcely discernible in the fog; sometimes from the top of each a point would show itself, as of a mighty hand, and they could hear an occasional plash and roar, as if this hand came downwards. Once they heard a cry, as if of sailors from another vessel. Then they strained their eyes to gaze into the fog, and a whole island seemed to be turning itself upside down, its peak coming down, while its base went uppermost, and the whole water boiled for leagues around, as if both earth and sea were upheaved.

The sun rose upon this chaos of waters. No demon hand was anywhere visible, nor any island, but a few icebergs were in sight, and the frightened sailors rowed away and made sail for home. It was rare to see icebergs so far south, and this naturally added to the general dismay. Amid the superstition of the sailors, the tales grew and grew, and all the terrors became mingled. But tradition says that there were some veteran Spanish sailors along that coast, men who had sailed on longer voyages, and that these persons actually laughed at the whole story of Satan's Hand, saying that any one who had happened to see an iceberg topple over would know all about it. It was more generally believed, however, that all this was mere envy and jealousy; the daring fishermen remained heroes for the rest of their days; and it was only within a century or two that the island of Satanaxio disappeared from the charts.

## ANTILLIA, THE ISLAND OF THE SEVEN CITIES

The young Spanish page, Luis de Vega, had been for some months at the court of Don Rodrigo, king of Spain, when he heard the old knights lamenting, as they came out of the palace at Toledo, over the king's last and most daring whim. "He means," said one of them in a whisper, "to penetrate the secret cave of the Gothic kings, that cave on which each successive sovereign has put a padlock,"

"Till there are now twenty-seven of them," interrupted a still older knight.

"And he means," said the first, frowning at the interruption, "to take thence the treasures of his ancestors."

"Indeed, he must do it," said another, "else the son of his ancestors will have no treasure left of his own."

"But there is a spell upon it," said the other. "For ages Spain has been threatened with invasion, and it is the old tradition that the only talisman which can prevent it is in this cave."

"Well," said the scoffer, "it is only by entering the cave that he can possess the talisman."

"But if he penetrates to it, his power is lost."

"A pretty talisman," said the other. "It is only of use to anybody so long as no one sees it. Were I the king I would hold it in my hands. And I have counselled him to heed no graybeards, but to seize the treasure for himself. I have offered to accompany him."

"May it please your lordship," said the eager Luis, "may I go with you?"

"Yes," said Don Alonzo de Carregas, turning to the ardent boy. "Where the king goes I go, and where I go thou shalt be my companion. See, señors," he said, turning to the others, "how the ready faith of boyhood puts your fears to shame. To his Majesty the terrors of this goblin cave are but a jest which frightens the old and only rouses the young to courage. The king may find the recesses of the cavern filled with gold and jewels; he who goes with him may share them. This boy is my first recruit: who follows?"

By this time a whole group of courtiers, young and old, had assembled about Don Alonzo, and every man below thirty years was ready to pledge himself to the enterprise. But the older courtiers and the archbishop Oppas were beseeching the king to refrain. "Respect, O king," they said, "the custom held sacred by twenty-seven of thy predecessors. Give us but an estimate of the sum that may, in thy kingly mind, represent the wealth that is within the cavern walls, and we will raise it on our own domains, rather than see the sacred tradition set at nought." The king's only answer was, "Follow me," Don Alonzo hastily sending the boy Luis to collect the younger knights who had already pledged themselves to the enterprise. A gallant troop, they made their way down the steep steps which led from the palace to the cave. The news had spread; the ladies had gathered on the balconies, and the bright face of one laughing girl looked from a bower window, while she tossed a rose to the happy Luis. Alas, it fell short of its mark and hit the robes of Archbishop Oppas, who stood with frowning face as the youngster swept by. The archbishop crushed it unwittingly in the hand that held the crosier.

The rusty padlocks were broken, and each fell clanking on the floor, and was brushed away by mailed heels. They passed from room to room with torches, for the cavern extended far beneath the earth; yet they found no treasure save the jewelled table of Solomon. But for their great expectations, this table alone might have proved sufficient to reward their act of daring. Some believed that it had been brought by the Romans from Solomon's temple, and from Rome by the Goths and Vandals who sacked that city and afterwards conquered Spain; but all believed it to be sacred, and now saw it to be gorgeous. Some describe it as being of gold, set with precious stones; others, as of gold and silver, making it yellow and white in hue, ornamented with a row of pearls, a row of rubies, and another row of emeralds. It is generally agreed that it stood on three hundred and sixty feet, each made of a single emerald. Being what it was, the king did not venture to remove it, but left it where it was. Traversing chamber after chamber and finding all empty, they at last found all passages leading to the inmost apartment, which had a marble urn in the centre. Yet all eyes presently turned from this urn to a large painting on the wall which displayed a troop of horsemen in full motion. Their horses were of Arab breed, their arms were scimitars and lances, with fluttering pennons; they wore turbans, and their coarse black hair fell over their shoulders; they were dressed in skins. Never had there been seen by the courtiers a mounted troop so wild, so eager, so formidable. Turning from them to the marble urn, the king drew from it a parchment, which said: "These are the people who, whenever this cave is entered and the spell contained in this urn is broken, shall possess this country. An idle curiosity has done its work.[2]

[Footnote 2: "Latinas letras á la margen puestas Decian:—'Cuando aquesta puerta y arca Fueran abiertas, gentes como estas Pondrán por tierra cuanto España abarca." —LOPE DE VEGA.]

The rash king, covering his eyes with his hands, fled outward from the cavern; his knights followed him, but Don Alonzo lingered last except the boy Luis. "Nevertheless, my lord," said Luis, "I should like to strike a blow at these bold barbarians." "We may have an opportunity," said the gloomy knight. He closed the centre gate of the cavern, and tried to replace the broken padlocks, but it was in vain. In twenty-four hours the story had travelled over the kingdom.

The boy Luis little knew into what a complex plot he was drifting. In the secret soul of his protector, Don Alonzo, there burned a great anger against the weak and licentious king. He and his father, Count Julian, and Archbishop Oppas, his uncle, were secretly brooding plans of wrath against Don Rodrigo for his ill treatment of Don Alonzo's sister, Florinda. Rumors had told them that an army of strange warriors from Africa, who had hitherto carried all before them, were threatening to cross the straits not yet called Gibraltar, and descend on Spain. All the ties of fidelity held these courtiers to the king; but they secretly hated him, and wished for his downfall. By the next day they had planned to betray him to the Moors. Count Julian had come to make his military report to Don Rodrigo, and on some pretext had withdrawn Florinda from the court. "When you come again," said the pleasure-loving king, "bring me some hawks from the south, that we may again go hawking." "I will bring you hawks enough," was the answer, "and such as you never saw before." "But Rodrigo," says the Arabian chronicler, "did not understand the full meaning of his words."

It was a hard blow for the young Luis when he discovered what a plot was being urged around him. He would gladly have been faithful to the king, worthless as he knew him to be; but Don Alonzo had been his benefactor, and he held by him. Meanwhile the conspiracy drew towards completion, and the Arab force was drawing nearer to the straits. A single foray into Spain had shown Musa, the Arab general, the weakness of the kingdom; that the cities were unfortified, the citizens unarmed, and many of the nobles lukewarm towards the king. "Hasten," he said, "towards that country where the palaces are filled with gold and silver, and the men cannot fight in their defence." Accordingly, in the early spring of the year 711, Musa sent his next in command, Tarik, to cross to Spain with an army of seven thousand men, consisting mostly of chosen cavalry. They crossed the straits then called the Sea of Narrowness, embarking the troops at Tangier and Ceute in many merchant vessels, and landing at that famous promontory called thenceforth by the Arab general's name, the Rock of Tarik, Dschebel-Tarik, or, more briefly, Gibraltar.

Luis, under Don Alonzo, was with the Spanish troops sent hastily down to resist the Arab invaders, and, as these troops were mounted, he had many opportunities of seeing the new enemies and observing their ways. They were a picturesque horde; their breasts were covered with mail armor; they wore white turbans on their heads, carried their bows slung across their backs, and their swords suspended to their girdles, while they held their long spears firmly grasped in their hands. The Arabs said that their fashion of mail armor had come to them from King David, "to whom," they said, "God made iron soft, and it became in his hands as thread." More than half of them were mounted on the swift horses which were peculiar to their people; and the white, red, and black turbans and cloaks made a most striking picture around the camp-fires. These men, too, were already trained and successful soldiers, held together both by a common religion and by the hope of spoil. There were twelve thousand of them by the most probable estimate,—for Musa had sent reinforcements,—and they had against them from five to eight times their number. But of the Spaniards only a small part were armed or drilled, or used to warfare, and great multitudes of them had to put their reliance in clubs, slings, axes, and short scythes. The cavalry were on the wings, where Luis found himself, with Count Julian and Archbishop Oppas to command them. Soon, however, Don Alonzo and Luis were detached, with others, to act as escort to the king, Don Rodrigo.

The battle began soon after daybreak on Sunday, July 19, 711. As the Spanish troops advanced, their trumpets sounded defiance and were answered by Moorish horns and kettledrums. While they drew near, the shouts of the Spaniards were drowned in the lelie of the Arabs, the phrase Lá ilá-ha ella-llah—there is no deity but God. As they came nearer yet, there is a tradition that Rodrigo looking on the Moslem, said, "By the faith of the Messi-Messiah, these are the very men I saw painted on the walls of the cave at Toledo." Yet he certainly bore himself like a king, and he rode on the battlefield in a chariot of ivory lined with gold, having a silken awning decked with pearls and rubies, while the vehicle was drawn by three white mules abreast. He was then nearly eighty, and was dressed in a silken robe embroidered with pearls. He had brought with him in carts and on mules his treasures in jewels and money; and he had trains of mules whose only load consisted of ropes, to bind the arms of his captives, so sure was he of making every Arab his prisoner. Driving along the lines he addressed his troops boldly, and arriving at the centre quitted his chariot, put on a horned helmet, and mounted his white horse Orelio.

This was before the invention of gunpowder, and all battles were hand to hand. On the first day the result was doubtful, and Tarik rode through the Arab ranks, calling on them to fight for their religion and their safety. As the onset began, Tarik rode furiously at a Spanish chief whom he took for the king, and struck him down. For a moment it was believed to be the king whom he had killed, and from that moment new energy was given to the Arabs. The line of the Spaniards wavered; and at this moment the whole wing of cavalry to which Luis belonged rode out from its place and passed on the flank of the army, avoiding both Spaniard and Arab. "What means this?" said Luis to the horseman by his side. "It means," was the answer, "that Bishop Oppas is betraying the king." At this moment Don Alonzo rode up and cheered their march with explanations. "No more," he said, "will we obey this imbecile old king who can neither fight nor govern. He and his troops are but so many old women; it is only these Arabs who are men. All is arranged with Tarik, and we will save our country by joining the only man who can govern it." Luis groaned in dismay; it seemed to him an act of despicable treachery; but those around him seemed mostly prepared for it, and he said to himself, "After all, Don Alonzo is my chief; I must hold by him;" so he kept with the others, and the whole cavalry wing followed Oppas to a knoll, whence they watched the fight. It soon became a panic; the Arabs carried all before them, and the king himself was either killed or hid himself in a convent.

Many a Spaniard of the seceding wing of cavalry reproached himself afterwards for what had been done; and while the archbishop had some influence with the conquering general and persuaded him to allow the Christians everywhere to retain a part of their churches, yet he had, after all, the reward of a traitor in contempt and self-reproach. This he could bear no longer, and organizing an expedition from a Spanish port, he and six minor bishops, with many families of the Christians, made their way towards Gibraltar. They did not make their escape, however, without attracting notice and obstruction. As they rode among the hills with their long train, soldiers, ecclesiastics, women, and children, they saw a galloping band of Arabs in pursuit. The archbishop bade them turn instantly into a deserted castle they were just passing, to drop the portcullis and man the walls. That they might look as numerous as possible, he bade all the women dress themselves like men and tie their long hair beneath their chins to resemble beards. He then put helmets on their heads and lances in their hands, and thus the Arab leader saw a formidable host on the walls to be besieged. In obedience, perhaps, to orders, he rode away and after sufficient time had passed, the archbishop's party rode onward towards their place of embarkation. Luis found himself beside a dark-eyed maiden, who ambled along on a white mule, and when he ventured to joke her a little on her late appearance as an armed cavalier, she said coyly, "Did you think my only weapons were roses?" Looking eagerly at her, he recognized the laughing face which he had once seen at a window; but ere he could speak again she had struck her mule lightly and taken refuge beside the archbishop, where Luis dared not venture. He did not recognize the maiden again till they met on board one of the vessels which the Arabs had left at Gibraltar, and on which they embarked for certain islands of which Oppas had heard, which lay in the Sea of Darkness. Among these islands they were to find their future home.

    The voyage, at first rough, soon became serene and quiet; the skies were clear, the moon shone; the veils of the Spanish maidens were convenient by day and useless at evening, and Luis had many a low-voiced talk on the quarter-deck with Juanita, who proved to be a young relative of the archbishop. It was understood that she was to take the veil, and that, young as she was, she would become, by and by, the lady abbess of a nunnery to be established on the islands; and as her kinsman, though severe to others, was gentle to her, she had her own way a good deal— especially beneath the moon and the stars. For the rest, they had daily services of religion, as dignified and sonorous as could have taken place on shore, except on those rare occasions when the chief bass voice was hushed in seasickness in some cabin below. Beautiful Gregorian masses rose to heaven, and it is certain that the Pilgrim fathers, in their two months on the Atlantic, almost a thousand years later, had no such rich melody as floated across those summer seas. Luis was a favorite of Oppas, the archbishop, who never seemed to recognize any danger in having an enamoured youth so near to the demure future abbess. He consulted the youth about many plans. Their aim, it seemed, was the great island called Antillia, as yet unexplored, but reputed to be large enough for many thousand people. Oppas was to organize the chief settlement, and he planned to divide the island into seven dioceses, each bishop having a permanent colony. Once established, they would trade with Spain, and whether it remained Moorish or became Christian, Oppas was sure of friendly relations.

The priests were divided among the three vessels, and among them there was that occasional jarring from which even holy men are not quite free. The different bishops had their partisans, but none dared openly face the imperial Oppas. His supposed favorite Luis was less formidable; he was watched and spied upon, while his devotion to the dignified Juanita was apparent to all. Yet he was always ready to leave her side when Oppas called, and then they discussed together the future prospects of the party: when they should see land, whether it would really be Antillia, whether they should have a good landfall, whether the island would be fertile, whether there would be native inhabitants, and if so, whether they should be baptized and sent to Spain as slaves, or whether they should be retained on the island. It was decided, on the whole, that this last should be done; and what with the prospect of winning souls, and the certainty of having obedient subjects, the prospect seemed inviting.

One morning, at sunrise, there lay before them a tropic island, soft and graceful, with green shrubs and cocoanut trees, and rising in the distance to mountains whose scooped tops and dark, furrowed sides spoke of extinct volcanoes—yet not so extinct but that a faint wreath of vapor still mounted from the utmost peak of the highest among them. Here and there were seen huts covered with great leaves or sheaves of grass, and among these they saw figures moving and disappearing, watching their approach, yet always ready to disappear in the recesses of the woods. Sounding carefully the depth of water with their imperfect tackle, they anchored off the main beach, and sent a boat on shore from each vessel, Luis being in command of one. The natives at first hovered in the distance, but presently came down to the shore to meet the visitors, some even swimming off to the boats in advance. They were of a yellow complexion, with good features, were naked except for goat-skins or woven palm fibres, or reeds painted in different colors; and were gay and merry, singing and dancing among themselves. When brought on board the ships, they ate bread and figs, but refused wine and spices; and they seemed not to know the use of rings or of swords, when shown to them. Whatever was given to them they divided with one another. They cultivated fruit and grain on their island, reared goats, and seemed willing to share all with their newly found friends. Luis, always thoughtful, and somewhat anxious in temperament, felt many doubts as to the usage which these peaceful islanders would receive from the ships' company, no matter how many bishops and holy men might be on board.

All that day there was exploring by small companies, and on the next the archbishop landed in solemn procession. The boats from the ships all met at early morning, near the shore, the sight bringing together a crowd of islanders on the banks; men, women, and children, who, with an instinct that something of importance was to happen, decked themselves with flowers, wreaths, and plumes, the number increasing constantly and the crowd growing more and more picturesque. Forming from the boats, a procession marched slowly up the beach, beginning with a few lay brethren, carrying tools for digging; then acolytes bearing tall crosses; and then white-robed priests; the seven bishops being carried on litters, the archbishop most conspicuously of all. Solemn chants were sung as the procession moved through the calm water towards the placid shore, and the gentle savages joined in kneeling while a solemn mass was said, and the crosses were uplifted which took possession of the new-found land in the name of the Church.

These solemn services occupied much of the day; later they carried tents on shore, and some of them occupied large storehouses which the natives had built for drying their figs; and to the women, under direction of Juanita, was allotted a great airy cave, with smaller caves branching from it, where the natives had made palm baskets. Day after day they labored, transferring all their goods and provisions to the land,—tools, and horses, and mules, clothing, and simple furniture. Most of them joined with pleasure in this toil, but others grew restless as they transferred all their possessions to land, and sometimes the women especially would climb to high places and gaze longingly towards Spain.

One morning a surprise came to Luis. Every night it was their custom to have a great fire on the beach, and to meet and sing chants around it. One night Luis had personally put out the blaze of the fire, as it was more windy than usual, and went to sleep in his tent. Soon after midnight he was awakened by a glare of a great light upon his tent's thin walls, and hastily springing up, he saw their largest caravel on fire. Rushing out to give the alarm, he saw a similar flame kindled in the second vessel, and then, after some delay, in the third. Then he saw a dark boat pulling hastily towards the shore, and going down to the beach he met their most trusty captain, who told him that the ships had been burnt by order of the archbishop, in order that their return might be hopeless, and that their stay on the island might be forever.

There was some lamentation among the emigrants when they saw their retreat thus cut off, but Luis when once established on shore did not share it; to be near Juanita was enough for him, though he rarely saw her. He began sometimes to feel that the full confidence of the archbishop was withdrawn from him, but he was still high in office, and he rode with Oppas over the great island, marking it out by slow degrees into seven divisions, that each bishop might have a diocese and a city of his own. Soon the foundations began to be laid, and houses and churches began to be built, for the soft volcanic rock was easily worked, though not very solid for building. The spot for the cathedral was selected with the unerring eye for a fine situation which the Roman Catholic Church has always shown, and the adjoining convent claimed, as it rose, the care of Juanita. As general superintendent of the works, it was the duty of Luis sometimes to be in that neighborhood, until one unlucky day when the two lovers, lingering to watch the full moon rise, were interrupted by one of the younger bishops, a black-browed Spaniard of stealthy ways, who had before now taken it upon himself to watch them. Nothing could be more innocent than their dawning loves, yet how could any love be held innocent on the part of a maiden who was the kinswoman of an archbishop and was his destined choice for the duties of an abbess? The fact that she had never yet taken her preliminary vows or given her consent to take them, counted for nothing in the situation; though any experienced lady-superior could have told the archbishop that no maiden could be wisely made an abbess until she had given some signs of having a vocation for a religious life.

From that moment the youthful pair met no more for weeks. It seemed always necessary for Luis to be occupied elsewhere than in the Cathedral city; as the best architect on the island, he was sent here, there, and everywhere; and the six other churches rose with more rapidity because the archbishop preferred to look after his own. The once peaceful natives found themselves a shade less happy when they were required to work all day long as quarry-men or as builders, but it was something, had they but known it, that they were not borne away as slaves, as happened later on other islands to so many of their race. To Luis they were always loyal for his cheery ways, although there seemed a change in his spirits as time went on. But an event happened which brought a greater change still.

A Spanish caravel was seen one day, making towards the port and showing signals of distress. Luis, having just then found an excuse for visiting the Cathedral city, was the first to board her and was hailed with joy by the captain. He was a townsman of the youth's and had given him his first lessons in navigation. He had been bound, it seemed, for the Canary Islands, and had put in for repairs, which needed only a few days in the quiet waters of a sheltered port. He could tell Luis of his parents, of his home, and that the northern part of Spain, under Arab sway, was humanely governed, and a certain proportion of Christian churches allowed. In a few days the caravel sailed again at nightfall; but it carried with it two unexpected passengers; the archbishop lost his architect, and the proposed convent lost its unwilling abbess.

From this point both the Island of the Seven Cities and its escaping lovers disappear from all definite records. It was a period when expeditions of discovery came and went, and when one wondrous tale drove out another. There exist legends along the northern coast of Spain in the region of Santander, for instance, of a youth who once eloped with a high-born maiden and came there to dwell, but there may have been many such youths and many such maidens—who knows? Of Antillia itself, or the Island of the Seven Cities, it is well known that it appeared on the maps of the Atlantic, sometimes under the one name and sometimes under another, six hundred years after the date assigned by the story that has here been told. It was said by Fernando Columbus to have been revisited by a Portuguese sailor in 1447; and the name appeared on the globe of Behaim in 1492.

The geographer Toscanelli, in his famous letter to Columbus, recommended Antillia as likely to be useful to Columbus as a way station for reaching India, and when the great explorer reached Hispaniola, he was supposed to have discovered the mysterious island, whence the name of Antilles was given to the group. Later, the first explorers of New Mexico thought that the pueblos were the Seven Cities; so that both the names of the imaginary island have been preserved, although those of Luis de Vega and his faithful Juanita have not been recorded until the telling of this tale.

HARALD THE VIKING

Erik the Red, the most famous of all Vikings, had three sons, and once when they were children the king came to visit Erik and passed through the playground where the boys were playing. Leif and Biorn, the two oldest, were building little houses and barns and were making believe that they were full of cattle and sheep, while Harald, who was only four years old, was sailing chips of wood in a pool. The king asked Harald what they were, and he said, "Ships of war." King Olaf laughed and said, "The time may come when you will command ships, my little friend." Then he asked Biorn what he would like best to have. "Corn-land," he said; "ten farms." "That would yield much corn," the king replied. Then he asked Leif the same question, and he answered, "Cows." "How many?" "So many that when they went to the lake to be watered, they would stand close round the edge, so that not another could pass." "That would be a large housekeeping," said the king, and he asked the same question of Harald. "What would you like best to have?" "Servants and followers," said the child, stoutly. "How many would you like?" "Enough," said the child, "to eat up all the cows and crops of my brothers at a single meal." Then the king laughed, and said to the mother of the children, "You are bringing up a king."

As the boys grew, Leif and Harald were ever fond of roaming, while Biorn wished to live on the farm at peace. Their sister Freydis went with the older boys and urged them on. She was not gentle and amiable, but full of energy and courage: she was also quarrelsome and vindictive. People said of her that even if her brothers were all killed, yet the race of Erik the Red would not end while she lived; that "she practised more of shooting and the handling of sword and shield than of sewing or embroidering, and that as she was able, she did evil oftener than good; and that when she was hindered she ran into the woods and slew men to get their property." She was always urging her brothers to deeds of daring and adventure. One day they had been hawking, and when they let slip the falcons, Harald's falcon killed two blackcocks in one flight and three in another. The dogs ran and brought the birds, and he said proudly to the others, "It will be long before most of you have any such success," and they all agreed to this. He rode home in high spirits and showed his birds to his sister Freydis. "Did any king," he asked, "ever make so great a capture in so short a time?" "It is, indeed," she said, "a good morning's hunting to have got five blackcocks, but it was still better when in one morning a king of Norway took five kings and subdued all their kingdoms." Then Harald went away very humble and besought his father to let him go and serve on the Varangian Guard of King Otho at Constantinople, that he might learn to be a warrior.

So Harald was brought from his Norwegian home by his father Erik the Red, in his galley called the Sea-serpent, and sailed with him through the Mediterranean Sea, and was at last made a member of the Emperor Otho's Varangian Guard at Constantinople. This guard will be well remembered by the readers of Scott's novel, "Count Robert of Paris," and was maintained by successive emperors and drawn largely from the Scandinavian races. Erik the Red had no hesitation in leaving his son among them, as the young man was stout and strong, very self-willed, and quite able to defend himself. The father knew also that the Varangian Guard, though hated by the people, held to one another like a band of brothers; and that any one brought up among them would be sure of plenty of fighting and plenty of gold,—the two things most prized by early Norsemen. For ordinary life, Harald's chief duties would be to lounge about the palace, keeping guard, wearing helmet and buckler and bearskin, with purple underclothes and golden clasped hose; and bearing as armor a mighty battle-axe and a small scimitar. Such was the life led by Harald, till one day he had a message from his father, through a new recruit, calling him home to join an expedition to the western seas. "I hear, my son," the message said, "that your good emperor, whom may the gods preserve, is sorely ill and may die any day. When he is dead, be prompt in getting your share of the plunder of the palace and come back to me."

The emperor died, and the order was fulfilled. It was the custom of the Varangians to reward themselves in this way for their faithful services of protection; and the result is that, to this day, Greek and Arabic gold crosses and chains are to be found in the houses of Norwegian peasants and may be seen in the museums of Christiania and Copenhagen. No one was esteemed the less for this love of spoil, if he was only generous in giving. The Norsemen spoke contemptuously of gold as "the serpent's bed," and called a generous man "a hater of the serpent's bed," because such a man parts with gold as with a thing he hates.

When the youth came to his father, he found Erik the Red directing the building of one of the great Norse galleys, nearly eighty feet long and seventeen wide and only six feet deep. The boat had twenty ribs, and the frame was fastened together by withes made of roots, while the oaken planks were held by iron rivets. The oars were twenty feet long, and were put through oar holes, and the rudder, shaped like a large oar, was not at the end, but was attached to a projecting beam on the starboard (originally steer-board) side. The ship was to be called a Dragon, and was to be painted so as to look like one, having a gilded dragon's head at the bow and a gilded tail on the stern; while the moving oars would look like legs, and the row of red and white shields, hung along the side of the boat, would resemble the scales of a dragon, and the great square sails, red and blue, would look like wings. This was the vessel which young Harald was to command.

He had already made trips in just such vessels with his father; had learned to attack the enemy with arrow and spear; also with stones thrown down from above, and with grappling-irons to clutch opposing boats. He had learned to swim, from early childhood, even in the icy northern waters, and he had been trained in swimming to hide his head beneath his floating shield, so that it could not be seen. He had learned also to carry tinder in a walnut shell, enclosed in wax, so that no matter how long he had been in the water he could strike a light on reaching shore. He had also learned from his father acts of escape as well as attack. Thus he had once sailed on a return trip from Denmark after plundering a town; the ships had been lying at anchor all night in a fog, and at sunlight in the morning lights seemed burning on the sea. But Erik the Red said, "It is a fleet of Danish ships, and the sun strikes on the gilded dragon crests; furl the sail and take to the oars." They rowed their best, yet the Danish ships were overtaking them, when Erik the Red ordered his men to throw wood overboard and cover it with Danish plunder. This made some delay, as the Danes stopped to pick it up, and in the same way Erik the Red dropped his provisions, and finally his prisoners; and in the delay thus caused he got away with his own men.

But now Harald was not to go to Denmark, but to the new western world, the Wonderstrands which Leif had sought and had left without sufficient exploration. First, however, he was to call at Greenland, which his father had first discovered. It was the custom of the Viking explorers, when they reached a new country, to throw overboard their "seat posts," or setstokka,—the curved part of their doorways,—and then to land where they floated ashore. But Erik the Red had lent his to a friend and could not get them back, so that he sailed in search of them, and came to a new land which he called Greenland, because, as he said, people would be attracted thither if it had a good name. Then he established a colony there, and then Leif the Lucky, as he was called, sailed still farther, and came to the Wonderstrand, or Magic Shores. These he called Vinland or Wine-land, and now a rich man named Karlsefne was to send a colony thither from Greenland, and the young Harald was to go with it and take command of it.

Now as Harald was to be presented to the rich Karlsefne, he thought he must be gorgeously arrayed. So he wore a helmet on his head, a red shield richly inlaid with gold and iron, and a sharp sword with an ivory handle wound with golden thread. He had also a short spear, and wore over his coat a red silk short cloak on which was embroidered, both before and behind, a yellow lion. We may well believe that the sixty men and five women who composed the expedition were ready to look on him with admiration, especially as one of the women was his own sister, Freydis, now left to his peculiar care, since Erik the Red had died. The sturdy old hero had died still a heathen, and it was only just after his death that Christianity was introduced into Greenland, and those numerous churches were built there whose ruins yet remain, even in regions from which all population has gone.

So the party of colonists sailed for Vinland, and Freydis, with the four older women, came in Harald's boat, and Freydis took easily the lead among them for strength, though not always, it must be admitted, for amiability.

The boats of the expedition having left Greenland soon after the year 1000, coasted the shore as far as they could, rarely venturing into open sea. At last, amidst fog and chilly weather, they made land at a point where a river ran through a lake into the sea, and they could not enter from the sea except at high tide. It was once believed that this was Narragansett Bay in Rhode Island, but this is no longer believed. Here they landed and called the place Hóp, from the Icelandic word hópa, meaning an inlet from the ocean. Here they found grape-vines growing and fields of wild wheat; there were fish in the lake and wild animals in the woods. Here they landed the cattle and the provisions which they had brought with them; and here they built their huts. They went in the spring, and during that summer the natives came in boats of skin to trade with them—men described as black, and ill favored, with large eyes and broad cheeks and with coarse hair on their heads. These, it is thought, may have been the Esquimaux. The first time they came, these visitors held up a white shield as a sign of peace, and were so frightened by the bellowing of the bull that they ran away. Then returning, they brought furs to sell and wished to buy weapons, but Harald tried another plan: he bade the women bring out milk, butter, and cheese from their dairies, and when the Skraelings saw that, they wished for nothing else, and, the legend says, "the Skraelings carried away their wares in their stomachs, but the Norsemen had the skins they had purchased." This happened yet again, but at the second visit one of the Skraelings was accidentally killed or injured.

The next time the Skraelings came they were armed with slings, and raised upon a pole a great blue ball and attacked the Norsemen so furiously that they were running away when Erik's sister, Freydis, came out before them with bare arms, and took up a sword, saying, "Why do you run, strong men as you are, from these miserable dwarfs whom I thought you would knock down like cattle? Give me weapons, and I will fight better than any of you." Then the rest took courage and began to fight, and the Skraelings were driven back. Once more the strangers came, and one of them took up an axe, a thing which he had not before seen, and struck at one of his companions, killing him. Then the leader took the axe and threw it into the water, after which the Skraelings retreated, and were not seen again.

The winter was a mild one, and while it lasted, the Norsemen worked busily at felling wood and house-building. They had also many amusements, in most of which Harald excelled. They used to swim in all weathers. One of their feats was to catch seals and sit on them while swimming; another was to pull one another down and remain as long as possible under water. Harald could swim for a mile or more with his armor on, or with a companion on his shoulder. In-doors they used to play the tug of war, dragging each other by a walrus hide across the fire. Harald was good at this, and was also the best archer, sometimes aiming at something placed on a boy's head, the boy having a cloth tied around his head, and held by two men, that he might not move at all on hearing the whistling of the arrow. In this way Harald could even shoot an arrow under a nut placed on the head, so that the nut would roll down and the head not be hurt. He could plant a spear in the ground and then shoot an arrow upward so skilfully that it would turn in the air and fall with the point in the end of the spear-shaft. He could also shoot a blunt arrow through the thickest ox-hide from a cross-bow. He could change weapons from one hand to the other during a fencing match, or fence with either hand, or throw two spears at the same time, or catch a spear in motion. He could run so fast that no horse could overtake him, and play the rough games with bat and ball, using a ball of the hardest wood. He could race on snowshoes, or wrestle when bound by a belt to his antagonist. Then when he and his companions wished a rest, they amused themselves with harp-playing or riddles or chess. The Norsemen even played chess on board their vessels, and there are still to be seen, on some of these, the little holes that were formerly used for the sharp ends of the chessmen, so that they should not be displaced.

They could not find that any European had ever visited this place; but some of the Skraelings told them of a place farther south, which they called "the Land of the Whiteman," or "Great Ireland." They said that in that place there were white men who clothed themselves in long white garments, carried before them poles to which white cloths were hung, and called with a loud voice. These, it was thought by the Norsemen, must be Christian processions, in which banners were borne and hymns were chanted. It has been thought from this that some expedition from Ireland—that of St. Brandan, for instance—may have left a settlement there, long before, but this has never been confirmed. The Skraelings and the Northmen were good friends for a time; until at last one of Erik's own warriors killed a Skraeling by accident, and then all harmony was at an end.

They saw no hope of making a lasting settlement there, and, moreover, Freydis who was very grasping, tried to deceive the other settlers and get more than her share of everything, so that Harald himself lost patience with her and threatened her. It happened that one of the men of the party, Olaf, was Harald's foster-brother. They had once had a fight, and after the battle had agreed that they would be friends for life and always share the same danger. For this vow they were to walk under the turf; that is, a strip of turf was cut and held above their heads, and they stood beneath and let their blood flow upon the ground whence the turf had been cut. After this they were to own everything by halves and either must avenge the other's death. This was their brotherhood; but Freydis did not like it; so she threatened Olaf, and tried to induce men to kill him, for she did not wish to bring upon herself the revenge that must come if she slew him.

This was the reason why the whole enterprise failed, and why Olaf persuaded Harald, for the sake of peace, to return to Greenland in the spring and take a load of valuable timber to sell there, including one stick of what was called massur-wood, which was as valuable as mahogany, and may have been at some time borne by ocean currents to the beach. It is hardly possible that, as some have thought, the colonists established a regular trade in this wood for no such wood grows on the northern Atlantic shores. However this may be, the party soon returned, after one winter in Vinland the Good; and on the way back Harald did one thing which made him especially dear to his men.

A favorite feat of the Norsemen was to toss three swords in the air and catch each by the handle as it came down. This was called the handsax game. The young men used also to try the feat of running along the oar-blades of the rowers as they were in motion, passing around the bow of the vessel with a spring and coming round to the stern over the oars on the other side. Few could accomplish this, but no one but Harald could do it and play the handsax game as he ran; and when he did it, they all said that he was the most skilful man at idrottie ever seen. That was their word for an athletic feat. But presently came a time when not only his courage but his fairness and justice were to be tried.

It happened in this way. There was nothing of which the Norsemen were more afraid than of the teredo, or shipworm, which gnaws the wood of ships. It was observed in Greenland and Iceland that pieces of wood often floated on shore which were filled with holes made by this animal, and they thought that in certain places the seas were full of this worm, so that a ship would be bored and sunk in a little while. It is said that on this return voyage Harald's vessel entered a worm-sea and presently began to sink. They had, however, provided a smaller boat smeared with sea-oil, which the worms would not attack. They went into the boat, but found that it would not hold more than half of them all. Then Harald said, "We will divide by lots, without regard to the rank; each taking his chance with the rest." This they thought, the Norse legend says, "a high-minded offer." They drew lots, and Harald was among those assigned to the safer boat. He stepped in, and when he was there a man called from the other boat and said, "Dost thou intend, Harald, to separate from me here?" Harald answered, "So it turns out," and the man said, "Very different was thy promise to my father when we came from Greenland, for the promise was that we should share the same fate."

Then Harald said, "It shall not be thus. Go into the boat, and I will go back into the ship, since thou art so anxious to live." Then Harald went back to the ship, while the man took his place in the boat, and after that Harald was never heard of more.

THE SEARCH FOR NORUMBEGA

Sir Humphrey Gilbert, colonel of the British forces in the Netherlands, was poring over the manuscript narrative of David Ingram, mariner. Ingram had in 1568-69 taken the widest range of travel that had ever been taken in the new continent, of which it was still held doubtful by many whether it was or was not a part of Asia. "Surely," Gilbert said to his half-brother, Walter Raleigh, a youth of twenty-three, "this knave hath seen strange things. He hath been set ashore by John Hawkins in the Gulf of Mexico and there left behind. He hath travelled northward with two of his companions along Indian trails; he hath even reached Norumbega; he hath seen that famous city with its houses of crystal and silver."

"Pine logs and hemlock bark, belike," said Raleigh, scornfully.

"Nay," said Gilbert, "he hath carefully written it down. He saw kings decorated with rubies six inches long; and they were borne on chairs of silver and crystal, adorned with precious stones. He saw pearls as common as pebbles, and the natives were laden down by their ornaments of gold and silver. The city of Bega was three-quarters of a mile long and had many streets wider than those of London. Some houses had massive pillars of crystal and silver."

"What assurance can he give?" asked Raleigh.

"He offers on his life to prove it."

"A small offer, mayhap. There be many of these lying mariners whose lives are as worthless as the stories they relate. But what said he of the natives?"

"Kindly disposed," was the reply, "so far as he went, but those dwelling farther north, where he did not go, were said to be cannibals with teeth like those of dogs, whereby you may know them."

"Travellers' tales," said Raleigh. "Omne ignotum pro mirifico."

"He returned," said Gilbert, disregarding the interruption, "in the Gargarine, a French vessel commanded by Captain Champagne."

"Methinks something of the flavor represented by the good captain's name hath got into your Englishman's brain. Good ale never gives such fantasies. Doth he perchance speak of elephants?"

"He doth," said Sir Humphrey, hesitatingly. "Perchance he saw them not, but heard of them only."

"What says he of them?" asked Raleigh.

"He says that he saw in that country both elephants and ounces; and he says that their trumpets are made of elephants' teeth."

"But the houses," said Raleigh; "tell me of the houses."

"In every house," said Gilbert, reading from the manuscript, "they have scoops, buckets, and divers vessels, all of massive silver with which they throw out water and otherwise employ them. The women wear great plates of gold covering their bodies, and chains of great pearls in the manner of curvettes; and the men wear manilions or bracelets on each arm and each leg, some of gold and some of silver."

"Whence come they, these gauds?"

"There are great rivers where one may find pieces of gold as big as the fist; and there are great rocks of crystal, sufficient to load many ships."

This was all which was said on that day, but never was explorer more eager than Gilbert. He wrote a "Discourse of a Discoverie for a New Passage to Cathaia and the East Indies"—published without his knowledge by George Gascoigne. In 1578 he had from Queen Elizabeth a patent of exploration, allowing him to take possession of any uncolonized lands in North America, paying for these a fifth of all gold and silver found. The next year he sailed with Raleigh for Newfoundland, but one vessel was lost and the others returned to England. In 1583, he sailed again, taking with him the narrative of Ingram, which he reprinted. He also took with him a learned Hungarian from Buda, named Parmenius, who went for the express purpose of singing the praise of Norumbega in Latin verse, but was drowned in Sir Humphrey's great flag-ship, the Delight. This wreck took place near Sable Island, and as most of the supplies for the expedition went down in the flagship, the men in the remaining vessels grew so impatient as to compel a return. There were two vessels, the Golden Hind of forty tons, and the Squirrel of ten tons, this last being a mere boat then called a frigate, a small vessel propelled by both sails and oars, quite unlike the war-ship afterwards called by that name. On both these vessels the men were so distressed that they gathered on the bulwarks, pointing to their empty mouths and their ragged clothing. The officers of the Golden Hind were unwilling to return, but consented on Sir Humphrey's promise that they should come back in the spring; they sailed for England on the 31st of August. All wished him to return in the Golden Hind as a much larger and safer vessel; the Squirrel, besides its smallness, being encumbered on the deck with guns, ammunition, and nettings, making it unseaworthy. But when he was begged to remove into the larger vessel, he said, "I will not forsake my little company going homeward with whom I have passed so many storms and perils." One reason for this was, the narrator of the voyage says, because of "hard reports given of him that he was afraid of the sea, albeit this was rather rashness than advised resolution, to prefer the wind of a vain report to the weight of his own life."

On the very day of sailing they caught their first glimpse of some large species of seal or walrus, which is thus described by the old narrator of the expedition:—

"So upon Saturday in the afternoone the 31 of August, we changed our course, and returned backe for England, at which very instant, euen in winding about, there passed along betweene vs and towards the land which we now forsooke a very lion to our seeming, in shape, hair and colour, not swimming after the maner of a beast by moouing of his feete, but rather sliding vpon the water with his whole body (excepting the legs) in sight, neither yet in diuing vnder, and againe rising aboue the water, as the maner is, of Whales, Dolphins, Tunise, Porposes, and all other fish: but confidently shewing himselfe aboue water without hiding: Notwithstanding, we presented our selues in open view and gesture to amase him, as all creatures will be commonly at a sudden gaze and sight of men. Thus he passed along turning his head to and fro, yawning and gaping wide, with ougly demonstration of long teeth, and glaring eies, and to bidde vs a farewell (comming right against the Hinde) he sent forth a horrible voyce, roaring or bellowing as doeth a lion, which spectacle wee all beheld so farre as we were able to discerne the same, as men prone to wonder at euery strange thing, as this doubtlesse was, to see a lion in the Ocean sea, or fish in shape of a lion. What opinion others had thereof, and chiefly the Generall himselfe, I forbeare to deliuer: But he tooke it for Bonum Omen [a good omen], reioycing that he was to warre against such an enemie, if it were the deuill."

When they came north of the Azores, very violent storms met them; most "outrageous seas," the narrator says; and they saw little lights upon the mainyard called then by sailors "Castor and Pollux," and now "St. Elmo's Fire"; yet they had but one of these at a time, and this is thought a sign of tempest. On September 9, in the afternoon, "the general," as they called him, Sir Humphrey, was sitting abaft with a book in his hand, and cried out more than once to those in the other vessel, "We are as near to heaven by sea as by land." And that same night about twelve o'clock, the frigate being ahead of the Golden Hind, the lights of the smaller vessel suddenly disappeared, and they knew that she had sunk in the sea. The event is well described in a ballad by Longfellow.

The name of Norumbega and the tradition of its glories survived Sir Humphrey Gilbert. In a French map of 1543, the town appears with castle and towers. Jean Allfonsce, who visited New England in that year, describes it as the capital of a great fur country. Students of Indian tongues defined the word as meaning "the place of a fine city"; while the learned Grotius seized upon it as being the same as Norberga and so affording a relic of the visits of the Northmen. As to the locality, it appeared first on the maps as a large island, then as a smaller one, and after 1569 no longer as an island, but a part of the mainland, bordering apparently on the Penobscot River. Whittier in his poem of "Norumbega" describes a Norman knight as seeking it in vain.

"He turned him back, 'O master dear,
We are but men misled;
And thou hast sought a city here
To find a grave instead.

"'No builded wonder of these lands
My weary eyes shall see;
A city never made with hands
Alone awaiteth me.'"

So Champlain, in 1604, could find no trace of it, and said that "no such marvel existed," while Mark Lescarbot, the Parisian advocate, writing in 1609, says, "If this beautiful town ever existed in nature, I would like to know who pulled it down, for there is nothing here but huts made of pickets and covered with the barks of trees or skins." Yet it kept its place on maps till 1640, and even Heylin in his "Cosmography" (1669) speaks of "Norumbega and its fair city," though he fears that the latter never existed.

It is a curious fact that the late Mr. Justin Winsor, the eminent historian, after much inquiry among the present descendants of the Indian tribes in Maine, could never find any one who could remember to have heard the name of Norumbega.

## THE GUARDIANS OF THE ST. LAWRENCE

When in 1611 the Sieur de Champlain went back to France to report his wonderful explorations in Canada, he was soon followed by a young Frenchman named Vignan, who had spent a whole winter among the Indians, in a village where there was no other white man. This was a method often adopted by the French for getting more knowledge of Indian ways and commanding their confidence. Vignan had made himself a welcome guest in the cabins, and had brought away many of their legends, to which he added some of his own. In particular, he declared that he had penetrated into the interior until he had come upon a great lake of salt water, far to the northwest. This was, as it happened, the very thing which the French government and all Europe had most hoped to find. They had always believed that sooner or later a short cut would be discovered across the newly found continent, a passage leading to the Pacific Ocean and far Cathay. This was the dream of all French explorers, and of Champlain in particular, and his interest was at once excited by anything that looked toward the Pacific. Now Vignan had prepared himself with just the needed information. He said that during his winter with the Indians he had made the very discovery needed; that he had ascended the river Ottawa, which led to a body of salt water so large that it seemed like an ocean; that he had just seen on its shores the wreck of an English ship, from which eighty men had been taken and slain by the savages, and that they had with them an English boy whom they were keeping to present to Champlain.

This tale about the English ship was evidently founded on the recent calamities of Henry Hudson, of which Vignan had heard some garbled account, and which he used as coloring for his story. The result was that Champlain was thoroughly interested in the tale, and that Vignan was cross-examined and tested, and was made at last to certify to the truth of it before two notaries of Rochelle. Champlain privately consulted the chancellor de Sillery, the old Marquis de Brissac, and others, who all assured him that the matter should be followed up; and he resolved to make it the subject of an exploration without delay. He sailed in one vessel, and Vignan in another, the latter taking with him an ardent young Frenchman, Albert de Brissac.

M. de Vignan, talking with the young Brissac on the voyage, told him wonderful tales of monsters which were, he said, the guardians of the St. Lawrence River. There was, he said, an island in the bay of Chaleurs, near the mouth of that river, where a creature dwelt, having the form of a woman and called by the Indians Gougou. She was very frightful, and so enormous that the masts of the vessel could not reach her waist. She had already eaten many savages and constantly continued to do so, putting them first into a great pocket to await her hunger. Some of those who had escaped said that this pocket was large enough to hold a whole ship. This creature habitually made dreadful noises, and several savages who came on board claimed to have heard them. A man from St. Malo in France, the Sieur de Prevert, confirmed this story, and said that he had passed so near the den of this frightful being, that all on board could hear its hissing, and all hid themselves below, lest it should carry them off. This naturally made much impression upon the young Sieur de Brissac, and he doubtless wished many times that he had stayed at home. On the other hand, he observed that both M. de Vignan and M. de Prevert took the tale very coolly and that there seemed no reason why he should distrust himself if they did not. Yet he was very glad when, after passing many islands and narrow straits, the river broadened and they found themselves fairly in the St. Lawrence and past the haunted Bay of Chaleurs. They certainly heard a roaring and a hissing in the distance, but it may have been the waves on the beach.

But this was not their last glimpse of the supposed guardians of the St. Lawrence. As the ship proceeded farther up the beautiful river, they saw one morning a boat come forth from the woods, bearing three men dressed to look like devils, wrapped in dogs' skins, white and black, their faces besmeared as black as any coals, with horns on their heads more than a yard long, and as this boat passed the ship, one of the men made a long address, not looking towards them. Then they all three fell flat in the boat, when Indians rowed out to meet them and guided them to a landing.

Then many Indians collected in the woods and began a loud talk which they could hear on board the ships and which lasted half an hour. Then two of their leaders came towards the shore, holding their hands upward joined together, and meanwhile carrying their hats under their upper garments and showing great reverence. Looking upward they sometimes cried, "Jesus, Jesus," or "Jesus Maria." Then the captain asked them whether anything ill had happened, and they said in French, "Nenni est il bon," meaning that it was not good. Then they said that their god Cudraigny had spoken in Hochelaga (Montreal) and had sent these three men to show to them that there was so much snow and ice in the country that he who went there would die. This made the Frenchmen laugh, saying in reply that their god Cudraigny was but a fool and a noddy and knew not what he said. "Tell him," said a Frenchman, "that Christ will defend them from all cold, if they will believe in him." The Indians then asked the captain if he had spoken with Jesus. He answered No; but that his priests had, and they had promised fair weather. Hearing this, they thanked the captain and told the other Indians in the woods, who all came rushing out, seeming to be very glad. Giving great shouts, they began to sing and dance as they had done before. They also began to bring to the ships great stores of fish and of bread made of millet, casting it into the French boats so thickly that it seemed to fall from heaven. Then the Frenchmen went on shore, and the people came clustering about them, bringing children in their arms to be touched, as if to hallow them. Then the captain in return arranged the women in order and gave them beads made of tin, and other trifles, and gave knives to the men. All that night the Indians made great fires and danced and sang along the shore. But when the Frenchmen had finally reached the mouth of the Ottawa and had begun to ascend it, under Vignan's guidance, they had reasons to remember the threats of the god Cudraigny.

Ascending the Ottawa in canoes, past cataracts, boulders, and precipices, they at last, with great labor, reached the island of Allumette, at a distance of two hundred and twenty-five miles. Often it was impossible to carry their canoes past waterfalls, because the forests were so dense, so that they had to drag the boats by ropes, wading among rocks or climbing along precipices. Gradually they left behind them their armor, their provisions, and clothing, keeping only their canoes; they lived on fish and wild fowl, and were sometimes twenty-four hours without food. Champlain himself carried three French arquebuses or short guns, three oars, his cloak, and many smaller articles; and was harassed by dense clouds of mosquitoes all the time. Vignan, Brissac, and the rest were almost as heavily loaded. The tribe of Indians whom they at last reached had chosen the spot as being inaccessible to their enemies; and thought that the newcomers had fallen from the clouds.

When Champlain inquired after the salt sea promised by Vignan, he learned to his indignation that the whole tale was false. Vignan had spent a winter at the very village where they were, but confessed that he had never gone a league further north. The Indians knew of no such sea, and craved permission to torture and kill him for his deceptions; they called him loudly a liar, and even the children took up the cry and jeered at him. They said, "Do you not see that he meant to cause your death? Give him to us, and we promise you that he shall not lie any more." Champlain defended him from their attacks, bore it all philosophically, and the young Brissac went back to France, having given up hope of reaching the salt sea, except, as Champlain himself coolly said, "in imagination." The guardians of the St. Lawrence had at least exerted their spell to the extent of saying, Thus far and no farther. Vignan never admitted that he had invented the story of the Gougou, and had bribed the Indians who acted the part of devils,—and perhaps he did not,—but it is certain that neither the giantess nor the god Cudraigny has ever again been heard from.

## THE ISLAND OF DEMONS

Those American travellers who linger with delight among the narrow lanes and picturesque, overhanging roofs of Honfleur, do not know what a strange tragedy took place on a voyage which began in that quaint old port three centuries and a half ago. When, in 1536, the Breton sailor Jacques Cartier returned from his early explorations of the St. Lawrence, which he had ascended as high as Hochelaga, King Francis I. sent for him at the lofty old house known as the House of the Salamander, in a narrow street of the quaint town of Lisieux. It now seems incredible that the most powerful king in Europe should have dwelt in such a meagre lane, yet the house still stands there as a witness; although a visitor must now brush away the rough, ready-made garments and fishermen's overalls which overhang its door. Over that stairway, nevertheless, the troubadours, Pierre Ronsard and Clement Marot, used to go up and down, humming their lays or touching their viols; and through that door De Lorge returned in glory, after leaping down into the lions' den to rescue his lady's glove. The house still derives its name from the great carved image of a reptile which stretches down its outer wall, from garret to cellar, beside the doorway.

In that house the great king deigned to meet the Breton sailor, who had set up along the St. Lawrence a cross bearing the arms of France with the inscription Franciscus Primus, Dei gratia Francorum Rex regnat; and had followed up the pious act by kidnapping the king Donnacona, and carrying him back to France. This savage potentate was himself brought to Lisieux to see his French fellow-sovereign; and the jovial king, eagerly convinced, decided to send Cartier forth again, to explore for other wonders, and perhaps bring back other kingly brethren. Meanwhile, however, as it was getting to be an affair of royalty, he decided to send also a gentleman of higher grade than a pilot, and so selected Jean François de la Roche, Sieur de Roberval, whom he commissioned as lieutenant and governor of Canada and Hochelaga. Roberval was a gentleman of credit and renown in Picardy, and was sometimes jocosely called by Francis "the little king of Vimeu." He was commissioned at Fontainebleau, and proceeded to superintend the building of ships at St. Malo.

Marguerite Roberval, his fair-haired and black-eyed niece, was to go with him on the voyage, with other ladies of high birth, and also with the widowed Madame de Noailles, her gouvernante. Roberval himself remained at St. Malo to superintend the building of the ships, and Marguerite and her gouvernante would sit for hours in a beautiful nook by the shipyards, where they could overlook the vessels in rapid construction, or else watch the wondrous swirl of the tide as it swept in and out, leaving the harbor bare at low tide, but with eight fathoms of water when the tide was full. The designer of the ships often came, cap in hand, to ask or answer questions—one of those frank and manly French fishermen and pilots, whom the French novelists describe as "un solide gaillard," or such as Victor Hugo paints in his "Les Travailleurs de la Mer." The son of a notary, Etienne Gosselin was better educated than most of the young noblemen whom Marguerite knew, and only his passion for the sea and for nautical construction had kept him a shipbuilder. No wonder that the young Marguerite, who had led the sheltered life of the French maiden, was attracted by his manly look, his open face, his merry blue eyes, and curly hair. There was about her a tinge of romance, which made her heart an easier thing to reach for such a lover than for one within her own grade; and as the voyage itself was a world of romance, a little more or less of the romantic was an easy thing to add. Meanwhile Madame de Noailles read her breviary and told her beads and took little naps, wholly ignorant of the drama that was beginning its perilous unfolding before her. When the Sieur de Roberval returned, the shipbuilder became a mere shipbuilder again.

Three tall ships sailed from Honfleur on August 22, 1541, and on one of them, La Grande Hermine,—so called to distinguish it from a smaller boat of that name, which had previously sailed with Cartier,—were the Sieur de Roberval, his niece, and her gouvernante. She also had with her a Huguenot nurse, who had been with her from a child, and cared for her devotedly. Roberval naturally took with him, for future needs, the best shipbuilder of St. Malo, Etienne Gosselin. The voyage was long, and there is reason to think that the Sieur de Roberval was not a good sailor, while as to the gouvernante, she may have been as helpless as the seasick chaperon of yachting excursions. Like them, she suffered the most important events to pass unobserved, and it was not till too late that she discovered, what more censorious old ladies on board had already seen, that her young charge lingered too often and too long on the quarter-deck when Etienne Gosselin was planning ships for the uncle. When she found it out, she was roused to just indignation; but being, after all, but a kindly dowager, with a heart softened by much reading of the interminable tales of Madame de Scudéry, she only remonstrated with Marguerite, wept over her little romance, and threatened to break the sad news to the Sieur de Roberval, yet never did so. Other ladies were less considerate; it all broke suddenly upon the angry uncle; the youth was put in irons, and threatened with flogging, and forbidden to approach the quarter-deck again. But love laughs at locksmiths; Gosselin was relieved of his irons in a day or two because he could not be spared from his work in designing the forthcoming ship, and as both he and Marguerite were of a tolerably determined nature, they invoked, through the old nurse, the aid of a Huguenot minister on board, who had before sailed with Cartier to take charge of the souls of some Protestant vagabonds on the ship, and who was now making a second trip for the same reason. That night, after dark, he joined the lovers in marriage; within twenty-four hours Roberval had heard of it, and had vowed a vengeance quick and sure.

The next morning, under his orders, the vessel lay to under the lee of a rocky island, then known to the sailors as l'Isle des Demons from the fierce winds that raged round it. There was no house there, no living person, no tradition of any; only rocks, sands, and deep forests. With dismay, the ship's company heard that it was the firm purpose of Roberval to put the offending bride on shore, giving her only the old nurse for company, and there to leave her with provisions for three months, trusting to some other vessel to take the exiled women away within that time. The very ladies whose love of scandal had first revealed to him the alleged familiarities, now besought him with many tears to abandon the thought of a doom so terrible. Vainly Madame de Noailles implored mercy for the young girl from a penalty such as was never imposed in any of Madame de Scudéry's romances; vainly the

Huguenot minister and the Catholic chaplain, who had fought steadily on questions of doctrine during the whole voyage, now united in appeals for pardon. At least they implored him to let the offenders have a man-servant or two with them to protect them against wild beasts or buccaneers. He utterly refused until, at last wearied out, his wild nature yielded to one of those sudden impulses which were wont to sweep over it; and he exclaimed, "Is it that they need a man-servant, then? Let this insolent caitiff, Gosselin, be relieved of his irons and sent on shore. Let him be my niece's servant or, since a Huguenot marriage is as good as any in the presence of bears and buccaneers, let her call the hound her husband, if she likes. I have done with her; and the race from which she came disowns her forever."

Thus it was done. Etienne was released from his chains and sent on shore. An arquebus and ammunition were given him; and resisting the impulse to send his first shot through the heart of his tyrant, he landed, and the last glimpse seen of the group as the Grande Hermine sailed away, was the figure of Marguerite sobbing on his shoulder, and of the unhappy nurse, now somewhat plethoric, and certainly not the person to be selected as a pioneer, sitting upon a rock, weeping profusely. The ship's sails filled, the angry Roberval never looked back on his deserted niece, and the night closed down upon the lonely Isle of Demons, now newly occupied by three unexpected settlers, two of whom at least were happy in each other.

A few boxes of biscuits, a few bottles of wine, had been put on shore with them, enough to feed them for a few weeks. They had brought flint and steel to strike fire, and some ammunition. The chief penalty of the crime did not lie, after all, in the cold and the starvation and the wild beasts and the possible visits of pirates; it lay in the fact that it was the Island of Demons where they were to be left; and in that superstitious age this meant everything that was terrible. For the first few nights of their stay, they fancied that they heard superhuman voices in every wind that blew, every branch that creaked against another branch; and they heard, at any rate, more substantial sounds from the nightly wolves or from the bears which ice-floes had floated to that northern isle. They watched Roberval sail away, he rejoicing, as the old legend of Thevet says, at having punished them without soiling his hands with their blood (ioueux de les auior puniz sans se souiller les mains en leurs sang). They built as best they could a hut of boughs and strewed beds of leaves, until they had killed wild beasts enough to prepare their skins. Their store of hard bread lasted them but a little while, but there were fruits around them, and there was fresh water near by. "Yet it was terrible," says Thevet's old narrative, "to hear the frightful sounds which the evil spirits made around them, and how they tried to break down their abode, and showed themselves in various forms of frightful animals; yet at last, conquered by the constancy and perseverance of these repentant Christians, the tormentors afflicted or disquieted them no more, save that often in the night they heard cries so loud that it seemed as if more than five thousand men were assembled together" (plus de cent mil homes qui fussent ensemble).

So passed many months of desolation, and alas! the husband was the first to yield. Daily he climbed the rocks to look for vessels; each night he descended sadder and sadder; he waked while the others slept. Feeling that it was he who had brought distress upon the rest, he concealed his depression, but it soon was past concealing; he only redoubled his care and watching as his wife grew the stronger of the two; and he faded slowly away and died. His wife had nothing to sustain her spirits except the approach of maternity—she would live for her child. When the child was born and baptized in the name of the Holy Church, though without the Church's full ceremonies, Marguerite felt the strength of motherhood; became a better huntress, a better provider. A new sorrow came; in the sixteenth or seventeenth month of her stay, the old nurse died also, and not long after the baby followed. Marguerite now seemed to herself deserted, even by Heaven itself; she was alone in that northern island without comradeship; her husband, child, and nurse gone; dependent for very food on the rapidly diminishing supply of ammunition. Her head swam; for months she saw visions almost constantly, which only strenuous prayer banished, and only the acquired habit of the chase enabled her, almost mechanically, to secure meat to support life. Fortunately, those especial sights and sounds of demons which had haunted her imagination during the first days and nights on the island, did not recur; but the wild beasts gathered round her the more when there was only one gun to alarm them; and she once shot three bears in a day,—one a white bear, of which she secured the skin.

What imagination can depict the terrors of those lonely days and still lonelier nights? Most persons left as solitary tenants of an island have dwelt, like Alexander Selkirk, in regions nearer the tropics, where there was at least a softened air, a fertile soil, and the Southern Cross above their heads; but to be solitary in a prolonged winter, to be alone with the Northern Lights,—this offered peculiar terrors. To be ice-bound, to hear the wolves in their long and dreary howl, to protect the very graves of her beloved from being dug up, to watch the floating icebergs, not knowing what new and savage visitor might be borne by them to the island, what a complication of terror was this for Marguerite!

For two years and five months in all she dwelt upon the Isle of Demons, the last year wholly alone. Then, as she stood upon the shore, some Breton fishing-smacks, seeking codfish, came in sight. Making signals with fire and calling for aid, she drew them nearer; but she was now dressed in furs only, and seemed to them but one of the fancied demons of the island. Beating up slowly and watchfully toward the shore, they came within hearing of her voice and she told her dreary tale. At last they took her in charge, and bore her back to France with the bearskins she had prepared; and taking refuge in the village of Nautron, in a remote province (Perigord), where she could escape the wrath of Roberval, she told her story to Thevet, the explorer, to the Princess Marguerite of Navarre (sister of Francis I.), and to others. Thevet tells it in his "Cosmographie," and Marguerite of Navarre in her "Cent Nouvelles Nouvelles."

She told Thevet that after the first two months, the demons came to her no more, until she was left wholly alone; then they renewed their visits, but not continuously, and she felt less fear. Thevet also records of her this touching confession, that when the time came for her to embark, in the Breton ship, for home, there came over her a strong impulse to refuse the embarkation, but rather to die in that solitary place, as her husband, her child, and her servant had already died. This profound touch of human nature does more than anything else to confirm the tale as substantially true. Certain it is that the lonely island which appeared so long on the old maps as the Isle of Demons (l'Isola de Demoni) appears differently in later ones as the Lady's Island (l'Isle de la Demoiselle).

The Princess Marguerite of Navarre, who died in 1549, seems also to have known her namesake at her retreat in Perigord, gives some variations from Thevet's story, and describes her as having been put on shore with her husband, because of frauds which he had practised on Roberval; nor does she speak of the nurse or of the child. But she gives a similar description of Marguerite's stay on the island, after his death, and says, that although she lived what might seem a bestial life as to her body, it was a life wholly angelic as regarded her soul (aînsî vivant, quant au corps, de vie bestiale, et quant à l'esprit, de vie angelîcque). She had, the princess also says, a mind cheerful and content, in a body emaciated and half dead. She was afterwards received with great honor in France, according to the princess, and was encouraged to establish a school for little children, where she taught reading and writing to the daughters of high-born families. "And by this honest industry," says the princess, "she supported herself during the remainder of her life, having no other wish than to exhort every one to love and confidence towards God, offering them as an example, the great pity which he had shown for her."

BIMINI AND THE FOUNTAIN OF YOUTH

When Juan Ponce de Leon set forth from Porto Rico, March 13, 1512, to seek the island of Bimini and its Fountain of Youth, he was moved by the love of adventure more than by that of juvenility, for he was then but about fifty, a time when a cavalier of his day thought himself but in his prime. He looked indeed with perpetual sorrow—as much of it as a Spaniard of those days could feel—upon his kinsman Luis Ponce, once a renowned warrior, but on whom age had already, at sixty-five, laid its hand in earnest. There was little in this slowly moving veteran to recall one who had shot through the lists at the tournament, and had advanced with his short sword at the bull fight,—who had ruled his vassals, and won the love of high-born women. It was a vain hope of restored youth which had brought Don Luis from Spain to Porto Rico four years before; and, when Ponce de Leon had subdued that island, his older kinsman was forever beseeching him to carry his flag farther, and not stop till he had reached Bimini, and sought the Fountain of Youth.

"For what end," he said, "should you stay here longer and lord it over these miserable natives? Let us go where we can bathe in those enchanted waters and be young once more. I need it, and you will need it ere long."

"How know we," said his kinsman, "that there is any such place?"

"All know it," said Luis. "Peter Martyr saith that there is in Bimini a continual spring of running water of such marvellous virtue that the water thereof, being drunk, perhaps with some diet, maketh old men young." And he adds that an Indian grievously oppressed with old age, moved with the fame of that fountain, and allured through the love of longer life, went to an island, near unto the country of Florida, to drink of the desired fountain, ... and having well drunk and washed himself for many days with the appointed remedies, by them who kept the bath, he is reported to have brought home a manly strength, and to have used all manly exercises. "Let us therefore go thither," he cried, "and be like him."

They set sail with three brigantines and found without difficulty the island of Bimini among the Lucayos (or Bahamas) islands; but when they searched for the Fountain of Youth they were pointed farther westward to Florida, where there was said to be a river of the same magic powers, called the Jordan. Touching at many a fair island green with trees, and occupied by a gentle population till then undisturbed, it was not strange if, nearing the coast of Florida, both Juan Ponce de Leon and his more impatient cousin expected to find the Fountain of Youth.

They came at last to an inlet which led invitingly up among wooded banks and flowery valleys, and here the older knight said, "Let us disembark here and strike inland. My heart tells me that here at last will be found the Fountain of Youth." "Nonsense," said Juan, "our way lies by water."

"Then leave me here with my men," said Luis. He had brought with him five servants, mostly veterans, from his own estate in Spain.

A fierce discussion ended in Luis obtaining his wish, and being left for a fortnight of exploration; his kinsman promising to come for him again at the mouth of the river St. John. The men left on shore were themselves past middle age, and the more eager for their quest. They climbed a hill and watched the brigantines disappear in the distance; then set up a cross, which they had brought with them, and prayed before it bareheaded.

Sending the youngest of his men up to the top of a tree, Luis learned from him that they were on an island, after all, and this cheered him much, as making it more likely that they should find the Fountain of Youth. He saw that the ground was pawed up, as if in a cattle-range and that there was a path leading to huts. Taking this path, they met fifty Indian bowmen, who, whether large or not, seemed to them like giants. The Spaniards gave them beads and hawk-bells, and each received in return an arrow, as a token of friendship. The Indians promised them food in the morning, and brought fish, roots, and pure water; and finding them chilly from the coldness of the night, carried them in their arms to their homes, first making four or five large fires on the way. At the houses there were many fires, and the Spaniards would have been wholly comfortable, had they not thought it just possible that they were to be offered as a sacrifice. Still fearing this, they left their Indian friends after a few days and traversed the country, stopping at every spring or fountain to test its quality. Alas! they all grew older and more worn in look, as time went on, and farther from the Fountain of Youth.

After a time they came upon new tribes of Indians, and as they went farther from the coast these people seemed more and more friendly. They treated the white men as if come from heaven,—brought them food, made them houses, carried every burden for them. Some had bows, and went upon the hills for deer, and brought half a dozen every night for their guests; others killed hares and rabbits by arranging themselves in a circle and striking down the game with billets of wood as it ran from one to another through the woods. All this game was brought to the visitors to be breathed upon and blessed, and when this had to be done for several hundred people it became troublesome. The women also brought wild fruit, and would eat nothing till the guests had seen and touched it. If the visitors seemed offended, the natives were terrified, and apparently thought that they should die unless they had the favor of these wise and good men. Farther on, people did not come out into the paths to gather round them, as the first had done, but stayed meekly in their houses, sitting with their faces turned to the wall, and with their property heaped in the middle of the room. From these people the travellers received many valuable skins, and other gifts. Wherever there was a fountain, the natives readily showed it, but apparently knew nothing of any miraculous gift; yet they themselves were in such fine physical condition, and seemed so young and so active, that it was as if they had already bathed in some magic spring. They had wonderful endurance of heat and cold, and such health that, when their bodies were pierced through and through by arrows, they would recover rapidly from their wounds. These things convinced the Spaniards that, even if the Indians would not disclose the source of all their bodily freshness, it must, at any rate, lie somewhere in the neighborhood. Yet a little while, no doubt, and their visitors would reach it.

It was a strange journey for these gray and careworn men as they passed up the defiles and valleys along the St. John's River, beyond the spot where now spreads the city of Jacksonville, and even up to the woods and springs about Magnolia and Green Cove. Yellow jasmines trailed their festoons above their heads; wild roses grew at their feet; the air was filled with the aromatic odors of pine or sweet bay; the long gray moss hung from the live-oak branches; birds and butterflies of wonderful hues fluttered around them; and strange lizards crossed their paths, or looked with dull and blinking eyes from the branches. They came, at last, to one spring which widened into a natural basin, and which was so deliciously aromatic that Luis Ponce said, on emerging: "It is enough. I have bathed in the Fountain of Youth, and henceforth I am young." His companions tried it, and said the same: "The Fountain of Youth is found."

No time must now be lost in proclaiming the great discovery. They obtained a boat from the natives, who wept at parting with the white strangers whom they had so loved. In this boat they proposed to reach the mouth of the St. John, meet Juan Ponce de Leon, and carry back the news to Spain. But one native, whose wife and children they had cured, and who had grown angry at their refusal to stay longer, went down to the water's edge and, sending an arrow from his bow, transfixed Don Luis, so that even his foretaste of the Fountain could not save him, and he died ere reaching the mouth of the river. If Don Luis ever reached what he sought, it was in another world. But those who have ever bathed in Green Cove Spring, near Magnolia, on the St. John's River, will be ready to testify that, had he but stayed there longer, he would have found something to recall his visions of the Fountain of Youth.

# NOTES

I. ATLANTIS

For the original narrative of Socrates, see Plato's "Timaeus" and "Critias," in each of which it is given. For further information see the chapter on the Geographical Knowledge of the Ancients by W. H. Tillinghast, in Winsor's "Narrative and Critical History of America," I. 15. He mentions (I. 19, note) a map printed at Amsterdam in 1678 by Kircher, which shows Atlantis as a large island midway between Spain and America. Ignatius Donnelly's "Atlantis, the Antediluvian World" (N. Y. 1882), maintains that the evidence for the former existence of such an island is irresistible, and his work has been very widely read, although it is not highly esteemed by scholars.

II. TALIESSIN

The Taliessin legend in its late form cannot be traced back beyond the end of the sixteenth century, but the account of the transformation is to be found in the "Book of Taliessin," a manuscript of the thirteenth century, preserved in the Hengwt Collection at Peniarth. The Welsh bard himself is supposed to have flourished in the sixth century. See Alfred Nutt in "The Voyage of Bram" (London, 1897), II. 86. The traditions may be found in Lady Charlotte Guest's translation of the "Mabinogion," 2d ed., London, 1877, p. 471. The poems may be found in the original Welsh in Skene's "Four Ancient Books of Wales," 2 vols., Edinburgh, 1868; and he also gives a facsimile of the manuscript.

III. CHILDREN OF LIR

The lovely legend of the children of Lir or Lear forms one of those three tales of the old Irish Bards which are known traditionally in Ireland as "The Three Sorrows of Story Telling." It has been told in verse by Aubrey de Vere ("The Foray of Queen Meave, and Other Legends," London, 1882), by John Todhunter ("Three Irish Bardic Tales," London, 1896); and also in prose by various writers, among whom are Professor Eugene O'Curry, whose version with the Gaelic original was published in "Atlantis," Nos. vii.

and viii.; Gerald Griffin in "The Tales of a Jury Room"; and Dr. Patrick Weston Joyce in "Ancient Celtic Romances" (London, 1879). The oldest manuscript copy of the tale in Gaelic is one in the British Museum, made in 1718; but there are more modern ones in different English and Irish libraries, and the legend itself is of much older origin. Professor O'Curry, the highest authority, places its date before the year 1000. ("Lectures on the Manuscript Materials of Irish History," p. 319.)

## IV. USHEEN

In the original legend, Oisin or Usheen is supposed to have told his tale to St. Patrick on his arrival in Ireland; but as the ancient Feni were idolaters, the hero bears but little goodwill to the saint. The Celtic text of a late form of the legend (1749) with a version by Brian O'Looney will be found in the transactions of the Ossianic Society for 1856 (Vol. IV. p. 227); and still more modern and less literal renderings in P. W. Joyce's "Ancient Celtic Romances" (London, 1879), p. 385, and in W. B. Yeats's "Wanderings of Oisin, and Other Poems" (London, 1889), p. 1. The last is in verse and is much the best. St. Patrick, who takes part in it, regards Niam as "a demon thing." See also the essays entitled "L'Elysée Transatlantique," by Eugene Beauvois, in the "Revue de L'Histoire des Religions," VII. 273 (Paris, 1885), and "L'Eden Occidental" (same, VII. 673). As to Oisin or Usheen's identity with Ossian, see O'Curry's "Lectures on the Manuscript Materials for Ancient Irish History" (Dublin, 1861), pp. 209, 300; John Rhys's "Hibbert Lectures" (London, 1888), p. 551. The latter thinks the hero identical with Taliessin, as well as with Ossian, and says that the word Ossin means "a little fawn," from "os," "cervus." (See also O'Curry, p. 304.) O'Looney represents that it was a stone which Usheen threw to show his strength, and Joyce follows this view; but another writer in the same volume of the Ossianic Society transactions (p. 233) makes it a bag of sand, and Yeats follows this version. It is also to be added that the latter in later editions changes the spelling of his hero's name from Oisin to Usheen.

## V. BRAN

The story of Bran and his sister Branwen may be found most fully given in Lady Charlotte Guest's translation of the "Mabinogion," ed. 1877, pp. 369, 384. She considers Harlech, whence Bran came, to be a locality on the Welsh seacoast still known by that name and called also Branwen's Tower. But Rhys, a much higher authority, thinks that Bran came really from the region of Hades, and therefore from a distant island ("Arthurian Legend," p.

250, "Hibbert Lectures," pp. 94, 269). The name of "the Blessed" came from the legend of Bran's having introduced Christianity into Ireland, as stated in one of the Welsh Triads. He was the father of Caractacus, celebrated for his resistance to the Roman conquest, and carried a prisoner to Rome. Another triad speaks of King Arthur as having dug up Bran's head, for the reason that he wished to hold England by his own strength; whence followed many disasters (Guest, p. 387).

There were many Welsh legends in regard to Branwen or Bronwen (White Bosom), and what is supposed to be her grave, with an urn containing her ashes, may still be seen at a place called "Ynys Bronwen," or "the islet of Bronwen," in Anglesea. It was discovered and visited in 1813 (Guest, p. 389).

The White Mount in which Bran's head was deposited is supposed to have been the Tower of London, described by a Welsh poet of the twelfth century as "The White Eminence of London, a place of splendid fame" (Guest, p. 392).

## VI. THE CASTLE OF THE ACTIVE DOOR

This legend is mainly taken from different parts of Lady Charlotte Guest's translation of the "Mabinogion," with some additions and modifications from Rhys's "Hibbert Lectures" and "The Arthurian Legend."

## VIII. MERLIN

In later years Merlin was known mainly by a series of remarkable prophecies which were attributed to him and were often said to be fulfilled by actual events in history. Thus one of the many places where Merlin's grave was said to be was Drummelzion in Tweeddale, Scotland. On the east side of the churchyard a brook called the Pansayl falls into the Tweed, and there was this prophecy as to their union:—

"When Tweed and Pansayl join at Merlin's grave,
Scotland and England shall one monarch have."

Sir Walter Scott tells us, in his "Border Minstrelsy," that on the day of the coronation of James VI. of Scotland the Tweed accordingly overflowed and joined the Pansayl at the prophet's grave. It was also claimed by one of the witnesses at the trial of Jeanne d'Arc, that there was a prediction by Merlin that France would be saved by a peasant girl from Lorraine. These prophesies have been often reprinted, and have been translated into different languages, and there was published in London, in 1641, "The Life of Merlin, surnamed Ambrosius, His Prophesies and Predictions interpreted, and their Truth made Good by our English Annals." Another book was also published in London, in 1683, called "Merlin revived in a Discourse of Prophesies, Predictions, and their Remarkable Accomplishments."

## VIII. LANCELOT

The main sources of information concerning Lancelot are the "Morte d'Arthur," Newell's "King Arthur and the Table Round," and the publications of the Early English Text Society. See also Rhys's "Arthurian Legend," pp. 127, 147, etc.

## IX. THE HALF-MAN

The symbolical legend on which this tale is founded will be found in Lady Charlotte Guest's translation of the "Mabinogion" (London, 1877), II. p. 344. It is an almost unique instance, in the imaginative literature of that period, of a direct and avowed allegory. There is often allegory, but it is usually contributed by modern interpreters, and would sometimes greatly astound the original fabulists.

## X. ARTHUR

The earliest mention of the island of Avalon, or Avilion, in connection with the death of Arthur, is a slight one by the old English chronicler, Geoffrey of Monmouth (Book XI. c. 2), and the event is attributed by him to the year 542. Wace's French romance was an enlargement of Geoffrey; and the narrative of Layamon (at the close of the twelfth century) an explanation of that of Wace. Layamon's account of the actual death of Arthur, as quoted in the text, is to be found in the translation, a very literal one, by Madden (Madden's "Layamon's Brut," III. pp. 140-146).

The earliest description of the island itself is by an anonymous author known as "Pseudo-Gildas," supposed to be a thirteenth-century Breton writer (Meyer's "Voyage of Bram," I. p. 237), and quoted by Archbishop Usher in his "British Ecclesiastical Antiquities" (1637), p. 273, who thus describes it in Latin hexameters:—

"Cingitur oceano memorabilis insula nullis
Desolata bonis: non fur, nec praedo, nec hostis
Insidiatur ibi: nec vis, nec bruma nec aestas,

Immoderata furit. Pax et concordia, pubes
Ver manent aeternum. Nec flos, nec lilia desunt,
Nec rosa, nec violae: flores et poma sub unâ
Fronde gerit pomus. Habitant sine labe cruoris
Semper ibi juvenes cum virgine: nulla senectus,
Nulla vis morbi, nullus dolor; omnia plena
Laetitiae; nihil hic proprium, communia quaeque.

Regit virgo locis et rebus praesidet istis,
Virginibus stipata suis, pulcherrima pulchris;
Nympha decens vultu, generosis patribus orta,
Consilio pollens, medicinas nobilis arte.
At simul Arthurus regni diadema reliquit,
Substitutique sibi regem, se transtulit illic;
Anno quingeno quadragenoque secundo
Post incarnatum sine patris semine natum.
Immodicè laesus, Arthurus tendit ad aulam
Regis Avallonis; ubi virgo regia vulnus
Illius tractans, sanati membra reservat
Ipsa sibi: vivuntque simul; si credere fas est."

A translation of this passage into rhyming English follows; both of these being taken from Way's "Fabliaux" (London, 1815), II. pp. 233-235.

"By the main ocean's wave encompass'd, stands
A memorable isle, fill'd with all good:
No thief, no spoiler there, no wily foe
With stratagem of wasteful war; no rage
Of heat intemperate, or of winter's cold;
But spring, full blown, with peace and concord reigns:
Prime bliss of heart and season, fitliest join'd!
Flowers fail not there: the lily and the rose,
With many a knot of fragrant violets bound;
And, loftier, clustering down the bended boughs,
Blossom with fruit combin'd, rich apples hang.

"Beneath such mantling shades for ever dwell
In virgin innocence and honour pure,
Damsels and youths, from age and sickness free,
And ignorant of woe, and fraught with joy,
In choice community of all things best.

O'er these, and o'er the welfare of this land,
Girt with her maidens, fairest among fair,
Reigns a bright virgin sprung from generous sires,
In counsel strong, and skill'd in med'cine's lore.
Of her (Britannia's diadem consign'd
To other brow), for his deep wound and wide
Great Arthur sought relief: hither he sped
(Nigh two and forty and five hundred years
Since came the incarnate Son to save mankind),
And in Avallon's princely hall repos'd.
His wound the royal damsel search'd; she heal'd;
And in this isle still holds him to herself
In sweet society,—so fame say true!"

## XI. MAELDUIN

This narrative is taken partly from Nutt's "Voyage of Bram" (I. 162) and partly from Joyce's "Ancient Celtic Romances." The latter, however, allows Maelduin sixty comrades instead of seventeen, which is Nutt's version. There are copies of the original narrative in the Erse language at the British Museum, and in the library of Trinity College, Dublin. The voyage, which may have had some reality at its foundation, is supposed to have taken place about the year 700 A.D. It belongs to the class known as Imrama, or sea-expeditions. Another of these is the voyage of St. Brandan, and another is that of "the sons of O'Corra." A poetical translation of this last has been made by T. D. Sullivan of Dublin, and published in his volume of poems. (Joyce, p. xiii.) All these voyages illustrated the wider and wider space assigned on the Atlantic ocean to the enchanted islands until they were finally identified, in some cases, with the continent which Columbus found.

## XII. ST. BRANDAN

THE legend of St. Brandan, which was very well known in the Middle Ages, was probably first written in Latin prose near the end of the eleventh century, and is preserved in manuscript in many English libraries. An English metrical version, written probably about the beginning of the fourteenth century, is printed under the editorship of Thomas Wright in the publications of the Percy Society, London, 1844 (XIV.), and it is followed in the same volume by an English prose version of 1527. A partial narrative in

Latin prose, with an English version, may be found in W. J. Rees's "Lives of the Cambro-British Saints" (Llandovery, 1853), pp. 251, 575. The account of Brandan in the Acta Sanctorum of the Bollandists may be found under May 16, the work being arranged under saints' days. This account excludes the more legendary elements. The best sketch of the supposed island appears in the Nouvelles Annales des Voyages for 1845 (p. 293), by D'Avezac. Professor O'Curry places the date of the alleged voyage or voyages at about the year 560 ("Lectures on the Manuscript Materials for Irish History," p. 289). Good accounts of the life in the great monasteries of Brandan's period may be found in Digby's "Mores Catholici" or "Ages of Faith"; in Montalembert's "Monks of the West" (translation); in Villemarqué's "La Legende Celtique et la Poésie des Cloistres en Irlande, en Cambrie et en Bretagne" (Paris, 1864). The poem on St. Brandan, stanzas from which are quoted in the text, is by Denis Florence McCarthy, and may be found in the Dublin University Magazine (XXXI. p. 89); and there is another poem on the subject—a very foolish burlesque—in the same magazine (LXXXIX. p. 471). Matthew Arnold's poem with the same title appeared in Fraser's Magazine (LXII. p. 133), and may be found in the author's collected works in the form quoted below.

The legends of St. Brandan, it will be observed, resemble so much the tales of Sindbad the Sailor and others in the "Arabian Nights"—which have also the island-whale, the singing birds, and other features—that it is impossible to doubt that some features of tradition were held in common with the Arabs of Spain.

In later years (the twelfth century), a geographer named Honoré d'Autun declared, in his "Image of the World," that there was in the ocean a certain island agreeable and fertile beyond all others, now unknown to men, once discovered by chance and then lost again, and that this island was the one which Brandan had visited. In several early maps, before the time of Columbus, the Madeira Islands appear as "The Fortunate Islands of St. Brandan," and on the famous globe of Martin Behaim, made in the very year when Columbus sailed, there is a large island much farther west than Madeira, and near the equator, with an inscription saying that in the year 565, St. Brandan arrived at this island and saw many wondrous things, returning to his own land afterwards. Columbus heard this island mentioned at Ferro, where men declared that they had seen it in the distance. Later, the chart of Ortelius, in the sixteenth century, carried it to the neighborhood of Ireland; then it was carried south again, and was supposed all the time to change its place through enchantment, and when Emanuel of Portugal, in 1519, renounced all claim to it, he described it as "The Hidden Island." In 1570 a Portuguese expedition was sent which claimed actually to have touched the mysterious island, indeed to have found there the vast impression of a human foot—doubtless of the baptized giant Mildus—and also a cross nailed to a tree, and three stones laid in a triangle for cooking food. Departing hastily from the island, they left two sailors behind, but could never find the place again.

Again and again expeditions were sent out in search of St. Brandan's island, usually from the Canaries—one in 1604 by Acosta, one in 1721 by Dominguez; and several sketches of the island, as seen from a distance, were published in 1759 by a Franciscan priest in the Canary Islands, named Viere y Clarijo, including one made by himself on May 3, 1759, about 6 A.M., in presence of more than forty witnesses. All these sketches depict the island as having its chief length from north to south, and formed of two unequal hills, the highest of these being at the north, they having between them a depression covered with trees. The fact that this resembles the general form of Palma, one of the Canary Islands, has led to the belief that it may have been an ocean mirage, reproducing the image of that island, just as the legends themselves reproduce, here and there, the traditions of the "Arabian Nights."

In a map drawn by the Florentine physician, Toscanelli, which was sent by him to Columbus in 1474 to give his impression of the Asiatic coast,—lying, as he supposed, across the Atlantic,—there appears the island of St. Brandan. It is as large as all the Azores or Canary Islands or Cape de Verde Islands put together; its southern tip just touches the equator, and it lies about half-way between the Cape de Verde Islands and Zipangu or Japan, which was then believed to lie on the other side of the Atlantic. Mr. Winsor also tells us that the apparition of this island "sometimes came to sailors' eyes" as late as the last century (Winsor's "Columbus," 112).

He also gives a reproduction of Toscanelli's map now lost, as far as can be inferred from descriptions (Winsor, p. 110).

The following is Matthew Arnold's poem:—

SAINT BRANDAN

Saint Brandan sails the northern main;
The brotherhoods of saints are glad.
He greets them once, he sails again;
So late!—such storms!—the Saint is mad!

He heard, across the howling seas,
Chime convent-bells on wintry nights;
He saw, on spray-swept Hebrides,

Twinkle the monastery lights;

But north, still north, Saint Brandan steer'd—
And now no bells, no convents more!
The hurtling Polar lights are near'd,
The sea without a human shore.

At last—(it was the Christmas-night;
Stars shone after a day of storm)—
He sees float past an iceberg white,
And on it—Christ!—a living form.

That furtive mien, that scowling eye,
Of hair that red and tufted fell—
It is—oh, where shall Brandan fly?—
The traitor Judas, out of hell!

Palsied with terror, Brandan sate;
The moon was bright, the iceberg near.
He hears a voice sigh humbly: "Wait!
By high permission I am here.

"One moment wait, thou holy man!
On earth my crime, my death, they knew;
My name is under all men's ban—
Ah, tell them of my respite, too!

"Tell them, one blessed Christmas-night—
(It was the first after I came,
Breathing self-murder, frenzy, spite,
To rue my guilt in endless flame)—

"I felt, as I in torment lay
'Mid the souls plagued by heavenly power,
An angel touch my arm and say:
Go hence, and cool thyself an hour!

"'Ah, whence this mercy, Lord?' I said;
The Leper recollect, said he,
Who ask'd the passers-by for aid,
In Joppa, and thy charity.

"Then I remember'd how I went,
In Joppa, through the public street,
One morn when the sirocco spent
Its storm of dust with burning heat;

"And in the street a leper sate,
Shivering with fever, naked, old;
Sand raked his sores from heel to pate,
The hot wind fever'd him five-fold.

"He gazed upon me as I pass'd,
And murmur'd: Help me, or I die!—
To the poor wretch my cloak I cast,
Saw him look eased, and hurried by.

"Oh, Brandan, think what grace divine,
What blessing must full goodness shower,
When fragment of it small, like mine,
Hath such inestimable power!

"Well-fed, well-clothed, well-friended, I
Did that chance act of good, that one!
Then went my way to kill and lie—
Forgot my good as soon as done.

"That germ of kindness, in the womb
Of mercy caught, did not expire;
Outlives my guilt, outlives my doom,
And friends me in this pit of fire.

"Once every year, when carols wake
On earth the Christmas-night's repose,
Arising from the sinner's lake,
I journey to these healing snows.

"I stanch with ice my burning breast,
With silence balm my whirling brain;
O Brandan! to this hour of rest
That Joppan leper's ease was pain."

Tears started to Saint Brandan's eyes;
He bow'd his head, he breathed a prayer—
Then look'd, and lo, the frosty skies!
The iceberg, and no Judas there!

The island of St. Brandan's was sometimes supposed to lie in the Northern Atlantic, sometimes farther south. It often appears as the Fortunate Isle or Islands, "Insulae Fortunatae" or "Beatae."

On some early maps (1306 to 1471) there is an inlet on the western coast of Ireland called "Lacus Fortunatus," which is filled with Fortunate Islands to the number of 358 (Humboldt, "Examen," II. p. 159), and in one map of 1471 both these and the supposed St. Brandan's group appear in different parts of the ocean under the same name. When the Canary Islands were discovered, they were supposed to be identical with St. Brandan's, but the latter was afterwards supposed to lie southeast of them. After the discovery of the Azores various expeditions were sent to search for St. Brandan's until about 1721. It was last reported as seen in 1759. A full bibliography will be found in Winsor's "Narrative and Critical History," I. p. 48, and also in Humboldt's "Examen," II. p. 163, and early maps containing St. Brandan's will be found in Winsor (I. pp. 54, 58). The first of these is Pizigani's (1387), containing "Ysolae dictae Fortunatae," and the other that of Ortelius (1587), containing "S. Brandain."

## XIII. HY-BRASAIL

"The people of Aran, with characteristic enthusiasm, fancy, that at certain periods, they see Hy-Brasail, elevated far to the west in their watery horizon. This has been the universal tradition of the ancient Irish, who supposed that a great part of Ireland had been swallowed by the sea, and that the sunken part often rose and was seen hanging in the horizon: such was the popular notion. The Hy-Brasail of the Irish is evidently a part of the Atlantis of Plato; who, in his 'Timaeus,' says that that island was totally swallowed up by a prodigious earthquake." (O'Flaherty's "Discourse on the History and Antiquities of the Southern Islands of Aran, lying off the West Coast of Ireland," 1824, p. 139.)

The name appeared first (1351) on the chart called the Medicean Portulana, applied to an island off the Azores. In Pizigani's map (1367) there appear three islands of this name, two off the Azores and one off Ireland. From this time the name appears constantly in maps, and in 1480 a man named John Jay went out to discover the island on July 14, and returned unsuccessful on September 18. He called it Barsyle or Brasylle; and Pedro d'Ayalo, the Spanish Ambassador, says that such voyages were made for seven years "according to the fancies of the Genoese, meaning Sebastian Cabot." Humboldt thinks that the wood called Brazil-wood was supposed to have come from it, as it was known before the South American Brazil was discovered.

A manuscript history of Ireland, written about 1636, in the Library of the Royal Irish Academy, says that Hy-Brasail was discovered by a Captain Rich, who saw its harbor but could never reach it. It is mentioned by Jeremy Taylor ("Dissuasives from Popery," 1667), and the present narrative is founded partly on an imaginary one, printed in a pamphlet in London, 1675, and reprinted in Hardiman's "Irish Minstrelsy" (1831), II. p. 369. The French Geographer Royal, M. Tassin, thinks that the island may have been identical with Porcupine Bank, once above water. In Jeffrey's atlas (1776) it appears as "the imaginary island of O'Brasil." "Brazil Rock" appears on a chart of Purdy, 1834 (Humboldt's "Examen Critique," II. p. 163). Two rocks always associated with it, Mayda and Green Rock, appear on an atlas issued in 1866. See bibliography in Winsor's "Narrative and Critical History," I. p. 49, where there are a number of maps depicting it (I. pp. 54-57). The name of the island is derived by Celtic scholars from breas, large, and i, island; or, according to O'Brien's "Irish Dictionary," its other form of O'Brasile means a large imaginary island (Hardiman's "Irish Minstrelsy," I. p. 369). There are several families named Brazil in County Waterford, Ireland ("Transactions of the Ossianic Society, Dublin," 1854, I. p. 81). The following poem about the island, by Gerald Griffin, will be found in Sparling's "Irish Minstrelsy" (1888), p. 427:—

HY-BRASAIL, THE ISLE OF THE BLEST

On the ocean that hollows the rocks where ye dwell
A shadowy land has appeared, as they tell;
Men thought it a region of sunshine and rest,
And they called it Hy-Brasail, the isle of the blest.
From year unto year on the ocean's blue rim,
The beautiful spectre showed lovely and dim;
The golden clouds curtained the deep where it lay,
And it looked like an Eden away, far away!

A peasant who heard of the wonderful tale,
In the breeze of the Orient loosened his sail;
From Ara, the holy, he turned to the west,
For though Ara was holy, Hy-Brasail was blest.

He heard not the voices that called from the shore—
He heard not the rising wind's menacing roar;
Home, kindred, and safety he left on that day,
And he sped to Hy-Brasail, away, far away!

Morn rose on the deep, and that shadowy isle,
O'er the faint rim of distance, reflected its smile;
Noon burned on the wave, and that shadowy shore
Seemed lovelily distant, and faint as before;
Lone evening came down on the wanderer's track,
And to Ara again he looked timidly back;
O far on the verge of the ocean it lay,
Yet the isle of the blest was away, far away!

Rash dreamer, return! O ye winds of the main,
Bear him back to his own peaceful Ara again,
Rash fool! for a vision of fanciful bliss,
To barter thy calm life of labor and peace.
The warning of reason was spoken in vain;
He never revisited Ara again!
Night fell on the deep, amidst tempest and spray,
And he died on the waters, away, far away!

## XIV. ISLAND OF SATAN'S HAND

The early part of this narrative is founded on Professor O'Curry's Lectures on the manuscript materials of Irish history; it being another of those "Imrama" or narratives of ocean expeditions to which the tale of St. Brandan belongs. The original narrative lands the three brothers ultimately in Spain, and it is a curious fact that most of what we know of the island of Satanaxio or Satanajio—which remained so long on the maps— is taken from an Italian narrative of three other brothers, cited by Formaleoni, "Il Pellegrinaccio di tre giovanni," by Christoforo Armeno (Gaffarel, "Les Iles Fantastiques," p. 91). The coincidence is so peculiar that it offered an irresistible temptation to link the two trios of brothers into one narrative and let the original voyagers do the work of exploration. The explanation given by Gaffarel to the tale is the same that I have suggested as possible. He says in "Iles Fantastiques de l'Atlantaque" (p. 12), "S'il nous était permis d'aventurer une hypothèse, nous croirions voluntiers que les navigateurs de l'époque rencontrèrent, en s'aventurant dans l'Atlantique, quelques-uns de ces gigantesques icebergs, ou montagnes de glace, arrachés aux banquises du pôle nord, et entraînés au sud par les courants, dont la rencontre, assez fréquente, est, même aujourd'hui, tellement redoutée par les capitaines. Ces icebergs, quand ils se heurtent contre un navire, le coulent à pic; et comme ils arrivent à l'improviste, escortés par d'épais brouillards, ils paraissent réellement sortir du sein des flots, comme sortait la main de Satan, pour précipiter au fond de l'abîme matelots et navires." As to the name itself there has been much discussion. On the map of Bianco (1436)— reproduced in Winsor, I. p. 54— the name "Ya de Lamansatanaxio" distinctly appears, and this was translated by both Formaleoni and Humboldt as meaning "the Island of the Hand of Satan." D'Avezac was the first to suggest that the reference was to two separate islands, the one named "De la Man" or "Danman," and the other "Satanaxio." He further suggests— followed by Gaffarel—that the name of the island may originally have been San Atanagio, thus making its baptism a tribute to St. Athanasius instead of to Satan. This would certainly have been a curious transformation, and almost as unexpected in its way as the original conversion of the sinful brothers from outlaws to missionaries.

## XV. ANTILLIA

The name Antillia appears first, but not very clearly, on the Pizigani map of 1367; then clearly on a map of 1424, preserved at Weimar, on that of Bianco in 1436, and on the globe of Beheim in 1492, which adds in an inscription the story of the Seven Bishops. On some maps of the sixteenth and seventeenth centuries there appears near it a smaller island under the name of Sette Cidade, or Sete Ciudades, which is properly another name for the same island. Toscanelli, in his famous letter to Columbus, recommended Antillia as a good way-station for his voyage to India. The island is said by tradition to have been re-discovered by a Portuguese sailor in 1447. Tradition says that this sailor went hastily to the court of Portugal to announce the discovery, but was blamed for not having remained longer, and so fled. It was supposed to be "a large, rectangular island extending from north to south, lying in the mid Atlantic about lat. 35 N." An ample bibliography will be found in Winsor's "Narrative and Critical History," I. p. 48, with maps containing Antillia, I. pp. 54 (Pizigani's), 56, 58.

After the discovery of America, Peter Martyr states (in 1493) that Hispaniola and the adjacent islands were "Antillae insulae," meaning that they were identical with the group surrounding the fabled Antillia (Winsor's "Narrative and Critical History," I. p. 49); and Schöner, in the dedicatory letter of his globe of 1523, says that the king of Castile, through Columbus, has discovered Antiglias Hispaniam Cubam quoque. It was thus that the name Antilles came to be applied to the islands discovered by Columbus;

just as the name Brazil was transferred from an imaginary island to the new continent, and the name Seven Cities was applied to the pueblos of New Mexico by those who discovered them. (See J. H. Simpson, "Coronado's March in Search of the Seven Cities of Cibola," Smithsonian Institution, 1869, pp. 209-340.)

The sailor who re-discovered them said that the chief desire of the people was to know whether the Moors still held Spain (Gaffarel, "Iles Fantastiques," p. 3). In a copy of "Ptolemy" addressed to Pope Urban VI. about 1380, before the alleged visit of the Portuguese, it was stated of the people at Antillia that they lived in a Christian manner, and were most prosperous, "Hie populus christianissime vivit, omnibus divitiis seculi hujus plenus" (D'Avezac, "Nouvelles Annales des voyages," 1845, II. p. 55).

It was afterwards held by some that the island of Antillia was identical with St. Michael in the Azores, where a certain cluster of stone huts still bears the name of Seven Cities, and the same name is associated with a small lake by which they stand. (Humboldt's "Examen Critique," Paris, 1837, II. p. 203; Gaffarel, "Iles Fantastiques," p. 3.)

### XVI. HARALD THE VIKING

The tales of the Norse explorations of America are now accessible in many forms, the most convenient of these being in the edition of E. L. Slafter, published by the Prince Society. As to the habits of the Vikings, the most accessible authorities are "The Age of the Vikings," by Du Chaillu, and "The Sea Kings of Norway," by Laing. The writings of the late Professor E. N. Horsford are well known, but his opinions are not yet generally accepted by students. His last work, "Leif's House in Vineland," with his daughter's supplementary essay on "Graves of the Northmen," is probably the most interesting of the series (Boston, 1893). In Longfellow's "Saga of King Olaf" (II.), included in "Tales of a Wayside Inn," there is a description of the athletic sports practised by the Vikings, which are moreover described with the greatest minuteness by Du Chaillu.

### XVII. NORUMBEGA

The narrative of Champlain's effort to find Norumbega in 1632 may be found in Otis's "Voyages of Champlain" (II. p. 38), and there is another version in the Magazine of American History (I. p. 321). The whole legend of the city is well analyzed in the same magazine (I. p. 14) by Dr. De Costa under the title "The Lost City of New England." In another volume he recurs to the subject (IX. p. 168), and gives (IX. p. 200) a printed copy of David

Ingram's narrative, from the original in the Bodleian Library. He also discusses the subject in Winsor's "Narrative and Critical History" (IV. p. 77, etc.), where he points out that "the insular character of the Norumbega region is not purely imaginary, but is based on the fact that the Penobscot region affords a continued watercourse to the St. Lawrence, which was travelled by the Maine Indians." Ramusio's map of 1559 represents "Nurumbega" as a large island, well defined (Winsor, IV. p. 91); and so does that of Ruscelli (Winsor, IV. p. 92), the latter spelling it "Nurumberg." Some geographers supposed it to extend as far as Florida. The name was also given to a river (probably the Penobscot) and to a cape. The following is Longfellow's poem on the voyage of Sir Humphrey Gilbert:—

SIR HUMPHREY GILBERT

Southward with fleet of ice
Sailed the corsair Death;
Wild and fast blew the blast,
And the east-wind was his breath.

His lordly ships of ice
Glisten in the sun;
On each side, like pennons wide,
Flashing crystal streamlets run.

His sails of white sea-mist
Dripped with silver rain;
But where he passed there were cast
Leaden shadows o'er the main.

Eastward from Campobello
Sir Humphrey Gilbert sailed;
Three days or more seaward he bore,
Then, alas! the land-wind failed.

Alas! the land-wind failed,
And ice-cold grew the night;
And nevermore, on sea or shore,
Should Sir Humphrey see the light.

He sat upon the deck,
The Book was in his hand;

"Do not fear! Heaven is as near,"
He said, "by water as by land!"

In the first watch of the night,
Without a signal's sound,
Out of the sea, mysteriously,
The fleet of Death rose all around.

The moon and the evening star
Were hanging in the shrouds;
Every mast, as it passed,
Seemed to rake the passing clouds.

They grappled with their prize,
At midnight black and cold!
As of a rock was the shock;
Heavily the ground-swell rolled.

Southward through day and dark,
They drift in close embrace,
With mist and rain, o'er the open main;
Yet there seems no change of place.

Southward, forever southward,
They drift through dark and day;
And like a dream, in the Gulf-Stream
Sinking, vanish all away.

### XVIII. GUARDIANS OF THE ST. LAWRENCE

For authorities for this tale see "Voyages of Samuel de Champlain," translated by Charles Pomeroy Otis, Ph.D., with memoir by the Rev. E. F. Slafter, A.M., Boston, 1880 (I. pp. 116, 289, II. p. 52). The incident of the disguised Indians occurred, however, to the earlier explorer, Jacques Cartier. (See my "Larger History of the United States," p. 112.)

### XIX. ISLAND OF DEMONS

The tale of the Isle of Demons is founded on a story told first by Marguerite of Navarre in her "Heptameron" (LXVII. Nouvelle), and then with much variation and amplification by the very untrustworthy traveller Thevet in his "Cosmographie" (1571), Livre XXIII. c. vi. The only copy of the latter work known to me is in the Carter-Brown Library at Providence, R.I., and the passage has been transcribed for me through the kindness of A. E. Winship, Esq., librarian, who has also sent me a photograph of a woodcut representing the lonely woman shooting at a bear. A briefer abstract of the story is in Winsor's "Narrative and Critical History" (IV. p. 66, note), but it states, perhaps erroneously, that Thevet knew Marguerite only through the Princess of Navarre, whereas that author claims—though his claim is never worth much—that he had the story from the poor woman herself, "La pauvre femme estant arriuvee en France ... et venue en la ville de Nautron, pays de Perigort lors que i'y estois, me feit le discours de toutes ses fortunes passées."

The Island of Demons appears on many old maps which may be found engraved in Winsor, IV. pp. 91, 92, 93, 100, 373, etc.; also as "Isla de demonios" in Sebastian Cabot's map (1544) reprinted in Dr. S. E. Dawson's valuable "Voyages of the Cabots," in the Transactions of the Royal Society of Canada for 1897. He also gives Ruysch's map (1508), in which a cluster of islands appears in the same place, marked "Insulae daemonum." Harrisse, in his "Notes sur la Nouvelle France" (p. 278), describes the three sufferers as having been abandoned by Roberval à trente six lieues des côtes de Canada, dans une isle deserte qui fut depuis désignée sous le nom de l'Isle de la Demoiselle, pres de l'embouchure de la Rivière St. Paul ou des Saumons. I have not, however, been able to identify this island. Parkman also says ("Pioneers of France," p. 205) that Roberval's pilot, in his routier, or logbook, speaks often of "Les Isles de la Demoiselle," evidently referring to Marguerite. The brief account by the Princess of Navarre follows:—

LXVII. NOUVELLE

Une pauvre femme, pour sauver la vie de son mary, hasarda la sienne, et ne l'abandonna jusqu'à la mort.

C'est que faisant le diet Robertval un voiage sur la mer, duquel il estoit chef par le commandement du Roy son maistre, en l'isle de Canadas; auquel lieu avoit délibéré, si l'air du païs euste esté commode, de demourer et faire villes et chasteaulx; en quoy il fit tel commencement, que chacun peut sçavoir. Et, pour habituer le pays de Chrestiens, mena avecq luy de toutes sortes d'artisans, entre lesquelz y avoit un homme, qui fut si malheureux, qu'il trahit son maistre et le mist en dangier d'estre prins des gens du pays. Mais Dieu voulut que son entreprinse fut si tost congneue, qu'elle ne peut nuyre au cappitaine Robertval, lequel feit prendre ce meschant traistre, le voulant pugnir comme il l'avoit mérité; ce qui eust esté faict, sans sa femme qui avoit suivy son mary par les périlz de la mer; et ne le voulut abandonner à la mort, mais avecq force larmes feit tant, avecq le cappitaine et toute la compaignye, que, tant pour la pitié d'icelle que pour le service qu'elle leur avoit faict, luy accorda sa requeste qui fut telle, que le mary et la femme furent laissez en une petite isle, sur la mer, où il n'habitoit que bestes saulvaiges; et leur fut permis de porter avecq eulx ce dont ilz avoient nécessité. Les pauvres gens, se trouvans tous seulz en la compaignye des bestes saulvaiges et cruelles, n'eurent recours que à Dieu seul, qui avoit esté toujours le ferme espoir de ceste pauvre femme. Et, comme celle qui avoit toute consolation en Dieu, porta pour sa saulve garde, nourriture et consolation le Nouveau Testament, lequel elle lisoit incessamment. Et, au demourant, avecq son mary, mettoit peine d'accoustrer un petit logis le mieulx qui'l leur estoit possible; et, quand les lyons et aultres bestes en aprochoient pour les dévorer, le mary avecq sa harquebuze, et elle, avecq les pierres, se défendoient si bien, que, non suellement les bestes ne les osoient approcher, mais bien souvent en tuèrent de très-bonnes à manger; ainsy, avecq telles chairs et les herbes du païs, vesquirent quelque temps, quand le pain leur fut failly. A la longue, le mary ne peut porter telle nourriture; et, à cause des eaues qu'ilz buvoient, devint si enflé, que en peu de temps il mourut, n'aiant service ne consolation que sa femme, laquelle le servoit de médecin et de confesseur; en sorte qu'il passa joieusement de ce désert en la céleste patrie. Et la pauvre femme, demourée seulle, l'enterra le plus profond en terre qu'il fut possible; si est-ce que les bestes en eurent incontinent le sentyment, qui vindrent pour manger la charogne. Mais la pauvre femme, en sa petite maisonnette, de coups de harquebuze défendoit que la chair de son mary n'eust tel sépulchre. Ainsy vivant, quant au corps, de vie bestiale, et quant à l'esperit, de vie angélicque, passoit son temps en lectures, contemplations, prières et oraisons ayant un esperit joieux et content, dedans un corps emmaigry et demy mort. Mais Celluy qui n'abandonne jamais les siens, et qui, au désespoir des autres, monstre sa puissance, ne permist que la vertu qu'il avoit myse en ceste femme fust ignorée des hommes, mais voulut qu'elle fust congneue à sa gloire; et fiet que, au bout de quelque temps, un des navires de ceste armée passant devant ceste isle, les gens qui estoient dedans advisèrent, quelque fumée qui leur feit souvenir de ceulx qui y avoient esté laissez, et délibérèrent d'aller veoir ce que Dieu en avoit faict. La pauvre femme, voiant approcher el navire, se tira au bort de la mer, auquel lieu la trouvèrent à leur arrivée. Et, après en avoir rendu louange à Dieu, les mena en sa pauvre maisonnette, et leur monstra de quoy elle vivoit durant sa demeure; ce que leur eust esté incroiable, sans la congnoissance qu'ilz avoient que Dieu est puissant de nourrir en un désert ses serviteurs, comme au plus grandz festins du monde. Et, ne pouvant demeurer en tel lieu, emmenèrent la pauvre femme avecq eulx droict à la Rochelle, où, après un navigage, ilz arrivèrent. Et quand ilz eurent faict entendre aux habitans la fidélité et persévérance de ceste femme, elle fut receue à grand honneur de toutes les Dames, qui voluntiers luy baillèrent leurs filles pour aprendre à lire et à escripre. Et, à cest honneste mestier-là, gaigna le surplus de sa vie, n'aiant autre désîr que d'exhorter un chaucun à l'amour et confiance de Nostre Seigneur, se proposant pour exemple la grande miséricorde dont il avoit usé envers elle.

## XX. BIMINI

Parkman says expressly that "Ponce de Léon found the Island of Bimini," but it is generally mentioned as having been imaginary, and is not clearly identified among the three thousand islands and rocks of the Bahamas. Peter Martyr placed the Fountain of Youth in Florida, which he may have easily supposed to be an island. Some of the features of my description are taken from the strange voyage of Cabeza da Vaca, which may be read in Buckingham Smith's translation of his narrative (Washington, D.C., 1851), or in a more condensed form in Henry Kingsley's "Tales of Old Travel," or in my own "Book of American Explorers" (N.Y., Longmans, 1894).

# Saga of King Harald Grafeld and of Earl Hakon Son of Sigurd by Snorri Sturluson

Preliminary remarks

*This saga might be called Gunhild's Saga, as she is the chief person in it. The reign of King Harald and Earl Hakon is more fully described in the next saga, that is, Olaf Trygvason's. Other literature on this epoch:*
*"Agrip" (chap. 8), "Historia Norvegia", (p. 12), "Thjodrek" (chap. 5), "Saxo" (pp. 479-482), "Egla" (chaps. 81, 82), "Floamanna" (chap. 12), "Fareyinga" (chaps. 2, 4, 10), "Halfred's Saga" (chap. 2), "Hord Grimkelsons Saga" (chaps. 13, 18), "Kormak" (chaps. 19-27), "Laxdaela" (chaps. 19-21), "Njala" (chaps, 3-6).*

*The skalds of this saga are:—Glum Geirason, Kormak Agmundson, Eyvind Skaldaspiller, and Einar Helgason Skalaglam.*

1. GOVERNMENT OF THE SONS OF EIRIK.

When King Hakon was killed, the sons of Eirik took the sovereignty of Norway. Harald, who was the oldest of the living brothers, was over them in dignity. Their mother Gunhild, who was called the King-mother, mixed herself much in the affairs of the country. There were many chiefs in the land at that time. There was Trygve Olafson in the Eastland, Gudrod Bjornson in Vestfold, Sigurd earl of Hlader in the Throndhjem land; but Gunhild's sons held the middle of the country the first winter. There went messages and ambassadors between Gunhild's sons and Trygve and Gudrod, and all was settled upon the footing that they should hold from Gunhild's sons the same part of the country which they formerly had held under King Hakon. A man called Glum Geirason, who was King Harald's skald, and was a very brave man, made this song upon King Hakon's death:—

"Gamle is avenged by Harald!
Great is thy deed, thou champion bold!
The rumour of it came to me
In distant lands beyond the sea,
How Harald gave King Hakon's blood

To Odin's ravens for their food."

This song was much favoured. When Eyvind Finson heard of it he composed the song which was given before, viz.:—

"Our dauntless king with Gamle's gore
Sprinkled his bright sword o'er and o'er," &c.

This song also was much favoured, and was spread widely abroad; and when King Harald came to hear of it, he laid a charge against Evyind affecting his life; but friends made up the quarrel, on the condition that Eyvind should in future be Harald's skald, as he had formerly been King Hakon's. There was also some relationship between them, as Gunhild, Eyvind's mother, was a daughter of Earl Halfdan, and her mother was Ingibjorg, a daughter of Harald Harfager. Thereafter Eyvind made a song about King Harald:—

"Guardian of Norway, well we know
Thy heart failed not when from the bow
The piercing arrow-hail sharp rang
On shield and breast-plate, and the clang
Of sword resounded in the press
Of battle, like the splitting ice;
For Harald, wild wolf of the wood,
Must drink his fill of foeman's blood."

Gunhild's sons resided mostly in the middle of the country, for they did not think it safe for them to dwell among the people of Throndhjem or of Viken, where King Hakon's best friends lived; and also in both places there were many powerful men. Proposals of agreement then passed between Gunhild's sons and Earl Sigurd, or they got no scat from the Throndhjem country; and at last an agreement was concluded between the kings and the earl, and confirmed by oath. Earl Sigurd was to get the same power in the Throndhjem land which he had possessed under King Hakon, and on that they considered themselves at peace. All Gunhild's sons had the character of being penurious; and it was said they hid their money in the ground. Eyvind Skaldaspiller made a song about this:—

"Main-mast of battle! Harald bold!
In Hakon's days the skald wore gold
Upon his falcon's seat; he wore

Rolf Krake's seed, the yellow ore
Sown by him as he fled away,
The avenger Adils' speed to stay.
The gold crop grows upon the plain;
But Frode's girls so gay (1) in vain
Grind out the golden meal, while those
Who rule o'er Norway's realm like foes,
In mother earth's old bosom hide
The wealth which Hakon far and wide
Scattered with generous hand: the sun
Shone in the days of that great one,
On the gold band of Fulla's brow,(2)
On gold-ringed hands that bend the bow,
On the skald's hand; but of the ray
Of bright gold, glancing like the spray
Of sun-lit waves, no skald now sings—
Buried are golden chains and rings."

Now when King Harald heard this song, he sent a message to Eyvind to come to him, and when Eyvind came made a charge against him of being unfaithful. "And it ill becomes thee," said the king, "to be my enemy, as thou hast entered into my service." Eyvind then made these verses:—

"One lord I had before thee, Harald!
One dear-loved lord! Now am I old,
And do not wish to change again,—
To that loved lord, through strife and pain,
Faithful I stood; still true to Hakon,—
To my good king, and him alone.
But now I'm old and useless grown,
My hands are empty, wealth is flown;
I am but fir for a short space
In thy court-hall to fill a place."

But King Harald forced Eyvind to submit himself to his clemency. Eyvind had a great gold ring, which was called Molde, that had been dug up out of the earth long since. This ring the King said he must have as the mulet for the offence; and there was no help for it. Then Eyvind sang:—

"I go across the ocean-foam,
Swift skating to my Iceland home

Upon the ocean-skates, fast driven
By gales by Thurse's witch fire given.
For from the falcon-bearing hand
Harald has plucked the gold snake band
My father wore—by lawless might
Has taken what is mine by right."

Eyvind went home; but it is not told that he ever came near the king again.

ENDNOTES:

(1) Menja and Fenja were strong girls of the giant race, whom Frode bought in Sweden to grind gold and good luck to him; and their meal means gold.—L.

(2) Fulla was one of Frig's attendants, who wore a gold band on the forehead, and the figure means gold,—that the sun shone on gold rings on the hands of the skalds in Hakon's days.—L.

## 2. CHRISTIANITY OF GUNHILD'S SONS.

Gunhild's sons embraced Christianity in England, as told before; but when they came to rule over Norway they made no progress in spreading Christianity—only they pulled down the temples of the idols, and cast away the sacrifices where they had it in their power, and raised great animosity by doing so. The good crops of the country were soon wasted in their days, because there were many kings, and each had his court about him. They had therefore great expenses, and were very greedy. Besides, they only observed those laws of King Hakon which suited themselves. They were, however, all of them remarkably handsome men—stout, strong, and expert in all exercises. So says Glum Geirason, in the verses he composed about Harald, Gunhild's son:—

"The foeman's terror, Harald bold,
Had gained enough of yellow gold;
Had Heimdal's teeth (1) enough in store,
And understood twelve arts or more."

The brothers sometimes went out on expeditions together, and sometimes each on his own account. They were fierce, but brave and active; and great warriors, and very successful.

ENDNOTES:

(1) Heimdal was one of the gods, whose horse was called Gold-top; and the horse's teeth were of gold.

## 3. COUNCILS BY GUNHILD AND HER SONS.

Gunhild the King-mother, and her sons, often met, and talked together upon the government of the country. Once Gunhild asked her sons what they intended to do with their kingdom of Throndhjem. "Ye have the title of king, as your forefathers had before you; but ye have little land or people, and there are many to divide with. In the East, at Viken, there are Trygve and Gudrod; and they have some right, from relationship, to their governments. There is besides Earl Sigurd ruling over the whole Throndhjem country; and no reason can I see why ye let so large a kingdom be ruled by an earl, and not by yourselves. It appears wonderful to me that ye go every summer upon viking cruises against other lands, and allow an earl within the country to take your father's heritage from you. Your grandfather, whose name you bear, King Harald, thought it but a small matter to take an earl's life and land when he subdued all Norway, and held it under him to old age."

Harald replied, "It is not so easy, mother, to cut off Earl Sigurd as to slay a kid or a calf. Earl Sigurd is of high birth, powerful in relations, popular, and prudent; and I think if the Throndhjem people knew for certain there was enmity between us, they would all take his side, and we could expect only evil from them. I don't think it would be safe for any of us brothers to fall into the hands of the Throndhjem people."

Then said Gunhild, "We shall go to work another way, and not put ourselves forward. Harald and Erling shall come in harvest to North More, and there I shall meet you, and we shall consult together what is to be done." This was done.

## 4. GUNHILD'S SONS AND GRJOTGARD.

Earl Sigurd had a brother called Grjotgard, who was much younger, and much less respected; in fact, was held in no title of honour. He had many people, however, about him, and in summer went on viking cruises, and gathered to himself property. Now King Harald sent messengers to Throndhjem with offers of friendship, and with presents. The messengers declared that King Harald was willing to be on the same friendly terms with the earl that King Hakon had been; adding, that they wished the earl to come to King Harald, that their friendship might be put on a firm footing. The Earl Sigurd received well the king's messengers and friendly message, but said that on account of his many affairs he could not come to the king. He sent many friendly gifts, and many glad and grateful words to the king, in return for his friendship. With this reply the messengers set off, and went to Grjotgard, for whom they had the same message, and brought him good presents, and offered him King Harald's friendship, and invited him to visit the king. Grjotgard promised to come and at the appointed time he paid a visit to King Harald and Gunhild, and was received in the most friendly manner. They treated him on the most intimate footing, so that Grjotgard had access to their private consultations and secret councils. At last the conversation, by an understanding between the king and queen, was turned upon Earl Sigurd; and they spoke to Grjotgard about the earl having kept him so long in obscurity, and asked him if he would not join the king's brothers in an attack on the earl. If he would join with them, the king promised Grjotgard that he should be his earl, and have the same government that Sigurd had. It came so far that a secret agreement was made between them, that Grjotgard should spy out the most favourable opportunity of attacking by surprise Earl Sigurd, and should give King Harald notice of it. After this agreement Grjotgard returned home with many good presents from the king.

### 5. SIGURD BURNT IN A HOUSE IN STJORADAL

Earl Sigurd went in harvest into Stjoradal to guest-quarters, and from thence went to Oglo to a feast. The earl usually had many people about him, for he did not trust the king; but now, after friendly messages had passed between the king and him, he had no great following of people with him. Then Grjotgard sent word to the king that he could never expect a better opportunity to fall upon Earl Sigurd; and immediately, that very evening, Harald and Erling sailed into Throndhjem fjord with several ships and many people. They sailed all night by starlight, and Grjotgard came out to meet them. Late in the night they came to Oglo, where Earl Sigurd was at the feast, and set fire to the house; and burnt the house, the earl, and all his men. As soon as it was daylight, they set out through the fjord, and south to More, where they remained a long time.

### 6. HISTORY OF HAKON, SIGURD'S SON.

Hakon, the son of Earl Sigurd, was up in the interior of the Throndhjem country when he heard this news. Great was the tumult through all the Throndhjem land, and every vessel that could swim was put into the water;

and as soon as the people were gathered together they took Earl Sigurd's son Hakon to be their earl and the leader of the troops, and the whole body steered out of Throndhjem fjord. When Gunhild's sons heard of this, they set off southwards to Raumsdal and South More; and both parties kept eye on each other by their spies. Earl Sigurd was killed two years after the fall of King Hakon (A.D. 962). So says Eyvind Skaldaspiller in the "Haleygjatal":—

"At Oglo, as I've heard, Earl Sigurd
Was burnt to death by Norway's lord,—
Sigurd, who once on Hadding's grave
A feast to Odin's ravens gave.
In Oglo's hall, amidst the feast,
When bowls went round and ale flowed fast,
He perished: Harald lit the fire
Which burnt to death the son of Tyr."

Earl Hakan, with the help of his friends, maintained himself in the Throndhjem country for three years; and during that time (A.D. 963-965) Gunhild's sons got no revenues from it. Hakon had many a battle with Gunhild's sons, and many a man lost his life on both sides. Of this Einar Skalaglam speaks in his lay, called "Vellekla," which he composed about Earl Hakon:—

"The sharp bow-shooter on the sea
Spread wide his fleet, for well loved he
The battle storm: well loved the earl
His battle-banner to unfurl,
O'er the well-trampled battle-field
He raised the red-moon of his shield;
And often dared King Eirik's son
To try the fray with the Earl Hakon."

And he also says:—

"Who is the man who'll dare to say
That Sigurd's son avoids the fray?
He gluts the raven—he ne'er fears
The arrow's song or flight of spears,
With thundering sword he storms in war,
As Odin dreadful; or from far

He makes the arrow-shower fly
To swell the sail of victory.
The victory was dearly bought,
And many a viking-fight was fought
Before the swinger of the sword
Was of the eastern country lord."

And Einar tells also how Earl Hakon avenged his father's murderer:—

"I praise the man, my hero he,
Who in his good ship roves the sea,
Like bird of prey, intent to win
Red vengeance for his slaughtered kin.
From his blue sword the iron rain
That freezes life poured down amain
On him who took his father's life,
On him and his men in the strife.
To Odin many a soul was driven,—
To Odin many a rich gift given.
Loud raged the storm on battle-field—
Axe rang on helm, and sword on shield."

The friends on both sides at last laid themselves between, and brought proposals of peace; for the bondes suffered by this strife and war in the land. At last it was brought to this, by the advice of prudent men, that Earl Hakon should have the same power in the Throndhjem land which his father Earl Sigurd had enjoyed; and the kings, on the other hand, should have the same dominion as King Hakon had: and this agreement was settled with the fullest promises of fidelity to it. Afterwards a great friendship arose between Earl Hakon and Gunhild, although they sometimes attempted to deceive each other. And thus matters stood for three years longer (A.D. 966-968), in which time Earl Hakon sat quietly in his dominions.

### 7. OF HARALD GRAFELD.

King Hakon had generally his seat in Hordaland and Rogaland, and also his brothers; but very often, also, they went to Hardanger. One summer it happened that a vessel came from Iceland belonging to Icelanders, and loaded with skins and peltry. They sailed to Hardanger, where they heard the greatest number of people assembled; but when the folks came to deal with them, nobody would buy their skins. Then the steersman went to King Harald, whom he had been acquainted with before, and complained of his ill luck. The king promised to visit him, and did so. King Harald was very condescending, and full of fun. He came with a fully manned boat, looked at the skins, and then said to the steersman, "Wilt thou give me a present of one of these gray-skins?" "Willingly," said the steersman, "if it were ever so many." On this the king wrapped himself up in a gray-skin, and went back to his boat; but before they rowed away from the ship, every man in his suite bought such another skin as the king wore for himself. In a few days so many people came to buy skins, that not half of them could be served with what they wanted; and thereafter the king was called Harald Grafeld (Grayskin).

## 8. EARL EIRIK'S BIRTH.

Earl Hakon came one winter to the Uplands to a feast, and it so happened that he had intercourse with a girl of mean birth. Some time after the girl had to prepare for her confinement, and she bore a child, a boy, who had water poured on him, and was named Eirik. The mother carried the boy to Earl Hakon, and said that he was the father. The earl placed him to be brought up with a man called Thorleif the Wise, who dwelt in Medaldal, and was a rich and powerful man, and a great friend of the earl. Eirik gave hopes very early that he would become an able man, was handsome in countenance, and stout and strong for a child; but the earl did not pay much attention to him. The earl himself was one of the handsomest men in countenance,—not tall, but very strong, and well practised in all kinds of exercises; and withal prudent, of good understanding, and a deadly man at arms.

## 9. KING TRYGVE OLAFSON'S MURDER.

It happened one harvest (A.D. 962) that Earl Hakon, on a journey in the Uplands, came to Hedemark; and King Trygve Olafson and King Gudrod Bjornson met him there, and Dale-Gudbrand also came to the meeting. They had agreed to meet, and they talked together long by themselves; but so much only was known of their business, that they were to be friends of each other. They parted, and each went home to his own kingdom. Gunhild and her sons came to hear of this meeting, and they suspected it must have been to lay a treasonable plot against the kings; and they often talked of this among themselves. When spring (A.D. 963) began to set in, King Harald and his brother King Gudrod proclaimed that they were to make a viking cruise, as usual, either in the West sea, or the Baltic. The people accordingly assembled, launched the ships into the sea, and made themselves ready to sail. When they were drinking the farewell ale,—and they drank bravely,—much and many things were talked over at the drink-table, and, among other things, were comparisons between different men, and at last between the kings themselves. One said that King Harald excelled his brothers by far, and in every way. On this King Gudrod was very angry, and said that he was in no respect behind Harald, and was ready to prove it. Instantly both parties were so inflamed that they challenged each other to battle, and ran to their arms. But some of the guests who were less drunk, and had more understanding, came between them, and quieted them; and each went to his ship, but nobody expected that they would all sail together. Gudrod sailed east ward along the land, and Harald went out to sea, saying he would go to the westward; but when he came outside of the islands he steered east along the coast, outside of the rocks and isles. Gudrod, again, sailed inside, through the usual channel, to Viken, and eastwards to Folden. He then sent a message to King Trygve to meet him, that they might make a cruise together in summer in the Baltic to plunder. Trygve accepted willingly, and as a friend, the invitation; and as heard King Gudrod had but few people with him, he came to meet him with a single boat. They met at Veggen, to the east of Sotanes; but just as they were come to the meeting place, Gudrod's men ran up and killed King Trygve and twelve men. He lies buried at a place called Trygve's Cairn (A.D. 963).

10. KING GUDROD'S FALL.

King Harald sailed far outside of the rocks and isles; but set his course to Viken, and came in the night-time to Tunsberg, and heard that Gudrod Bjornson was at a feast a little way up the country. Then King Harald set out immediately with his followers, came in the night, and surrounded the house. King Gudrod Bjornson went out with his people; but after a short resistance he fell, and many men with him. Then King Harald joined his brother King Gudrod, and they subdued all Viken.

11. OF HARALD GRENSKE.

King Gudrod Bjornson had made a good and suitable marriage, and had by his wife a son called Harald, who had been sent to be fostered to Grenland to a lenderman called Hroe the White. Hroe's son, called Hrane Vidforle (the Far-travelled), was Harald's foster-brother, and about the same age. After his father Gudrod's fall, Harald, who was called Grenske, fled to the Uplands, and with him his foster-brother Hrane, and a few people. Harald staid a while there among his relations; but as Eirik's sons sought after every man who interfered with them, and especially those who might oppose them, Harald Grenske's friends and relations advised him to leave the country. Harald therefore went eastward into Svithjod, and sought shipmates, that he might enter into company with those who went out a cruising to gather property. Harald became in this way a remarkably able man. There was a man in Svithjod at that time called Toste, one of the most powerful and clever in the land among those who had no high name or dignity; and he was a great warrior, who had been often in battle, and was therefore called Skoglar-Toste. Harald Grenske came into his company, and cruised with Toste in summer; and wherever Harald came he was well thought of by every one. In the winter Harald, after passing two years in the Uplands, took up his abode with Toste, and lived five years with him. Toste had a daughter, who was both young and handsome, but she was proud and high-minded. She was called Sigrid, and was afterwards married to the Swedish king, Eirik the Victorious, and had a son by him, called Olaf the Swede, who was afterwards king of Svithjod. King Eirik died in a sick-bed at Upsala ten years after the death of Styrbjorn.

## 12. EARL HAKON'S FEUDS.

Gunhild's sons levied a great army in Viken (A.D. 963), and sailed along the land northwards, collecting people and ships on the way out of every district. They then made known their intent, to proceed northwards with their army against Earl Hakon in Throndhjem. When Earl Hakon heard this news, he also collected men, and fitted out ships; and when he heard what an overwhelming force Gunhild's sons had with them, he steered south with his fleet to More, pillaging wherever he came, and killing many people. He then sent the whole of the bonde army back to Throndhjem; but he himself, with his men-at-arms, proceeded by both the districts of More and Raumsdal, and had his spies out to the south of Stad to spy the army of Gunhild's sons; and when he heard they were come into the Fjords, and were waiting for a fair wind to sail northwards round Stad, Earl Hakon set out to sea from the north side of Stad, so far that his sails could not be seen from the land, and then sailed eastward on a line with the coast, and came to Denmark, from whence he sailed into the Baltic, and pillaged there during the summer. Gunhild's sons conducted their army north to Throndhjem, and remained there the whole summer collecting the scat and duties. But when summer was advanced they left Sigurd Slefa and Gudron behind; and the other brothers returned eastward with the levied army they had taken up in summer.

## 13. OF EARL HAKON AND GUNHILD'S SONS.

Earl Hakon, towards harvest (A.D. 963), sailed into the Bothnian Gulf to Helsingjaland, drew his ships up there on the beach, and took the landways through Helsingjaland and Jamtaland, and so eastwards round the dividing ridge (the Kjol, or keel of the country), and down into the Throndhjem district. Many people streamed towards him, and he fitted out ships. When the sons of Gunhild heard of this they got on board their ships, and sailed out of the Fjord; and Earl Hakon came to his seat at Hlader, and remained there all winter. The sons of Gunhild, on the other hand, occupied More; and they and the earl attacked each other in turns, killing each other's people. Earl Hakon kept his dominions of Throndhjem, and was there generally in the winter; but in summer he sometimes went to Helsingjaland, where he went on board of his ships and sailed with them down into the Baltic, and plundered there; and sometimes he remained in Throndhjem, and kept an army on foot, so that Gunhild's sons could get no hold northwards of Stad.

## 14. SIGURD SLEFA'S MURDER.

One summer Harald Grayskin with his troops went north to Bjarmaland, where be forayed, and fought a great battle with the inhabitants on the banks of the Vina (Dwina). King Harald gained the victory, killed many people, plundered and wasted and burned far and wide in the land, and made enormous booty. Glum Geirason tells of it thus:—

"I saw the hero Harald chase
With bloody sword Bjarme's race:
They fly before him through the night,
All by their burning city's light.
On Dwina's bank, at Harald's word,
Arose the storm of spear and sword.
In such a wild war-cruise as this,
Great would he be who could bring peace."

King Sigurd Slefa came to the Herse Klyp's house. Klyp was a son of Thord, and a grandson of Hordakare, and was a man of power and great family. He was not at home; but his wife Alof give a good reception to the king, and made a great feast at which there was much drinking. Alof was a daughter of Asbjorn, and sister to Jarnskegge, north in Yrjar. Asbjorn's brother was called Hreidar, who was father to Styrkar, whose son was

Eindride, father of Einar Tambaskielfer. In the night the king went to bed to Alof against her will, and then set out on his journey. The harvest thereafter, King Harald and his brother King Sigurd Slefa went to Vors, and summoned the bondes to a Thing. There the bondes fell on them, and would have killed them, but they escaped and took different roads. King Harald went to Hardanger, but King Sigurd to Alrekstader. Now when the Herse Klyp heard of this, he and his relations assembled to attack the king; and Vemund Volubrjot (1) was chief of their troop. Now when they came to the house they attacked the king, and Herse Klyp, it is said, ran him through with his sword and killed him; but instantly Klyp was killed on the spot by Erling Gamle (A.D. 965).

ENDNOTES:

(1) Volubrjotr.—Literally "the one who breaks the vala", that is, breaks the skulls of witches.

15. GRJOTGARD'S FALL.

King Harald Grafeld and his brother King Gudrod gathered together a great army in the east country, with which they set out northwards to Throndhjem (A.D. 968). When Earl Hakon heard of it he collected men, and set out to More, where he plundered. There his father's brother, Grjotgard, had the command and defence of the country on account of Gunhild's sons, and he assembled an army by order of the kings. Earl Hakon advanced to meet him, and gave him battle; and there fell Grjotgard and two other earls, and many a man besides. So says Einar Skalaglam:—

"The helm-crown'd Hakon, brave as stout,
Again has put his foes to rout.
The bowl runs o'er with Odin's mead, (1)
That fires the skald when mighty deed
Has to be sung. Earl Hakon's sword,
In single combat, as I've heard,
Three sons of earls from this one fray
To dwell with Odin drove away." (2)

Thereafter Earl Hakon went out to sea, and sailed outside the coast, and came to Denmark. He went to the Danish King, Harald Gormson, and was well received by him, and staid with him all winter (A.D. 969). At that time there was also with the Danish king a man called Harald, a son of Knut

Gormson, and a brother's son of King Harald. He was lately come home from a long viking cruise, on which he had gathered great riches, and therefore he was called Gold Harald. He thought he had a good chance of coming to the Danish kingdom.

ENDNOTES:
(1) Odin's mead, called Bodn, was the blood or mead the sons of Brage, the god of poets, drank to inspire them. —L.
(2) To dwell with Odin,—viz. slew them.—L.

16. KING ERLING'S FALL.

King Harald Grafeld and his brothers proceeded northwards to Throndhjem, where they met no opposition. They levied the scat-duties, and all other revenues, and laid heavy penalties upon the bondes; for the kings had for a long time received but little income from Throndhjem, because Earl Hakon was there with many troops, and was at variance with these kings. In autumn (A.D. 968) King Harald went south with the greater part of the men-at-arms, but King Erlin remained behind with his men. He raised great contributions from the bondes, and pressed severely on them; at which the bondes murmured greatly, and submitted to their losses with impatience. In winter they gathered together in a great force to go against King Erling, just as he was at a feast; and they gave battle to him, and he with the most of his men fell (A.D. 969).

17. THE SEASONS IN NORWAY AT THIS TIME.

While Gunhild's sons reigned in Norway the seasons were always bad, and the longer they reigned the worse were the crops; and the bondes laid the blame on them. They were very greedy, and used the bondes harshly. It came at length to be so bad that fish, as well as corn, were wanting. In Halogaland there was the greatest famine and distress; for scarcely any corn grew, and even snow was lying, and the cattle were bound in the byres (1) all over the country until midsummer. Eyvind Skaldaspiller describes it in his poem, as he came outside of his house and found a thick snowdrift at that season:—

"Tis midsummer, yet deep snows rest
On Odin's mother's frozen breast:
Like Laplanders, our cattle-kind
In stall or stable we must bind."

ENDNOTES: (1) Byres = gards or farms.

## 18. THE ICELANDERS AND EYVIND THE SKALD.

Eyvind composed a poem about the people of Iceland, for which they rewarded him by each bonde giving him three silver pennies, of full weight and white in the fracture. And when the silver was brought together at the Althing, the people resolved to have it purified, and made into a row of clasps; and after the workmanship of the silver was paid, the row of clasps was valued at fifty marks. This they sent to Eyvind; but Eyvind was obliged to separate the clasps from each other, and sell them to buy food for his household. But the same spring a shoal of herrings set in upon the fishing ground beyond the coast-side, and Eyvind manned a ship's boat with his house servants and cottars, and rowed to where the herrings were come, and sang:—

"Now let the steed of ocean bound
O'er the North Sea with dashing sound:
Let nimble tern and screaming gull
Fly round and round—our net is full.
Fain would I know if Fortune sends
A like provision to my friends.
Welcome provision 'tis, I wot,
That the whale drives to our cook's pot."

So entirely were his movable goods exhausted, that he was obliged to sell his arrows to buy herrings, or other meat for his table:—

"Our arms and ornaments of gold
To buy us food we gladly sold:
The arrows of the bow gave we
For the bright arrows of the sea." (1)


ENDNOTES:

(1) Herrings, from their swift darting along, are called *arrows of the sea*.

# The Death of Baldur by Jean Song

"I heard a voice, that cried,
'Baldur the Beautiful
Is dead, is dead!'
And through the misty air
Passed like the mournful cry
Of sunward sailing cranes."
- Longfellow.

Among the gods of Greece we find gods and goddesses who do unworthy deeds, but none to act the permanent part of villain of the play. In the mythology of the Norsemen we have a god who is wholly treacherous and evil, ever the villain of the piece, cunning, malicious, vindictive, and cruel—the god Loki. And as his foil, and his victim, we have Baldur, best of all gods, most beautiful, most greatly beloved. Baldur was the Galahad of the court of Odin the king, his father.

"My strength is of the strength of ten,
Because my heart is pure."

No impure thing was to be found in his dwelling; none could impugn his courage, yet ever he counselled peace, ever was gentle and infinitely wise, and his beauty was as the beauty of the whitest of all the flowers of the Northland, called after him Baldrsbrá. The god of the Norsemen was essentially a god of battles, and we are told by great authorities that Baldur was originally a hero who fought on the earth, and who, in time, came to be deified. Even if it be so, it is good to think that a race of warriors could worship one whose chief qualities were wisdom, purity, and love.

In perfect happiness, loving and beloved, Baldur lived in Asgard with his wife Nanna, until a night when his sleep was assailed by horrible dreams of evil omen. In the morning he told the gods that he had dreamed that Death, a thing till then unknown in Asgard, had come and cruelly taken his life away. Solemnly the gods debated how this ill happening might be averted, and Freya, his mother, fear for her best beloved hanging heavy over her heart, took upon herself the task of laying under oath fire and water, iron and all other metals, trees and shrubs, birds, beasts and creeping things, to do no harm to Baldur. With eager haste she went from place to place, nor did she fail to exact the oath from anything in all nature, animate or inanimate, save one only.

"A twig of mistletoe, tender and fair, grew high above the field," and such a little thing it was, with its dainty green leaves and waxen white berries, nestling for protection under the strong arm of a great oak, that the goddess passed it by. Assuredly no scathe could come to Baldur the Beautiful from a creature so insignificant, and Freya returned to Asgard well pleased with her quest.

Then indeed was there joy and laughter amongst the gods, for each one tried how he might slay Baldur, but neither sword nor stone, hammer nor battle-axe could work him any ill.

Odin alone remained unsatisfied. Mounted on his eight-footed grey steed, Sleipnir, he galloped off in haste to consult the giant prophetess Angrbotha, who was dead and had to be followed to Niflheim, the chilly underworld that lies far north from the world of men, and where the sun never comes. Hel, the daughter of Loki and of Angrbotha, was queen of this dark domain.

"There, in a bitterly cold place, she received the souls of all who died of sickness or old age; care was her bed, hunger her dish, starvation her knife. Her walls were high and strong, and her bolts and bars huge; 'Half blue was her skin, and half the colour of human flesh. A goddess easy to know, and in all things very stern and grim.'"
- Dasent.

In her kingdom no soul that passed away in glorious battle was received, nor any that fought out the last of life in a fierce combat with the angry waves of the sea. Only those who died ingloriously were her guests.

When he had reached the realm of Hel, Odin found that a feast was being prepared, and the couches were spread, as for an honoured guest, with rich tapestry and with gold. For many a year had Angrbotha rested there in peace, and it was only by chanting a magic spell and tracing those runes which have power to raise the dead that Odin awoke her. When she raised herself, terrible and angry from her tomb, he did not tell her that he was the mighty father of gods and men. He only asked her for whom the great feast was prepared, and why Hel was spreading her couches so gorgeously. And to the father of Baldur she revealed the secret of the future, that Baldur was the expected guest, and that by his blind brother Hodur his soul was to be hastened to the Shades.

"Who, then, would avenge him?" asked the father, great wrath in his heart. And the prophetess replied that his death should be avenged by Vali, his youngest brother, who should not wash his hands nor comb his hair until he had brought the slayer of Baldur to the funeral pyre. But yet another question Odin would fain have answered.

"Who," he asked, "would refuse to weep at Baldur's death?"

Thereat the prophetess, knowing that her questioner could be none other than Odin, for to no mortal man could be known so much of the future, refused for evermore to speak, and returned to the silence of her tomb. And Odin was forced to mount his steed and to return to his own land of warmth and pleasure.

On his return he found that all was well with Baldur. Thus he tried to still his anxious heart and to forget the feast in the chill regions of Niflheim, spread for the son who was to him the dearest, and to laugh with those who tried in vain to bring scathe to Baldur.

Only one among those who looked at those sports and grew merry, as he whom they loved stood like a great cliff against which the devouring waves of the fierce North Sea beat and foam and crash in vain, had malice in his heart as he beheld the wonder. In the evil heart of Loki there came a desire to overthrow the god who was beloved by all gods and by all men. He hated him because he was pure, and the mind of Loki was as a stream into which all the filth of the world is discharged. He hated him because Baldur was truth and loyalty, and he, Loki, was treachery and dishonour. He hated him because to Loki there came never a thought that was not full of meanness and greed and cruelty and vice, and Baldur was indeed one sans peur et sans reproche.

Thus Loki, taking upon himself the form of a woman, went to Fensalir, the palace, all silver and gold, where dwelt Freya, the mother of Baldur.

The goddess sat, in happy majesty, spinning the clouds, and when Loki, apparently a gentle old woman, passed by where she sat, and then paused and asked, as if amazed, what were the shouts of merriment that she heard, the smiling goddess replied:

"All things on earth have sworn to me never to injure Baldur, and all the gods use their weapons against him in vain. Baldur is safe for evermore."

"All things?" queried Loki.

And Freya answered, "All things but the mistletoe. No harm can come to him from a thing so weak that it only lives by the lives of others."

Then the vicious heart of Loki grew joyous. Quickly he went to where the mistletoe grew, cut a slender green branch, shaped it into a point, and sought the blind god Hodur.

Hodur stood aside, while the other gods merrily pursued their sport.

"Why dost thou not take aim at Baldur with a weapon that fails and so join in the laughter?" asked Loki.

And Hodur sadly made answer:

"Well dost thou know that darkness is my lot, nor have I ought to cast at my brother."

Then Loki placed in his hand the shaft of mistletoe and guided his aim, and well and surely Hodur cast the dart. He waited, then, for the merry laughter that followed ever on the onslaught of those against him whom none could do harm. But a great and terrible cry smote his ears. "Baldur the Beautiful is dead! is dead!"

On the ground lay Baldur, a white flower cut down by the scythe of the mower. And all through the realm of the gods, and all through the land of the Northmen there arose a cry of bitter lamentation.

"That was the greatest woe that ever befell gods and men," says the story.

The sound of terrible mourning in place of laughter brought Freya to where

"...on the floor lay Baldur dead; and round lay thickly strewn swords, axes, darts, and spears, which all the gods in sport had lightly thrown at Baldur, whom no weapon pierced or clove; but in his breast stood fixed the fatal bough of mistletoe."

- Matthew Arnold.

When she saw what had befallen him, Freya's grief was a grief that refused to be comforted, but when the gods, overwhelmed with sorrow, knew not what course to take, she quickly commanded that one should ride to Niflheim and offer Hel a ransom if she would permit Baldur to return to Asgard.

Hermoder the Nimble, another of the sons of Odin, undertook the mission, and, mounted on his father's eight-footed steed, he speedily reached the ice-cold domain of Hel.

There he found Baldur, sitting on the noblest seat of those who feasted, ruling among the people of the Underworld. With burning words Hermoder pled with Hel that she would permit Baldur to return to the world of gods and the world of men, by both of whom he was so dearly beloved. Said Hel:

"Come then! if Baldur was so dear beloved,
And this is true, and such a loss is Heaven's—
Hear, how to Heaven may Baldur be restored.

Show me through all the world the signs of grief!
Fails but one thing to grieve, here Baldur stops!
Let all that lives and moves upon the earth
Weep him, and all that is without life weep;
Let Gods, men, brutes, beweep him; plants and stones,
So shall I know the loss was dear indeed,
And bend my heart, and give him back to Heaven."

- Matthew Arnold.


Gladly Hermoder made answer:
"All things shall weep for Baldur!"
Swiftly he made his perilous return journey, and at once, when the gods heard what Hel had said, messengers were despatched all over the earth to beg all things, living and dead, to weep for Baldur, and so dear to all nature was the beautiful god, that the messengers everywhere left behind them a track of the tears that they caused to be shed.

Meantime, in Asgard, preparations were made for Baldur's pyre. The longest of the pines in the forest were cut down by the gods, and piled up in a mighty pyre on the deck of his great ship Ringhorn, the largest in the world.

"Seventy ells and four extended
On the grass the vessel's keel;
High above it, gilt and splendid,
Rose the figure-head ferocious
With its crest of steel."

- Longfellow.

Down to the seashore they bore the body, and laid it on the pyre with rich gifts all round it, and the pine trunks of the Northern forests that formed the pyre, they covered with gorgeous tapestries and fragrant flowers. And when they had laid him there, with all love and gentleness, and his fair young wife, Nanna, looked on his beautiful still face, sorrow smote her heart so that it was broken, and she fell down dead. Tenderly they laid her beside him, and by him, too, they laid the bodies of his horse and his hounds, which they slew to bear their master company in the land whither his soul had fled; and around the pyre they twined thorns, the emblem of sleep.

Yet even then they looked for his speedy return, radiant and glad to come home to a sunlit land of happiness. And when the messengers who were to have brought tidings of his freedom were seen drawing near, eagerly they crowded to hear the glad words, "All creatures weep, and Baldur shall return!"

But with them they brought not hope, but despair. All things, living and dead, had wept, save one only. A giantess who sat in a dark cave had laughed them to scorn. With devilish merriment she mocked:

"Neither in life, nor yet in death,
Gave he me gladness.
Let Hel keep her prey."

Then all knew that yet a second time had Baldur been betrayed, and that the giantess was none other than Loki, and Loki, realising the fierce wrath of Odin and of the other gods, fled before them, yet could not escape his doom. And grief unspeakable was that of gods and of men when they knew that in the chill realm of the inglorious dead Baldur must remain until the twilight of the gods had come, until old things had passed away, and all things had become new.

Not only the gods, but the giants of the storm and frost, and the frost elves came to behold the last of him whom they loved. Then the pyre was set alight, and the great vessel was launched, and glided out to sea with its sails of flame.

"They launched the burning ship!
It floated far away
Over the misty sea,
Till like the sun it seemed,
Sinking beneath the waves,
Baldur returned no more!"

Yet, ere he parted from his dead son, Odin stooped over him and whispered a word in his ear. And there are those who say that as the gods in infinite sorrow stood on the beach staring out to sea, darkness fell, and only a fiery track on the waves showed whither he had gone whose passing had robbed Asgard and the Earth of their most beautiful thing, heavy as the weight of chill Death's remorseless hand would have been their hearts, but for the knowledge of that word. They knew that with the death of Baldur the twilight of the gods had begun, and that by much strife and infinite suffering down through the ages the work of their purification and hallowing must be wrought. But when all were fit to receive him, and peace and happiness reigned again on earth and in heaven, Baldur would come back. For the word was Resurrection.

"So perish the old Gods!
But out of the sea of time
Rises a new land of song,
Fairer than the old."

- Longfellow.

"Heartily know,
When half-gods go,
The gods arrive."

- Emerson.

# The Story of the Magic Mead by Emilie Kip Baker

THERE once lived on the earth a man named Kvasir; and he was much beloved by the gods because they had given him the wonderful gift of poetry. Kvasir was a great traveller, and wherever he went men begged him to tell them, in his singing words, of the life of the gods and of the brave deeds of heroes. So the poet went from cottage to castle sharing his gift with rich and poor alike. Sometimes he told the familiar tales that had grown old on men's lips; and sometimes he sang of heroes in far-off forgotten lands.

Every one loved Kvasir—every one except the spiteful little dwarfs who grew jealous of him, and longed to do him some evil. So one day when the poet was walking on the seashore, two of the dwarfs named Fialar and Galar came up to him and begged him to visit their cave in the rocks. Now Kvasir never suspected wrong of any one, so he willingly followed the dwarfs into a dark cavern underground. Here the treacherous brothers slew him, and drained his blood into three jars in which they had already placed some honey. Thus of sweetness mingled with a poet's life-blood they brewed the Magic Mead, [19] which would give to any one who drank of it gentleness and wisdom and the gift of poesy.

When the dwarfs had mixed the mead, they took great care to hide it in a secret cave; and then, proud of their cruel cunning, they set off in search of further adventures. Soon they found the giant Gilling asleep on the seashore; and after pinching him awake, they asked him to row them a little way in his boat. The giant, who was both good-natured and stupid, took the dwarfs into his boat, and began to row vigorously. Then Galar suddenly steered the boat so that it struck on a sharp rock and was overturned. The poor giant, who could not swim, was immediately drowned; while the wicked little dwarfs climbed upon the keel of the boat and finally drifted ashore.

Not content with this cruel act, they went straightway to the giant's house and called to his wife to come quickly, for Gilling was drowning. The giantess at once hurried to her husband's aid; and as she came through the doorway, Fialar, who had climbed up above the lintel, suddenly dropped a millstone on her head, killing her instantly.

As the dwarfs were jumping up and down exulting over their success, the giant's son—whose name was Suttung—came along. When he saw his mother stretched dead upon the ground, and the little men skipping about in their wicked glee, he [20] guessed who was guilty of this shameful deed. So he seized Galar and Fialar, one in each hand; and, wading far out into the sea, he set them on a certain rock which was sure to be covered with water when the tide rose. As he turned to go away, the dwarfs screamed to him in terror and begged him to take them back to land. In their fright they promised to give him anything he might ask if only he would put them safe on shore.

Now Suttung had heard of the Magic Mead, and he longed very much to possess it; so he made the dwarfs promise to give him the three jars in exchange for their lives. Much as Galar and Fialar hated to do this, they had no choice but to agree to the giant's demand; so as soon as they were on land again, they delivered the precious mead into his hands. As Suttung could not be at home all day to guard his treasure, he hid the jars in a deep recess in the rocks, and bade his daughter Gunlod watch over them night and day. The mouth of the cavern was sealed up with an enormous stone so that no one could enter except by a passageway known only to Gunlod, and Suttung felt that his treasure was safe from both gods and men.

Odin disguised as a Traveller

Meanwhile the news of Kvasir's death had been brought to Odin by his ravens Hugin and Munin, and he determined to get possession of the wonderful mead that had been brewed from the poet's blood. [21] So he disguised himself as a traveller, pulled his gray hat well over his face and set out for the country where the Magic Mead was hidden. As he neared the giant's home, he saw a field in which nine sturdy thralls[10] were mowing hay. These men did not belong to Suttung, but were the servants of his brother Baugi. This suited Odin's purpose just as well, so he went quickly up to the thralls and said: "Your scythes seem very dull. How much faster you could work if they were sharper. Shall I whet them for you?" The men were surprised at this unexpected offer of help; but they accepted the stranger's assistance gladly. When they found how sharp he had made their scythes, they begged him to sell or give them the marvellous whetstone. To this Odin replied, "Whoever can catch it, may have it as a gift," and with these words he threw the stone among them. Then began a fierce battle among the thralls for the possession of the prize; and they cut at each other so fiercely with their scythes that by evening every one of them lay dead in the field.

[10] Thralls; servants.

While they were fighting thus savagely, Odin sought out Baugi's house and begged for supper and a night's lodging. The giant received him hospitably; and as they sat eating, word was brought to Baugi that his nine thralls were dead. For a time [22] Odin listened to his host's complaints of his evil luck and of how much wealth he would lose through his unmowed fields. Then he offered his services to Baugi, promising to do as much work as the nine thralls. The giant was very doubtful whether his visitor could make good this boast; but he accepted the offer quickly, and next morning Odin set to work in the fields.

Before many days had passed, all the hay on Baugi's land was carefully stored away in the barns, and Odin came to the giant to demand his wages. "What payment shall I make you?" asked Baugi, fearing that a great sum would be named as the price of such remarkable service. He was surprised, therefore, when Odin answered, "All I ask is a draught of the Magic Mead which your brother Suttung keeps hidden in a cavern."

"That is not an easy thing to get," replied the giant, "for though I would be glad to fetch you some of the mead, my brother has never let me enter the cave. However, I will ask him to bring you a single draught." So Baugi went in search of his brother, and told him of the wonderful service that Odin had rendered. Then he asked for one drink of the Magic Mead for his servant. At this Suttung flew into a great rage and cried:—

"Do you think I would give any of the mead to a stranger who can do the work of nine thralls? No [23] man could have such wonderful power. It is a god that you have been calling your servant, and the gods have been our enemies since the beginning of time."

Now Baugi feared and hated the gods as much as his brother; but he had given his word to Odin to help him get the Magic Mead, and he did not dare to break his promise. So when he returned to his one-time servant, and told of the ill success of his visit to Suttung, Odin answered: "Then we must try some other way. Take me to the cavern where the mead is hidden; but see that your brother knows nothing of our going."

Very unwillingly Baugi consented to show Odin the secret cave; and as they walked, he plotted how to get rid of his troublesome servant. It seemed to take the giant a very long time to find the cavern; but when they finally reached it, Odin drew an augur from his pocket, and began to bore a hole in the great stone that stood at the cave's mouth. As soon as he grew tired, he made Baugi take his turn at the augur; and, owing to the giant's great strength, a hole was soon bored through the rock. Then Odin quickly turned himself into a snake and crept into the opening while Baugi, seeing his servant no longer beside him, and realizing what the sudden transformation meant, made a stab at the snake with the augur, hoping to kill it. But Odin [24] had slid safely through the hole, and was already inside the cave.

Taking his rightful form, Odin now began to look eagerly about him, and when his eyes grew accustomed to the dimness of the cavern, he saw the daughter of Suttung seated in the furthest corner beside the three jars that contained the Magic Mead. He came softly to Gunlod's side, and spoke to her so gently that she was not frightened at the sudden appearance of a stranger; and when he smiled at her with a reassuring look, she asked, "Who are you, and why are you here?"

"I am a traveller, tired and thirsty after my long journey," answered Odin. "Will you not give me something to drink?"

Gunlod shook her head. "I have nothing here save the Magic Mead, and that I dare not give you," she said sadly. Then Odin begged for just a single draught, but the giant's daughter firmly refused to let him touch the jars.

At last, after much coaxing and soft words, Gunlod allowed her visitor to take one sip of the mead; but as soon as Odin got the jars in his hands, he drained each one dry before the astonished maiden had realized what had happened. Then he changed himself quickly into a snake, and glided out through the opening in the rock. It was now but a moment's work to assume an eagle's form, and start at once on [25] his journey back to Asgard. He knew well that there was no time to lose, for Baugi had already gone to his brother with the news of what had happened at the cave's mouth.

When Suttung heard Baugi's story and realized that his precious mead was being stolen by one of the gods, he hurried at once to the cavern. Just as he reached it, he saw an eagle rise heavily up from the earth, and he knew this was some god in disguise bearing away the Magic Mead to Asgard. So he quickly changed himself into an eagle, and started in pursuit of the one with slowly moving wings. Odin could not fly very fast, for the mead made him heavy; and he was much distressed to see that the giant was easily gaining on him. As they both neared the gates of Asgard, some of the gods were looking out, and they saw the two birds approaching. They wondered what the pursuit might mean; but it was not until the eagles neared the outer walls that the watchers realized that it was Odin fleeing from an enemy, and straining his weary wings to reach Asgard.

Then they laid a great pile of wood on the inner walls, and to this they applied a torch the moment that the first eagle had passed safely over. The flames shot up with a roar just as the pursuer had almost caught his prey. The fire scorched Baugi's great wings, and the smoke blinded his eyes so that [26] he fluttered helplessly down to the earth. Meanwhile the Magic Mead was safe in Asgard, and there it was put in care of Bragi, the white-haired son of Odin. Thus the mead remained forever with the gods; but sometimes a favoured mortal is given, at his birth, a drop of this divine drink; and then, in later years, men find that a poet has been born among them.

# The Viking's Code by Florence Holbrook

Over the foaming sea Frithiof sailed, seeking strange lands and adventures. Like a falcon in search of its prey flew the good boat, Ellide, over the waves.

To the champions on board Frithiof gave this law of the viking:—
Make no tent on thy ship, never sleep in a house, for a foe
within doors you may view;
On his shield sleeps the viking; his sword in his hand, and
his tent is the heavenly blue.
When the storm rageth fierce, hoist the sail to the top—
O how merry the storm-king appears;
Let her drive! let her drive! better founder than strike,
for who strikes is a slave to his fears.
If a merchant sail by, you must shelter his ship, but the
weak will not tribute withhold;
You are king of the waves, he a slave to his gains; and
your steel is as good as his gold.
Let your goods be divided by lot or by dice, how it falls
you may never complain;
But the sea-king himself takes no part in the lots—he
considers the honour his gain.
If a viking-ship come, there is grappling and strife, and
the fight 'neath the shields will rejoice;
If you yield but a pace you are parted from us; 'tis the
law, you may act by your choice.
If you win, be content: he who, praying for peace, yields
his sword, is no longer a foe!
Prayer's a Valhalla-child, hear the suppliant voice; he's
a coward who answereth no.
Wounds are viking's reward, and the pride of the man
on whose breast or whose forehead they stand;
Let them bleed on unbound till the close of the day, if you
wish to be one of our band.

# The Pre-Columbian Discovery of America by the Northmen by Benjamin Franklin DeCosta

Before the plains of Europe, or even the peaks of Choumalarie, rose above the primeval seas, the Continent of America emerged from the watery waste that encircled the whole globe, and became the scene of animate life. The so-called New World is in reality the Old, and bears abundant proofs of hoary age. But at what period it became the abode of man we are unable even to conjecture. Down to the close of the tenth century of the Christian era it had no written history. Traces of a rude civilization that suggest a high antiquity are by no means wanting. Monuments and mounds remain that point to periods the contemplation of which would cause Chronos himself to grow giddy; yet among all these great and often impressive memorials there is no monument, inscription, or sculptured frieze, that solves the mystery of their origin. Tradition itself is dumb, and the theme chiefly kindles when brought within the realm of imagination. We can only infer that age after age nations and tribes continued to rise to greatness and then fall into decline, and that barbarism and a rude culture held alternate sway.

Nevertheless, men have enjoyed no small degree of satisfaction in conjuring up theories to explain the origin of the early races on the Western Continent. What a charm lingers around the supposed trans-Atlantic voyages of the hardy Phenician, the luxurious sailors of Tyre, and, later, of the bold Basque. What stories might the lost picture-records of Mexico and the chronicles of Dieppe tell. Now we are presented with the splendid view of great fleets, the remnant of some conquered race, bearing across the ocean to re-create in new and unknown lands the cities and monuments they were forever leaving behind;[1] and now it is simply the story of some storm-tossed mariner who blindly drives across to the western strand, and lays the foundation of empire. Again it is the devotee of mammon, in search of gainful traffic or golden fleece. How romantic is the picture of his little solitary bark setting out in the days of Roman greatness, or in the splendid age of Charlemagne, sailing trustingly away between the Pillars of Hercules, and tossing towards the Isles of the Blessed and the Fountains of Eternal Youth. In time the Ultima Thule of the known world is passed, and favoring gales bear the merchant-sailor to new and wondrous lands. We see him coasting the unknown shores passing from cape to cape, and from bay to inlet, gazing upon the marvels of the New World, trafficking with the bronzed Indian, bartering curious wares for barbaric gold; and then shaping his course again for the markets of the distant East to pour strange tales into incredulous ears. Still this may not be all fancy.

In early times the Atlantic ocean, like all things without known bounds, was viewed by man with mixed feelings of fear and awe. It was called the Sea of Darkness. Yet, nevertheless, there were those who professed to have some knowledge of its extent, and of what lay beyond. The earliest reference to this sea is that by Theopompus, in the fourth century before the Christian era, given in a fragment of Ælian,[2] where a vast island is described, lying far in the west, and peopled by strange races. To this we may add the reference of Plato[3] to the island called Atlantis, which lay west of the Pillars of Hercules, and which was estimated to be larger than Asia and Africa combined. Aristotle[4] also thought that many other lands existed beyond the Atlantic. Plato supposed that the Atlantis was sunk by an earthquake, and Crantor says that he found the same account related by the Priests of Sais three hundred years after the time of Solon, from whom the grandfather of Critias had his information. Plato says, that after the Atlantis disappeared navigation was rendered too difficult to be attempted by the slime which resulted from the sinking of the land. It is probable that he had in mind the immense fields of drifting sea-weed found in that locality, and which Humboldt estimates to cover a portion of the Atlantic ocean six times as large as all Germany.

It is thought that Homer[5] obtained the idea of his Elysium in the Western ocean from the voyages of the Phenicians, who, as is well known, sailed regularly to the British Islands. They are also supposed by some to have pushed their discoveries as far as the Western Continent. Cadiz, situated on the shore of Andalusia, was established by the Tyrians twelve centuries before the year of Christ; and when Cadiz, the ancient Gadir, was full five hundred years old, a Greek trader, Colæus, there bought rare merchandise, a long and severe gale having driven his ships beyond the Pillars of Hercules.

In the ninth century before the Christian Era, the Phenicians had established colonies on the western coast of Africa; and three hundred years later, according to Herodotus, Pharaoh Necho, son of Psammiticus, sent an expedition, manned by Phenician sailors, around the entire coast of Africa. Vivien de St. Martin fixes the date of this expedition at 570 before Christ. St. Martin, in his account of the voyage, improves slightly upon the views of Carl Müller, and is followed by Bougainville.[6] This voyage, performed by Hanno under the direction of Pharaoh, was inscribed in the Punic language in a Carthagenian temple, being afterwards translated into Greek, and was thus preserved.

That the Canary Islands were discovered and colonized by the Phenicians, there need be no doubt. Tradition had always located islands in that vicinity. Strabo speaks of the Islands of the Blessed, as lying not far from Mauritania, opposite Gadir or Cadiz. And he distinctly says, "That those who pointed out these things were the Phenicians, who, before the time of Homer, had possession of the best part of Africa and Spain."[7] And when we remember that the Phenicians sought to monopolize trade, and hold the knowledge of their commercial resorts a secret, it is not surprising that we should hear nothing more of the Fortunate Isles until about eighty-two years before Christ, when the Roman Sertorius met some Lusitanian sailors on the coast of Spain who had just returned from the Fortunate Isles. They are described as two delightful islands, separated by a narrow strait, distant from Africa five hundred leagues. Twenty years after the death of Sertorius, Statius Sebosus drew up a chart of a group of five islands, each mentioned by name, and which Pliny calls the Hesperides, including the Fortunate Isles. This mention of the Canaries was sixty-three years before Christ.

When King Juba II returned to Mauritania, he sent an expedition to the Fortunate Isles. A fragment of the narratives of this expedition still survives in the works of Pliny. They are described as lying southwest, six hundred and twenty-five miles from Purpurariæ. To reach them from this place, they first sailed two hundred and fifty miles westward and then three hundred and seventy-five miles eastward. Pliny says: "The first is called Ombrios, and contains no traces of buildings. There is in it a pool in the midst of mountains, and trees like ferules, from which water may be pressed, which is bitter from the black kinds, but from the light kinds pleasant to drink. The second is called Junonia, and contains a small temple built entirely of stone. Near it is another smaller island having the same name. Then comes Capraria, which is full of large lizards. Within sight of these is Nivaria, so called from the snow and fogs with which it is always covered. Not far from Nivaria is Canaria, so called on account of the great number of large dogs therein, two of which were brought to King Juba. There were traces of buildings in these islands. All the islands abound in apples, and in birds of every kind, and in palms covered with dates, and in the pine nut. There is also plenty of fish. The papyrus grows there, and the silurus fish is found in the rivers."[8] The author of Prince Henry the Navigator,[9] says that in Ombrios, we recognize the Pluvialia of Sebosus. Convallis of Sebosus, in Pliny, becomes Nivaria, the Peak of Teneriffe, which lifts itself up to the majestic height of nine thousand feet, its snow-capped pinnacle seeming to pierce the sky. Planaria is displaced by Canaria, which term first applied to the great central island, now gives the name to the whole group. Ombrios or Pluvialia, evidently means the island of Palma, which had "a pool in the midst of mountains," now represented by the crater of an extinct volcano. This the sailors of King Juba evidently saw. Major says: "The distance of this island [Palma] from Fuerteventura, agrees with that of the two hundred and fifty miles indicated by Juba's navigators as existing between Ombrios and the Purpurariæ. It has already been seen that the latter agree with Lancerote and Fuerteventura, in respect of their distance from the continent and from each other, as described by Plutarch. That the Purpurariæ are not, as M. Bory de St. Vincent supposed, the Madeira group, is not only shown by the want of inhabitants in the latter, but by the orchil, which supplies the purple dye, being derived from and sought for especially from the Canaries, and not from the Madeira group, although it is to be found there. Junonia," he continues, "the nearest to Ombrios, will be Gomera. It may be presumed that the temple found therein, was, like the island, dedicated to Juno. Capraria, which implies the island of goats, agrees correctly with the island of Ferro, ... for these animals were found there in large numbers when the island was invaded by Jean de Bethencourt, in 1402. But a yet more striking proof of the identity of this island with Capraria, is the account of the great number of lizards found therein. Bethencourt's chaplains, describing their visit to the islands, in 1402, state: 'There are lizards in it as big as cats, but they are harmless, although very hideous to look at.'"[10]

We see, then, that the navigators of Juba visited the Canaries[11] at an early period, as Strabo testifies was the case with the Phenicians, who doubtless built the temple in the island of Junonia. And, for aught we know, early navigators may have passed over to the Western continent and laid the foundation of those strange nations whose monuments still remain. Both Phenician and Tyrian voyages to the Western Continent, have been warmly advocated; while Lord Kingsborough published his magnificent volumes on the Mexican Antiquities, to show that the Jews settled this continent at an early day.[12] And if it is true that all the tribes of the earth sprang from one central Asiatic family, it is more than likely that the original inhabitants of the American continent crossed the Atlantic, instead of piercing the frozen regions of the north, and coming in by the way of Behring Straits. From the Canaries to the coast of Florida, it is a short voyage, and the bold sailors of the Mediterranean, after touching at the Canaries, need only spread their sails before the steady-breathing monsoon, to find themselves wafted safely to the western shore.

There was even a tradition that America was visited by St. Columba,[13] and also by the Apostle St. Thomas,[14] who penetrated even as far as Peru. This opinion is founded on the resemblance existing between certain rites and doctrines which seem to have been held in common by Christians and the early inhabitants of Mexico. The first Spanish missionaries were surprised to find the Mexicans bowing in adoration before the figure of the cross, and inferred that these people were of a Christian origin. Yet the inference has no special value, when we remember that Christianity is far less ancient than the symbol of the cross, which also existed among the Egyptians and other ancient people.

Claims have also been made for the Irish. Broughton brings forward a passage in which St. Patrick is represented as sending missionaries to the Isles of America.[15] Another claim has been urged of a more respectable character, which is supported by striking, though not conclusive allusions in the chronicles of the North, in which a distant land is spoken of as "Ireland the Great." The Irish, in the early times, might easily have passed over to the Western continent, for which voyage they undoubtedly had the facilities. And Professor Rafn, after alluding to the well known fact that the Northmen were preceded in Iceland by the Irish, says, that it is by no means improbable that the Irish should also have anticipated them in America. The Irish were a sea-faring people, and have been assigned a Phenician origin by Moore and others who have examined the subject.[16] If this is so, the tradition would appear to be some what strengthened. Even as early as the year 296, the Irish are said to have invaded Denmark with a large fleet. In 396, Niall made a descent upon the coast of Lancashire with a considerable navy, where he was met by the Roman, Stilicho, whose achievements were celebrated by Claudian in the days of the Roman occupation of England. At that period the Irish were in most respects in advance of the Northmen, not yet having fallen into decline, and quite as likely as any people then existing to brave the dangers of an ocean voyage.[17] The Icelandic documents, possibly referring to the Irish, will be given in their proper place, and in the meanwhile it need only to be added that the quotation given by Beamish from such an authority as the Turkish Spy will hardly tend to strengthen their claims, especially where its author, John Paul Marana, says that in Mexico "the British language is so prevalent," that "the very towns, bridges, beasts, birds, rivers, hills, etc., are called by the British or Welch[18] names."[19] In truth, as the wish is so often father to the thought, it would be an easy task to find resemblance in the languages of the aborigines to almost any language that is spoken in our day.

But notwithstanding the probabilities of the case, we have no solid reason for accepting any of these alleged voyages as facts. Much labor has been given to the subject, yet the early history of the American continent is still veiled in mystery, and not until near the close of the tenth century of the present era can we point to a genuine trans-Atlantic voyage.

The first voyage to America, of which we have any account, was performed by Northmen. But who were the Northmen?

The Northmen were the descendants of a race that in early times migrated from Asia and traveled towards the north, finally settling in what is now the kingdom of Denmark. From thence they overran Norway and Sweden, and afterwards colonized Iceland and Greenland. Their language was the old Danish (Dönsk túnga) once spoken all over the north,[20] but which is now preserved in Iceland alone, being called the Icelandic or old North,[21] upon which is founded the modern Swedish, Danish and Norse or Norwegian.

After the Northmen had pushed on from Denmark to Norway, the condition of public affairs gradually became such that a large portion of the better classes found their life intolerable. In the reign of Harold Harfagr (the Fair-haired), an attempt was made by the king to deprive the petty jarls of their ancient udal or feudal rights, and to usurp all authority for the crown. To this the proud jarls would not submit; and, feeling themselves degraded in the eyes of their retainers, they resolved to leave those lands and homes which they could now hardly call their own. Whither, then, should they go?

In the cold north sea, a little below the arctic circle, lay a great island. As early as the year 860, it had been made known to the Northmen by a Dane of Swedish descent named Gardar, who called it Gardar's island, and four years later by the pirate Nadodd, who sailed thither in 864 and called it Snowland. Presenting in the main the form of an irregular elipse, this island occupies an area of about one hundred and thirty-seven square miles, affording the dull diversity of valleys without verdure and mountains without trees.[22] Desolation has there fixed its abode. It broods among the dells, and looks down upon the gloomy fiords. The country is threaded with streams and dotted with tarns, yet the geologist finds but little evidence in the structure of the earth to point to the action of water. On the other hand, every rock and hillside is covered with signs that prove their igneous origin, and indicate that the entire island, at some distant period, has already seethed and bubbled in the fervent heat, in anticipation of the long promised Palingenesia. Even now the ground trembles in the throes of the earthquake, the Geyser spouts scalding water, and the plain belches mud; while the great jokull, clad in white robes of eternal snow—true priest of Ormuzd—brandishes aloft its volcanic torch, and threatens to be the incendiary of the sky.

The greater portion of the land forms the homestead of the reindeer and the fox, who share their domain with the occasional white bear that may float over from Greenland on some berg. Only two quadrupeds, the fox and the moose, are indigenous. Life is here purchased with a struggle. Indeed the neighboring ocean is more hospitable than the dry land, for of the thirty-four species of mammalia twenty-four find their food in the roaring main. The same is true of the feathered tribes, fifty-four out of ninety being water fowl. Here and there may be seen patches of meadow and a few sheep pastures and tracts of arable land warmed into fruitfulness by the brief summer's sun; yet, on the whole, so poor is the soil that man, like the lower orders, must eke out a scanty subsistence by resorting to the sea.

It was towards this land, which the settlers called Iceland, that the proud Norwegian jarl turned his eyes, and there he resolved to found a home.

The first settler was Ingolf. He approached the coast in the year 875, threw overboard his seat-posts,[23] and waited to see them touch the land. But in this he was disappointed, and those sacred columns, carved with the images of the gods, drifted away from sight. He nevertheless landed on a pleasant promontory at the southeastern extremity of the island, and built his habitation on the spot which is called Ingolfshofdi to this day. Three years after, his servants found the seat-posts in the southwestern part of the island, and hither, in obedience to what was held to be the expressed wish of the gods, he removed his household, laying the foundation of Reikiavik, the capital of this ice-bound isle. He was rapidly followed by others, and in a short time no inconsiderable population was gathered here.

But the first settlers did not find this barren country entirely destitute of human beings. Ari Frode,[24] than whom there is no higher authority, says: "Then were here Christian people, whom the Northmen called papas, but they afterwards went away, because they would not be here among heathens; and left behind them Irish books, and bells, and croziers, from which it could be seen that they were Irishmen." He repeats substantially the same thing in the Landanama Book, the authority of which, no one acquainted with the subject, will question, adding that books and other relics were found in the island of Papey and Papyli, and that the circumstance is also mentioned in English books. The English writings referred to are those of the Venerable Bede. This is also stated in an edition of King Olaf Tryggvesson's Saga, made near the end of the fourteenth century.[25]

The monks or Culdees, who had come hither from Ireland and the Isles of Iona, to be alone with God, all took their departure on the arrival of the heathen followers of Odin and Thor, and the Northmen were thus left in undisputed possession of the soil. In about twenty years the island became quite thickly settled, though the tide of immigration continued to flow in strongly for fifty years, so that at the beginning of the tenth century Iceland possessed a population variously estimated from sixty to seventy thousand souls. But few undertook the voyage who were not able to buy their own vessels, in which they carried over their own cattle, and thralls, and household goods. So great was the number of people who left Norway at the outset that King Harold tried to prevent emigration by royal authority, though, as might have been predicted, his efforts were altogether in vain. Here, therefore, was formed a large community, taking the shape of an aristocratic republic, which framed its own laws, and for a long time maintained a genuine independence, in opposition to all the assumptions and threats of the Norwegian king.

But as time passed on, the people of Iceland felt a new impulse for colonization in strange lands, and the tide of emigration began to tend towards Greenland in the west. This was chiefly inaugurated by a man named Eric the Red, born in Norway in the year 935. On account of manslaughter, he was obliged to flee from Jardar and take up his abode in Iceland. The date of removal to Iceland is not given, though it is said that at the time the island was very generally inhabited. Here, however, he could not live in peace, and early in the year 982, he was again outlawed for manslaughter by the public Thnig, and condemned to banishment. He accordingly fitted out a ship, and announced his determination to go in search of the land lying in the ocean at the west, which, it was said, Gunnbiorn,[26] Ulf Krage's son, saw, when, in the year 876, he was driven out to sea by a storm. Eric sailed westward and found land, where he remained and explored the country for three years. At the end of this period he returned to Iceland, giving the newly discovered land the name of Greenland,[27] in order, as he said, to attract settlers, who would be favorably impressed by so pleasing a name.

The summer after his return to Iceland, he sailed once more for Greenland, taking with him a fleet of thirty-five ships, only fourteen of which reached their destination, the rest being either driven back or lost. This event took place, as the Saga says, fifteen winters[28] before the introduction of Christianity into Iceland, which we know was accomplished in the year A. D. 1000. The date of Eric's second voyage must therefore be set down at 985.[29]

But, before proceeding to the next step in Icelandic adventure, it will be necessary to give a brief sketch of the progress of the Greenland colony, together with a relation of the circumstances which led to its final extinction.

There is but little continuity in the history of the Icelandic occupation of Greenland. We have already seen that the second voyage of Eric the Red took place in the year 985. Colonists appear to have followed him in considerable numbers, and the best portions of the land were soon appropriated by the principal men, who gave the chief bays and capes names that indicated the occupants, following the example of Eric, who dwelt in Brattahlid, in Ericsfiord.

In the year 999, Leif, son of Eric, sailed out to Norway and passed the winter at the court of King Olaf Tryggvesson, where he accepted the Christian faith, which was then being zealously propagated by the king. He was accordingly baptized, and when the spring returned the king requested him to undertake the introduction of Christianity in Greenland, urging the consideration that no man was better qualified for the task. Accordingly he set sail from Norway, with a priest and several members of the religious order, arriving at Brattahlid, in Greenland, without any accident.[30] His pagan father was incensed by the bringing in of the Christian priest, which act he regarded as pregnant with evil; yet, after some persuasion on the part of Leif, he renounced heathenism and nominally accepted Christianity, being baptized by the priest. His wife Thorhild made less opposition, and appears to have received the new faith with much willingness. One of her first acts was to build a church, which was known far and wide as Thorhild's church.[31] These examples appear to have been very generally followed, and Christianity was adopted in both Iceland and Greenland at about the same period,[32] though its acceptance did not immediately produce any very radical change in the spiritual life of the people. In course of time a number of churches were built, the ruins of which remain down to our own day.

In the year 1003, the Greenlanders became tributary to Norway. The principal settlement was formed on the western coast, and what was known as the eastern district, did not extend farther than the southern extremity towards Cape Farewell. For a long time it was supposed that the east district was located on the eastern coast of Greenland; but the researches of Captain Graah, whose expedition went out under the auspices of the Danish government, proved very conclusively that no settlement ever existed on the eastern shore, which for centuries has remained blocked up by vast accumulations of ice that floated down from the arctic seas. In early times, as we are informed by the Sagas, the eastern coast was more accessible, yet the western shores were so superior in their attractions that the colonist fixed his habitation there. The site of the eastern settlement is that included in the modern district of Julian's Hope, now occupied by a Danish colony. The western settlement is represented by the habitation of Frederikshab, Godthaab, Sukkertoppen and Holsteinborg.

In process of time the Christians in Greenland multiplied to such an extent, both by conversions and by the immigration from Iceland, that it was found necessary, in the beginning of the twelfth century to take some measures for the better government of the church, especially as they could not hope much for regular visits from the bishops of Iceland. They therefore resolved to make an effort to secure a bishop of their own. Eric Gnupson, of Iceland, was selected for the office, and proceeded to Greenland about the year 1112, without being regularly consecrated. He returned to Iceland in

1120, and afterwards went to Denmark, where he was consecrated in Lund, by Archbishop Adzer. Yet he probably never returned to his duties in Greenland, but soon after resigned that bishopric and accepted another,[33] thus leaving Greenland without a spiritual director.

In the year 1123, Sokke, one of the principal men of Greenland, assembled the people and represented to them that both the welfare of the Christian faith and their own honor demanded that they should follow the example of other nations and maintain a bishop. To this view they gave their unanimous approval; and Einar, son of Sokke, was appointed a delegate to the court of King Sigurd, of Norway. He carried a present of ivory and fur, and a petition for the appointment of a bishop. His mission was successful, and in the year 1126 Arnald, the successor of Eric,[34] came into Greenland, and set up the Episcopal seat at Gardar.[35] Torfæus and Baron Holberg,[36] give a list of seventeen bishops who ruled in Greenland, ending with Andrew. The latter was consecrated and went thither in 1408, being never heard of afterwards.

The history of Old Greenland is found in the Ecclesiastical Annals, and consists of a mere skeleton of facts. As in Iceland and Norway there was no end of broils and bloodshed. A very considerable trade was evidently carried on between that country and Norway, which is the case at the present time with Denmark. As the land afforded no materials for ships, they depended in a great measure upon others for communication with the mother countries, which finally proved disastrous.

Their villages and farms were numerous. Together they probably numbered several hundred, the ruins now left being both abundant and extensive. Near Igaliko, which is supposed to be the same as the ancient Einarsfiord, are the ruins of a church, probably the cathedral of Gardar. It is called the Kakortok church. It was of simple but massive architecture, and the material was taken from the neighboring cliffs. The stone is rough hewn, and but few signs of mortar are visible. It is fifty-one feet long and twenty-five wide. The north and south walls are over four feet thick, while the end walls are still more massive.

Nor are other monuments wanting. At Igalikko, nine miles from Julian's Hope, a Greenlander being one day employed in obtaining stones to repair his house, found among a pile of fragments a smooth stone that bore, what seemed to him, written characters. He mentioned the circumstance to Mr. Mathieson, the colonial director at Julian's Hope, who inferred that it must be a runic stone. He was so fortunate as to find it afterwards, and he accordingly sent it to Copenhagen, where it arrived in the year 1830. The runes, which were perfectly distinct, showed that it was a tombstone. The inscription was translated as follows:

"Vigdis Mars Daughter Rests Here.
May God Gladden Her Soul."

Another found in 1831, by the Rev. Mr. De Fries, principal of the Moravian Mission, bore the following inscription in the runic letter:

"Here Rests Hroar Kolgrimsson."

This stone, now in the museum at Copenhagen, was found built into the wall over the entrance of a Greenland house, having been taken for that purpose from a heap of ruins, about two miles north of Friederichsthal. This stone is more than three feet long, being eighteen inches wide in the narrowest part, and about five inches thick. It bears every sign of a high antiquity.

But one of the most interesting remains which prove the Icelandic occupation of Greenland is the runic stone found by Parry, in 1824, in the island of Kingiktorsoak, lying in 72° 55′ N. and 56° 51′ W. It contained a somewhat lengthy inscription, and copies of it were sent to three of the first scholars of the age, Finn Magnusson, Professor Rask, and Dr. Bryniulfson, who, without consultation, at once arrived at the same conclusion and united in giving the following translation:

*"Erling Sighvatson and Biorn Thordarson and Eindrid Oddson, on Saturday before Ascension week, raised these marks and cleared ground. 1135."*[37]

The Icelandic colonists in Greenland do not appear to have been confined to a small portion of territory. We find considerable relating to this subject in the chronicle attributed to Ivar Bert,[38] the steward of one of the bishops of Greenland; yet, though used extensively by Torfæus, modern researches in this country prove that it is in some respects faulty. In this chronicle, as in the Sagas, the colonists are spoken of as possessing horses, sheep and oxen; and their churches and religious houses appear to have been well supported.

Much was done, it appears, in the way of exploring the extreme northern portions of the country known as Nordrsetur. In the year 1266, a voyage was made under the auspices of some of the priests, and the adventurers penetrated north of Lancaster sound, reaching about the same latitude that was attained by Parry in 1827. This expedition was of sufficient importance to justify some notice of it here. The account is found in Antiquitates Americanæ (p. 269), and it sets out with the statement that the narrative of the expedition was sent by Haldor, a priest, to Arnald, the chaplain of King Magnus in Norway. They sailed out of Kroksfiardarheidi in an open boat, and met with southerly winds and thick weather, which forced them to let the boat drive before the wind. When the weather cleared, they saw a number of islands, together with whales and seals and bears. They made their way into the most distant portion of the sea, and saw glaciers south of them as far as the eye could reach. They also saw indications of the natives, who were called Skrællings, but did not land, on account of the number of the bears. They therefore put about, and laid their course southward for nearly three days, finding more islands, with traces of the natives. They saw a mountain which they call Snæfell, and on St. James day, July 25, they had a severe weather, being obliged to row much and very hard. It froze during the night in that region, but the sun was above the horizon both day and night. When the sun was on the southern meridian, and a man lay down crosswise in a six-oared boat, the shadow of the gunwale[Pg xxxiii] towards the sun would reach as far as his feet, which, of course, indicates that the sun was very low. Afterwards they all returned in safety to Gardar.[39] Rafn fixes the position of the point attained by the expedition in the parallel of 75° 46′. Such an achievement at that day indicates a degree of boldness quite surprising.

Of the reality and importance of the Greenland colony there exists no doubt, notwithstanding the records are so meagre and fragmentary.[40] It maintained its connection with the mother countries for a period of no less than four hundred years; yet it finally disappeared and was almost forgotten.

The causes which led to the suspension of communication were doubtless various, though it is difficult to account for the utter extinction of the colony, which does not appear ever to have been in much danger from the Skrællings. On one occasion, in 1349 or later, the natives attacked the western settlement, it is said, and killed eighteen Greenlanders of Icelandic lineage, carrying away two boys captives.

We hear from the eastern colony as late as the middle of the fifteenth century. Trade was carried on with Denmark until nearly the end of the fourteenth century, although the voyages were not regular. The last bishop, Andreas, was sent out in 1406, and Professor Finn Magnussen has established the fact that he officiated in the cathedral at Gardar in 1409.[41]

From this time the trade between Norway and Greenland appears to have been given up, though Wormius told Peyrere of his having read in a Danish manuscript that down to the year 1484 there was a company of more than forty sailors at Bergen, in Norway, who still traded with Greenland.[42] But as the revenue at that time belonged to Queen Margaret of Denmark, no one could go to Greenland without the royal permission. One company of sailors who were driven upon the Greenland coast, came near suffering the penalty of the law on their return. Crantz[43] says, that "about the year 1530, Bishop Amund of Skalholt in Iceland is said to have been driven by a storm, on his return from Norway, so near the coast of Greenland by Heriulfness, that he could see the people driving in their cattle. But he did not land, because just then a good wind arose, which carried the ship the same night to Iceland. The Icelander, Biærnvon Skardfa, who relates this, also says further, that a Hamburgh mariner, Jon Greenlander by name, was driven three times on the Greenland island, where he saw such fisher's huts for drying fish as they have in Iceland, but saw no men; further, that pieces of shattered boats, nay, in the year 1625, an entire boat, fastened together with sinews and wooden pegs, and pitched with seal blubber, have been driven ashore at Iceland from time to time; and since then they found once an oar with a sentence written in Runic letters: 'Oft var ek dasa, dur elk drothik,' that is, 'Oft was I tired when I drew thee.'"[44]

But, whatever may be the value of the preceding extract, it is clear that Greenland was never wholly forgotten. The first person who proposed to reopen communication was Eric Walkendorf, Archbishop of Drontheim, who familiarized himself with the subject, and made every preparation necessary in order to reestablish the colony; but, having fallen under the displeasure of King Christian II, he left the country and went to Rome, where he died in the year 1521. Thus his plans came to nothing.[45] Christian III abrogated the decree of Queen Margaret, prohibiting trade with Greenland without the royal permission, and encouraged voyages by fitting out a vessel to search for Greenland, which, however, was not found. In 1578, Frederic II sent out Magnus Henningsen. He came in sight of the land, but does not appear to have had the courage to proceed further. Crantz, in his work on Greenland, gives an account of a number of voyages undertaken to the coast, but says that "at last Greenland was so buried in oblivion that one hardly would believe that such a land as Greenland was inhabited by Christian Norwegians."[46]

It remained, therefore, for Hans Egede,[47] in 1721, to reopen communication, and demonstrate the reality of the previous occupation. Columbus himself did not meet with greater trials and mortification than did this good man for the space of eleven years, during which period he labored to persuade the authorities to undertake the rediscovery. But his faith and zeal finally overcame all hostility and ridicule, and on the second day of May, 1721, he went on board the Hope, with his wife and four young children, and landed at Ball's river in Greenland on the third of the following month. Here he spent the best portion of his life in teaching the natives Christianity, which had been first introduced seven centuries before, and in making those explorations the results of which filled the mind of Europe with surprise, and afforded a confirmation of the truthfulness of the Icelandic Sagas.

Let us now return to the consideration of the Icelandic voyages to the American Continent, though not without first seeking a better acquaintance with the men by whom they were performed.

We have already seen that the Northmen were a people of no inferior attainments. Indeed, they constituted the most enterprising portion of the race, and, on general principles, we should therefore view them as fitted even above all the men of their time for the important work of exploration beyond the seas. They had made themselves known in every part of the civilized world[48] by their daring as soldiers and navigators. Straying away into the distant east from whence they originally came, we see them laying the foundation of the Russian empire, swinging their battle-axes in the streets of Constantinople, carving their mystic runes upon the Lions of the Areopagus, and filling the heart of even the great Charlemagne with dismay. Says Dasent, when summing up their achievements: "In Byzantium they are the leaders of the Greek emperor's body guard, and the main support of his[Pg xxxvii] tottering throne. From France, led by Rollo, they tear away her fairest province and found a long line of kings. In Saxon England they are the bosom friends of such kings as Athelstane, and the sworn foes of Ethelred the Unready. In Danish England they are the foremost among the thanes of Canute, Swein and Hardicanute, and keep down the native population with an iron heel. In Norman England," he continues, "the most serious opposition the conqueror meets with is from the colonists of his own race settled in Northumbria. He wastes their lands with fire and sword, and drives them across the border, where we still find their energy, their perseverance, and their speech existing in the lowland Scotch. In Norway they dive into the river with King Olaf Tryggvesson, the best and strongest champion of his age, and hold him down beneath the waves so long that the bystanders wonder whether either king or Icelander will ever reappear on the surface.[49] Some follow Saint Olaf in his crusades against the old [pagan] faith.[50] Some are his obstinate foes, and assist at his martyrdom. Many follow Harold the Stern to England when he goes to get his 'seven feet' of English earth, and almost to a man they get their portion of the same soil, while their names grow bright in song and story." And finally, "From Iceland as a base, they push on to Greenland and colonize it: nay, they discover America in those half-decked barks."[51]

The Northmen were excellent navigators. They were, moreover, it has been claimed, the first to learn the art of sailing on the wind. They had good sea-going vessels, some of which were of large size. We have an account in the Saga of Olaf Tryggvesson of one that in some respects was remarkable.

It is said that "the winter after King Olaf Tryggvesson came from Halogeland. He had a great ship built at Ledehammer,[52] which was larger than any ship in the country, and of which the beam-knees are still to be seen. The length of the keel that rested upon the grass was seventy-four ells. Thorberg Skafting was the man's name who was the master builder of the ship, but there were many others besides; some to fell the wood, some to shape it, some to make nails, some to carry timber, and all that was used was the best. The ship was both long and broad and high sided, and strongly timbered.... The ship was a dragon, built after the one that the king had captured in Halogaland, but it was far longer and more carefully put together in all her parts. The Long Serpent [her name] had thirty-four benches for rowers. The head and arched tail were both gilt, and the bulwarks were as high as in sea-going ships. This ship was the best and most costly ever built in Norway."[53]

Laing computes the tonnage of this ship at about nine hundred and forty-two tons, thus giving a length of about one hundred feet, which is nearly the size of a forty-two gun ship. By steam tonnage it would give a capacity of a little less than three hundred tons, and one hundred and twenty horse power. We apprehend, however, that the estimate is sufficiently large; yet we are not concerned to show any great capacity for the Icelandic ships. All the vessels employed in the early times on the American coasts were small. Cabot sailed in Baffins Bay with a vessel of thirty tons; and the Anna Pink, the craft that accompanied Lord Anson in his expedition around the world, was only sixteen tons.[54] The vessels possessed by the Northmen were everyway adapted for an ocean voyage.

In nautical knowledge, also, they were not behind the age. The importance of cultivating the study of navigation was fully understood. The Raudulf of Oesterdal, in Norway, taught his son to calculate the course of the sun and moon, and how to measure time by the stars. In 1520 Olaus Magnus complained that the knowledge of the people in this respect had been diminished. In that noble work called Speculum Regale the Icelander is taught to make an especial study of commerce and navigation, of the divisions of time and the movements of the heavenly bodies, together with arithmetic, the rigging of vessels and morals.[55] Without a high degree of knowledge they could never have achieved their eastern voyages.

We find that the Northmen were well acquainted with other parts of the world, and that they possessed all the means of reaching the continent in the west. We come, therefore, to the question: Did the Northmen actually discover and explore the coast of the country now known as America?

No one can say that the idea wears any appearance of improbability; for there is certainly nothing wonderful in the exploit. And after conceding the fact that the colonies of the Northmen existed in Greenland for at least three hundred years we must prepare ourselves for something of this kind. Indeed it is well nigh, if not altogether unreasonable, to suppose that a sea-faring people like the Northmen could live for three centuries within a short voyage of this vast continent, and never become aware of its existence. A supposition like this implies a rare credulity, and whoever is capable of believing it must be capable of believing almost anything.

But on this point we are not left to conjecture. The whole decision, in the absence of monuments like those of Greenland, turns upon a question of fact. The point is this: Do the manuscripts which describe these voyages belong to the pre-Columbian age? If so, then the Northmen are entitled to the credit of the prior discovery of America. That these manuscripts belong to the pre-Columbian age, is as capable of demonstration as the fact that the writings of Homer existed prior to the age of Christ. Before intelligent persons deny either of these points they must first succeed in blotting out numberless pages of well known history. The manuscript in which we have versions of all the Sagas relating to America is found in the celebrated Codex Flatöiensis, a work that was finished in the year 1387, or 1395 at the latest. This collection, made with great care and executed in the highest style of art, is now preserved in its integrity[56] in the archives of Copenhagen. These manuscripts were for a time supposed to be lost, but were ultimately found safely lodged in their repository in the monastery library of the island of Flatö, from whence they were transferred to Copenhagen with a large quantity of other literary material collected from various localities. If these Sagas which refer to America were interpolations, it would have early become apparent, as abundant means exist for detecting frauds; yet those who have examined the whole question do not find any evidence that invalidates their historical statements. In the absence, therefore, of respectable testimony to the contrary, we accept it as a fact that the Sagas relating to America are the productions of the men who gave them in their present form nearly, if not quite, an entire century before the age of Columbus.

It might also be argued, if it were at all necessary, that, if these Sagas were post-Columbian compositions drawn up by Icelanders who were jealous of the fame of the Geneose navigator, we should certainly be able to point out something either in their structure, bearing, or style by which it would be indicated. Yet such is not the case. These writings reveal no anxiety to show the connection of the Northmen with the great land lying at the west. The authors do not see anything at all remarkable or meritorious in the explorations, which were conducted simply for the purpose of gain. Those marks which would certainly have been impressed by a more modern writer forging a historical composition designed to show an occupation of the country before the time of Columbus, are wholly wanting. There is no special pleading or rivalry, and no desire to show prior and superior knowledge of the country to which the navigators had from time to time sailed. We only discover a straightforward, honest endeavor to tell the story of certain men's lives. This is done in a simple, artless way, and with every indication of a desire to mete out even handed justice to all. And candid readers who come to the subject with minds free from prejudice, will be powerfully impressed with the belief that they are reading authentic histories written by honest men.[57]

Before speaking particularly of the substance of the Sagas it will be necessary to trace briefly the origin and history of Icelandic literature in general.

We have already mentioned the fact that Iceland was mainly settled by Norwegians of superior qualities. And this superiority was always maintained, though it was somewhat slow in manifesting itself in the form of literature. Prior to the year 1000, the Runic alphabet had existed in Iceland, but it was generally used for the simplest purposes.[58] History and literature derived no advantage, as the runes were used chiefly for monumental inscriptions, and for mottoes and charms on such things as drinking cups, sacrifical vessels and swords. Yet the people were not without a kind of intellectual stimulus. It had long been the custom to preserve family and general histories, and recite them from memory as occasion seemed to warrant. This was done with a wonderful degree of accuracy and fidelity, by men more or less trained for the purpose, and whose performances at times were altogether surprising. They also had their scalds or poets, who were accustomed both to repeat the old songs and poems and extemporize new ones. Every good fighter was expected to prove himself a poet when the emergency required it. This profession was strongly encouraged. When Eyvind Skialdespilder sang his great song in praise of Iceland every peasant in the island, it is said, contributed three pieces of silver to buy a clasp for his mantel of fifty marks weight. These scalds were sometimes employed by the politicians, and on one occasion a satire so nettled Harold, king of Denmark, that he sent a fleet to ravage the island, and made the repetition an offense punishable with death. These poets also went to England, to the Orkneys and to Norway, where at the king's court they were held in the highest estimation, furnishing poetical effusions on every public or private occasion which demanded the exercise of their gifts. The degree to which they had cultivated their memories was surprising. Old Blind Skald Stuf could repeat between two and three hundred poems without halting; while the Saga-men had the same power of memory, which we know may be improved to almost any extent by cultivation. But with the advent of Christianity came the Roman alphabet, which proved an easy method of expressing thought. Christianity, however, did not stop here. Its service was a reasonable service, and demanded of its votaries a high intelligence. The priest of Odin need do no more than to recite a short vow, or mutter a brief prayer. He had no divine records to read and to explain. But the minister of the new religion came with a system that demanded broader learning and culture than that implied in extemporaneous songs. His calling required the aid of books, and the very sight of such things proved a mental stimulus to this hard-brained race. Besides, Christianity opened to the minds of the people new fields of thought. These rude sons of war soon began to understand there were certain victories, not to be despised, that might be gained through peace, and soon letters came to be some what familiar to the public mind. The earliest written efforts very naturally related to the lives of the Saints, which on Sundays and holy days were read in public for the edification of the people. During the eleventh century these exercises shared the public attention with those of the professional Saga-man, who still labored to hand down the oral versions of the national history and traditions. But in the beginning of the twelfth century the use of letters was extended, and, ere-long, the Saga-man found his occupation gone, the national history now being diligently gathered up by zealous students and scribes and committed to the more lasting custody of the written page. Among these was Ari Frode, who began the compilation of the Icelandic Dooms-day Book, which contained the records of all the early settlers. Scarcely less useful was Sæmund the Wise, who collected the poetical literature of the North and arranged it in a goodly tome. The example of these great men was followed, and by the end of the twelfth century all the Sagas relating to the pagan period of the country had been reduced to writing. This was an era of great literary activity, and the century following showed the same zeal. Finally Iceland possessed a body of prose literature superior in quantity and value to that of any other modern nation of its time.[59] Indeed, the natives of Europe at this period had no prose or other species of literature hardly worthy of the name; and, taken altogether, the Sagas formed the first prose literature in any modern language spoken by the people.[60] Says Sir Edmund Head, "No doubt there were translations in Anglo-Saxon from the Latin, by Alfred, of an earlier date, but there was in truth no vernacular literature. I cannot name," he says, "any work in high or low German prose which can be carried back to this period. In France, prose writing cannot be said to have begun before the time of Villehardouin (1204), and Joinville (1202). Castilian prose certainly did not commence before the time of Alfonso X (1252). Don Juan Manvel, the author of the Conde Lucanor, was not born till 1282. The Cronica General de España was not composed till at least the middle of the thirteenth century. About the same time the language of Italy was acquiring that softness and strength which were destined to appear so conspicuously in the prose of Boccaccio, and the writers of the next century."[61]

Yet while other nations were without a literature the intellect of Iceland was in active exercise, and works were produced like the Eddas and the Heimskringla, works which being inspired by a lofty genius will rank with the writings of Homer and Herodotus while time itself endures.

But in the beginning of the sixteenth century the literature of Iceland ultimately reached the period of its greatest excellence and began to decline. Books in considerable numbers always continued to be written, though works of positive genius were wanting. Yet in Iceland there has never been an absence of literary industry, while during the recent period the national reputation has been sustained by Finn Magnussen and similar great names. One hundred years before the Plymouth colonists, following in the track of Thorwald Ericson, landed on the sands of Cape Cod, the people of Iceland had set up the printing press, and produced numerous works both in the native language and the Latin tongue

It is to this people, whom Saxo Grammaticus points out as a people distinguished for their devotion to letters, that we are indebted for the narratives of the pre-Columbian voyages to America. Though first arranged for oral recitation, these Sagas were afterwards committed to manuscript, the earliest of which do not now exist, and were finally preserved in the celebrated Flatö collection nearly a century before the rediscovery of America by Columbus.

But it is no longer necessary to spend much time on this point, since the character and value of the Icelandic writings have come to be so generally acknowledged, and especially since scholars and antiquarians like Humbolt have fully acknowledged their authenticity and authority.

It is proper to notice here the fact that not a few have imagined that the claims of the Northmen have been brought forward to detract from the fame of Columbus;[62] yet, nothing could be farther from the truth, since no one denies that it was by the discovery of America by Columbus that the continent first became of value to the Old World. The Northmen came and went away without accomplishing any thing of lasting value; yet, because the world at large derived no benefit from their discovery, it is certainly unjust to deny its reality.

The fact that the Northmen knew of the existence of the Western Continent, prior to the age of Columbus, was prominently brought before the people of this country in the year 1837, when the Royal Society of Northern Antiquarians at Copenhagen published their work on the Antiquities of North America, under the editorial supervision of that great Icelandic scholar, Professor Rafn. But we are not to suppose that the first general account of these voyages was then given, for it has always been known that the history of certain early voyages to America by the Northmen were preserved in the libraries of Denmark and Iceland.[63] Torfæus, as early as 1706, published his work on Greenland, which threw much light on the subject. We find accounts of these discoveries in the works of Egede and Crantz. A very intelligent sketch, at least for those times, was given by J. Reinhold Forster, who frankly concedes the pre-Columbian discovery of America, in a History of the Voyages and Discoveries made in the North. Robertson speaks of them in his History of America, but says that he is unable to give an intelligent opinion. Indeed, the most of the older and more comprehensive writers give the Northmen recognition. Yet, owing to the fact that the Icelandic language, though simple in construction and easy of acquisition, was a tongue not understood by scholars, the subject has until recent years been suffered to lie in the back ground, and permitted, through a want of interest, to share, in a measure, the treatment meted out to vague and uncertain reports. But the well-directed efforts of the Northern Antiquarians of Denmark, supported by the enlightened zeal of scholars and historians in England, France and Germany, have done much to dispel popular ignorance, and to place the whole question in its true bearing before the people of all the principal civilized nations. In our own country, the work of Professor Rafn, already alluded to, has created a deep and wide-spread conviction of the reality of the Northman's claim, and has elicited confessions like that of Palfrey, who is obliged to say of the Icelandic records that, "their antiquity and genuineness appear to be well established, nor is there anything to bring their credibility into question, beyond the general doubt which always attaches to what is new or strange."[64]

It now remains to give the reader some general account of the contents of the narratives which relate more or less to the discovery of the Western continent. In doing this, the order followed will be that which is indicated by the table of contents at the beginning of the volume.

The first extracts given are very brief. They are taken from the Landanama Book, and relate to the report in general circulation, which indicated one Gunnbiorn as the discoverer of Greenland, an event which has been fixed at the year 876. These fragments also give an account of a voyage to what was called Gunnbiorn's Rocks, where the adventurers passed the winter, and found in a hole, or excavation, a sum of money, which indicated that others had been there before them.

The next narrative relates to the rediscovery of Greenland by the outlaw, Eric the Red, in 983, who there passed three years in exile, and afterwards returned to Iceland. About the year 986, he brought out to Greenland a considerable colony of settlers, who fixed their abode at Brattahlid, in Ericsfiord.

Then follows two versions of the voyage of Biarne Heriulfson, who, in the same year, 986, when sailing for Greenland, was driven away during a storm, and saw a new land at the southward, which he did not visit.

Next is given three accounts of the voyage of Leif, son of Eric the Red, who in the year 1000 sailed from Brattahlid to find the land which Biarne saw. Two of these accounts are hardly more than notices of the voyage, but the third is of considerable length, and details the successes of Leif, who found and explored this new land, where he spent the winter, returning to Greenland the following spring.

After this follows the voyage of Thorvald Ericson, brother of Leif, who sailed to Vinland from Greenland, which was the point of departure in all these voyages. This expedition was begun in 1002, and it cost him his life, as an arrow from one of the natives pierced his side, causing death.

Thorstein, his brother, went to seek Vinland, with the intention of bringing home his body, but failed in the attempt, and was driven back, passing the winter in a part of Greenland remote from Brattahlid, where he died before the spring fully opened.

The most distinguished explorer was Thorfinn Karlsefne, the Hopeful, an Icelander whose genealogy runs back in the old Northern annals, through Danish, Swedish, and even Scotch and Irish ancestors, some of whom were of royal blood. In the year 1006 he went to Greenland, where he met Gudrid, widow of Thorstein, whom he married. Accompanied by his wife, who urged him to the undertaking, he sailed to Vinland in the spring of 1007, with three vessels and one hundred and sixty men, where he remained three years. Here his son Snorre was born. He afterwards became the founder of a great family in Iceland, which gave the island several of its first bishops. Thorfinn finally left Vinland because he found it difficult to sustain himself against the attacks of the natives. They spent the most of their time in the vicinity of Mount Hope Bay in Rhode Island. Of this expedition we have three narratives, all of which are given.

The next to undertake a voyage was a wicked woman named Freydis, a sister to Leif Ericson, who went to Vinland in 1011, where she lived for a time with her two ships' crews in the same places occupied by Leif and Thorfinn. Before she returned, she caused the crew of one ship to be cruelly murdered, assisting in the butchery with her own hands.

After this we have what are called the Minor Narratives, which are not essential, yet they are given that the reader may be in the possession of all that relates to the subject. The first of these refers to a voyage of Are Marson to a land southwest of Ireland, called Hvitrammana-land, or Great

Ireland. This was prior to Leif's voyage to Vinland, or New England, taking place in the year 983. Biorn Asbrandson is supposed to have gone to the same place in 999. The voyage of Gudleif, who went thither, is assigned to the year 1027. The narrative of Asbrandson is given for the sake of the allusion at the close.

Finally we have a few scraps of history which speak of a voyage of Bishop Eric to Vinland in 1121, of the rediscovery of Helluland (Newfoundland) in 1285, and of a voyage to Markland (Nova Scotia) in 1347, whither the Northmen came to cut timber. With such brief notices the accounts come to an end.

The reader will occasionally find in these narratives instances of a marvelous and supernatural character, but there is nothing at all mythological, as persons ignorant of their nature have supposed. Besides there are multitudes of narratives of a later date, to be found in all languages, which contain as many statements of a marvelous nature as these Sagas, which are nevertheless believed to contain a substantial and reliable ground-work of truth. All early histories abound in the supernatural, and these things are so well known that illustrations are hardly needed here. The relation of prodigies in no wise destroys the credibility of historical statement. If this were not so, we should be obliged to discard the greater portion of well known history, and even suspect plain matters of fact in the writings of such men as Dr. Johnson, because that great scholar fully believed in the reality of an apparition known in London as the Cock-Lane Ghost. The Sagas are as free from superstition and imagination as any other reliable narratives of that age, and just as much entitled to belief.

There will also, in certain cases, be found contradictions. The statements of the different narratives do not always coincide. The disagreements are, however, neither very numerous nor remarkable. The discrepancies are exactly what we should expect to find in a series of narratives, written at different times and by different hands. The men who recorded the various expeditions to New England in the eleventh century agree, on the whole, quite as well as the writers of our own day, who, with vastly greater advantages, undertake to narrate the events of the second colonization in the seventeenth century.[65]

Therefore these marvelous statements and occasional contradictions in nowise detract from the historic value of the documents themselves, which, even in their very truthfulness to the times, give every evidence of authenticity and great worth. To this general appearance of truthfulness we may, however, add the force of those undesigned coincidences between writers widely separated and destitute of all means of knowing what had been already said. The same argument may be used with the Sagas which has been so powerfully employed by Paley and others in vindicating the historical character of the New Testament. In these narratives, as in those of Paul and John, it may be used with overwhelming effect. Yet we do not fear to dispense with all auxiliary aids. We are willing to rest the whole question of the value of these narratives upon their age; for if the Sagas date back to a period long prior to the voyage of Columbus, then the Northmen are entitled to the credit of having been the first Europeans to land upon these shores. But the date of these narratives has now been settled beyond reasonable question. The doubts of the ablest critical minds, both in Europe and America, have been effectually laid to rest, and the only reply now given to the Northern Antiquarian is some feeble paragraph pointed with a sneer.

We need not, therefore, appear before the public to cry, Place for the Northmen. They can win their own place, as of old. They are as strong today in ideas, as anciently in arms.

That the Northmen left no monuments or architectural remains in New England is true, notwithstanding Professor Rafn supposed that he found in the celebrated Dighton rock[66] and the stone mill at Newport, indubitable evidences of the Icelandic occupation. Any serious efforts to identify the Dighton inscription and the Newport Mill with the age of the Northmen can only serve to injure a good cause. If Professor Rafn could have seen these memorials himself, he would doubtless have been among the first to question the truth of the theory which he set forth.

In regard to the structure at Newport, Professor Rafn says that he is inclined to believe "that it had a sacred destination, and that it belonged to some monastery or Christian place of worship of one of the chief parishes in Vinland. In Greenland," he says, "there are to be found ruins of several round buildings in the vicinity of the churches. One of this description, in diameter about twenty-six feet, is situated at the distance of three hundred feet to the eastward of the great church in Igalliko; another of forty-four feet in diameter, at the distance of four hundred and forty feet to the eastward of the church in Karkortok; ... a third, of thirty-two feet diameter amongst the ruins of sixteen buildings at Kanitsok."[67] He supposes that all these ancient remains of the Icelanders, which are to be seen in Greenland to-day, are baptisteries, similar to those of Italy.

According to this view, there must have been a considerable ecclesiastical establishment in Vinland, which is not clearly indicated by the Sagas, from which we learn no more than the simple fact that Bishop Eric sailed on a voyage to this place in the year 1121. But is it probable that the Northmen would have erected a baptistery like this, and, at the same time, left no other monument? It seems hardly reasonable. Besides, whoever examines this ancient structure must be impressed by its modern aspect, so especially apparent in the preservation of the mortar, which does not bear the marks of seven centuries. The displacement of a portion of the masonry might perhaps reveal some peculiarity that would effectually settle the question of its antiquity to the satisfaction of all.[68]

In treating this subject we shall run into needless errors and difficulties, if we attempt the task of discovering monuments of the Northmen in New England. In Greenland these evidences of their occupation are abundant, because they were regularly established on the ground for generations, and formed their public and private edifices of the only material at hand, which was well nigh imperishable. But their visits to New England were comparatively few, and were scattered over many years. Owing to the weakness of their numbers, they found permanent colonies impracticable. Thorfinn Karlsefne deliberately gave up the attempt at the end of a three years experiment, saying that it would be impossible to maintain themselves against the more numerous bands of natives. Their habitations were temporary. The various companies that came into Vinland, instead of building new houses, took possession of Leif's booths, and simply added others like them when they afforded insufficient quarters. To ask for monuments of the Northmen is therefore unreasonable, since their wooden huts and timber crosses must soon have disappeared. The only memorial we have a right to expect is some trifling relic, a coin or amulet, perhaps, that chance may yet throw in the antiquarian's way.[69] In the meanwhile among scholars the Icelandic narratives are steadily winning their way to unquestioned belief. This is all the more gratifying in an age like the present, in which large portions of history are being dismissed to the realms of hoary fable, and all the annals of the past are being studied in a critical spirit, with true aims and a pure zeal.

# Major Narratives (Pre-Columbian Discovery)

I. FRAGMENTS FROM LANDNAMA-BOK.

The following extracts from the *Landnama*,[70] give us the earliest information on record, in regard to the westward movements of the Icelanders. The men referred to were well known, and the mention of their names and exploits in this great work, than which no higher authority could be produced, is gratifying. These extracts, which are given in the order in which they stand in vol. I. of Grönland's *Historiske Mindesmærker*, the greater portion of which work is the labor of Finn Magnusen, have probably never appeared before in an English dress. The first extract simply mentions Gunnbiorn and his Rocks; the second shows that Eric the Red obtained his knowledge of the existence of Greenland through this person; the third again gives the name of Gunnbiorn: while the fourth furnishes a brief account of an early voyage to the Rocks. It appears from these references, that, previous to the sailing of Eric the Red, the existence of land at the west was well understood, the report of Gunnbiorn's adventure having been quite generally circulated amongst the people.

1. There was a man named Grimkel, [A. D. 876.] son of Ulf Hreidarson, called Krage, and brother to Gunnbiorn,[71] after whom Gunnbiorn's Rocks[72] are named. He took possession of that piece of land that extends from Berevigs Röin to Ness Röin, and out round the point of the cape. And he lived on Saxahval. He drove away Saxe, a son of Alfarin Valeson, and he lived on the Röin of Saxahval. Alfarin Valeson had first taken possession of the cape between Berevigs Röin and Enne.

2. Eric Red [A. D. 983.] said that he intended to find the land that was seen by Gunnbiorn,[73] Ulf Krage's son, when he was driven by a storm west from Iceland, and found Gunnbiorn's Rocks. [A. D. 876.] At the same time he said if he did not find the land he would return to his friends.

3. Two sons of Gunnbiorn, Ulf Krage's son, after whom Gunnbiorn's Rocks were named, were called Gunstein and Haldor. They took possession of Skötufiorden, Löigardelen and Ogursvigen to Mjorfiord. Berse was Haldor's son, father to Thormod Kalbrunarskald.

Snæbiorn (Holmstein's son), called Galte, owned a ship [A. D. 970.] that lay in the mouth of Grimsar (in Borgafiorden). Rolf, from Rödesand,

162

bought a half of the ship. Each of the parties mustered twelve men. With Snæbiorn, was Thorkel and Sumarlide, sons of Thorgier Red, son of Einar, from Stafholdt.

Snæbiorn also took Thorod from Thingness, his step-father and his five sons, and Rolf took Stærbiorn. The last named recited the following verse, after he had a dream:

Both ours
dead I see;
all empty
in Northwestern Sea;
cold weather,
great suffering,
I expect
Snæbiorn's death.[74]

They sought Gunnbiorn's Rocks and found land. Snæbiorn would not permit any one to go ashore in the night. Stærbiorn landed, notwithstanding, and found a purse[75] with money in an earth hole, and concealed it. Snæbiorn hit him with an axe so that the purse fell down.

They built a cabin to live in, and it was all covered with snow. Thorkel Red's son, found that there was water on a shelf that stood out of the cabin window. This was in the month of Goe.[76] They shovelled the snow away. Snæbiorn rigged the ship; Thorod and five of his party were in the hut, and Stærbiorn and several men of Rolf's party. Some hunted.[77] Stærbiorn killed Thorod, but both he and Rolf killed Snæbiorn. Red's sons and all the rest were obliged to take the oath of allegiance to save their lives. They arrived on their return at Helgeland, Norway, and later at Vadil in Iceland.[78]

## II. THE COLONIZATION OF GREENLAND.

The first document relating to the settlement of Greenland by the Northmen, is taken from the Saga of Eric the Red, as given in Professor Rafn's Antiquitates Americanæ. Besides the history of Eric and his sons, that Saga contains notices of other voyages. The following are simply extracts. The whole Saga does not necessarily apply to the subject under examination—the Discovery of America. The second extract, which gives more of the particulars, is from Grönland's Historiske Mindesmærker, vol. ii, p. 201. The third is also taken from the same great historical depository.

First Narrative

There was a man named Thorvald, son of Osvald, son of Ulf-Oexna-Thorerisson. Thorvald and his son were obliged to leave Jardar[79] and go to Iceland, on account of manslaughter. At that time Iceland was generally colonized.[80] They first lived in Drangey, where Thorvald died. Then Eric married Thorhild, daughter of Jorund and Thorbiarg Knarrabringa, whom afterwards Thorbiorn of Haukdale married. Eric moved from the north, and fixed his abode in Ericstad opposite Vatshorn. The son of Eric and Thorhold was named Leif. But after Eyulf Soers and Holm-Gang Rafn's murder, Eric was banished from Haukdale. Eric went westward to Breidafiord and lived at Oexney in Ericstad. He lent Thorgest his seat-posts,[81] and he could not get them again. He then demanded them. Then came disputes and hostility between him and Thorgest, which is told in the history of Eric. Styr Thorgrim's son, Eyulf of Svinoe, the sons of Brand of Aptelfiord and Thorbiorn Vifilsson plead the cause of Eric; Thorder Gellurson and Thorgeir of Hitardale plead for Thorgest. Eric was declared outlawed by the Thing, and prepared his ship for sea in Eric's Bay. Styr and the others went with him beyond the island. [A. D. 982.] Then Eric declared it to be his resolution to seek the land which Gunnbiorn, Ulf Krage's son, saw [A. D. 876.] when driven into the Western ocean, where he found Gunnbiorn's Rocks, saying, that if he did not find the land he would return to his friends. Eric set sail from Snæfellsjokul, and found land which from its height he called Midjokul, now called Blaaserk. Thence he sailed along the shore in a southerly direction, seeking for the nearest habitable land. The first winter he passed in Ericseya,[82] near the middle of the east district. The following year he came into Ericsfiord, where he fixed his seat. The same summer he explored the western desert, and gave names to many places. The following winter he passed on a holm opposite Rafnsgnipa, and the third year he came into Iceland and brought his ship into Breidafiord. The land which he found, he named Greenland, saying that men would be persuaded to go to a land with so good a name. Eric stayed in Iceland that winter, and the summer after he went over to the land which he had found, and fixed his abode in Brattahlid in Ericsfiord. [A. D. 986.] Men acquainted with affairs, say, that this same summer in which Eric went to settle in Greenland, thirty-five ships sailed from Breidafiord and Bogafjord, of which only fourteen arrived, and the rest were driven back or lost. This event took place fifteen winters[83] before the Christian religion was established in Iceland. The same summer, Bishop Frederick and Thorvold Kodranson went from Iceland.[84] Among those who emigrated with Eric and established themselves, were Heriulf Heriulfsfiord who took Heriulfsness, and abode in Heriulfsness, Ketil

Ketilsfiord, Rafn Rafnsfiord, Solvi Solvidale, Helgi Thorbrandson Alptafiord, Thorbjornglora Siglefjord, Einar Einarsfiord, Hafgrim Hafgrimsfiord and Vatnahver, Arnlaug Arnlaugsfiord; and other men went to the west district.

And when the sixth[85] winter had passed [A. D. 999.] since Eric Red went to live in Greenland, Leif, son of Eric, went over from Greenland to Norway, and in the autumn arrived in Throndheim and came north to King Olaf Trygvesson,[86] from Hegeland. He brought his ship to Nidaros and went at once to King Olaf. The king commanded Leif and some other pagan men to come to him. They were exhorted to accept religion, which the king having easily arranged with Leif, he and all his sailors were baptized, and passed the winter with the king, being liberally entertained.

Second Narrative

Thorvold the son of Usvold, son of Ulf, son of Oexne-Thorer, and his son, Eric Red, left Jardar in Norway on account of manslaughter, and took possession of a piece of land on Hornastrand [Iceland], and lived there at Drangey. There Thorvold died. Eric then married Thorhild, daughter of Jorund Atleson and Thorbiarg Knarrabringa, who was then married to Thorbiorn of Haukdale. Then Eric went from the north and ploughed the fields in Haukdale. Then he lived in Ericstadt by Vatshorn. There his thralls[87] let a piece of rock tumble down over Valthiof's house in Valthiofstadt. But his relation, Eyulf Söirs, killed the thralls at Kneide-Brinke above Vatshorn. For this cause, Eric killed Eyulf Söirs. He also killed Holm-Gang Rafn at Leikskaale. Geirstein and Odd at Jörund Eyulf Söirs relations brought a suit against the slayer. Eric was then banished from Hauksdale, and took possession of the islands, Brokö and Oexno, but lived in Todum at Sydero, the first winter. Then he loaned Thorgest his seat-posts. Then Eric moved to Oexno and lived in Ericstadt. Then he demanded his seat-posts, but did not get them. Eric took them thereafter from Bredobolstad, but Thorgest followed him. They fought near the house at Drangey. Two sons of Thorgest fell, and some other men. Thereafter they both kept their followers with them. Styr, Eyulf of Svino, Thorbrand's sons of Alptefiord, and Thorbiorn Vifilsson, were of Eric's party. But Thord Gelleirson, Thorgeir from Hitardale, Aslak of Langedale, and Illuge's son helped Thorgest. Eric and his party were sentenced to be banished at Thorsness Thing. He fitted out a ship in Ericsfiord, but Eyulf concealed him in Dimonsvaag, while Thorgest and his men sought after him on the highlands. Thorbiorn, Eyulf and Styr followed with Eric out to sea beyond the islands. He said that he meant to seek the land Gunnbiorn, Ulf Krage's son, saw [A. D. 876.] when he was

165

driven by a storm west from Iceland, and found Gunnbiorn's Rocks; though he said at the same time if he discovered the land he would return to his friends. [A. D. 982.] Eric laid his course to the west from Snæfieldness, and approached [Greenland] from the sea to land at Midjokul, in that place that is called Blæsark. From thence he went along the coast to the south, to see if the land was fit to live in. The first year he stayed all winter in Ericksö, nearly in the middle of the west bygd. In the next spring [A. D. 983.] he went to Ericsfiord, and there found a dwelling. Next summer he went to the western bygd, and gave certain names to many places. The second winter he lived in Ericsholm, at Hvarfo Fiedspidæ, and at the third summer [A. D. 984.] he went north to Snæfield, inside of Rafnsfiord. He thought then that the place where Ericsfiord bent was opposite the place where he came. He then returned and spent the third winter in Ericksö opposite the mouth of Ericsfiord. The next summer [A. D. 985.] he went to Iceland, and landed at Breidafiord. The next winter he stayed at Holmstater, with Ingolf. Next spring he fought with Thorgest and lost the battle. That summer, Eric began to settle the land which he had discovered [A. D. 986.] and which he called Greenland, because he said that the people would not like to move there, if the land did not have a good name. Learned men say that twenty-five ships went that summer to Greenland from Breidafiord and Borgafjord, but only fourteen arrived. Of the rest, some were driven back and others were wrecked. This happened fifteen winters before Christianity was introduced into Iceland.

Third Narrative

The land some call Greenland, was discovered and settled from Iceland. Eric the Red was the name of the Breidafiord man, who [A. D. 986.] went from here [Iceland] to there, and took possession of that part of the land, which later was called Ericsfiord. He named the land and called it Greenland, and said it would encourage people to come there, if the land had a good name. They found there, both east and west, ruins of houses and pieces of boats, and begun stonework. From which it is to be seen what kind of people have lived in Vinland, and which the Greenlanders call Skrælings and who had been there. He [Eric] began to settle the land fourteen or fifteen years before the introduction of Christianity in Iceland. Afterwards this was told of Greenland to Thorkel Gelleirson, by a man who had himself followed Eric Red.

## III. THE VOYAGE OF BIARNE.

The voyage of Biarne to Greenland was attended by many hardships. His vessel was blown away from the course during a storm, at which time he saw the shores of the American continent, yet he made no attempt to land. Of this voyage we have two versions. The first is a translation of a passage from Codex Flatöiensis, given in *Antiquitates Americæ*, p. 17. The second is taken from Grönland's *Historiske Mindesmærker*. The date of this voyage is fixed by the fact that Biarne sailed the same season that his father settled in Greenland, which, as we learn from the narrative of Eric, was in the year 985. There is a complete agreement between this account and the preceding.

First Narrative

Heriulf was the son of Bard, Heriulf's son, who was a relation of Ingolf the Landnamsman.[88] Ingolf gave Heriulf land between Vog and Reikianess. Heriulf dwelt first at Dropstock. His wife was called Thorgird, and their son was called Biarne. He was a promising young man. In his earliest youth he had a desire to go abroad, and he soon gathered property and reputation; and was by turns a year abroad, and a year with his father. Biarne was soon in possession of a merchant ship of his own. The last winter [A. D. 985.] while he was in Norway, Heriulf prepared to go to Greenland with Eric, and gave up his dwelling. There was a Christian man belonging to the Hebudes along with Heriulf, who composed the lay called the Hafgerdingar[89] Song, in which is this stave:

May he whose hand protects so well
The simple monk in lonely cell,
And o'er the world upholds the sky,
His own blue hall, still stand me by.[90]

Heriulf settled at Heriulfness [A. D. 985.] and became a very distinguished man. Eric Red took up his abode at Bratthalid, and was in great consideration, and honored by all. These were Eric's children: Leif, Thorvold, and Thorstein; and his daughter was called Ferydis. She was married to a man called Thorvald; and they dwelt at Gardar, which is now a bishop's seat. She was a haughty, proud woman; and he was but a mean man. She was much given to gathering wealth. The people of Greenland were heathen at this time. Biarne came over the same summer [A. D. 985.] with his ship to the strand[91] which his father had sailed abroad from in the spring. He was much struck with the news, and would not unload his vessel.

When his crew asked him what he intended to do, he replied that he was resolved to follow his old custom by taking up his winter abode with his father. "So I will steer for Greenland if ye will go with me." They one and all agreed to go with him. Biarne said, "Our voyage will be thought foolish, as none of us have been on the Greenland sea before." Nevertheless they set out to sea as soon as they were ready, and sailed for three days, until they lost sight of the land they left. But when the wind failed, a north wind with fog set in, and they knew not where they were sailing to; and this lasted many days. At last they saw the sun, and could distinguish the quarters of the sky; so they hoisted sail again, and sailed a whole day and night, when they made land. They spoke among themselves what this land could be, and Biarne said that, in his opinion, it could not be Greenland. On the question, if he should sail nearer to it, he said, "It is my advice that we sail up close to the land." They did so; and they soon saw that the land was without mountains, was covered with woods, and that there were small hills inland. They left the land on the larboard side, and had their sheet on the land side. Then they sailed two days and nights before they got sight of land again. They asked Biarne if they thought this would be Greenland; but he gave his opinion that the land was no more Greenland, than the land they had seen before. "For on Greenland, it is said, there are great snow mountains." They soon came near to the land, and saw that it was flat and covered with trees. Now, as the wind fell, the ship's people talked of its being advisable to make for the land; but Biarne would not agree to it. They thought that they would need wood and water; but Biarne said: "Ye are not in want of either." And the men blamed him for this. He ordered them to hoist the sail, which was done. They now turned the ship's bow from the land, and kept the sea for three days and nights, with a fine breeze from southwest. Then they saw a third land, which was high and mountainous, and with snowy mountains. Then they asked Biarne if he would land here; but he refused altogether: "For in my opinion this land is not what we want."[92] Now they let the sails stand and kept along the land and saw it was an island. Then they turned from the land and stood out to sea with the same breeze; but the gale increased, and Biarne ordered a reef to be taken in, and not to sail harder than the ship and her tackle could easily bear. After sailing three days and nights, they made, the fourth time, land; and when they asked Biarne if he thought this was Greenland or not, Biarne replies: "This is most like what has been told me of Greenland; and here we shall take to the land." They did so, and came to the land in the evening, under a ness, where they found a boat. On this ness dwelt Biarne's father, Heriulf; and from that it is called Heriulfness. Biarne went to his father's, gave up sea-faring, and after his father's death, continued to dwell there when at home.

Second Narrative

A man named Heriulf, son of Bard, son of Heriulf, a relation to Landnamsman Ingolf, who gave the last named Heriulf the piece of land that lies between Vaag and Reikianess. The younger Heriulf went to Greenland, when Eric Red began to settle there, and on his ship was a Christian man from the South Islands [the Hebrides] who was the author of the poem, Havgerdingar, in which was the following verse:

I to the monk's protector pray
That he will give my voyage luck!
The heaven's great Ruler
Save me from danger.

Heriulf took possession of Heriulfsfiord, and became one of the chief men. Eric Red took to himself Ericsfiord, and lived in Brattahlid, and Leif, his son, after his death. Those men who at the same time went away with Eric took possession of the following pieces of land: Heriulf Heriulfsfiord, and he lived in Heriulfness, Ketil Ketilsfiord, Rafn Rafnsfiord, Sölve Sölvedale, Snorro Thorbrandson Alptefiord, Thorbiornglora Siglefiord, Einar Einarsfiord, Havgrim Havgrimsfiord and Vatnahverf, Arnlaug Arnlaugfiord; but some went to the west bygd. A man named Thorkel Forsark, cousin to Eric Red on their mother's side, went to Greenland with Eric, and took possession of Hvalsöfiord, together with the greater part of the piece of land between Eyolfsfiord and Einarsfiord, and lived in Hvalosöfne. From him came the Hvalsöfiord people. He was very strong. Once Eric Red visited him, and he would welcome his guest in the best way possible, but he had no boats at hand which he could use. He was compelled to swim out to Hvalsö, and get a full-grown sheep,[93] and carry it on his back home to his house. It was a good half mile. Thorkel was buried in a cave in the field of Hvalsöfiord.

## IV. LEIF'S VOYAGE TO VINLAND.

This voyage is recorded in the Flatö Manuscript, and is given in Antiquitates Americanæ, pp. 26-40. It contains the account of the voyage of Leif, son of Eric the Red, who, following out the hints of Biarne, sailed to discover the new land, which he called Vinland, on account of the quantity of vines that he found growing wild. Several extracts are appended, because of interest in connection with the subject.

First narrative

[A. D. 984.] It is next to be told that Biarne Heriulfson came over from Greenland to Norway, on a visit to Earl Eric, who received him well. Biarne tells of this expedition of his, in which he had discovered unknown land; and people thought he had not been very curious to get knowledge, as he could not give any account of those countries, and he was somewhat blamed on this account. [A. D. 986.] Biarne was made a Court man of the earl, and the summer after he went over to Greenland; and afterwards there was much talk about discovering unknown lands. Leif, a son of Eric Red of Brattahlid, went over[94] to Biarne Heriulfson, and bought the ship from him, and manned the vessel, so that in all, there were thirty-five men on board. Leif begged his father Eric to go as commander of the expedition; but he excused himself, saying he was getting old, and not so able as formerly to undergo the hardship of a sea voyage. Leif insisted that he among all their relations was the most likely to have good luck on such an expedition; and Eric consented, and rode from home with Leif, when they had got all ready for sea; but when they were coming near to the ship,[95] the horse on which Eric was riding, stumbled, and he fell from his horse[96] and hurt his foot. "It is destined," said Eric, "that I should never discover more lands than this of Greenland, on which we live; and now we must not run hastily into this adventure."[97] Eric accordingly returned home to Brattahlid, but Leif, with his comrades, in all thirty-five men, rigged out their vessel. There was a man from the south country called Tyrker,[98] with the expedition. [A. D. 1000.] They put the ship in order, and put to sea when they were ready. They first came to the land which Biarne had last discovered, sailed up to it, cast anchor, put out a boat and went on shore; but there was no grass to be seen. There were large snowy mountains[99] up the country; but all the way from the sea up to these snowy ridges, the land was one field of snow, and it appeared to them a country of no advantages. Leif said: "It shall not be said of us, as it was of Biarne, that we did not come upon the land; for I will give the country a name, and call it Helluland."[100] Then they went on board again and put to sea, and found another land. They sailed in towards it, put out a boat, and landed. The country was flat,[101] and overgrown with wood; and the strand far around, consisted of a white sand, and low towards the sea. Then Leif said: "We shall give this land a name according to its kind, and called it Markland."[102] Then they hastened on board, and put to sea again with the wind from the northeast, and were out for two days and made land. They sailed towards it, and came to an island[103] which lay on the north side of the land, where they disembarked[104] to wait for good weather. There was dew upon the grass; and having accidentally gotten some of the dew upon their hands and put it in their mouths, they thought that they had never tasted anything so sweet as it was.[105] Then they went on board and sailed into a sound[106] that was between the island and a ness[107] that went out northwards from the land, and sailed westward[108] past the ness. There was very shallow[109] water in ebb tide, so that their ship lay dry; and there was a long way between their ship and the water. They were so desirous to get to the land that they would not wait till their ship floated, but ran to the land, to a place where a river comes out of a lake. As soon as their ship was afloat they took the boats, rowed to the ship, towed her up the river,[110] and from thence into the lake,[111] where they cast anchor, carried their beds out of the ship, and set up their tents. They resolved to put things in order for wintering there, and they erected a large house. They did not want for salmon,[112] both in the river and in the lake; and they thought the salmon larger than any they had ever seen before. The country appeared to them of so good a kind, that it would not be necessary to gather fodder for the cattle for winter.[113] There was no frost in winter,[114] and the grass was not much withered. Day and night were more equal than in Greenland and Iceland; for on the shortest day the sun was in the sky between Eyktarstad[115] and the Dagmalastad. Now when they were ready with their house building, [A. D. 1001.] Leif said to his fellow travellers: "Now I will divide the crew into two divisions, and explore the country. Half shall stay at home and do the work, and the other half shall search the land; but so that they do not go farther than they can come back in the evening, and that they do not wander from each other." This they continued to do for some time. Leif changed about, sometimes with them, and sometimes with those at home. Leif was a stout and strong man, and of manly appearance; and was, besides, a prudent and sagacious man in all respects.

It happened one evening that a man of the party was missing; and it was the south country man, Tyrker. Leif was very sorry for this, because Tyrker had long been in his father's house, and he loved Tyrker in his childhood. Leif blamed his comrades very much, and proposed to go with twelve men on an expedition to find him; but they had gone only a short way from the station when Tyrker came to meet them, and he was joyfully received. Leif soon perceived that his foster father[116] was quite merry.[117] Tyrker had a high forehead, sharp eyes, with a small face, and was little in size, and ugly; but was very dexterous in all feats. Leif said to him, "Why art thou so late, my foster-father? and why didst thou leave thy comrades?" He spoke at first long in German, rolled his eyes and knit his brows; but they could not make out what he was saying. After a while, and some delay, he said in Norse, "I did not go much farther than they; and yet I have something altogether new to relate, for I found vines and grapes."[118] "Is that true, my foster-father?" said Leif. "Yes, true it is," answered he, "for I was born where there was no scarcity of grapes." Now they slept all night, and the next morning Leif said to his men, "Now we shall have two occupations to attend to, and day about; namely, to gather grapes or cut vines, and to fell wood in the forest to lade our vessel." And this advice was followed. It is related that their stern boat was filled with grapes, and then a cargo of wood was hewn for the vessel.[119] Towards spring they made ready and sailed sway, and Leif gave the country a name from its products, and called it Vinland.[120] They now sailed into the open sea and had a fair wind until they came in sight of Greenland and the lands below the ice mountains.[121] Then a man put in a word and said to Leif, "Why do you steer so close on the wind?" Leif replied: "I mind my helm and tend to other things too; do you notice anything?" They said that they saw nothing remarkable. "I do not know," said Leif, "whether I see a ship or a rock." Then they looked and saw that it was a rock. But he saw so much better than they, that he discovered men upon the rock. "Now I will," said Leif, "that we hold to the wind, that we may come up to them if they should need help; and if they should not be friendly inclined, it is in our power to do as we please and not theirs." Now they sailed under the rock, lowered their sails, cast anchor, and put out another small boat which they had with them. Then Tyrker asked who their leader was. He said his name was Thorer, and said he was a Northman;[122] "But what is your name?" said he. Leif told his name. "Are you the son of Eric the Red of Brattahlid?" he asked. Leif said that was so. "Now I will," said Leif, "take ye and all on board my ship, and as much of the goods as the ship will store." They took up this offer, and sailed away to Ericfiord with the cargo, and from thence to Brattahlid, where they unloaded the ship. Leif offered Thorer and his wife, Gudrid, and three others, lodging with himself, and offered lodging elsewhere for the rest of the people, both of Thorer's crew and his own. Leif took fifteen men from the rock, and thereafter was called, Leif the Lucky. After that time Leif advanced greatly in wealth and consideration. That winter, sickness came among Thorer's people, and he himself, and a great part of his crew, died. The same winter Eric Red died. This expedition to Vinland was much talked of, and Leif's brother, Thorvald, thought that the country had not been explored enough in different places. Then Leif said to Thorvald, "You may go, brother, in my ship to Vinland if you like; but I will first send the ship for the timber which Thorer left upon the rock." And so it was done.

Second Narrative

The same spring, King Olaf, as said before, sent Gissur[123] and Hialte[124] to Iceland. The king also sent Leif to Greenland to proclaim Christianity there. The king sent with him, a priest, and some other religious men, to baptize the people and teach them the true faith. Leif sailed the same summer to Greenland; he took up out of the ocean, the people of a ship who were on a wreck completely destroyed, and in a perishing condition. And on this same voyage he discovered Vinland the Good,[125] and came at the close of summer to Brattahlid, to his father Eric. After that time the people called him, Leif the Fortunate; but his father Eric said that these two things went against one another; that Leif had saved the crew of the ship, and delivered them from death, and that he had [brought] that bad man into Greenland, that is what he called the priest; but after much urging, Eric was baptized,[126] as well as all the people of Greenland.

Third Narrative

The same winter, Leif, the son of Eric the Red, was in high favor with King Olaf, and embraced Christianity. But the summer that Gissur went to Iceland, King Olaf sent Leif to Greenland, to proclaim Christianity. He sailed the same summer for Greenland. He found some men in the sea on a wreck, and helped them; the same voyage,[127] he discovered Vinland the Good, and came at harvest time to Greenland. He brought with him a priest and other religious[128] men, and went to live at Brattahlid with his father Eric. He was afterwards called, Leif the Fortunate. But his father Eric said, that these two things were opposed to one another, because Leif had saved the crew of the ship, and brought evil men to Greenland, meaning the priests.

V. THORVALD ERICSON'S EXPEDITION.

The greater portion of this voyage appears to have been performed during two summers, the expedition finally returning to Greenland on account of the death of their leader. The narrative is taken from *Codex Flatöiensis*, as given in *Antiquitates Americanæ*.

Now Thorvald [A. D. 1002.] made ready for his voyage with thirty men, after consulting his brother Leif. They rigged their ship, and put to sea. Nothing is related of this expedition until they came to Vinland, to the booths put up by Leif, where they secured the ship and tackle, and remained quietly all winter and lived by fishing. In spring [A. D. 1003.] Thorvald ordered the vessel to be rigged, and that some men should proceed in the longboat westward along the coast, and explore it during the summer. They thought the country beautiful and well wooded, the distance small between the forest and the sea, and the strand full of white sand. There were also many islands and very shallow water. They found no abode for man or beast, but on an island far towards the west, they found a corn barn constructed of wood. They found no other traces of human work, and came back in autumn to Leif's booths. The following spring, [A. D. 1004.] Thorvald, with his merchant ship, proceeded eastwards, and towards the north along the land.[129] Opposite to a cape[130] they met bad weather, and drove upon the land and broke their keel, and remained there a long time to repair the vessel. Thorvald said to his companions: "We will stick up the keel here upon the ness, and call the place Kialarness," which they did. Then they sailed away eastward along the country, to a point of land,[131] which was everywhere covered with woods. They moored the vessel to the land, laid out gangways to the shore, and Thorvald with all his ship's company, landed. He said, "Here it is beautiful, and I would willingly set up my abode here." They afterwards went on board, and saw three specks upon the sand within the point, and went to them and found there were three skin boats with three men under each boat. They divided their men and took all of them prisoners, except one man, who escaped with his boat. They killed eight of them, and then went to the point and looked about them. Within this bay they saw several eminences, which they took to be habitations. Then a great drowsiness came upon them and they could not keep themselves awake, but all of them fell asleep. A sudden scream came to them, and they all awoke; and mixed with the scream they thought they heard the words: "Awake, Thorvald, with all thy comrades, if ye will save your lives. Go on board your ship as fast as you can, and leave this land without delay." In the same moment an innumerable multitude, from the interior of the bay, came in skin boats and laid themselves alongside. Then said Thorvald, "We shall put up our war screens[132] along the gunwales and defend ourselves as well as we can, but not use our weapons much against them." They did so accordingly. The Skrællings[133] shot at them for a while, and then fled away as fast as they could. Then Thorvald asked if anyone was wounded, and they said nobody was hurt. He said: "I have a wound under the arm.[134] An arrow flew between the gunwale and the shield under my arm: here is the arrow, and it will be my death wound. Now I advise you to make ready with all speed to return; but ye shall carry me to the point which I thought would be so convenient for a dwelling. It may be that it was true what I said, that here would I dwell for a while. Ye shall bury me there, and place a cross at my head and one at my feet, and call the place Crossness." Christianity had been established in Greenland at this time;[135] but Eric Red was dead[136] before Christianity was introduced. Now Thorvald died, and they did everything as he had ordered. Then they went away in search of their fellow voyagers; and they related to each other all the news. They remained in their dwelling all winter, and gathered vines and grapes, and put them on board their ships. Towards spring, they prepared to return to Greenland, where they arrived with their vessel, and landed at Ericsfiord, bringing heavy tidings to Leif.

## VI. THORSTEIN ERICSON'S ATTEMPT TO FIND VINLAND.

This version is from Codex Flatöiensis, and is given in Antiquitates Americanæ, pp. 47-55. The expedition was wholly unsuccessful, and the leader finally died without reaching the desired land. One cannot help feeling, notwithstanding the marvellous events recorded, that the basis of this account, is formed of solid fact. The main narrative is not one likely to have been invented by an impostor.

In the meantime it had happened in Greenland, that Thorstein of Ericsfiord had married, and taken to wife, [A. D. 1005.] Gudrid, the daughter of Thorbiorn, who had been married, as before related, to Thorer, the Eastman.[137] Thorstein Ericsson bethought him now, that he would go to Vinland, for his brother Thorvald's body. He rigged out the same vessel, and chose an able and stout crew. He had with him, twenty-five men, and his wife Gudrid; and as soon as they were ready he put to sea, and they quickly lost sight of the land. They drove about on the ocean the whole summer, without knowing where they were; and in the first week of winter,[138] they landed at Lysifiord in Greenland, in the western settlement. Thorstein looked for lodgings for his men, and got his whole ship's crew accommodated, but not himself and wife; so that for some nights they had to sleep on board. At that time Christianity was but recent in Greenland. One day, early in the morning, some men came to their tent, and the leader asked them what people were in the tent? Thorstein replies, "Two; who is it that asks?" "Thorstein," was the reply, "and I am called Thorstein the Black, and it is my errand here, to offer thee and thy wife lodging beside me." Thorstein said he would speak to his wife about it; and as she gave her consent, he agreed to it. "Then I shall come for you to-morrow with my horses,[139] for I do not want means to entertain you; but few care to live in my house, for I and my wife live lonely, and I am very melancholy. I have also a different religion[140] from yours, although I think the one you have, the best." Now the following morning he came for them with horses; and they took up their abode with Thorstein Black, who was very friendly towards them. Gudrid had a good outward appearance, and was knowing, and understood well how to behave with strangers. Early in the winter, a sickness prevailed among Thorstein Ericsson's people, and many of his ship men died. He ordered that coffins should be made for the bodies of the dead, and that they should be brought on board, and stowed away carefully; for he said, "I will transport all the bodies to Ericsfiord in summer." It was not long before sickness broke out in Thorstein Black's house, and his wife, who was called Grimhild, fell sick first. She was very stout, and as strong as a man, but yet she could not bear up against the illness. Soon after, Thorstein Ericksson also fell sick, and they both lay ill in bed at the same time; but Grimhild, Thorstein Black's wife died first. When she was dead, Thorstein went out of the room for a skin to lay over the corpse. Then Gudrid said, "My dear Thorstein, be not long away;" which he promised. Then said Thorstein Ericsson, "Our housewife is wonderful, for she raises herself up with her elbows, moves herself forward over the bed-frame, and is feeling for her shoes." In the same moment, Thorstein the Goodman, came back, and instantly, Grimhild laid herself down, so that it made every beam that was in the house, crack. Thorstein now made a coffin for Grimhild's corpse, removed it outside, and buried it. He was a stout and strong man, but it required all his strength to remove the corpse from the house. Now Thorstein Ericsson's illness increased upon him, and he died, which Gudrid his wife took with great grief. They were all in the room, and Gudrid had set herself upon a stool before the bench on which her husband Thorstein's body lay. Now Thorstein the goodman took Gudrid from the stool in his arms, and set himself with her upon a bench just opposite to Thorstein's body,[141] and spoke much with her. He consoled her, and promised to go with her in summer to Ericsfiord, with her husband Thorstein's corpse, and those of his crew. "And," said he, "I shall take with me many servants to console and assist." She thanked him for this. Thorstein Ericsson then raised himself up and said, "Where is Gudrid?" And thrice he said this; but she was silent. Then she said to Thorstein the Goodman, "Shall I give answer or not?" He told her not to answer. Then went Thorstein the Goodman across the room, and sat down in a chair, and Gudrid set herself on his knee; and Thorstein the Goodman said: "What wilt thou make known?" After a while the corpse replies, "I wish to tell Gudrid her fate beforehand, that she may be the better able to bear my death; for I have come to a blessed resting place. And this I have now to tell thee, Gudrid, that thou wilt be married to an Iceland man, and ye will live long together; and from you will descend many men, brave, gallant and wise, and a well pleasing race of posterity. Ye shall go from Greenland to Norway, and from thence to Iceland, where ye shall dwell. And long will ye live together, but thou wilt survive him; and then thou shalt go abroad, and go southwards, and shall return to thy home in Iceland. And there must a church be built, and thou must remain there and be consecrated a nun, and there end thy days."[142] And then Thorstein sank backwards, and his corpse was put in order and carried to the ship. Thorstein the Goodman did all that he had promised. He sold in spring [A. D. 1006.] his land and cattle, and went with Gudrid and all her goods; made ready the ship, got men for it, and then went to Ericsfiord. The body was buried at the church.[143] Gudrid went to Leif's at Brattahlid, and Thorstein the Black took his abode in Ericsfiord, and dwelt there as long as he lived; and was reckoned an able man.

## VII. THORFINN KARLSEFNE'S EXPEDITION TO VINLAND.

This was in many respects the most important expedition to New England, both as regards the numbers engaged, and the information and experience derived. We have three different accounts of this expedition. The first is from the somewhat lengthy Saga of Thorfinn Karlsefne, from the Arnæ-Magnæan Collection; the second is from the Saga of Eric the Red, being called "The Account of Thorfinn:" while the third is a briefer relation from Codex Flatöiensis. The two first may be found in Rafn's Antiquitates Americanæ, pp. 75-200; while the last is also given in the same work, on pp. 55-64.

The Saga of Karlsefne is occupied largely at the beginning with accounts of various matters connected with social life; yet, as such subjects are not essential to the treatment of the subject, they are all omitted, except the account of Thorfinn's marriage with the widow of Thorstein Ericson.

The notes to the narrative of Leif's expedition, which precedes this in the chronological order, supersede the necessity of treating a number of important points suggested again in the present narrative.

It is believed that the principal manuscript of Thorstein Karlsefne is a genuine autograph by one of his descendants, the celebrated Hauk Erlander, the Governor or Lagman of Iceland, in 1295, who was also one of the compilers of the Landnama-bok. Erlander was the ninth in descent from Thorfinn. Torfæus, who supposed that this manuscript was lost, knew it only through corrupt extracts in the collection of Biörn Johnson.

There will be found a substantial agreement between the different accounts, notwithstanding they are not the work of eye witnesses. The differences are evidently such as would not appear in the case of three writers who had banded together for the purpose of carrying out a historical fraud. The Saga of Thorfinn was written in Iceland, while that of Eric was composed in Greenland. The account from the Flatö Manuscript, was, of course, written in the island which bears that name, and is extremely brief, wanting many essential particulars.

Narrative of Thorfinn Karlsefne

There was a man named Thord, who dwelt at Höfda, in Höfda-Strand. He married Fridgerda, daughter of Thorer the Idle, and of Fridgerda the daughter of Kiarval, King of the Irish. Thord was the son of Biarne Byrdusmjör,[144] son of Thorvald, son of Aslak, son of Biarne Ironsides, son of Ragnar Lodbrok. They had a son named Snorre, who married Thorhild the Partridge, daughter of Thord Geller. They had a son named Thord Horsehead. Thorfinn Karlsefne was his son, whose mother's name was Thoruna. Thorfinn occupied his time in merchant voyages, and was thought a good trader. One summer he fitted out his ship for a voyage to Greenland, attended by Snorre Thorbrandson of Alptafiord, and a crew of forty men. There was a man named Biarne Grimolfson of Breidafiord, and another named Thorhall Gamlason of Austfiord. The men fitted out a ship at the same time, to voyage to Greenland. They also had a crew of forty men. This ship, and that of Thorfinn, as soon as they were ready, put to sea. It is not said how long they were on the voyage; it is only told that both ships arrived at Ericsfiord in the autumn of that year. Leif[145] and other people rode down to the ships, and friendly exchanges were made. The captains requested Leif to take whatever he desired of their goods. Leif in return, entertained them well, and invited the principal men of both ships to spend the winter with him at Brattahlid. The merchants accepted his invitation with thanks. Afterwards their goods were moved to Brattahlid, where they had every entertainment that they could desire; therefore their winter quarters pleased them much. When the Yule feast began, Leif was silent and more depressed than usual. Then Karlsefne said to Leif: "Are you sick friend Leif? you do not seem to be in your usual spirits. You have entertained us most liberally, for which we desire to render you all the service in our power. Tell me what it is that ails you." "You have received what I have been able to offer you," said Leif, "in the kindest manner and there is no idea in my mind that you have been wanting in courtesy; but I am afraid lest when you go away, it may be said that you never saw a Yule[146] feast so meanly celebrated as that which draws near, at which you will be entertained by Leif of Brattahlid." "What shall never be the case, friend," said Karlsefne, "we have ample stores in the ship; take of these what you wish, and make a feast as splendid as you please." Leif accepted this offer, and the Yule began; and so well were Leif's plans made, that all were surprised that such a rich feast could be prepared in so poor a country. After the Yule feast, Karlsefne began to treat with Leif, as to the marriage of Gudrid,[147] Leif being the person to whom the right of betrothal belonged. Lief gave a favorable reply, and said she must fulfill that destiny which fate had assigned, and that he had heard of none except a good report of him; and in the end it turned out that Karlsefne married Gudrid, and their wedding was held at Brattahlid, this same winter.

[A. D. 1007.] The conversation often turned at Brattahlid, on the discovery of Vinland the Good, and they said that a voyage there had great hope of gain. And after this Karlsefne and Snorre made ready for going on a voyage there, the following spring. Biarne and Thorhall Gamlason, before mentioned, joined him with a ship. There was a man named Thorvard, who married Freydis, natural daughter of Eric Red, and he decided to go with them, as did also Thorvald, son[148] of Eric. And Thorhall, commonly called the Hunter, who had been the huntsman of Eric in the summer, and his steward in the winter, also went. This Thorhall was a man of immense size and of great strength, and dark complexion and taciturn, and when he spoke, it was always jestingly. He was always inclined to give Leif evil advice, and was an enemy of Christianity. He knew much about desert lands; and was in the same ship with Thorvord and Thorvald. These used the ship which brought Thorbiorn from Iceland. There were in all, forty men and a hundred.[149] They sailed to the West district [of Greenland], and thence to Biarney;[150] hence they sailed south a night and a day. Then land was seen, and they launched a boat and explored the land; they found great flat stones, many of which were twelve ells broad. There were a great number of foxes there. They called the land Helluland.[151] Then they sailed a day and a night in a southerly course, and came to a land covered with woods, in which there were many wild animals. Beyond this land to the southeast, lay an island on which they slew a bear. They called the island Bear island,[152] and the land, Markland. Thence they sailed south two days and came to a cape. The land lay on the right [starboard] side of the ship, and there were long shores of sand. They came to land, and found on the cape, the keel of a ship, from which they called the place Kiarlarness,[153] and the shores they also called Wonder-strand, because it seemed so long sailing by. Then the land became indented with coves, and they ran the ship into a bay,[154] whither they directed their course. King Olaf Tryggvesson had given Leif two Scots,[155] a man named Haki and a woman named Hekia; they were swifter of foot than wild animals. These were in Karlfsefne's ship. And when they had passed beyond Wonder-strand, they put these Scots ashore, and told them to run over the land to the southwest, three days, and discover the nature of the land, and then return. They had a kind of garment that they called kiafal, that was so made that a hat was on top, and it was open at the sides, and no arms; fastened between the legs with a button and strap, otherwise they were naked. When they returned, one had in his hand a bunch of grapes, and the other an ear of corn. They went on board, and afterwards the course was obstructed by another bay.[156] Beyond this bay was an island,[157] on each side of which was a rapid current, that they called the Isle of Currents.[158] There was so great a number of eider ducks[159] there, that they could hardly step without treading on their eggs. They called this place Stream Bay.[160] Here they brought their ships to land, and prepared to stay. They had with them all kinds of cattle. The situation of the place[161] was pleasant, but they did not care for anything, except to explore the land. Here they wintered without sufficient food. The next summer [A. D. 1008.] failing to catch fish, they began to want food. Then Thorhall the Hunter disappeared.

They found Thorhall, whom they sought three days, on the top of a rock, where he lay breathing, blowing through his nose and mouth, and muttering. They asked why he had gone there. He replied that this was nothing that concerned them.[162] They said that he should go home with them, which he did. Afterwards a whale was cast ashore[163] in that place; and they assembled and cut it up, not knowing what kind of a whale it was. They boiled it with water, and devoured it, and were taken sick. Then Thorhall said: "Now you see that Thor[164] is more prompt to give aid than your Christ. This was cast ashore as a reward for the hymn which I composed to my patron Thor, who rarely forsakes me." When they knew this, they cast all the remains of the whale into the sea, and commended their affairs to God. After which the air became milder, and opportunities were given for fishing; and from that time there was an abundance of food; and there were beasts on the land, eggs in the island, and fish in the sea.

They say that Thorhall desired to go northward around Wonder-strand to explore Vinland, but Karlsefne wished to go along the shore south. Then Thorhall prepared himself at the island, but did not have more than nine men in his whole company, and all the others went in the company of Karlsefne. When Thorhall was carrying water to his ship, he sang this verse:

> "People said when hither I
> Came, that I the best
> Drink would have, but the land
> It justly becomes me to blame;
> I, a warrior, am now obliged
> To bear the pail;
> Wine touches not my lips,
> But I bow down to the spring."

And when they had made ready and were about to sail, Thorhall sang:

"Let us return
Thither where [our] country-men rejoice,
Let the ship try
The smooth ways of the sea;
While the strong heroes
Live on Wonder-strand
And there boil whales
Which is an honor to the land."

Afterwards he sailed north to go around Wonder-strand and Kiarlarness, but when he wished to sail westward, they were met by a storm from the west and driven to Ireland, where they were beaten and made slaves. And, as merchants[165] reported, there Thorhall died.

It is said that Karlsefne, with Snorre and Biarne and his comrades, sailed along the coast south. They sailed long until they came to a river flowing out from the land through a lake into the sea, where there were sandy shoals, where it was impossible to pass up, except with the highest tide. Karlsefne sailed up to the mouth of the river with his folk, and called the place Hop.[166] Having come to the land, they saw that where the ground was low corn[167] grew, and where it was higher, vines were found. Every river was full of fish.

They dug pits where the land began, and where the land was highest; and when the tide went down, there were sacred fish[168] in the pits. There were a great number of all kinds of wild beasts in the woods. They stayed there half a month and enjoyed themselves, and did not notice anything; they had their cattle with them. And early one morning, when they looked around, they saw a great many skin boats, and poles were swung upon them, and it sounded like reeds shaken by the wind, and they pointed to the sun. Then said Karlsefne, "What may this mean?" Snorre Thorbrandson replied, "It may be that this is a sign of peace, so let us take a white shield and hold it towards them." They did so. Thereupon they rowed towards them, wondering at them, and came to land. These people were swarthy and fierce, and had bushy hair on their heads; they had very large eyes and broad cheeks. They stayed there for a time, and gazed upon those they met, and afterwards rowed away southward around the ness.

Karlsefne and his people had made their houses above the lake, and some of the houses were near the lake, and others more distant. They wintered there, and there was no snow, and all their cattle fed themselves on the grass.[169] But when spring came [A. D. 1009.] they saw one morning early, that a number of canoes rowed from the south round the ness; so many, as if the sea were sown with coal; poles were also swung on each boat. Karlsefne and his people then raised up the shield, and when they came together they began to trade; and these people would rather have red cloth; for this they offered skins and real furs. They would also buy swords and spears, but this, Karlsefne and Snorre forbade. For a whole fur skin, the Skrællings took a piece of red cloth, a span long, and bound it round their heads. Thus went on their traffic for a time; then the cloth began to be scarce with Karlsefne and his people, and they cut it up into small pieces, which were not wider than a finger's breath, and yet the Skrællings gave just as much as before, and more.

It happened that a bull, which Karlsefne had, ran out of the wood and roared aloud; this frightened the Skrællings, and they rushed to their canoes and rowed away toward the south; and after that they were not seen for three whole weeks. But at the end of that time, a great number of Skrælling's ships were seen coming from the south like a rushing torrent, all the poles turned from the sun, and they all yelled very loud. Then Karlsefne's people took a red[170] shield and held it towards them. The Skrællings leaped out of their vessels, and after this, they went against each other and fought. There was a hot shower of weapons, because the Skrællings had slings. Karlsefne's people saw that they raised up on a pole, a very large ball, something like a sheep's paunch, and of a blue color; this they swung from the pole over Karlsefne's men, upon the ground, and it made a great noise as it fell down.[171] This caused great fear with Karlsefne and his men, so that they only thought of running away, and they retreated along the river, for it seemed to them that the Skrællings pressed them on all sides; they did not stop until they came to some rocks, where they made a bold stand. Freydis came out and saw that Karlsefne's people fell back, and she cried out, "Why do you run, strong men as you are, before these miserable creatures, whom I thought you would knock down like cattle? And if I had arms, methinks I could fight better than any of you." They gave no heed to their words. Freydis would go with them, but she was slower, because she was pregnant; still she followed after them into the woods. She found a dead man in the woods; it was Thorbrand Snorreson, and there stood a flat stone stuck in his head; the sword lay naked by his side. This she took up, and made ready to defend herself. Then came the Skrællings toward her; she drew out her breasts from under her clothes, and dashed them against the naked sword;[172] by this the Skrællings became frightened and ran off to their ships, and rowed away. Karlsefne and his men then came up and praised her courage. Two men fell on Karlsefne's side, but a number of the Skrællings.

Karlsefne's band was overmatched. And now they went home to their dwellings and bound up their wounds; and considered what crowd that was that pressed upon them from the land side, and it now seemed to them that it could have hardly been real people from the ships, but that these must have been optical illusions. The Skrællings also found a dead man, and an axe lay by him; one of them took up the axe and cut wood with it; and then one after another did the same, and thought it was a fine thing and cut well. After that, one took it and cut at a stone, so that the axe broke, and then they thought that it was of no use, because it would not cut stone, and they cast it away.

Karlsefne and his people now thought that they saw, although the land had many good qualities, that they still would always be exposed there to the fear of attacks from the original dwellers.[173] They decided, therefore, to go away, and to return to their own land. They coasted northward along the shore,[174] and found five Skrællings clad in skins, sleeping near the sea. They had with them vessels containing animal marrow, mixed with blood.[175] Karlsefne's people thought that these men had been banished from the land; they killed them. After that they came to a ness, and many wild beasts were there, and the ness was covered all over with dung, from the beasts which had lain there during the night. Now they came back to Straumfiord, and there was a plenty of everything that they wanted to have. [It is thus that some men say, that Biarne and Gudrid stayed behind, and one hundred men with them, and did not go farther; but that Karlsefne and Snorre went southward, and forty men with them, and were not longer in Hop than barely two months, and the same summer came back.][176] Karlsefne then went with one ship to seek Thorhall the Hunter, but the rest remained behind, and they sailed northward past Kiarlarness, and thence westward, and the land was upon their larboard hand. There were wild woods over all, as far as they could see, and scarcely any open places. And when they had sailed long a river ran out of the land from east to west. They sailed into the mouth of the river, and lay by its banks.[177]

It chanced one morning that Karlsefne and his people saw opposite in an open place in the woods, a speck which glittered in their sight, and they called out towards it, and it was a Uniped,[178] which thereupon hurried down to the bank of the river, where they lay. Thorvald Ericson stood at the helm, and the Uniped shot an arrow into his bowels. Thorvald drew out the arrow and said: "It has killed me! To a rich land we have come, but hardly shall we enjoy any benefit from it." Thorvald soon after died[179] of his wound. Upon this the Uniped ran away to the northward; Karlsefne and his people went after him, and saw him now and then, and the last time they saw him, he ran out into a bay. Then they turned back, and a man sang these verses:

> The people chased
> A uniped
> Down to the beach.
> Behold he ran
> Straight over the sea—
> Hear thou, Thorfinn!

They drew off to the northward, and saw the country of the Unipeds; they would not then expose their men any longer. They looked upon the mountain range that was at Hop, and that which they now found,[180] as all one, and it also appeared to be of equal length from Straumfiord to both places. The third winter they were in Straumfiord. They now became much divided by party feeling, and the women were the cause of it, for those who were unmarried would injure those who were married, and hence arose great disturbance. There was born the first autumn, Snorre, Karlsefne's son, and he was three years old when they went away. When they sailed from Vinland they had a south wind, and then came to Markland, and found there, five Skrællings, and one was bearded; two were females, and two boys; they took the boys, but the others escaped, and the Skrællings sank down in the ground.[181] These boys they took with them; they taught them the language, and they were baptized. They called their mother Vathelldi, and their father, Uvæge. They said that two kings ruled over the Skrællings, and that one was named Avalldania, but the other Valldidia. They said that no houses were there; people lay in caves or in holes. They said there was a land on the other side, just opposite their country, where people lived who wore white clothes, and carried poles before them, and to these were fastened flags, and they shouted loud; and the people think that this was White-man's land, or Great Ireland.[182]

Biarne Grimolfson was driven with his ship into the Irish ocean, and they came into a worm sea,[183] and soon the ship began to sink under them. They had a boat which was smeared with sea oil, for the worms do not attack that. They went into the boat, and then saw that it could not hold them all. Then said Biarne: "As the boat will not hold more than half of our men, it is my counsel that lots should be drawn for those to go in the boat, for it shall not be according to rank." This, they all thought so generous an offer, that no one would oppose it. They then did so that lots were drawn, and it fell to Biarne to go in the boat, and the half of the men with him, for the boat had not room for more. But when they had gotten into the boat, an Icelandic man that was in the ship, and had come with Biarne from Iceland, said: "Dost thou mean, Biarne, to leave me here?" Biarne said: "So it seems." Then said the other: "Very different was the promise to my father, when I went with thee from Iceland, than thus to leave me, for thou said that we should both share the same fate." Biarne said, "It shall not be thus; go down into the boat, and I will go up into the ship, since I see that thou art so anxious to live."[184] Then Biarne went up into the ship, and this man down into the boat, and after that they went on their voyage, until they came to Dublin, in Ireland, and there told these things; but it is most people's belief that Biarne and his companions were lost in the worm sea, for nothing was heard of them after that time.

The Account of Thorfinn

That same winter [A. D. 1006-7.] there was much discussion about the affairs of Brattahlid; and they set up the game of chess, and sought amusement in the reciting of history,[185] and in many other things, and were able to pass life joyfully. And Karlsefne and Snorre resolved to seek Vinland, but there was much discussion about it. But it turned out that Karlsefne and Snorre prepared their ships to seek Vinland the following summer. [A. D. 1007.] And in this enterprise Biarne and Thorhall joined as comrades with their own ship and crew, who were their followers. There was a man named Thorvald, a relation[186] of Eric. Thorhall was called the Hunter; he long had hunted with Eric in summer, and had the care of many things. Thorhall was of great stature, large and swarthy face, of a hard nature, taciturn, saying little of affairs, and nevertheless crafty and malicious, always inclined to evil, and opposed in his mind to the Christian religion, from its first introduction into Greenland. Thorhall indulged in trifling, but nevertheless Eric was used to his familiarity. He went in the ship with Thorvald, and was well acquainted with uninhabitable places. He used the ship in which Thorbiorn came; and Karlsefne engaged comrades for the expedition; and the best part of the sailors of Greenland were with him. They carried in their ships, forty and a hundred men. Afterwards they sailed to West bygd and Biarney-isle. They sailed from Biarney-isle with a north wind, and were on the sea day and night, when they found land, and sending a boat to the shore, explored the land, where they found many flat stones of such great size, that they exceeded in length the size of two men. There were foxes there. And they gave the land a name, and called it Helluland. After this, they sailed a night and a day with a north wind. They came to a land in which were great woods and many animals. Southwest, opposite the land, lay an island. Here they found a bear, and called the island, Bear island. This land, where there were woods, they called Markland. After a voyage of a day and a night, they saw land, and they sailed near the land and saw that it was a cape; they kept close to the shore with the wind on the starboard side, and left the land upon the right side of the ship. There were places without harbors, long shores and sands. When they went to the shore with a boat, they found the keel of a ship, and they called the place, Kiarlarness;[187] and they gave the shore a name, and called it Wonder-strand, because they were so long going by. Then another bay extended into the land, and they steered into the bay.[188] When Leif was with King Olaf Tryggvesson, he sent him to establish the Christian religion in Greenland; then the king gave him two Scots-folk, a man named Hake, and a woman named Hekia. The king told Leif to take them with his men, if he would have his commands done quickly, as they were swifter than beasts. These folk, Leif and Eric gave to Karlsefne, as followers. When they were come opposite Wonder-strand, they put the Scots on the shore, and told them to run southward and explore the country, and return before the end of three days. They were thus clothed, having a garment called a Biafal;[189] it was made so that a hat was on top, open at the sides, without arms, buttoned between the legs, and fastened with a button and strap; and the rest was bare.

They came to anchor and lay by, until the three days passed, when they returned, one having in his hand a vine, and the other, self-sown wheat. Karlsefne said that they had found a fruitful land. Afterwards they were received into the ship, and they went on their way until a bay intersected the land. They steered the ship into the bay. On the outside was an island, and there was a great tide around the island. This they called, Straumey.[190] There was a great number of birds, and it was scarcely possible to find a place for their feet among the eggs. Then they steered into a long bay which they called Straumfiord, where they landed from their ships and began to prepare habitations. They brought with them all kinds of cattle, and they found sufficient pasturage. There were mountains, and the prospect was pleasant. But they cared for nothing, except to explore the land; there was a great abundance of grass. Here they wintered, and the winter was severe, and they did not have stores laid up, they began to be in want of food, and failed to catch fish. So they sailed over to the island,[191] hoping that they might find means of subsistence, either on what they could catch, or what was cast ashore. But they found but little better fare, though the cattle were better off. [A. D. 1008.] Afterwards they prayed to God, to send them food; which prayer was not answered as soon as desired. Then Thorhall disappeared, and a search was made, which lasted three days. On the morning of the fourth day, Karlsefne and Biarne found him lying on the top of a rock;

there he lay stretched out, with open eyes, blowing through his mouth, and muttering to himself. They asked him why he had gone there. He replied that it did not concern them and not to wonder, as he was old enough to take care of himself, without their troubling themselves with his affairs. They asked him to go home with them; this he did. After that a whale was cast up, and they ran down to cut it up; nevertheless they did not know what kind it was. Neither did Karlsefne, though acquainted with whales, know this one. Then the cooks dressed the whale, and they all ate of it, and it made them all sick. Then Thorhall said, "It is clear now that the Red-beard is more prompt to give aid than your Christ. This food is a reward for a hymn which I made to my god Thor, who has seldom deserted me." When they heard this, none would eat any more, and threw what was left from the rock, committing themselves to God. After this the opportunity was given of going after fish, and there was no lack of food. They sailed into Straumfiord, and had abundance of food and hunting on the mainland, with many eggs, and fish from the sea.

And now they began to consider where they should settle next. Thorhall the Hunter wished to go northward around Wonder-strand and Kiarlarness to explore Vinland, but Karlsefne wished to go southwest, thinking likely that there would be larger tracts of country the further they went south. Thorhall made ready at the island, and only nine men went with him, all the rest of the ship folk went with Karlsefne. One day Thorhall was carrying water to his ship; he drank it and sang this verse:

"People promised me when hither I
Came, then the best drink
I should have; but the country
I must denounce to all;
Here you are forced by hand
To bear the pail to the water,
I must bend me down to the spring;
Wine did not come to my lips."

Afterwards they left the land, and Karlsefne went with them to the island. Before they hoisted sail, Thorhall sang these verses:

"Let us return
Home to our countrymen,
Let the vessel try
The broad path of the sea;
While the persevering

Men, who praise the land  
Are building, and boil the whales  
Here on Wonder-strand."

Thereupon they sailed northward around Wonder-strand and Kialarness. But when they wished to cruise westward, a storm came against them, and drove them to Ireland, where they were beaten and made slaves. There Thorhall passed his life.[192]

Karlsefne, with Snorre and Biarne and the rest of his comrades, sailed south. They sailed long until they came to a river, which flowed from the land through a lake, and passed into the sea. Before the mouth of the river were great islands, and they were not able to enter the river except at the highest tide.[193] Karlsefne sailed into the mouth of the river, and called the land Hop. There they found fields, where the land was low, with wild corn, and where the land was high, were vines. And every river was full of fish. They made pits in the sand, where the tide rose highest, and at low tide, sacred fish were found in these pits, and in the woods was a great number of all kinds of beasts. Here they stayed half a month, enjoying themselves, but observing nothing new. Early one morning, on looking around, they saw nine skin boats, in which were poles that, vibrating towards the sun, gave out a sound like reeds shaken by the wind. Then Karlsefne said: "What, think you, does this mean?" Snorre said: "It is possible that it is a sign of peace; let us raise up a white shield and hold it towards them:" this they did. Then they rowed towards them, wondering at them, and came to land. These men were small of stature and fierce, having a bushy head of hair, and very great eyes and wide cheeks. They remained some time wondering at them, and afterwards rowed southward around the cape. They built dwellings beyond the lake, others made houses near the mainland, and others near the lake. Here they spent the winter. No snow fell,[194] and all their cattle fed under the open sky. They decided to explore all the mountains[195] that were in Hop; which done, they [A. D. 1009.] went and passed the third winter in Straum bay. At this time they had much contention among themselves, and the unmarried women vexed the married. The first autumn, Snorre, Karlsefne's son, was born, and he [was three years old] when they went away. They had a south wind, and came to Markland, and found five Skrællings, of whom one was a man, and two women, and two were boys. Karlsefne took the boys, and the others escaped and sank down into the earth. They carried the boys away with them, and taught them the language, and they were baptized. And the name of their mother was Vatheldi, and their father, Uvæge. They said that two kings ruled over the Skrællinger's land, one was named Avalldania, and the other, Valldidia; that they had no houses, but lived in dens and caves. In another part of the country, there was a region where the people wore white clothes, and shouted loud, and carried poles with flags. This they thought to be White-man's land. After this they came into Greenland, and passed the winter with Leif, son of Eric Red. Biarne Grimolfson was carried out into the Greenland[196] sea, and came into a worm sea, which they did not observe, until their ship was full of worm holes. They considered what should be done. They had a stern boat, smeared with oil; they say that wood covered with oil, the worms will not bore. The result of the council was, that as many should go into the boat as it would hold. It then appeared that the boat would not hold more than one-half of the men. Then Biarne ordered that the men should go in the boat by lot, and not according to rank. And as it would not hold all, they accepted the proposition, and when the lots were drawn, the men went out of the ship into the boat. And the lot was that Biarne should go down from the ship to the boat with one-half of the men. Then those to whom the lot fell, went down from the ship to the boat. And when they had come into the boat, a young Icelander, who was the companion of Biarne, said: "Now thus do you intend to leave me, Biarne?" Biarne replied, "That now seems necessary." He replied with these words: "Thou art not true to the promise made when I left my father's house in Iceland." Biarne replied: "In this thing I do not see any other way;" continuing, "What course can you suggest?" He said, "I see this, that we change places and thou come up here and I go there." Biarne replied: "Let it be so, since I see that you are so anxious to live, and are frightened by the prospect of death." Then they changed places, and he descended into the boat with the men, and Biarne went up into the ship. And it is related that Biarne, and the sailors with him in the ship, perished in the worm sea. Those who went in the boat, went on their course until they came to land, where they told all these things.

After the next summer, Karlsefne went to Iceland with his son Snorre, and he went to his own home at Reikianess. The daughter of Snorre, son of Karlsefne, was Hallfrida, mother to Bishop Thorlak Runolfson. They had a son named Thorbiorn, whose daughter was named Thoruna, mother of Bishop Biarne. Thorgeir was the name of the other son of Snorre Karlsefne's son, father to Ingveld, and mother of the first bishop of Brand. And this is the end of the history.

Third Narrative

That same summer came a ship from Norway to Greenland. The man was called Thorfinn Karlsefne, who steered the ship. He was a son of Thord Hesthöfde, a son of Snorre Thordarson, from Höfda. Thorfinn Karlsefne was a man of great wealth, and was in Brattahlid with Leif Ericsson. Soon he fell in love with Gudrid, and courted her, and she referred to Leif to answer for her. Afterwards she was betrothed to him, and their wedding was held the same winter. At this time, as before, much was spoken about a Vinland voyage; and both Gudrid and others persuaded Karlsefne much to that expedition. Now this expedition was resolved upon, and they got ready a crew of sixty men, and five women;[197] and then they made the agreement, Karlsefne and his people, that each of them should have equal share in what they made of gain. They had with them all kinds of cattle,[198] having the intention to settle in the land, if they could. Karlsefne asked Leif for his houses in Vinland, but he said he would lend them, but not give them. Then they put to sea with the ship, and came to Leif's houses[199] safe, and carried up their goods, They soon had in hand a great and good prize, for a whale had been driven on shore, both large and excellent.[200] They went to it and cut it up, and had no want of food. Their cattle went up into the land; but soon they were unruly, and gave trouble to them, They had one bull with them. Karlsefne let wood be felled and hewed for shipping it, and had it laid on a rock to dry. They had all the good of the products of the land, which were these: both grapes and wood, and other products. After that first winter, and when summer came, [A. D. 1008.] they were aware of Skrællings being there; and a great troop of men came out of the woods. The cattle were near to them, and the bull began to bellow and roar very loud, and with that the Skrællings were frightened, and made off with their bundles—and these were of furs and sables and all sorts of skins; and they turned and wanted to go into the houses, but Karlsefne defended the doors. Neither party understood the language of the other. Then the Skrællings took their bundles and opened them, and wanted to have weapons in exchange for them, but Karlsefne forbade his men to sell weapons. Then he adopted this plan with them, that he told the women to bear out milk and dairy products to them; and when they saw these things, they would buy them and nothing else. And now the trade for the Skrællings was such, that they carried away their winnings in their stomachs; and Karlsefne and his comrades got both their bags and skin goods, and so they went away. And now it is to be told, that Karlsefne let a good strong fence be made around the habitation, and strengthened it for defense. At this time, Gudrid,[201] Karlsefne's wife, lay in of a male child, and the child was called Snorre. In the beginning of the next winter, came the Skrællings again to them, and in much greater numbers than before, and with the same kind of wares. Then said Karlsefne to the women, "Now ye shall carry out the same kind of food as was best liked the last time, and nothing else." And when they saw that they threw their bundles in over the fence: and Gudrid sat in the door within, by the cradle of

Snorre, her son. Then came a shadow to the door, and a woman went in with a black kirtle on, rather short, with a snood around her head; clear, yellow hair; pale; with large eyes, so large that none ever saw such eyes in a human head. She went to where Gudrid was sitting, and said: "What art thou called?" "I am called Gudrid; and what art thou called?" "I am called Gudrid, said she." Then the goodwife, Gudrid, put out her hand to her, that she might sit down beside her. And at the same time Gudrid heard a great noise, and the woman had vanished;[202] and at the same time one of the Skrællings was killed by one of Karlsefne's house men, because he was about to take one of their weapons; and they made off as soon as possible, leaving behind them goods and clothes. No one had seen this woman but Gudrid. "Now," says Karlsefne, "we must be cautious, and take counsel; for I think they will come the third time with hostility and many people. We shall now take the plan, that ten men go out to the ness and show themselves there, and the rest of our men shall go into the woods and make a clearance for our cattle against the time the enemy comes out of the forest; and we shall take the bull before us, and let him go in front." And it happened so that at the place where they were to meet, there was a lake on the one side, and the forest on the other. The plan which Karlsefne had laid down, was adopted. The Skrællings came to the place where Karlsefne proposed to fight; and there was a battle there, and many of the Skrællings fell. There was one stout, handsome man among the Skrællings people, and Karlsefne thought that he must be their chief. One of the Skrællings had taken up an axe and looked at it awhile, and wielded it against one of his comrades and cut him down, so that he fell dead instantly. Then the stout man took the axe,[203] looked at it awhile, and threw it into the sea as far as he could. They then fled to the woods as fast as they could, and so ended the fight. Karlsefne stayed there with his men the whole winter; but towards spring he made known that he would not stay there any longer, and would return to Greenland.[204] Now they prepared for their voyage and took much goods from thence—vines, grapes and skin wares. They put to sea, and their ship came to Ericsfiord, and they there passed the winter.

The following summer,[205] [A. D. 1011.] Karlsefne went to Iceland and Gudrid with him, and he went home to Reikianess. His mother felt that he had made a poor match, and for this reason Gudrid was not at home the first winter. But when she saw that Gudrid was a noble woman, she went home, and they got on well together. Halfrid was the daughter of Snorre Karlsefnesson, mother to Bishop Thorlak Runolfson. Their son was named Thorbiorn, and his daughter, Thoruna, mother to Bishop Biorne. Thorgeir was the son of Snorre Karlsefnesson, father to Ingveld, mother of the first Bishop Brand. Snorre Karlsefnesson had a daughter, Steinun, who married

Einar, son of Grundarketil, son of Thorvald Krok, the son of Thorer, of Espihol; their son was Thorstein Rauglatr. He was father to Gudrun, who married Jorund of Keldum. Halla was their daughter, and she was mother to Flose, father of Valgerda, who was mother of Herr Erland Sterka, father of Herr Hauk, the Lagman.[206] Another daughter of Flose was Thordis, mother of Fru Ingigerd the Rich; her daughter was Fru Hallbera, Abbess of Stad, in Reikianess. Many other distinguished men in Iceland are the descendants of Karlsefne and Thurid, who are not here mentioned. God be with us. Amen.

## VIII. THE VOYAGE OF FREYDIS, HELGE AND FINBOGE.

This narrative is found in Antiquitates Americanæ, p. 65. It shows that history, among the Icelanders, was not made subservient to family interests. At the conclusion we have a (supplementary) notice of Thorfinn and Gudrid, after their return to Iceland.

Now the conversation began again to turn upon a Vinland voyage, as the expedition was both gainful and honorable. The same summer [A. D. 1010.] that Karlsefne returned from Vinland, a ship arrived in Greenland from Norway. Two brothers commanded the ship, Helge and Finboge; and they remained that winter in Greenland. The brothers were of Icelandic descent from Earlfiord. It is now to be told, that Freydis, Eric's daughter, came home from Garda,[207] and went to the abode of Finboge and Helge, and proposed to them that they should go to Vinland with their vessel, and have half with her of all the goods they could get there. They agreed to this. Then she went to the abode of her brother Leif, and asked him to give her the houses he had built in Vinland; and he answered as before, that he would lend, but not give the houses. It was agreed upon between the brothers and Freydis, that each should have thirty fighting men, besides women. But Freydis broke this, and had five men more, and concealed them; and the brothers knew nothing of it until they arrived in Vinland.[208] They went to sea, and had agreed beforehand to sail in company, if they could do so: and the difference was little, although the brothers came a little earlier, and had carried up their baggage to Leif's houses. And when Freydis came to the land, her people cleared the ship, and carried her baggage also up to the house. Then said Freydis: "Why are you carrying your things in here?" "Because we thought," said they, "that the whole of the agreement with us should be held." She said, "Leif lent the houses to me, not to you." Then said Helge, "In evil, we brothers cannot strive with thee:" and bore out their luggage and made a shed, and built it farther from the sea, on the borders of a lake,[209] and set all about it in order. Freydis let trees be cut down for her ship's cargo. Now winter set in, and the brothers proposed to have some games for amusement to pass the time. So it was done for a time, till discord came among them, and the games were given up, and none went from one house to the other; and things went on so during a great part of the winter. It happened one morning that Freydis got out of her berth, and put on her clothes, but not her shoes; and the weather was such that much dew had fallen. She took the cloak of her husband over her, and went out, and went to the house of the brothers, and to the door. A man had gone out a little before and left the door behind him, half shut. She opened the door, and stood in the doorway a little, and was silent. Finboge lay the farthest inside the hut, and was awake. He said: "What wilt thou have here, Freydis?" She said, "I want thee to get up and go out with me, for I would speak with thee." He did so: they went to a tree that was lying under the eaves of the hut, and sat down. "How dost thou like this place?" said she. He said, "The country, methinks, is good; but I do not like this quarrel that has arisen among us, for I think there is no cause for it." "Thou art right," says she, "and I think so too; and it is my errand to thy dwelling, that I want to buy the ship of your brothers, as your ship is larger than mine, and I would break up from hence." "I will let it be so," said he, "if that will please thee." Now they parted so, and she went home, and Finboge to his bed. She went up into her berth, and with her cold feet awakened Thorvard, who asked why she was so cold and wet. She answered with great warmth, "I went to these brothers," said she, "to treat about their ship, for I want a larger ship;[210] and they took it so ill, that they struck and abused me. And, thou, useless man! wilt neither avenge my affront, nor thy own; and now must I feel that I am away from Greenland, but I will separate[211] from thee if thou dost not avenge this." And now he could not bear her reproaches, and told his men to rise as fast as possible, and take their weapons. They did so, and went to the tents of the brothers, and went in as they lay asleep, and seized them all, bound them, and led them out bound, one after the other, and Freydis had each of them put to death, as he came out. Now all the men were killed; but the women were left, and nobody would kill them. Then said Freydis, "Give me an axe in my hand." This was done, and she turned on those five women, and did not give over until they were all dead. Now they returned to their own hut after this evil deed; and the people could only observe that Freydis thought she had done exceedingly well; and she said to her comrades, "If it be our lot to return to Greenland, I shall take the life of the man who speaks of this affair; and we shall say that we left them here when we went away." Now they got ready the ship early in spring [A. D. 1011.] which had belonged to the brothers, with all the goods they could get on, that the ship would carry, sailed out to sea, and had a good voyage; and the ship came early in the summer to Ericsfiord. Karlsefne was there still,[212] and had his ship ready for sea, but waited a wind; and it was a common saying that never a richer ship sailed from Greenland than that which he steered.

Freydis went home now to her house, which had stood without damage in the meanwhile. She bestowed many gifts on her followers, that they might conceal her wickedness; and she remained now on her farm. All were not so silent about their misdeeds and wickedness, that something did not come up about it. This came at last to the ears of Leif, her brother, and he thought this report was very bad. Leif took three men of Freydis's followers, and tortured them to speak, and they acknowledged the whole affair, and their tales agreed together. "I do not care," says Leif, "to treat my sister as she deserves; but this I will foretell them, that their posterity will never thrive." And it went so that nobody thought anything of them but evil, from that time.[213] Now we have to say that Karlsefne got ready his ship, and sailed out to sea.[214] He came on well, and reached Norway safely, and remained there all winter and sold his wares; and he, and his wife, were held in esteem by the best people in Norway. Now in the following spring, he fitted out his ship for Iceland, and when he was quite ready, and his ship lay outside the pier waiting a wind, there came to him a south-country man, from Bremen, in Saxon land, who would deal with him for his housebar.[215] "I will not sell it," said he. "I will give thee half a mark of gold for it," said the south-country man. Karlsefne thought it was a good offer, and sold it accordingly. The south-country man went away with his house-bar, and Karlsefne did not know what wood it was. It was massur-wood[216] from Vinland. Now Karlsefne put to sea, [A. D. 1012.] and his ship came to land north at Skagafiord,[217] and there he put up his vessel for winter. In spring he purchased Glambæirland,[218] where he took up his abode, and dwelt there as long as he lived, and was a man of great consideration; and many men are descended from him and his wife Gudrid, and it was a good family. When Karlsefne died, Gudrid took the management of his estates, and of Snorre her son, who was born in Vinland. And when Snorre was married, Gudrid went out of the country, and went to the south,[219] and came back again to Snorre's estate, and he had built a church at Glambæ. Afterwards Gudrid became a nun, and lived a hermit's life, and did so as long as she lived.[220] Snorre had a son called Thorgeir, who was father to Bishop Brand's mother, Ingveld. The daughter of Snorre Karlsefnesson was called Halfrid. She was mother of Runolf, the father of Bishop Thorlak. Karlsefne and Gudrid also had a son called Biörn. He was father of Thoruna, the mother of Bishop Biörn. Many people are descended from Karlsefne, and

194

his kin have been lucky; and Karlsefne has given the most particular accounts of all these travels, of which something is here related.

# Minor Narratives

I. ARE MARSON IN HVITRAMANNA-LAND.

This narrative is from the *Landnama-bok*, No. 107. Folio; collated with Hauksbok, Melabok and other manuscripts, in the Arnæ-Magnæan Collection.

It has frequently been observed that the Landnama-bok is of the highest authority; yet we must remember that it only proves the fact, that Rafn, the Limerick merchant, conveyed the narrative to Iceland from Ireland, where the circumstances were well known. The Landnama-bok, while it gives a tacit approval of the statements of the narrative, does not enter upon the question of the locality of the place to which Are Marson went. Therefore while we accept the narrative as genuine history, we should exercise due caution in determining the locality of Hvitramanna-land. Nothing is to be gained by making any forced deductions from the narrative; especially as the pre-Columbian discovery of America is abundantly proved, without the aid of this, or any other of the Minor Narratives.

Ulf the Squinter, son of Hogni the White, took the whole of Reikianess between Thorkafiord and Hafrafell; he married Biörg, daughter of Eyvind the Eastman,[221] sister to Helge the Lean. They had a son named Atli the Red, who married Thorbiorg, sister of Steinolf the Humble. Their son was named Mar of Holum, who married Thorkatla, daughter of Hergil Neprass. She had a son named Are, who [A. D. 928.] was driven by a storm to Whiteman's land,[222] which some call Ireland the Great, which lies in the Western ocean opposite Vinland, six[223] days sail west of Ireland. Are was not allowed to go away, and was baptized[224] there. This was first told by Rafn, the Limerick trader, who lived for a long time in Ireland. So also Thorkel, son of Geller, tells that certain Icelanders said, who heard Thorfinn, Earl of the Orkneys, say, that Are had been seen and known in White-man's land, and that, though not allowed to leave, he was held in much honor. Are had a wife named Thorgeir, daughter of Alf of Dolum. Their sons were Thorgils, Gudleif and Illuge, which is the family of Reikianess. Jorund was the son of Ulf the Squinter. He married Thorbiorg Knarrabringa. They had a daughter, Thorhild, whom Eric the Red married. They had a son, Leif the Fortunate of Greenland. Jorund was the name of the son of Atli the Red; he married Thordis, daughter of Thorgeir Suda; their daughter was Thorkatla, who married Thorgils Kollson. Jorund was also the father of Snorre.[225]

## II. BIÖRN ASBRANDSON.

This narrative is taken from Eyrbyggia Saga, which contains the early history of that part of Iceland lying around Snæfells, on the west coast. The Saga is not of a later date than the thirteenth century. It is given here, not because it applies largely to the question under consideration, the pre-Columbian discovery of America, but rather because it will make the reader fully acquainted with the hero, who afterwards appears.

Bork the Fat, and Thordis, daughter of Sur, had a daughter named Thurid, who married Thorbiörn the Fat, living on the estate of Froda. He was a son of Orne the Lean, who held and tilled the farm of Froda. Thorbiörn had before been married to Thurid, daughter of Asbrand, of Kamb, in Breidavik, and sister of Biörn Breidaviking the Athlete, soon to be mentioned in this Saga, and of Arnbiörn the Handy. The sons of Thorbiörn and Thurid, were Ketil the Champion, Gunnlaug and Hallstein.

Now this must be related of Snorre the Priest,[226] that he undertook the suit for the slaying of Thorbiörn, his kinsman. He also caused his sister to remove to his own home, at Helgefell, because it was reported that Biörn Asbrand, of Kamb, had come to pay her improper attention.

There was a man named Thorodd, of Medalfells Strand, an upright man and a good merchant. He owned a trading vessel in which he sailed to distant lands. Thorodd had sailed to the west,[227] to Dublin, on a trading voyage. At that time, Sigurd[228] Hlodverson, Earl of the Orkneys, had made an expedition towards the west, to the Hebrides and the Man, and had laid a tribute upon the habitable part of Man. Having settled the peace, he left men to collect the tribute; the earl himself returned to the Orkneys. Those who were left to collect the tribute, got all ready and set sail with a southwest wind. But after they had sailed some time, to the southeast and east, a great storm arose, which drove them to the northward as far as Ireland, and their vessel was cast away on a barren, uninhabited island. Just as they reached the island, Thorodd the Icelander came sailing by from Dublin. The shipwrecked men begged for aid. Thorodd put out a boat and went to them himself. When he reached them, the agents of Sigurd promised him money if he would carry them to their home in the Orkneys. When he told them that he could by no means do so, as he had made all ready to go back to Iceland, they begged the harder, believing that neither their money nor their liberty would be safe in Ireland or the Hebrides, whither they had just before been with a hostile army. At length Thorodd came to this, that he would sell them his ship's long-boat for a large sum of the tribute money; in this they reached the Orkneys, and Thorodd sailed to Iceland without a boat. Having reached the southern shores of the island, he laid his course along the coast to the westward, and entered Breidafiord, and came to the harbor at Dögurdarness. The same autumn he went to Helgefell to spend the winter with Snorre the Priest; and from that time he was called Thorodd the Tribute Taker. This took place just after the murder of Thorbiörn the Fat. During the same winter, Thurid, the sister of Snorre the Priest, who had been the wife of Thorbiörn the Fat, was at Helgefell. Thorodd made proposals of marriage to Snorre the Priest, with respect to Thurid. Being rich, and known by Snorre to be of good repute, and that he would be useful in supporting his administration of affairs, he consented. Therefore their marriage was celebrated during this winter, at Snorre's house, at Helgefell. In the following spring, Thorodd set himself up at Froda, and was thought an upright man. But when Thurid went to Froda, Biörn Asbrandson often paid her visits, and it was commonly reported that he had corrupted her chastity. Thorodd vainly tried to put an end to these visits. At that time Thorodd Wooden Clog lived at Arnahval. His sons, Ord and Val were men grown and youths of the greatest promise. The men blamed Thorodd for allowing himself to be insulted so greatly by Biörn, and offered him their aid, if desired, to end his coming. It chanced one time when Biörn came to Froda, that he sat with Thurid talking. It was Thorodd's custom when Biörn was there to sit in the house. But he was now nowhere to be seen. Then Thurid said, "Take care, Biörn, for I fear Thorodd means to put a stop to your visits here; I think he has secured the road, and means to attack you, and overpower you with unequal numbers." Biörn replied, "That is possible," and then sang these verses:

O Goddess[229] whom bracelet adorns,
This day (I linger
In my beloved's arms)
Stay longest in the heavens,
As we both must wish;
For I this night am drawn
To drink myself the parentals[230]
Of my oft-departing joys.

Having done this, Biörn took his weapons, and went to return home. As he went up the hill Digramula, five men jumped out upon him from their hiding place. These were Thorodd and two of his men, and the sons of Thoror Wooden Clog. They attacked Biörn, but he defended himself bravely and well. The sons of Thoror pressed him sharply, but he slew them both. Thorodd then fled with his men, though he himself had only a slight wound, and the others not any. Biörn went on until he reached home, and entered the house. The lady of the house[231] ordered a maid to place food before him. When the maid came into the room with the light, and saw Biörn wounded, she went and told Asbrand his father, that Biörn had returned, covered with blood. Asbrand came into the room, and inquired what was the cause of his wounds. He said, "Have you and Thorodd had a fight!" Biörn replied that it was so. Asbrand asked how the affair ended. Biörn replied with these verses:

Not so easy against a brave man
It is to fight;
(Wooden Clog's two sons
Now I have slain).
As for the ship's commander,
A woman to embrace,
Or for the cowardly,
A golden tribute to buy.[232]

Asbrand bound up his son's wounds, and his strength was soon restored. Thorodd went to Snorre the Priest, to talk with him about setting a suit on foot against Biörn, on account of the killing of Thoror's sons. This suit was laid in the court of Thorsnesthing. It was settled that Asbrand, who became surety for his son, should pay the usual fines. Biörn was exiled for three years,[233] and went abroad the same summer. During that summer, a son was born to Thurid, who was called Kiarten. He grew up at home, in Froda, and early gave great hope and promise.

When Biörn crossed the sea he came into Denmark, and went thence to Jomsberg. At that time, Palnatoki was captain of the Jomsberg[234] Vikings. Biörn was admitted into the crew, and won the name of the Athlete. He was at Jomsberg when Styrbiörn the Hardy, assaulted it. He went into Sweden, when the Jomsberg Vikings aided Styrbiörn;[235] he was in the battle of Tynsvall, in which Styrbiörn was killed, and escaped with the other Joms-vikings in the woods. While Palnatoki lived, Biörn remained with him, distinguished among all, as a man of remarkable courage.

The same summer [A. D. 996.] the brothers, Biörn and Arnbiörn returned into Iceland to Rönhavnsos. Biörn was always afterwards called the Athlete of Breidavik. Arnbiörn, who had gotten much wealth abroad, bought the Bakka estate in Raunhavn, the same summer. He lived there with little show or ostentation, and in most affairs was silent, but was, nevertheless, a man active in all things. Biörn, his brother, after his return from abroad, lived in splendor and elegance, for during his absence, he had truly adopted the manners of courtiers. He much excelled Arnbiörn in personal appearance, and was none the less active in execution. He was far more expert than his brother in martial exercises, having improved much abroad. The same summer after his return, there was a general meeting near Headbrink,[236] within the bay of Froda. All the merchants rode thither, clothed in colored garments, and there was a great assembly. Housewife Thurid, of Froda, was there, with whom Biörn began to talk; no one censuring, because they expected their conversation would be long, as they had not seen each other for a great while. On the same day there was a fight, and one of the Nordenfield men was mortally wounded, and was carried down under a bush on the beach; so much blood flowed out of the wound, that there was a large pool of blood in the bush. The boy Kiarten, Thurid of Froda's son, was there; he had a little axe in his hand, and ran to the bush and dipped the axe in the blood. When the Sondensfield's men rode from the beach south, Thord Blig asked Biörn how the conversation between him and Thurid of Froda, ended. Biörn said that he was well satisfied. Then Thord asked if he had seen the boy Kiarten, their and Thorodd's son. "I saw him," said Biörn: "What is your opinion of him?" asked Thord. Biörn answered with the following song:

"I saw a boy run
With fearful eyes,
The woman's image, to
The wolf's well[237] in the wood;
People will say,
That his true father [was]
He that ploughed the sea,
This the boy does not know."

Thord said: "What will Thorodd say when he hears that the boy belongs to you?" Then Biörn sung:

"Then will the noble born woman [make]
Thorodd's suspicion
Come true, when she gives me
The same kind of sons;
Always the slender,
Snow-white woman loved me,
I still to her
Am a lover."

Thord said, it will be best for you not to have anything to do with each other, and that you turn your thoughts. "It is certainly a good idea," said Biörn, "but it is far from my intention; though there is some difference when I have to do with such men as her brother Snorre." "You must take care of your own business," said Thord, and that ended their talk. Biörn afterwards went home to Kamb, and took the affairs of the family into his own hands, for his father was now dead. The following winter he determined to make a journey over the hills, to Thurid. Although Thorodd disliked this, he nevertheless saw that it was not easy to prevent its occurrence, since before he was defeated by him, and Biörn was much stronger, and more skilled in arms than before. Therefore he bribed Thorgrim Galdrakin to raise a snow storm against Biörn when he crossed the hills. When a day came, Biörn made a journey to Froda. When he proposed to return home, the sky was dark and the snow storm began. When he ascended the hills, the cold became intense, and the snow fell so thickly that he could not see his way. Soon the strength of the storm increased so much that he could hardly walk. His clothes, already wet through, froze around his body, and he wandered, he did not know where. In the course of the night he reached a cave, and in this cold house he passed the night. Then Biörn sung:

"Woman that bringest
Vestments,[238] would
Not like my
Dwelling in such a storm
If she knew that
He who before steered ships,
Now in the rock cave
Lay stiff and cold."

Again he sang:

"The cold field of the swans,
From the east with loaded ship I ploughed,
Because the woman inspired me with love;
I know that I have great trouble suffered,
And now, for a time, the hero is,
Not in a woman's bed, but in a cave."

Biörn stayed three days in the cave, before the storm subsided; and on the fourth day he came home from the mountain to Kamb. He was very weary. The domestic asked him where he was during the storm. Biörn sung:

"My deeds under
Styrbiörn's proud banner are known.
It came about that steel-clad Eric
Slew men in battle;
Now I on the wide heath,
Lost my way [and],
Could not in the witch-strong
Storm, find the road."[239]

Biörn passed the rest of the winter at home; the following spring his brother Arnbiörn fixed his abode in Bakka, in Raunhafn, but Biörn lived at Kamb, and had a grand house....

This same summer, Thorodd the Tribute Taker invited Snorre the Priest, his kinsman, to a feast at his house in Froda. Snorre went there with twenty men. In the course of the feast, Thorodd told Snorre how much he was hurt and disgraced by the visits of Biörn Asbrandson, to Thurid, his wife, Snorre's sister, saying that it was right for Snorre to do away with this scandal. Snorre after passing some days feasting with Thorodd went home with many presents. Then Snorre the Priest rode over the hills and spread the report that he was going down to his ship in the bay of Raunhafn. This happened in summer, in the time of haymaking. When he had gone as far south as the Kambian hills, Snorre said: "Now let us ride back from the hills to Kamb; let it be known to you," he added, "what I wish to do. I have resolved to attack and destroy Biörn. But I am not willing to attack and destroy him in his house, for it is a strong one, and Biörn is stout and active, while our number is small. Even those who with greater numbers, have attacked brave men in their houses, have fared badly; an example of which you know in the case of Gissur the White; who, when with eighty men, they attacked Gunnar[240] of Lithend, alone in his house, many were wounded and many were killed, and they would have been compelled to give up the attack, if Geir the Priest had not learned that Gunnar was short of arrows. Therefore," said he, "as we may expect to find Biörn out of doors, it being the time of haymaking, I appoint you my kinsman, Mar, to give him the first wound; but I would have you know this, that there is no room for child's play, and you must expect a contest with a hungry wolf, unless your first wound shall be his death blow." As they rode from the hills towards his homestead, they saw Biörn in the fields; he was making a sledge,[241] and no one was near him. He had no weapon but a small axe, and a large knife in his hand of a span's length, which he used to round the holes in the sledge. Biörn saw Snorre riding down from the hills, and recognized them. Snorre the Priest had on a blue cloak, and rode first. The idea suddenly occurred to Biörn, that he ought to take his knife and go as fast as he could to meet them, and as soon as he reached them, lay hold of the sleeve of Snorre with one hand, and hold the knife in the other, so that he might be able to pierce Snorre to the heart, if he saw that his own safety required it. Going to meet them, Biörn gave them hail; and Snorre returned the salute. The hands of Mar fell, for he saw that if he attacked Biörn, the latter would at once kill Snorre. Then Biörn walked along with Snorre and his comrades, asked what was the news, keeping his hands as at first. Then he said: "I will not try to conceal, neighbor Snorre, that my present attitude and look seem threatening to you, which might appear wrong, but for that I have understood that your coming is hostile. Now I desire that if you have any business to transact with me, you will take another course than the one you intended, and that you will transact it openly. If none, I will that you make peace, which when done, I will return to my work, as I do not wish to be led about like a fool." Snorre replied: "Our meeting has so turned out that we shall at this time part in the same peace as before; but I desire to get a pledge from you, that from this time you will leave off visiting Thurid, because if you go on in this, there can never be any real friendship between us." Biörn replied: "This I will promise, and will keep it; but I do not know how I shall be able to keep it, so long as Thurid and I live in the same land." "There is nothing so great binding you here," said Snorre, "as to keep you from going to some other land." "What you now say is true," replied Biörn, "and so let it be, and let our meeting end with this pledge, that neither you nor Thorodd shall have any trouble from my visits to Thurid, in the next year." With this they parted. Snorre the Priest rode down to his ship, and then went home to Helgefell. The day after, Biörn rode south to Raunhafn, and engaged his passage in a ship for the same summer. [A. D. 999.] When all was ready they set sail with a northeast wind which blew during the greater part of that summer. Nothing was heard of the fate of the ship for a very long time.[242]

### III. GUDLEIF GUDLAUGSON.

This narrative, which shows what became of Biörn Asbrandson, whose adventures are partially related in the previous sketch, is from the Eyrbyggia Saga. Notwithstanding the somewhat romantic character of these two narratives, there can be no doubt but that they are true histories. Yet that they relate to events in America, is not altogether so certain.

There was a man named Gudleif, the son of Gudlaug the Rich, of Straumfiord and brother of Thorfinn, from whom the Sturlingers are descended. Gudleif was a great merchant. He had a trading vessel, and Thorolf Eyrar Loptson had another, when they fought with Gyrid, son of Sigvald Earl. Gyrid lost an eye in that fight. It took place near the end of the reign of King Olaf the Saint, that Gudleif went on a trading voyage to the west to Dublin. On his return to Iceland, sailing from the west of Ireland, he met with northeast winds, and was driven far into the ocean west, and southwest, so that no land was seen, the summer being now nearly gone. Many prayers were offered that they might escape from the sea. At length they saw land. It was of great extent, but they did not know what land it was. They took counsel and resolved to make for the land, thinking it unwise to contend with the violence of the sea. They found a good harbor, and soon after they went ashore, a number of men came down to them. They did not recognize the people, but thought that their language resembled the Irish.[243] In a short time such a number of men had gathered around them as numbered many hundred. These attacked them and bound them all and drove them inland. Afterwards they were brought before an assembly, and it was considered what should be done with them. They thought that some wished to kill and that others were for dividing them among the villages as slaves. While this was going on, they saw a great number of men riding[244] towards them with a banner conspicuously lifted up, whence they inferred that some great man was among them. And when the company drew near, they saw a man riding under the banner, tall and with a martial air, aged and grayhaired. All present treated this man with the utmost honor and deference. They soon saw that their case was referred to the decision of this man. He commanded Gudleif and his comrades to be brought before him, and coming into his presence he addressed them in the Northern tongue, and asked from what land they came. They replied that the chief part were Icelanders. The man asked which of them were Icelanders. Gudleif declared himself to be an Icelander, and saluted the old man, which he received kindly, and asked what part of Iceland he came from. He replied that he came from the district some called Bogafiord. He asked who lived in Bogafiord, to which Gudleif replied at some length. Afterwards this man inquired particularly about all the principal men of Bogafiord and Breidafiord; and of these he inquired with special interest into everything relating to Snorre the Priest, and of his sister Thurid, of Froda, and for the great Kiarten, her son. In the meanwhile the natives grew impatient about the disposition of the sailors. Afterwards the great man left him and took twelve of the natives apart, and conferred with them. Afterwards he returned. Then the old man spoke to Gudleif and his comrades, and said: "We have had some debate concerning you, and the people have left the matter to my decision; I now permit you to go where you will, and although summer is nearly gone, I advise you to leave at once; for these people are of bad faith, and hard to deal with, and now think they have been deprived of their right." Then Gudleif asked, "Who shall we say, if we reach our own country again, to have given us our liberty?" He replied: "That, I will not tell you, for I am not willing that any of my friends or kindred should come here, and meet with such a fate as you would have met, but for me. Age now comes on so fast, that I may almost expect any hour to be my last. Though I may live some time longer, there are other men of greater influence than myself, though now at some distance from this place, and these would not grant safety or peace to any strange men." Then he looked to the fitting out of their ship, and stayed at this place until a fair wind sprang up, so that they might leave the port. Before they went away, this man took a gold ring from his hand and gave it to Gudleif, and also a good sword. Then he said to Gudleif: "If fortune permits you to reach Iceland, give this sword to Kiarten, hero of Froda, and this ring to Thurid, his mother." Gudleif asked, "Who shall I say was the sender of this valuable gift?" He replied: "Say that he sent it who loved the lady of Froda, better than her brother, the Priest of Helgafell. And if any man desires to know who sent this valuable gift, repeat my words, that I forbid any one to seek me, for it is a dangerous voyage, unless others should meet with the same fortune as you. This region is large, but has few good ports, and danger threatens strangers on all sides from the people, unless it shall fall to others as yourselves." After this they separated. Gudleif, with his comrades, went to sea, and reached Ireland the same autumn, and passed the winter in Dublin. The next spring they sailed to Iceland, and Gudleif delivered the jewel into the hand of Thurid. It was commonly believed that there was no doubt but that the man seen, was Biörn Breidaviking Kappa. And there is no other reliable report to prove this.

## IV. ALLUSIONS TO VOYAGES FOUND IN ANCIENT MANUSCRIPTS.

Professor Rafn, in Antiquitates Americanæ, gives brief notices of numerous Icelandic voyages to America, and other lands at the west, of which there is now no record. The works in which they are found are of the highest respectability. It is only necessary here to give the facts, which have been collected with much care. They show that the pre-Columbian discovery of America has tinged nearly the whole body of Icelandic history, in which the subject is referred to, not as a matter of doubt, but as something perfectly well known. All these revelations combine to furnish indisputable proof of the positions maintained in this work, showing as they do, beyond all reasonable question, that the impression which so generally prevailed in regard to the discovery of this land, was not the result of a literary fraud. Some of the facts are given below:

1121. Eric, Bishop of Greenland,[245] went to search out Vinland.
Bishop Eric Upse sought Vinland.
1285. A new land is discovered west from Iceland.
New land is found....[246]
Adalbrand and Thorvald, the sons of Helge, found the new land.
Adalbrand and Thorvald found new land west of Iceland.
The Feather[247] Islands are discovered.
1288. Rolf is sent by King Eric to search out the new land, and called on people of Iceland to go with him.
1289. King Eric sends Rolf to Iceland to seek out the new land.
1290. Rolf traveled through Iceland, and called out men for a voyage to the new land.[248]
1295. Landa-Rolf died.
1357. There came thirteen large ships to Iceland. Eindridesuden was wrecked in East Borgafiord, near Langeness. The crew and the greater part of the cargo was saved. Bessalangen was wrecked outside of Sida. Of its crew, Haldor Magre and Gunthorm Stale, and nineteen men altogether, were drowned. The cargo suffered also. There were also six ships driven back. There came likewise a ship from Greenland,[249] smaller than the smallest of Iceland ships, that came in the outer bay. It had lost its anchor. There were seventeen men on board, who had gone to Markland,[250] and on their return were drifted here. But here altogether that winter, were eighteen large ships, besides the two that were wrecked in the summer.

There came a ship from Greenland that had sailed to Markland, and there were eight men on board.

V. GEOGRAPHICAL FRAGMENTS.

The first of these documents is from a work which professes to give a description of the earth in the middle age. From this it appears that the Icelanders had a correct idea of the location of Vinland in New England, though they did not comprehend the fact that they had discovered a new Continent. The document may be found in Antiquitates Americanæ, p. 283. In the appendix of that work may be seen a fac simile of the original manuscript. The second document is from (Antiquitates Americanæ, p. 292). It was found originally in the miscellaneous collection called the Gripla.

The earth is said to be divided into three parts. One of these is called Asia, and extends from northeast to southwest, and occupies the middle of the earth. In the eastern part are three separate regions, called Indialand. In the farthest India, the Apostle Bartholomew preached the faith; and where he likewise gave up his life (for the name of Christ). In the nearest India, the Apostle Thomas preached, and there also he suffered death for the cause of God. In that part of the earth called Asia, is the city of Nineveh, greatest of all cities. It is three days' journey in length and one day's journey in breadth. There is also the city of Babylon, ancient and very large. There King Nebuchadnezzar formerly reigned, but now that city is so thoroughly destroyed that it is not inhabited by men, on account of serpents and all manner of noxious creatures. In Asia is Jerusalem, and also Antioch; in this city Peter the Apostle founded an Episcopal seat, and where he, the first of all men, sang Mass. Asia Minor is a region of Great Asia. There the Apostle John preached, and there also, in the city Ephesus, is his tomb. They say that four rivers flow out of Paradise. One is called Pison or Ganges; this empties into the sea surrounding the world. Pison rises under a mountain called Orcobares. The second river flowing from Paradise, is called Tigris, and the third, Euphrates. Both empty into the Mediterranean (sea), near Antioch. The Nile, also called Geon, is the fourth river that runs from Paradise. It separates Asia from Africa, and flows through the whole of Egypt. In Egypt is New Babylon (Cairo), and the city called Alexandria. The second part of the earth is called Africa, which extends from the southwest to the northwest. There are Serkland, and three regions called Blaland (land of blackmen or negroes). The Mediterranean sea divides Europe from Africa. Europe is the third part of the earth, extended from west and northwest to the northeast. In the east of Europe is the kingdom of Russia. There are Holmgard, Palteskia and Smalenskia. South of Russia lies the kingdom of Greece. Of this kingdom, the chief city is Constantinople, which our people call Miklagard. In Miklagard is a church, which the people call St. Sophia, but the Northmen call it, Ægisif. This church exceeds all the other churches in the world, both as respects its structure and size. Bulgaria and a great many islands, called the Greek islands, belong to the kingdom of Greece. Crete and Cyprus are the most noted of the Greek islands. Sicily is a great kingdom in that part of the earth called Europe. Italy is a country south of the great ridge of mountains, called by us Mundia [Alps]. In the remotest part of Italy is Apulia, called by the Northmen, Pulsland. In the middle of Italy is Rome. In the north of Italy is Lombardy, which we call Lombardland. North of the mountains on the east, is Germany, and on the southwest is France. Hispania, which we call Spainland, is a great kingdom that extends south to the Mediterranean, between Lombardy and France. The Rhine is a great river that runs north from Mundia, between Germany and France. Near the outlets of the Rhine is Friesland, northward from the sea. North of Germany is Denmark. The ocean runs into the Baltic sea, near Denmark. Sweden lies east of Denmark, and Norway at the north. North of Norway is Finnmark. The coast bends thence to the northeast, and then towards the east, until it reaches Permia, which is tributary to Russia. From Permia, desert tracts extend to the north, reaching as far as Greenland. Beyond Greenland, southward, is Helluland; beyond that is Markland; from thence it is not far to Vinland, which some men are of the opinion, extends to Africa.[251] England and Scotland are one island; but each is a separate kingdom. Ireland is a great island. Iceland is also a great island north of Ireland. All these countries are situated in that part of the world called Europe. Next to Denmark is Lesser Sweden; then is Oeland, then Gottland, then Helsingeland, then Vermeland, and the two Kvendlands, which lie north of Biarmeland. From Biarmeland stretches desert land towards the north, until Greenland begins. South of Greenland is Helluland; next is Markland, from thence it is not far to Vinland the Good, which some think goes out to Africa; and if this is so, the sea must extend between Vinland and Markland. It is told that Thorfinn Karlsefne cut wood here to ornament his house,[252] went afterwards to seek out Vinland the Good, and came there where they thought the land was, but did not reach it, and got none of the wealth of the land.[253] Leif the Lucky first discovered Vinland, and then he met some merchants in distress at sea, and by God's grace, saved their lives; and he introduced Christianity into Greenland, and it flourished so there that an Episcopal seat was set up in the place, called Gardar. England and Scotland are an island, and yet each is a separate kingdom. Ireland is a great island. These countries are all in that part of the world called Europe.

Bavaria is bounded by Saxony; Saxony is bounded by Holstein, and next is Denmark. The sea runs between the eastern countries. Sweden is east of Denmark. Norway is to the north; Finmark is east of Norway; from thence the land extends to the northeast and east, until you come to Biarmeland; this land is under tribute to Gardaridge. From Biarmeland lie desert places all northward to the land which is called Greenland, [which, however, the Greenlanders do not affirm, but believe to have seen it otherwise, both from drift timber, that is known and cut down by men, and also from reindeer which have marks upon their ears, or bands upon their horns, likewise from sheep which stray here, of which there are some remaining in Norway, for one head hangs in Throndheim, and another in Bergen, and many others are to be found.][254] But there are bays, and the land stretches out towards the southwest; there are ice mountains, and bays, and islands lie out in front of the ice mountains; one of the ice mountains cannot be explored, and the other is half a month's sail, to the third, a week's sail. This is nearest to the settlement called Hvidserk. Thence the land trends north; but he who desires to go by the settlement, steers to the southwest. Gardar, the bishop's seat, is at the bottom of Ericsfiord; there is a church consecrated to holy Nicholas. There are twelve churches in the eastern settlement, and four in the western.

Now it should be told what is opposite Greenland, out from the bay, which was before named. Furdustrandur[255] is the name of the land; the cold is so severe that it is not habitable, so far as is known. South from thence is Helluland, which is called Skrællings land. Thence it is not far to Vinland the Good, which some think goes out to Africa.[256] Between Vinland and Greenland, is Ginnungagah, which runs from the sea called Mare Oceanum, and surrounds the whole earth.

FOOTNOTES:

[1] See Jones on The Tyrian Period of America.
[2] Var. Hist., lib. iii, cap. xviii.
[3] See Plato's Critias and Timæas.
[4] De Mundo, cap. iii. See Prince Henry the Navigator, chap. vii, by Major: London, 1868.
[5] Odyssey, book iv, l. 765.
[6] See Prince Henry the Navigator, p. 90.
[7] Strobo. lib. iii.—Plutarch.
[8] Pliny's Natural History, lib. vi, cap. 37.
[9] See p. 137.
[10] Prince Henry the Navigator, p. 137.
[11] After this mention by Pliny, the Canaries, or Fortunate Isles, are lost sight of for a period of thirteen hundred years. In the reign of Edward III of England, at the beginning of the fourteenth century, one Robert Machin sailed from Bristol for France, carrying away a lady of rank, who had eloped with him, and was driven by a storm to the Canaries, where he landed, and thus rediscovered the lost Fortunate Isles. This fact is curiously established by Major, in the Life of Prince Henry, so that it can no longer be regarded as an idle tale (see pp. 66-77). In 1341, a voyage was also made to the Canaries, under the auspices of King Henry of Portugal. The report, so widely circulated by De Barros, that the islands were rediscovered by Prince Henry is therefore incorrect. His expedition reached Porto Santo and Madeira in 1418-20.
[12] He also speculates upon the probability of this continent having been visited by Christian missionaries. See vol. vi, p. 410.

[13] Kingsborough's Mexican Antiquities, vol. vi, p. 285.

[14] Ibid., p. 332.

[15] Monastikon Britannicum, pp. 131-2-187-8. The fact that the word America is here used, seems quite sufficient to upset the legend.

[16] The Irish were early known as Scots, and O'Halloran derives the name from Scota, high priest of Phœnius, and ancestor of Mileseuis.

Me quoque vicins pereuntem gentibus, inquit,
Munivit Stilicho. Totam cum Scotus Iernem,
Movit et infesto spumavit remige Thetys.
By him defended, when the neighboring hosts
Of warlike nations spread along our coasts;
When Scots came thundering from the Irish shores,
And the wide ocean foamed with hostile oars.

[17] Speaking of Britain and Ireland, Tacitus says of the latter, that "the approaches and harbors are better known, by reason of commerce and the merchants."—Vit. Agri., c. 24. The Irish, doubtless, mingled with the Carthagenians in mercantile transactions, and from them they not unlikely received the rites of Druidism.

[18] As the tradition of a Welch voyage to America under Prince Madoc, relates to a period following the Icelandic voyages, the author does not deem it necessary to discuss the subject. This voyage by the son of Owen Gwyneth, is fixed for the year 1170, and is based on a Welch chronicle of no authority. See Hackluyt, vol. iii, p. 1.

[19] Turkish Spy, vol. viii, p. 159.

[20] See "Northmen in Iceland," Socièta des Antiquaires du Nord, Seance du 14 Mai, 1859, pp. 12-14.

[21] It is sometimes, though improperly, called the Norse.

[22] In the time when the Irish monks occupied the island, it is said that it was "covered with woods between the mountains and the shores."

[23] Setstakkar. These were wooden pillars carved with images usually of Thor and Odin. In selecting a place for a settlement these were flung overboard, and wherever they were thrown up on the beach, there the settlement was to be formed. Ingolf, the first Norse settler of Iceland, lost sight of the seat-posts after they were thrown into the water, and was obliged to live for the space of three years at Ingolfshofdi. In another case a settler did not find his posts for twelve years, nevertheless he changed his abode then. In Frithiof's Saga (American edition) chap. iii, p. 18, we find the following allusion:

"Through the whole length of the hall shone forth the table of oak wood,
Brighter than steel, and polished; the pillars twain of the high seats

Stood on each side thereof; two gods deep carved out of elm wood:
Odin with glance of a king, and Frey with the sun on his forhead."

[24] Ari Hinn Frode, or the Wise. The chief compiler of the famous Landnama Book, which contains a full account of all the early settlers in Iceland. It is of the same character, though vastly superior to the English Doomsday Book, and is probably the most complete record of the kind ever made by any nation.

It contains the names of 3000 persons, and 1,400 places. It gives a correct account of the genealogies of the families, and brief notices of personal achievements. It was begun by Frode (born 1067, died 1148), and was continued by Kalstegg, Styrmer and Thordsen, and completed by Hauk Erlandson, Lagman, or Governor of Iceland, who died in the year 1334.

[25] "Thus saith the holy priest Bede.... Therefore learned men think that it is Iceland which is called Thule.... But the holy priest Bede died dccxxxv. years after the birth of our Lord Jesus Christ, more than a hundred years before Iceland was inhabited by the Northmen."—Antiquitates Americanæ, p. 202. This extract is followed by the statement of Ari Frode, and shows that the Irish Christians retired to Iceland at a very early day. The Irish monk Dicuil also refers to this solitary island, which, about the year 795, was visited by some monks with whom he had conversed.

[26] All the information which we possess relating to the discovery by Gunnbiorn is given in the body of this work, in extracts from Landanamabok.

[27] Claudius Christophessen, the author of some Danish verses relating to the history of Greenland, supposes that Greenland was discovered in the year 770, though he gave no real reason for his belief. M. Peyrere also tells us of a Papal Bull, issued in 835, by Gregory IV, which refers to the conversion of the Icelanders and Greenlanders. Yet this is beyond question fraud. Gunnbiorn was undoubtedly the first to gain a glimpse of Greenland.

[28] The Northmen reckoned by winters.

[29] See the Saga of Eric the Red.

[30] The statement, found in several places, that he discovered Vinland while on his way to Greenland, is incorrect. The full account of his voyages shows that his Vinland voyage was an entirely separate thing.

[31] The author designs shortly to give some full account of the early Christianity on the Western Continent in a separate work, now well advanced towards completion. It will include both the Pre and Post-Columbian eras.

[32] Gissur the White and Hialte, went on the same errand to Iceland in the year 1000, when the new religion was formally adopted at the public Thnig.

[33] It will be seen hereafter that he went and established himself in Vinland.

[34] See Memoires des Antiquaires du Nord, p. 383.

[35] The location of Gardar is now uncertain. At one time it was supposed to have been situated on the eastern coast; but since it became so clear that the east coast was never inhabited, that view has been abandoned, though the name appears in old maps.

[36] See Crantz's Greenland, vol. i, p. 252.

[37] These inscriptions are all in fair runic letters, about which there can be no mistake, and are totally unlike the imaginary runes, among which we may finally feel obliged to class those of the Dighton rock.

[38] See Egede's Greenland, p. xxv; Crantz's Greenland, vol. i, pp. 247-8; Purchas, His Pilgrimes, vol. iii, p. 518; Antiquitates Americanæ, p. 300.

[39] Antiquitates Americanæ, p. xxxix.

[40] For the account of the manuscripts upon which our knowledge of Greenland is founded, see Antiquitates Americanæ, p. 255.

[41] In that year parties are known to have contracted marriage at Gardar, from whom Finn Magnussen and other distinguished men owe their descent.

[42] Egede's Greenland, p. xlvii.

[43] Ibid., xlviii.

[44] Crantz's Greenland, vol. i, p. 264.

[45] Crantz's Greenland, p. 274.

[46] Ibid., p. 279.

[47] Hans Egede was a clergyman in priest's orders, and minister of the congregation at Vogen in the northern part of Norway, where he was highly esteemed and beloved. He spent fifteen years as a missionary in Greenland, and died at Copenhagen, 1758.

[48] The motto on the sword of Roger Guiscard was: "Appulus et Calaber Siculus mihi Servit et Afer."

[49] See Laing's Heimskringla, vol. ii, p. 450. This refers to his swimming match with Kiarten the Icelander, in which the king was beaten.

[50] See Saga of Saint (not king) Olaf.

[51] Des Antiquaires du Nord, 1859.

[52] Ledehammer. The point of land near the house of Lede, just below Drontheim.

[53] Laing's Heimskringla, vol. I, p. 457. It is related that while they were planking the ship, "it happened that Thorberg had to go home to his farm upon some urgent business; and as he stayed there a long time, the ship was planked upon both sides when he came back. In the evening the king went out and Thorberg with him, to see how the ship looked, and all said

that never was seen so large and fine a ship of war. Then the king went back to the town. Early the next morning the king came back again to the ship, and Thorberg with him. The carpenters were there before them, but all were standing idle with their hands across. The king asked, 'What is the matter?' They said the ship was ruined; for somebody had gone from stem to stern, and cut one deep notch after another down the one side of the planking. When the king came nearer he saw that it was so, and said with an oath, 'The man shall die who has thus ruined the ship out of malice, if he can be found, and I will give a great reward to him who finds him out.' 'I can tell you, king,' says Thorberg, 'who has done this piece of work.' 'I don't think that any one is so likely to find it out as thou art.' Thorberg says: 'I will tell you, king, who did it, I did it myself.' The king says, 'Thou must restore it all to the same condition as before, or thy life shall pay for it.' Then Thorberg went and chipped the planks until the deep notches were all smoothed and made even with the rest; and the king and all present declared that the ship was much handsomer on the side of the hull which Thorberg had chipped, and bade him shape the other side in the same way and gave him great thanks for the improvement."

[54] A few years ago two very ancient vessels which probably belonged to the seventh century were exhumed on the coast of Denmark, seven thousand feet from the sea, where they were scuttled and sunk. The changes in the coast finally left them imbedded in the sand. One vessel was seventy-two feet long, and nine feet wide amid ships. The other was forty-two feet long, and contained two eight-sided spars, twenty-four feet long. The bottoms were covered with mats of withes for the purpose of keeping them dry. Among the contents was a Damascened sword, with runes, showing that the letter existed among the Northmen in the seventh century.

[55] The people of Iceland were always noted for their superiority in this respect over their kinsmen in Denmark and Norway. There is one significant fact bearing on this point, which is this: that, while a few of the people of Iceland went at an early period to engage in piratical excursions with the vikings of Norway, not a single pirate ship ever sailed from Iceland. Such ways were condemned altogether at an early day, while various European nations continued to sanction piracy down to recent periods. Again it should be remembered that in Iceland duelling was also solemnly declared illegal as early as 1011, and in Norway the following year; while in England it did not cease to be a part of the judicial process until 1818. See Sir Edmund Head's Viga-Glum Saga, p. 120.

[56] Those who imagine that these manuscripts, while of pre-Columbian origin, have been tampered with and interpolated, show that they have not the faintest conception of the state of the question. The accounts of

the voyages of the Northmen to America form the framework of Sagas which would actually be destroyed by the elimination of the narratives. There is only one question to be decided, and that is the date of these compositions.

[57] The fact that Mr. Bancroft has in times past expressed opinions in opposition to this view will hardly have weight with those persons familiar with the subject. When that writer composed the first chapter of his History of the United States, he might have been excused for setting down the Icelandic narratives as shadowy fables; but, with all the knowledge shed upon the subject at present, we have a right to look for something better. It is therefore unsatisfactory to find him perpetuating his early views in each successive edition of the work, which show the same knowledge of the subject betrayed at the beginning. He tells us that these voyages "rest on narratives mythological in form, and obscure in meaning," which certainly cannot be the case. Furthermore they are "not contemporary;" which is true, even with regard to Mr. Bancroft's own work. Again, "The chief document is an interpolation in the history of Sturleson." This cannot be true in the sense intended, for Mr. Bancroft conveys the idea that the principal narrative first appeared in Sturleson's history when published at a late day. It is indeed well known that one version, but not the principal version, was interpolated in Peringskiold's edition of Sturleson's Heimskringla, printed at Copenhagen. But Bancroft teaches that these relations are of a modern date, while it is well known that they were taken verbatim from Codex Flatöiensis, finished in the year 1395. He is much mistaken in supposing that the northern Antiquarians think any more highly of the narratives in question, because they once happened to be printed in connection with Sturleson's great work. He tells us that Sturleson "could hardly have neglected the discovery of a continent," if such an event had taken place. But this, it should be remembered, depends upon whether or not the discovery was considered of any particular importance. This does not appear to have been the case. The fact is nowhere dwelt upon for the purpose of exalting the actors. Besides, as Laing well observes, the discovery of land at the west had nothing to do with his subject, which was the history of the kings of Norway. The discovery of America gave rise to a little traffic, and nothing more. Moreover the kings of Norway took no part, were not the patrons of the navigators, and had no influence whatever in instituting a single voyage. Mr. Bancroft's last objection is that Vinland, the place discovered, "has been sought in all directions from Greenland and the St. Lawrence to Africa." This paragraph also conveys a false view of the subject, since the location of Vinland was as well known to the Northmen as the situation of Ireland, with which island they had uninterrupted communication. It is to be earnestly hoped that in the

next edition, Mr. Bancroft may be persuaded to revise his unfounded opinions.

Washington Irving has expressed the same doubt in his Life of Columbus, written before the means of examining this question were placed within his reach, and in the appendix of his work he mixes the idle tales of St. Brandan's Isle with the authentic histories of the Northmen. A very limited inquiry would have led him to a different estimate.

[58] The word rune comes from ryn, a furrow. Odin has the credit of the invention, yet they are probably of Phenician origin. They were sometimes used for poetical purposes. Halmund, in the Grettir Saga (see Sabing Baring Gould's Iceland), says to his daughter: "Thou shalt now listen whilst I relate my deeds, and sing thereof a song, which thou shalt afterwards cut upon a staff." This indicates the training the memory must have undergone among the Northmen.

[59] For a list of many Icelandic works, see the Introduction of Laing's Heimskringla.

[60] See Sir Edmund Head's Viga Glum Saga, pp. viii and ix.

[61] Ibid. Of course there was more or less poetry, yet poetry is something that is early developed among the rudest nations, while good prose tells that a people have become highly advanced in mental culture.

[62] As early as 1411, there was a considerable trade between Bristol and Iceland, and Columbus visited Iceland in the spring of the year 1477, where he might have met Magnus Eyolfson, the bishop of Skalholt, or learned from some other scholar the facts in relation to the early Icelandic discoveries. Though Rafn supposes that by his visit, his opinions, previously formed regarding the existence of the Western continent, were confirmed, this is not altogether clear, for the reason that Columbus was not seeking a new continent, but a route to the Indies, which he believed he should find by sailing west. Accordingly when he found land he called it the West Indies, supposing that he had reached the extreme boundary of the East Indies. Irving tells us that Columbus founded his theory on (1), the nature of things; (2), the authority of learned writers; (3), the reports of navigators.

[63] Adam of Bremen even heard of the exploits of the Northmen in Vinland, and made mention of that country. But as it might be said that his work did not appear until after the voyage of Columbus, and that the reference may be an interpolation, the author does not rest anything upon it. Still he unquestionably knew of the voyages of the Northmen, as he lived near the time they were made, and wrote his ecclesiastical history in about the year 1075, after he had made a visit to King Sweno of Denmark, and had accumulated much material. The passage in question is as follows: "Besides, it was stated [by the king] that a region had been discovered by many in that

[the western] ocean, which was called Winland, because vines grow there spontaneously, making excellent wine; for that fruits, not planted, grow there of their own accord, we know not by false rumor, but by the certain testimony of the Danes."

The very ancient Faroese ballad of Finn the Handsome (see Rafn's Antiquitates Americanæ, p. 319), also contains references to Vinland, which indicates that the country was known as well by the Irish as by the Icelanders.

[64] History of New England, vol. ii, p. 53.

[65] The liability of the best historians to fail into error, is illustrated by Paley, who shows the serious blunders in the accounts of the Marquis of Argyle's death, in the reign of Charles II: "Lord Clarendon relates that he was condemned to be hanged, which was performed the same day; on the contrary, Burnet, Woodrow, Heath, Echard concur in stating that he was beheaded, and that he was condemned upon Saturday and executed on Monday."—Evidences of Christianity, part iii, chap. i. So Mr. Bancroft found it impossible to give with any accuracy the location of the French colony of St. Savion, established on the coast of Maine, by Saussaye, in 1613. Bancroft tells us that it was on the north bank of the Penobscot, while it is perfectly well known that it was located on the island of Mount Desert, a long way off in the Atlantic Ocean.

[66] Dighton Rock known as the Writing Rock, is situated six and a half miles south of Taunton, Mass., on the east side of Taunton river, formed by Assonnet Neck. It lies in the edge of the river, and is left dry at low water. It is a boulder of fire graywack, twelve feet long and five feet high, and faces the bed of the river. Its front is now covered with chiseled inscriptions of what appear to be letters and outlines of men, animals and birds. As early as the year 1680, Dr. Danforth secured a drawing of the upper portion; Cotton Mather made a full copy in 1712; and in 1788, Professor Winthrop, of Harvard College, took a full-sized impression on prepared paper. Various other copies have been made at different times, all of which present substantially the same features. Yet in the interpretation of the inscription there has been little agreement. The old rock is a riddle, dumb as the Sphinx. A copy of the inscription was shown to a Mohawk chief, who decided that it was nothing less than the representation of a triumph by Indians over a wild beast which took place on this spot. Mr. Schoolcraft also showed a copy to Chingwank, an Algonquin well versed in picture-writing, who gave a similar interpretation. The Roman characters in the central part of the composition he was finally induced to reject, as having no connection with the rest. And whoever compares this inscription with those of undeniably Indian origin found elsewhere, cannot fail to be impressed with the similari-

ty. Nevertheless, members of the Royal Society of Antiquarians, to whose notice it was brought by the Rhode Island Historical Society, felt strongly persuaded that the rock bears evidence of the Northman's visit to these shores. Mr. Laing, the accomplished translator of the Heimskringla, in discussing the theories in regard to the inscription, says, that the only real resemblance to letters is found in the middle of the stone, in which antiquarians discover the name of Thorfinn, that is, Thorfinn Karlsefne, the leader of the expedition which came to New England in 1007. Just over these letters is a character supposed to be Roman also, which may signify NA, or MA, the letter A being formed by the last branch of M. Now MA in Icelandic is used as an abbreviation of Madr, which signifies the original settler of a country. Close to these two letters are several numerals, construed to mean one hundred and fifty-one. And according to the account of the voyage, Thorfinn lost nine of the hundred and sixty men with whom it is presumed he started, and therefore one hundred and fifty-one would exactly express the number with him at the time he is supposed to have cut the inscription. This, then, would mean altogether, that Thorfinn Karlsefne established himself here with one hundred and fifty-one men. Yet, as the testimony of this rock is not needed, we may readily forego any advantage that can be derived from its study. Besides, the history of similar cases should serve to temper our zeal. In the time of Saxo Grammatticus (1160), there was a stone at Hoby, near Runamoe, in the Swedish province of Bleking, which was supposed to be sculptured with runes. At a late day copies were furnished the antiquarians, who came to the conclusion, as Laing tells us, that it was a genuine inscription, referring to the battle of Braaville, fought in the year 680. It afterwards turned out that the apparent inscription was made by the disintegration of veins of a soft material existing in the rock. Yet the Dighton inscription is beyond question the work of man. Mr. A. E. Kendal, writing in 1807, says that there was a tradition that Assonnet Neck, on which tongue of land the rock is situated, was once a place of banishment among the Indians. He states, further, that the Indians had a tradition to the effect, that in ancient times some white men in a bird landed there and were slaughtered by the aborigines. They also said thunder and lightening issued from the bird, which fact indicates that this event, if it occurred at all, must be referred to the age of gunpowder. Mr. Kendal mentions the story of a ship's anchor having been found there at an early day. In former years the rock was frequently dug under by the people, in the hope of finding concealed treasures. It is said that a small rock once existed near by which also bore marks of human hands. The Portsmouth and Tiverton Rocks, described by Mr. Webb (Antiquitates Americanæ, pp. 355-71), are doubtless Indian inscriptions; while that on the island of Monhegan, off the coast of Maine, may perhaps be classed with the rock of Hoby. Yet after all, it is possible that the central portion of the inscription on the Dighton Rock, may be the work of the Northmen. That two distinct parties were concerned in making the inscription is clear from the testimony of the Indians, who did not pretend to understand the portion thought to refer to Karlsefne. For the full discussion, see Antiquitates Americanæ, p. 378, et seq.

[67] Memoirs des Antiquaires du Nord, 1839-9, p. 377.

[68] The Old Mill at Newport stands on an eminence in the centre of the town, being about twenty-four feet high, and twenty-three feet in diameter. It rests upon eight piers and arches. It has four small windows, and, high up the wall, above the arches, was a small fire place. It is first distinctly mentioned in the will of Governor Benedict Arnold, of Newport, where it is called, "my stone-built wind mill." It is known that during the eighteenth century it served both as a mill and powder house. Edward Pelham, who married Governor Arnold's granddaughter, in 1740 also called it "an old stone mill." Peter Easton, who early went to live in Newport, wrote in 1663, that "this year we built the first windmill;" and August 28, 1675, he says, "A storm blew down our windmill." What Easton relates occurred before Governor Arnold writes about his stone windmill, and it is not unreasonable to suppose that when the one spoken of by Easton was destroyed he built something more substantial. Yet we cannot say that this was actually the case. The old tower existing at the beginning of the settlement may have been adapted by him for the purposes of a mill, when the one mentioned by Easton was destroyed.

The family of the Governor is said to have come from Warwickshire, England, and one of his farms was called the Leamington farm, as is supposed, from the place by that name near Warwick. In addition to this, in the Chesterton Parish, three miles from Leamington, there is an old windmill similar in construction to that at Newport. It is supposed that it was erected on pillars for pneumatic reasons, and also that carts might thus go underneath and be loaded and unloaded with greater ease. And it has been suggested, that if Gov. Arnold came from Warwickshire, of which the proof is not given, and if the Chesterton Mill was standing at the time of his departure for New England, he might have built a mill at Newport after the same model. Yet this is something we know little about. And whence came the Chesterton Mill itself? There was a tradition that it was built after a design by Inigo Jones, but this is only a tradition. That structure also might have belonged to the class of Round Towers in Ireland, of which one at least was built by Northmen. All is therefore, in a measure, doubtful. It will hardly help the Northmen to class this Newport relic with their works. See Palfrey's New England, vol. i, pp. 57-9.

[69] Many have supposed that the skeleton in armor, dug up near Fall River, was a relic of the Northmen, and one of those men killed by the natives in the battle with Karlsefne. But it would be far more reasonable to look for traces of the Northmen among the Indians of Gaspe, who, at an early day, were distinguished for an unusual degree of civilization. Malte Brun tells us that they worshiped the sun, knew the points of the compass, observed the position of some of the stars, and traced maps of their country. Before the French missionaries went among them they worshiped the figure of the Cross, and had a tradition that a venerable person once visited them, and during an epidemic cured many by the use of that symbol. See Malte Brun's Geography (English edition), vol. v, p. 135. Malte Brun's authority is Father Leclerc's Nouvelle Relation de la Gaspesie, Paris, 1672.

[70] The Landnama-bok. This is probably the most complete record of the kind ever made by any nation. It is of the same general character as the English Doomsday Book, but vastly superior in interest and value. It contains the names of three thousand persons and one thousand four hundred places. It gives a correct account of genealogies of the first settlers, with brief notices of their achievements. It was commenced by the celebrated Frode, the Wise, who was born 1067, and died 1148, and was continued by Kalstegg, Styrmer and Thordsen, and completed by Hauk Erlendson, Lagman, or Governor of Iceland, who died in the year 1334.

[71] Gunnbiorn appears to have been a Northman who settled in Iceland at an early day. Nothing more is known of him.

[72] Torfæus says that these rocks lie six sea miles out from Geirfuglesker, out from Reikiavek, and twelve miles south of Garde in Greenland, yet they cannot now be found. It is not too much to suppose that they have been sunk by some of those fearful convulsions which have taken place in Iceland; yet it is quite as reasonable to conclude that these rocks were located elsewhere, probably nearer the east coast, which was formerly more accessible than now. In the version of the Account of Greenland, by Ivar Bardason (see Antiquitates Americanæ, p. 301), given from a Faroese Manuscript, and curiously preserved by Purchas, His Pilgrimage, vol. iii, p. 518, we read as follows:

"Item, men shall know, that, between Island and Greenland, lyeth a Risse called Gornbornse-Skare. There were they wont to haue their passage for Gronland. But as they report there is Ice upon the same Risse, come out of the Long North Bottome, so that we cannot use the same old Passage as they thinke."

[73] Torfæus says (Greenlandia, p. 73), that "Eric the Red first lived in Greenland, but it was discovered by the man called Gunnbiorn. After him Gunnbiorn's Rocks are called."

[74] The translation is literal or nearly so, and the sense is obscure.

[75] This shows that others had been there before. They were doubtless Icelanders who were sailing to Greenland. The place of concealment appears to have been an excavation covered with stone or wood. That the people were sometimes accustomed to hide money in this way, is evident. We read in the Saga of Eric the Red, that this person at first intended to go with his son, Leif, on his voyage to discover the land seen by Heriulf, and which Leif named Vinland. On his way to the ship, Eric's horse stumbled, and he fell to the ground seriously injured, and was obliged to abandon the voyage. He accepted this as a judgment for having, as one preparation for his absence, buried his money, where his wife, Thorhild, would not be able to find it.

[76] This is believed to have been about February, which affords one of many indications that the climate of that region has become more rigorous than formerly. The fact that water did not freeze, indicates mild weather, which we might infer from the rigging of their vessels, and the preparation for sea. In regard to the term Goe, Grönland's Historiske Mindesmærker (vol. i, p. 7), says: "This name was before used in Denmark, which Etatsraad Werlauf has discovered on the inscription of a Danish Rune-Stone."

[77] The facts that they engaged in hunting, and that they built a cabin to live in, might at first lead some to suppose that the place contained a forest or more or less trees, to supply wood. Yet this does not follow, as drift wood might supply all their wants for building purposes, where they could not obtain or use stone. Regarding drift wood, Crantz says, in speaking of Greenland: "For as He has denied this frigid, rocky region the growth of trees, He has bid the storms of the ocean to convey to its shores a great deal of wood, which accordingly comes floating thither, part without ice, but the most part along with it, and lodges itself between the islands. Were it not for this, we Europeans should have no wood to burn there.... Among this wood are great trees torn up by the roots, which by driving up and down for many years, and dashing and rubbing on the ice, are quite bare of branches. A small part of this drift wood are willows, alder and birch trees, which come out of the bays in the south; also large trunks of aspen trees, ... but the greatest part is pine and fir. We find also, a good deal of a sort of wood, finely veined, and with few branches; this, I fancy, is larchwood.... There is also a solid, reddish wood of a more agreeable fragrancy than the common fir, with visible cross veins, which I take to be the same species as the beautiful silver firs, or zirbel, that have the smell of cedar, and grow on the high Grison hills, and the Switzers wainscot their rooms with them."—History of Greenland, vol. i, p. 37.

[78] If any confirmation were needed of the truth of this narrative, or of the killing of Snæbiorn and Thorod, we might look for it in the equally well

known fact, that after the return of the voyagers to Iceland, the death of these two men was fearfully revenged by their friends.

[79] In the southwest of Norway.

[80] See Colonization of Iceland, in the Introduction.

[81] See notes to Introduction.

[82] It is now impossible to identify these localities. The old view, that what is called the East-bygd, or District, was on the eastern coast of Greenland, is now abandoned. It is probable that no settlement was ever effected on the east coast, though once it was evidently more approachable than now. See Graah's Expedition.

[83] As we certainly know that Christianity was established in Iceland in the year A. D. 1000, the final settlement of Eric and his followers must have taken place during the year assigned, viz: 985.

[84] See Antiquitates Americanæ, p. 15, note a.

[85] Evidently an error. See Antiquitates Americanæ, p. 15, note 3.

[86] This king propagated Christianity by physical force, and marked the course of his missionary tours with fire and blood; which might have been expected from a barbarian just converted from the worship of Odin and Thor.

[87] These thralls were slaves, though slavery in Iceland assumed peculiar features. The following from the Saga of Gisli the Outlaw, shows the relation that slaves held to freemen. We read, that on one occasion, Gisli had borrowed a famous sword of Koll, and the latter asked to have it back, but Gisli in reply asks if he will sell it, receiving a negative reply. Then he says: "I will give thee thy freedom and goods, so that thou mayest fare whither thou wilt with other men." This is also declined, when Gisli continues: "Then I will give thee thy freedom, and lease, or give thee land, and besides I will give thee sheep, and cattle and goods, as much as thou needest." This he also declines, and Kol, when Gisli asks him to name a price, offering any sum of money, besides his freedom, and "a becoming match, if thou hast a liking for any one." But Kol refused to sell it at any price, which refusal led to a fight, and in the first onset, the slave's axe sank into Gisli's brain, while the disputed sword, Graysteel, clove the thick skull of Kol. See the Saga of Gisli the Outlaw, p, 6, Edinburgh, 1866. Also the Saga of Eric Red, where Thorbiorn thinks it an indignity that Einar should ask for the hand of his daughter in marriage, Einar being the son of a slave.

[88] Original settler or freeholder, whose name and possessions were recorded in the Landnama-bok.

[89] This poem no longer exists. Its subject, the Hafgerdingar, is described as a fearful body of water, "which sometimes rises in the sea near Greenland in such a way that three large rows of waves inclose a part of the

sea, so that the ship that finds itself inside, is in the greatest danger."—Grönland's Historiske Mindismærker, vol. i, p. 264. There does not appear to be any better foundation for this motion of the Hafgerdingar than of the old accounts of the Maelstrom, once supposed to exist on the coast of Norway. The Hafgardingar may have originated from seeing the powerful effect of a cross sea acting on the tide.

[90] To this translation may be added another in metre, by Beamish:
O thou who triest holy men!
Now guide me on my way;
Lord of the earth's wide vault, extend
Thy gracious hand to me.
This appears to be the earliest Christian prayer thus far found in connection with this period of American history.

[91] Æyrar. This is not the name of a place—for Heriulf dwelt in Iceland at a place called Dropstock—but of a natural feature of ground; eyri, still called an ayre in the Orkney islands, being a flat, sandy tongue of land, suitable for landing and drawing up boats upon. All ancient dwellings in those islands, and probably in Iceland also, are situated so as to have the advantage of this kind of natural wharf, and the spit of land called an ayre, very often has a small lake or pond inside of it, which shelters boats.—Laing.

[92] The details of this voyage are very simple, yet whoever throws aside his old time prejudices, and considers the whole subject with the care which it deserves, cannot otherwise than feel persuaded that Biarne was driven upon this Continent, and that the land seen was the coast of that great territory which stretches between Massachusetts and Newfoundland, for there is no other land to answer the description. Of course, no particular merit can be claimed for this discovery. It was also accidental, something like the discovery of America by Columbus, who, in looking for the East Indies, stumbled upon a new world. Yet Biarne's discovery soon led to substantial results.

[93] Considerable has been said at various times in opposition to these accounts, because cattle and sheep, and sometimes horses, are mentioned in connection with Greenland. Some have supposed that, for these reasons, the Saga must be incorrect. Yet, in more modern times, there has been nothing to prevent the people from keeping such animals, though it has been found better to substitute dogs for horses. Crantz says, that in "the year 1759, one of our missionaries brought three sheep with him from Denmark to New Herrnhuth. These have so increased by bringing some two, some three lambs a year, that they have been able to kill some every year since, to send some to Lichtenfels, for a beginning there, and, after all, to winter ten at pre-

sent. We may judge how vastly sweet and nutritive the grass is here, from the following tokens: that tho' three lambs come from one ewe, they are larger, even in autumn, than a sheep of a year old in Germany." He says that in the summer they could pasture two hundred sheep around New Herrnhuth; and that they formerly kept cows, but that it proved too much trouble.—History of Greenland, vol. i, p. 74.

[94] He must have gone over to Greenland from Norway then, as in the year 1000, he returned and introduced Christianity into Greenland. The language used is indefinite.

[95] One recension of the Saga of Eric the Red, states that he went with Leif on his voyage to Vinland. Finn Magnusen says that the error arose from a change of one letter in a pair of short words. See Grönland's Historiske Mindesmærker, vol. i, p. 471.

[96] Horses could be kept in Greenland now, only with much expense. It appears that anciently it was not so. Undoubtedly there has been more or less of change in climate. Geologists find evidence that at one period, a highly tropical climate must have existed in the northern regions.

[97] Superstition was the bane of the Northman's life. He was also a firm believer in Fate. The doctrines of Fate held the finest Northern minds in a vice-like grasp, so that in many cases their lives were continually overshadowed by a great sorrow. One of the saddest illustrations of this belief, may be found in the Saga of Grettir the Strong (given in Baring-Gould's work on Iceland), a Saga in which the doctrine appears with a power that is well nigh appalling.

[98] Some suppose that he was a German, others claim that he was a Turk, as his name might indicate.

[99] Snowy mountains, Jöklar miklir, such as Chappell mentions having been seen on the coast, June 14, 1818.

[100] Helluland, from Hella, a flat stone, an abundance of which may be found in Labrador and the region round about.

[101] This agrees with the general features of the country. The North American Pilot describes the land around Halifax, as "low in general, and not visible twenty miles off; except from the quarter-deck of a seventy-four. Apostogon hills have a long, level appearance, between Cape Le Have and Port Medway, the coast to the seaward being level and low, and the shores with white rocks and low, barren points; from thence to Shelburne and Port Roseway, are woods. Near Port Haldiman are several barren places, and thence to Cape Sable, which makes the southwest point into Barrington Bay, a low and woody island."—Antiquitates Americanæ, p. 423.

[102] Markland is supposed, with great reason, to be Nova Scotia, so well described, both in the Saga, and in the Coast Pilot. Markland means

woodland. Two days sail thence, brought them in view of Cape Cod, though very likely the sailing time is not correct.

[103] This island has given the interpreters considerable trouble, from the fact that it is said to lie to the northward of the land. And Professor Rafn, in order to identify this island with Nantucket, shows that the north point of the Icelandic compass lay towards the east. But this does not fairly meet the case. There would, perhaps, have been no difficulty in the interpretation, if the Northern Antiquarians had been acquainted with the fact, that in early times an island existed northward from Nantucket, on the opposite coast of Cape Cod. This island, together with a large point of land which now has also disappeared, existed in the times of Gosnold, who sailed around Cape Cod, in 1602. The position of this island, together with the point of land, is delineated in the map given in the Appendix. At one time, some doubt existed in regard to the truthfulness of the accounts, for the reason that those portions of land described, no longer existed. Yet their positions were laid down with scientific accuracy; the outer portion of the island being called Point Care, while the other point was called Point Gilbert. Neither Archer nor Brereton in their accounts of Gosnold's voyage, give the name of the island; but Captain John Smith, in 1614, calls it "Isle Nawset." Smith's History of Virginia, vol. ii, p. 183. This island was of the drift formation, and as late as half a century ago, a portion of it still remained, being called Slut Bush. The subject has been very carefully gone into by Mr. Otis, in his pamphlet on the Discovery of an Ancient Ship on Cape Cod. Professor Agassiz, writing December 17, 1863, says: "Surprising and perhaps incredible as the statements of Mr. Amos Otis may appear, they are nevertheless the direct and natural inference of the observations which may be easily made along the eastern coast of Cape Cod. Having of late felt a special interest in the geological structure of that remarkable region, I have repeatedly visited it during the past summer, and, in company with Mr. Otis, examined, on one occasion, with the most minute care, the evidence of the former existence of Isle Nauset and Point Gilbert. I found it as satisfactory as any geological evidence can be. Besides its scientific interest," he adds, "this result has some historical importance. At all events it fully vindicates Archer's account of the aspect of Cape Cod, at the time of its discovery in 1602, and shows him to have been a truthful and accurate observer." But possibly the vindication may extend back even to the Northmen, whom the learned professor and his colaborers did not have in mind; especially as this discovery will help very materially to explain their descriptions. Now, in the first account of Thorfinn Karlsefne's passage around this part of the Vinland, it is said that they called the shore Wonder-strand, "because they were so long going by," Yet any one in sailing past the coast to-day will not be struck with its

length. But by glancing at the reconstructed map of Cape Cod (see Appendix), the reader will find that the coast line is greatly increased, so that in order to pass around the cape, the navigator must sail a long distance; and, comparing this distance travelled with the distance actually gained, the Northmen might well grow weary, and call it Wonder-strand. This quite relieves the difficulty that was felt by Professor Rafn, who labored to show that the island in question was Nantucket, notwithstanding the fact that it lay too far east. For a fuller knowledge of Isle Nauset, see New England Historic and Genealogical Register, vol. xviii, p. 37; and Massachusetts Historical Collections, vol. viii, series iii, pp. 72-93.

[104] In speaking of the immediate vicinity of Wonder-strand, the second account of Thorfinn's expedition says, "There were places without harbors," which has always been the case, this coast being dangerous; yet it is said above that "they landed to wait for good weather." This would be impracticable now, except at Chatham; yet at that day, notwithstanding the absence of harbors, they would find accommodation for their small vessel somewhere between the island and the mainland. From Bradford's History, p. 217, we learn that in 1626-7, there was at this place "a small blind harbore" that "lyes aboute ye middle of Manamoyake Bay," which to-day is filled up by recently formed sandy wastes and salt meadows. This "blind harbore," had at its mouth a treacherous bar of sand. If this harbor had existed in the days of the Northmen, they would not of necessity discover it; and hence while Leif might have landed here and found protection, Thorfinn, in his much larger ship, might have found it needful to anchor, as he appears to have done, in the grounds between Isle Nauset and Point Gilbert, while explorations were being made on the land.

[105] "Honey dew," says Dr. Webb, "occurs in this neighborhood."— Antiquitates Americanæ, p. 443.

[106] This sound may have been the water between Point Gilbert and Isle Nauset.

[107] Archer says in his account of Gosnold's voyage: "Twelve leagues from [the end of] Cape Cod, we descried a point [Point Gilbert] with some beach, a good distance off." It is said that the ness, or cape, went out northward but we must remember that eastward is meant.

[108] This is precisely the course they would steer after doubling that ness or cape which existed in Gosnold's day, and which he named Point Gilbert. The author does not agree with Professor Rafn, in making this point to be at the eastern entrance to Buzzard's bay. If he had known of the existence of the Isle Nauset, he would not have looked for the ness in that neighborhood. At that time Cape Malabar probably did not exist, as we know how

rapidly land is formed in that vicinity; yet it would not have attracted notice in comparison with the great broad point mentioned by Archer.

[109] After passing Point Gilbert, shoal water may almost anywhere be found, which appears to have been the case anciently.

[110] The river was evidently Seaconnet passage and Pocasset river.

[111] This lake is Mount Hope Bay. The writer of the Saga passes over that part of the voyage immediately following doubling of the ness. The tourist in travelling that way by rail will at first take Mount Hope Bay for a lake.

[112] Salmon were formerly so plentiful in this vicinity, that it is said a rule was made, providing that masters should not oblige their apprentices to eat this fish more than twice a week.

[113] It is well known that cattle in that vicinity can pass the winter with little or no shelter, and the sheep on Nantucket, can, when necessary, take care of themselves.

[114] This is an exaggeration, or, possibly, the writer, who was not with the expedition, meant to convey the idea that there was no frost, compared with what was experienced in Greenland and Iceland. The early narrator of the voyage unquestionably tried to make a good impression as regards the climate. In so doing, he has been followed by nearly all who have come after him. Eric the Red told some almost fabulous stories about the climate of Greenland; and yet, because his accounts do not agree with facts, who is so foolish as to deny that he ever saw Greenland? And with as much reason we might deny that Leif came to Vinland. With equal reason, too, we might deny that Morton played the rioter at Merry Mount; for he tells us in his New English Canaan, that coughs and colds are unknown in New England. Lieutenant Governor Dudley of Massachusetts complained of these false representations in his day.

[115] This passage was misunderstood by Torfæus, the earliest writer who inquired into these questions, and he was followed by Peringskiold, Malte-Brun and others, who, by their reckoning, made the latitude of Vinland somewhere near Nova Scotia. Yet the recent studies of Rafn and Finn Magnussen, have elucidated the point: "The Northmen divided the heavens or horizons, into eight principal divisions, and the times of the day according to the sun's apparent motion through these divisions, the passage through each of which they supposed to occupy a period of three hours. The day was therefore divided into portions of time corresponding with these eight divisions, each of which was called an eykt, signifying an eighth part. This eykt was again divided, like each of the grand divisions of the heavens, into two smaller and equal portions, called stund or mal. In order to determine these divisions of time, the inhabitant of each place carefully observed the diurnal

course of the sun, and noted the terrestrial objects over which it seemed to stand. Such an object, whether artificial or natural, was called by the Icelanders, dagsmark (daymark). They were also led to make these daymarks by a division of the horizon according to the principal winds, as well as by the wants of their domestic economy. The shepherd's rising time, for instance, was called Hirdis rismál, which corresponds with half-past four o'clock a. m., and this was the beginning of the natural day of twenty-four hours. Reckoning from Hirdis rismál the eight stund or eighth half eykt ended at just half-past four p. m.; and therefore this particular period was called κατ' εξοχήν, eykt. This eykt, strictly speaking, commenced at three o'clock p. m., and ended at half-past four p. m., when it was said to be in eyktarstadr or the termination of the eykt. The precise moment that the sun appeared in this place indicated the termination of the artificial day (dagr), and half the natural day (dagr), and was therefore held especially deserving of notice: the hours of labor, also, are supposed to have ended at this time. Six o'clock a. m. was called midr morgun; half-past seven a. m., Dagmal; nine a. m., Dagverdarmal. Winter was considered to commence in Iceland about the seventeenth of October, and Bishop Thorlacius, the calculator of the astronomical calendar, fixes sun-rise in the south of Iceland, on the seventeenth of October, at half past seven a. m. At this hour, according to the Saga, it rose in Vinland on the shortest day, and set at half-past four p. m., which data fix the latitude of the place at $41° 43' 10''$, being nearly that of Mount Hope Bay." See Mem. Antiq. du Nord, 1836-7, p. 165. Rafn's calculation makes the position $41° 24' 10''$. It is based on the view that the observation was made in Vinland when only the upper portion of the disc had appeared above the horizon. The difference, of course, is not important. Thus we know the position of the Icelandic settlement in New England. See Antiquitates Americanæ, p. 436.

[116] In those turbulent times children were not brought up at home, but were sent to be trained up in the families of trusty friends. This was done to preserve the family line. Often, in some bloody feud, a whole household would be destroyed; yet the children being out at foster, would be preserved, and in due time come to represent the family. In Leif's day, heathenism and lawlessness were on the decline. We have a true picture given us by Dasent, of the way in which children were treated in the heathen age.

He says: "With us, an old house can stand upon a crooked, as well as upon a straight support. But in Iceland, in the tenth century, as in all the branches of that great family, it was only healthy children that were allowed to live. The deformed, as a burden to themselves, their friends, and to society, were consigned to destruction by exposure to the violence of the elements. This was the father's stern right, and, though the mothers of that age were generally blessed with robust offspring, still the right was often exercised. As soon as it was born, the infant was laid upon the bare ground, and, until the father came and looked at it, heard and saw that it was strong in lung and limb, took it up in his arms, and handed it over to the nurse; its fate hung in the balance, and life or death depended upon the sentence of its sire. That danger over, it was duly washed, signed with the Thunderer's [Thor's] holy hammer—the symbol of all manliness and strength—and solemnly received into the family as the faithful champion of the ancient gods. When it came to be named, there was what we should call the christening ale. There was saddling, mounting and riding among kith and kin. Cousins came in bands from all points of the compass: dependents, freedmen and thralls all mustered strong. The ale is broached, the board is set, and the benches are thronged with guests; the mirth and revelry are at the highest, when in strides into the hall, a being of awful power, in whom that simple age set full faith. This was the Norne, the wandering prophetess, sybil, fortune teller, a woman to whom it was given to know the weirds of men, and who had come to do honor to the child, and tell his fortune.... After the child was named, he was often put out to foster with some neighbor, his father's inferior in power, and there he grew up with the children of the house, and contracted those friendships and affections which were reckoned better and more binding than the ties of blood."—Antiquaires du Nord, 1859, pp. 8-9.

[117] There is nothing in this to indicate that Tyrker was intoxicated, as some have absurdly supposed. In this far off land he found grapes, which powerfully reminded him of his native country, and the association of ideas is so strong, that when he first meets Leif, he breaks out in the language of his childhood, and, like ordinary epicures, expresses his joy, which is all the more marked on account of his grotesque appearance. Is not this a stroke of genuine nature, something that a writer, framing the account of a fictitious voyage, would not dream of?

[118] Grapes grow wild almost everywhere on this coast. They may be found on Cape Cod ripening among the scrub oaks, even within the reach of the ocean spray, where the author has often gathered them.

[119] In Peringskiold's *Heimskringla*, which Laing has followed in translating Leif's voyage for his appendix, this statement of the cutting of wood is supplemented by the following statement: "There was also self-sown wheat in the fields, and a tree which is called massur. Of all these they took samples; and some of the trees were so large that they were used in houses." It is thought that the massur wood was a species of maple. Others have declared that it must have been mahogany, and that therefore the account of Leif's discovery is false. They forget that even George Popham, in writing home to his patron from Sagadahoc, in 1607, says that among the

productions of the country are "nutmegs and cinnamon." Yet shall we infer from this that Popham never saw New England?

[120] See Adam of Bremen's testimony in the Introduction.

[121] It will be noticed that they were close upon the Greenland coast.

[122] They were evidently Norwegian traders who were shipwrecked while approaching the coast and sailing for the Greenland ports.

[123] Gissur, called the White, was one of the greatest lawyers of Iceland. We read that "there was a man named Gissur White, he was Teit's son, Kettlebiarne the Old's son, of Mossfell [Iceland]. Bishop Isleif was Gissur's son. Gissur the White kept house at Mossfell, and was a great Chief."—Saga of Burnt Nial, vol. i, p. 146.

[124] Hialte was doubtless the same person who entered the swimming match with King Olaf. See Saga of Olaf Tryggvesson.

[125] This is an error, unless the writer means that the voyage to Vinland, afterwards undertaken, was a part of the same general expedition. Leif went to Greenland first, as we have already seen.

[126] These pagans did not always yield even so readily as Eric. Some in Norway became martyrs to the faith of Odin. See Saga of Olaf Tryggvesson (passim), in vol. i of Heimskringla.

[127] See note to foregoing account.

[128] These appear to have been married men or secular clergy.

[129] This clearly indicates a voyage around Cape Cod.

[130] This cape was evidently, not Point Gilbert, but the terminus of Cape Cod, known as Race Point, a dangerous place for navigation. It would seem that this was the place referred to, for the reason that the next place mentioned is the east shore, meaning the shore near Plymouth, which is readily seen from the end of Cape Cod in a clear day. It was undoubtedly the vicinity of Race Point that they called Kialarness, or Keel Cape.

[131] Here the version in Antiquitates Americanæ, p. 42, is followed, instead of Peringskiold, whose version does not mention the point of land. This place is regarded as Point Alderton, below Boston Harbor. Thorvald evidently sailed along the shore to this point, which is the most remarkable on the east coast.

[132] These screens were made of planks which could be quickly arranged above the bulwarks, thus affording additional protection against arrows and stones.

[133] These people are sometimes called Smællingar, or small men. Others deduce their name from skræla, to dry, alluding to their shriveled aspect; and others from skrækia to shout. It is evident from the accounts of Egede and Crantz, that they formerly inhabited this part of the country, but were gradually obliged to go northward. It is well known that in other parts

of America, these migrations were common. And these people were more likely to take a refuge in Greenland than the Northmen themselves.

[134] The conduct of Thorvald indicates magnanimity of character, thinking first of his men, and afterwards of himself.

[135] Christianity was introduced by Leif, Thorvald's brother, in 1001-2.

[136] This is evidently an error, for Christianity was introduced by Leif, before he sailed on his voyage to Vinland. Errors like this abound in all early annals, and why should the Icelandic chronicles be free from them? Every such case will be impartially pointed out. The treatment of this passage by Smith, in his Dialogues on the Northmen, p. 127, is far from being candid. He translates the passage thus: "But Eric the Red had died without professing Christianity," and refers the English reader to the Saga of Thorfinn Karlsefne, Antiquitates Americanæ, pp. 119-20, as if he would there find a reason for his rendering of the text, which is unequivocal, and is translated literally above. On turning to the authority in question, we find nothing more said than that "Eric was slow to give up his [pagan] religion," and that the affair caused a separation between him and his wife. That he was slow to give up his pagan belief, would seem to indicate that he did give it up eventually. Moreover, we have the direct statement that he was baptized. Second Narrative of Leif, p. 38.

[137] Norway lay east of Iceland, and hence the people of that country were sometimes called Eastmen.

[138] Winter began October 17. See p. 32, note 6.

[139] They probably had diminutive horses in Greenland, like this of Iceland to-day.

[140] Thorstein Black was a pagan, who nevertheless saw the superior value of the new faith.

[141] We must here remember the simplicity of manners, which then (as now) prevailed among the Icelanders. The tourist in Iceland is always surprised by the absence of all prudery.

[142] Whoever inclines to dismiss this whole narrative as an idle fiction, must remember that all history is more or less pervaded by similar stories. The Rev. Cotton, Mather, in his Magnalia of New England, gives the account of a great number of supernatural events of no better character than this related in the Saga. Some are ludicrous in the extreme, and others are horrible, both in their inception and end. Among other stories, is that of Mr. Philip Smith, deacon of the church at Hadley, Mass., and a member of the General Court, who appears to have been bewitched. He was finally obliged to keep his bed. Then it is said that the people "beheld fire sometimes on the bed; and when the beholders began to discourse of it, it vanished away. Di-

vers people actually felt something often stir in the bed, at a considerable distance from the man; it seemed as big as a cat, but they could never grasp it. Several trying to lean on the bed's head, tho' the sick man lay wholly still, the bed would shake so as to knock their heads uncomfortably. A very strong man could not lift the sick man, to make him lie more easily, tho' he apply'd his utmost strength unto it; and yet he could go presently and lift the bedstead and a bed, and a man lying on it, without any strain to himself at all. Mr. Smith dies.... After the opinion of all had pronounc'd him dead, his countenance continued as lively as though he had been alive.... Divers noises were heard in the room where the corpse lay; as the clattering of chairs and stools, whereof no account could be given."—Magnalia, ed. 1853, vol. i, p. 455. The account is vouched for by the author, who was one of the most learned divines of his day. Another is given, among the multitude of which he had the most convincing proof. He writes: "It was on the second day of May, in the year 1687, that a most ingenious, accomplish'd and well-dispos'd young gentleman, Mr. Joseph Beacon by Name, about 5 o'clock in the morning, as he lay, whether sleeping or waking he could not say (but he judged the latter of them), had a view of his brother, then at London, although he was himself at our Boston, distanc'd from him a thousand leagues. This his brother appear'd to him in the morning (I say) about 5 o'clock, at Boston, having on him a Bengale gown, which he usually wore, with a napkin ty'd about his head; his countenance was very pale, ghastly, deadly, and he had a bloody wound on the side of his forhead. 'Brother,' says the affrighted Joseph, 'Brother,' answered the apparition. Said Joseph, 'What's the matter Brother? how came you here?' The apparition replied: 'Brother I have been most barbarously and inhumanly murdered by a debauch'd fellow, to whom I never did any wrong in my life.' Whereupon he gave a particular description of the murderer; adding, 'Brother, this fellow, changing his name, is attempting to come over to New England, in Foy or Wild: I would pray you on the arrival of either of these, to get an order from the governour to seize the person whom I now have describ'd, and then do you indict him for the murder of your brother.' And so he vanished." Mather then adds an account, which shows that Beacon's brother was actually murdered as described, dying within the very hour in which his apparition appeared in Boston. He says that the murderer was tried, but, with the aid of his friends, saved his life. Joseph himself, our author says, died "a pious and hopeful death," and gave him the account written and signed with his own hand. And now, while New England history abounds with stories like this, men incline to question an Icelandic writer, because he occasionally indulges in fancies of the same sort. Rather should we look for them, as authentic contemporary signs.

[143] Thorhild's Church. See Antiquitates Americanæ, p. 119.

[144] Literally, Biarne Butter-tub, from which we may, perhaps, infer his personal peculiarity.

[145] Throughout this narrative of Thorfinn, the name of Eric occurs where that of Leif should be given. Eric died five years before Thorfinn came over to Greenland. This account having been written in Iceland, the author made a very natural mistake in supposing that Eric was still at the head of the family. The proper change has been made in the translation, to avoid confusion.

[146] Yule was a pagan festival, held originally in honor of Thor, the god of War, at the beginning of February, which was the opening of the Northman's year. But as Christianity had been established in Greenland for five years, the festival was now probably changed to December, and held in honor of Christ.

[147] Widow of Thorstein Ericson. Rafn thinks, as she is mentioned in this Saga by two names, Gudrid and Thurid, that one was her name in childhood, and the other in her maturer years, when Christianity came to have a practical bearing. Her father's name was Thorbiorn, derived from Thor. It was supposed that those who bore the names of gods would find in these names a charm or special protection from danger.

[148] This is a mistake, Eric's son was dead. It must have been another Thorvald.

[149] The Northmen had two ways of reckoning a hundred, the short and the long. The long hundred was a hundred and twenty. We read in Tegner's Frithiof's Saga:

"But a house for itself was the banquet hall, fashioned in fir wood;

Not five hundred, though told ten dozen to every hundred,

Filled that chamber so vast, when they gathered for Yule-tide carousing."

American ed., chap. iii, p. 13.

Professor Rafn infers that the long hundred was here meant, because he thinks that the inscription on Dighton Rock indicates CLI., the number of men Karlsefne had with him, after losing nine.

[150] The present island of Disco, also called by the Northmen, Biarney, or Bear island.

[151] The northern coast of America was called Helluland the Great, and Newfoundland, Helluland, or Little Helluland.—Antiquitates Americanæ, p. 419.

[152] Supposed from the distance to be the Isle of Sable.

[153] Leif had left the keel of his vessel here on the point of this cape, which was Cape Cod. In calling it by this name, they simply followed his example.

[154] This bay was the bay then situated between Point Gilbert and Isle Nauset, which Professor Agassiz proves to have existed. The writers do not mention this island in either of the accounts of Thorfinn's voyage; but it has been shown that Isle Nauset lay close to the shore, so that they would not know that it was an island without particular examination; and if they were aware of its existence, it was not necessary to speak of it. Leif landed upon it, therefore it was mentioned by the author who wrote the account of his voyage. Yet Thorfinn's chroniclers help to prove its existence, by showing that beyond Wonder-strand there was a bay where they could safely ride at anchor for three days.

It must be noticed that the events are not set down in their exact order, for after the writer gets the vessels into the bay, he goes back to speak of the landing of the Scots. Gosnold anchored in this same place in the night, and in the morning he remarked the number of coves, or as he calls them "breaches," in the land. The Saga mentions the same thing, saying that the land "became indented with coves." These coves have now disappeared, yet the testimony of Gosnold shows how accurately the Northmen observed this part of the coast. Like Gosnold, they found it convenient and safe to lie here for a while.

[155] This is the first time we hear of slaves being brought into Vinland. We have already seen that with the proud Northman, slavery was a reality. One of the near relatives of Ingolf, the first Northman who settled in Iceland, was murdered by his Scotch (Irish) slaves.

[156] This was Nantucket or Martha's Vineyard, then probably united, forming one island.

[157] Nantucket island, which then was probably united with Martha's Vineyard.

[158] Straumey, or Straum Isle, which, perhaps, indicates their knowledge of the Gulf stream.

[159] The gull, or some similar bird is here referred to.

[160] Buzzards Bay. The general positions are fixed by the astronomical calculations from the data given in Leif's voyage. See note to p. 33.

[161] The shore opposite Martha's Vineyard.

[162] It would appear from what follows that he was engaged in a heathen invocation. This is the only instance on record of honor being paid to this heathen god on the shores of New England, yet we unwittingly recognize him every time we say Thursday, that is, Thor's Day.

[163] In olden times a certain portion of every whale cast ashore on Cape Cod, formed a perquisite of the clergy.

[164] Literally the Red-beard, as Thor is supposed to have had a beard of that color. The principal deity of the Northmen was Odin, a king who died in his bed in Sweden, and was afterwards apotheosized. He was called the "Terrible god." The souls of men slain in battle were received by him into the hall of the gods. Next was Frigga or Frey, his wife, considered the goddess of earth and mother of the gods. She finally fell into the place occupied by the classic Venus. Next was Thor the Red-beard, synonymous with Jupiter. These three composed the supreme council of the gods. Afterwards came the good and gentle Balder, the Northman's Christ; then came Brage, patron of eloquence and poetry, and his wife Iduna, charged with the care of certain apples, with Heimdal the porter of the gods and builder of the rainbow, and Loke, a kind of Satan or evil principle, aided by his children, the Wolf Fenris, the Serpent Midgard, and Hela, or Death.

[165] We shall see from another part of this work, that the trade at that period between Ireland and Iceland, was very large.

[166] This corresponds precisely to Mount Hope bay. The Taunton river runs through it, and thence flows to the sea by Pocasset river and Seaconnet passage. Hop is from the Icelandic I Hópi, to recede, hence to form a bay. The coincidence in the names is striking.

[167] Perhaps wheat. Sialfsana hveitiakrar.

[168] In Iceland the halibut is called the sacred fish. Pliny uses the same name, which indicates that the water is safe where they were found. The halibut and most of the flat fish, such as flounders, are plentiful in that vicinity. The flounders are easily taken, and those who know how, often find them in very shoal water, burrowing just under the surface of the sand like the king crab.

[169] This is language that might be employed by an Icelander, to indicate the difference between the new country and his own. It may have been an intentional exaggeration, similar to those of Eric in describing Greenland. Yet even if it were a serious attempt at history, it could not be regarded as farther from the truth, than Dr. Cotton Mather's description of the climate of New England, where he tells us that water tossed up in the air, came down ice; and that in one place in Massachusetts, it actually snowed wool, some of which, he tells us, he preserved in a box in his study.

[170] The red shield was the sign of war, and the white, of peace.

[171] This account can hardly be explained. These people, doubtless, had their own ideas of the best method of conducting a fight. They were evidently Esquimaux, and formerly, according to Crantz, appear to have lived

on this coast before it was occupied by the Indians, who, being a superior race, soon drove them away.

[172] This appears childish, yet there is nothing to indicate that it was not so.

[173] Thiorfinn's experience was similar to that of most early colonists in America.

[174] This, very likely, was a short exploration up Narragansett bay.

[175] The ancient Mexicans mixed human blood with bread offered on the altar of their deities.

[176] The lines inclosed in brackets, convey what the writer understood to be a mere rumor. This report was evidently untrue, yet it shows his honest intentions.

[177] They appear to have sailed around Cape Cod, then steered across to Plymouth, coasted up the shore towards Point Alderton, and entered Scituate harbor, or some other river mouth on that coast.

[178] Einfoetingr, from ein, one, and fótr, foot. This term appears to have been given by some old writers, to one of the African tribes, on account of a peculiarity of dress, which Wormskiold describes as a triangular cloth, hanging down so low, both before and behind, that the feet were concealed. In an old work called Rimbigla, a tribe of this class, dwelling in Blaland, Ethiopia, are thus described.—Beamish's Northmen, p. 101. We do not say how far the Saga writer employs his fancy on the Uniped, yet he is quite excusable, considering the weakness of modern writers. In 1634, Hans Egede wrote as follows about a hideous monster: "July 6th, a most hideous sea monster was seen, which reared itself so high above the water, that its head overtopped our mainsail.... Instead of fins, it had broad flaps like wings; its body seemed to be overgrown like shell work.... It was shaped like a serpent behind, and when it dived, ... raised its tail above the water, a whole ship's length."—Egede's Greenland, p. 85; Crantz's Greenland, vol. iii, p. 116. Hudson even describes a mermaid.

The Rev. Dr. Cotton Mather, who has before been quoted, gives among other notable facts in his Magnalia, the statement, that in June, 1682, Mary Hortado, of Salmon Falls, was going with her husband "over the river in her canoe, when they saw the head of a man, and about three foot off, the tail of a cat, swimming before the canoe, but no body to join them.... A stone thrown by an invisible hand after this, caus'd a swelling and a soreness in her head: and she was bitten on both arms black and blue, and her breast scratch'd. The impression of the teeth, which were like a man's teeth, were seen by many."—Magnalia, vol. i, p. 454.

[179] See p. 41. This may be a wrong version of the death of the son of Eric.

[180] The Blue Hills, which extend to Mount Hope.

[181] That is, they fled into their abodes.

[182] The location of this place will be discussed in the Minor Narratives.

[183] This was the teredo, which is often so destructive, and which caused Columbus to abandon a ship at Puerto Bello, because he could not keep her afloat. See Irving's Columbus, p. 287.

[184] This was truly in accordance with the noble spirit of the great Northmen, who had no fear of death, which to heroes, is the shining gate of Valhalla.

[185] This is one evidence that history was cultivated in Greenland.

[186] Here the writer is correct. See note 2, p. 51.

[187] See page 52.

[188] The same bay referred to in the previous account, and which lay between Point Gilbert and Isle Nauset. Archer, in his account of Gosnold's voyage, says, that when they rounded Point Care, the extremity of Isle Nauset, "We bore up again with the land, and in the night, came with it anchoring in eight fathoms, the ground good." Here it will be seen that the Northmen lay safely for three days.

[189] In the first account it is called a Kiafal.

[190] The agreement with the first account is substantial.

[191] This was probably Martha's Vineyard.

[192] The first narrative says substantially the same thing, that Thorhall died in Ireland.

[193] The first narrative speaks of the shoals. The islands and shoals both doubtless existed then. Since that time great changes have taken place in the physical aspects of that region.

[194] This might have been the case on some remarkable season.

[195] This range extends to the Blue Hills of Massachusetts, which indicates considerable activity in exploration.

[196] Also called the Irish sea, and the sea before Vinland.

[197] There were three ships in the expedition, and this was doubtless the company that went in one of them.

[198] These could be easily carried, especially as their cattle were small. All the early Portuguese expeditions carried their live stock with them. See Prince Henry the Navigator.

[199] The different events are here stated with some rapidity, and we seem to reach Leif's booths or huts sooner than necessary. According to the two previous accounts, they did not reach the locality of Leif's booths until the summer after they found the whale. These booths were at Mt. Hope Bay. This is either the result of confusion in the mind of the writer, or else it is

founded on the fact that Leif erected habitations at both places. In the two first accounts of Thorfinn Karlsefne's expedition, they are not alluded to. There may be no real contradiction after all.

[200] The other accounts say that the whale made them sick; but that was not because the flesh of the whale was spoiled. Beamish, in his translation of the song of Thorhall, indeed makes that disagreeable pagan tell his comrades, that, if they wish, they

"Fetid whales may boil
Here on Furdustrand
Far from Fatherland;"

but there is nothing in the text to throw suspicion upon the whale. The trouble was, that a sudden overfeeding caused nausea, and the whale was thrown away afterwards in religious disgust. Yet the event is out of its chronological order, and properly belongs in the account of the next year.

[201] This event belongs to the previous year. These facts are not given in the other accounts, the writer appearing to have different information.

[202] This is another somewhat marvelous occurrence, similar to those with which Cotton Mather and others were accustomed to embellish New England history.

[203] For the previous versions of this affair of the axe, see pp. 60. This last account appears a little plainer.

[204] It is true that he decided to leave the country, but he did not carry out his intention until the following year, 1010. This narrative skips over all the events of the third year. It is nevertheless given, in order that the reader may have the fullest possible knowledge of any shortcomings that may exist in the manuscripts. This is done with the more confidence, for the reason that there is no doubt but that all the narratives contain a broad substratum of solid truth.

[205] From the statement at the end of the voyage of Freydis (see p. 80), we learn that the summer in which he returned from Iceland, Karlsefne went to Norway, and from thence the following spring, to Iceland. This does not conflict with the statement in the above narrative, though at first it may appear to. It does not say that he went the following summer from Greenland to Iceland, but that on that summer, he went to Iceland, which is perfectly true, though poorly stated, and his previous voyage to Norway being ignored.

[206] See p. 48.

[207] Garda was the Episcopal seat of Greenland. Freydis and her husband went to Vinland with Karlsefne. It was she who frightened the Skrællings.

[208] It appears that the route to Vinland had become so well known, that the Saga writers no longer thought it necessary to describe it.

[209] Mount Hope bay is still often called a lake. These waters always appear like lakes. Brereton, in his account of Gosnold's voyage, calls these same bays, lakes. He writes: "From this [Elizabeth] island, we went right over to the mayne, where we stood awhile as ravished at the beautie and dilicacy of the sweetnesse, besides divers cleare lakes, whereof we saw no end."

[210] Freydis was evidently the principal in all things.

[211] By the Icelandic law, a woman could separate from her husband for a slight cause.

[212] According to this statement, the expedition returned very early, as Karlsefne went to Norway the same season, as previously told.

[213] If this transaction had occurred during the previous century, when paganism universally prevailed, this atrocious act of the cold-blooded Freydis, would have been the prelude to almost endless strife.

[214] This account is supplementary to the foregoing, and is taken from the same work. Karlsefne, of course, sailed from Greenland.

[215] Húsasnotru has been translated "house-besom." The exact meaning is not known. A besom-shaft would be too small, however rare the wood, to be made into anything of value. The bar for securing the house door was as common as necessary in every house, and this, perhaps, is what is referred to.

[216] See note 1, p. 36.

[217] In the north of Iceland.

[218] Not far from Skagafiord.

[219] It is understood that she went to Rome. It may be asked why she did not spread the news of her son's voyage in those parts of Europe whither she went, and make known the discovery of the New World. To this it may be replied, that the Icelanders had no idea that they had found a New World, and did not appreciate the value of their geographical knowledge. Besides, there is nothing to prove that Gudrid, and others who went to Europe at this period, did not make known the Icelandic discoveries. At that time no interest was taken in such subjects, and therefore we have no right to expect to find traces of discussion in relation to what, among a very small class, would be regarded, at the best, as a curious story. See note on Adam of Bremen in the General Introduction.

[220] It will be remembered that all this was foretold by her former husband, Thorstein Ericson, when he returned to life in the house of Thorstein Black, in Greenland; from which we must infer that the voyage of Thorstein Ericson was composed after, or during, the second widowhood of

Gudrid, and that the circumstance of Thorstein's prophecy, was, in accordance with the spirit of the age, imagined in order to meet the circumstances of the case. See p. 46.

[221] That is, a Norwegian.

[222] Hvitramanna-land. It will be remembered that in the Saga of Thorfinn Karlsefne (p. 63), this land was referred to by the natives whom he took prisoners. They described it as a land inhabited by a people who wore white clothes, carried poles before them, and shouted. Yet the Saga writer there says no more than that the people think that this was the place known as Ireland the Great. What the Skrællings say does not identify it with the land of Are Marson. Yet, in order to allow Professor Rafn, who held that this country was America, the full benefit of his theory, we give the following extract from Wafer's Voyage, which shows that in the year 1681, when he visited the Isthmus of Darien, there were people among the natives who answered tolerably well to the description given in Karlsefne's narrative. Wafer says: "They are white, and there are them of both sexes; yet there were few of them in comparison of the copper colored, possibly but one, to two or three hundred. They differ from the other Indians, chiefly in respect of color, though not in that only. Their skins are not of such a white, as those of fair people among Europeans, with some tincture of a blush or sanguine complexion; neither is their complexion like that of our paler people, but 'tis rather a Milk-white, lighter than the color of any Europeans, and much like that of a white horse.... Their bodies are beset all over, more or less, with a fine, short, milk-white down.... The men would probably have white bristles for beards, did they not prevent them by their custom of plucking the young beard up by the roots.... Their eyebrows are milk-white also, and so is the hair of their heads." p. 107.

He also adds, that "The men have a value for Cloaths, and if any of them had an old shirt given him by any of us, he would be sure to wear it, and strut about at no ordinary rate. Besides this, they have a sort of long cotton garments of their own, some white, and others of a rusty black, shaped like our carter's frocks, hanging down to their heels, with a fringe of the same of cotton, about a span long, and short, wide, open sleeves, reaching but to the middle of their arms.... They are worn on some great occasions.... When they are assembled, they will sometimes walk about the place or plantation where they are, with these, their robes on. And once I saw Tacenta thus walking with two or three hundred of these attending him, as if he was mustering them. And I took notice that those in the black gowns walked before him, and the white after him, each having their lances of the same color with their robes." But notwithstanding these resemblances, historians will ask for more solid proof of the identity of the two people.

[223] Professor Rafn in, what seems to the author, his needless anxiety to fix the locality of the White-man's land in America, says that, as this part of the manuscript is difficult to decipher, the original letters may have got changed, and vi inserted instead of xx, or xi, which numerals would afford time for the voyager to reach the coast of America, in the vicinity of Florida. Smith in his Dialogues, has even gone so far as to suppress the term six altogether, and substitutes, "by a number of days sail unknown." This is simply trifling with the subject. In Grönland's Historiske Mindesmærker, chiefly the work of Finn Magnussen, no question is raised on this point. The various versions all give the number six, which limits the voyage to the vicinity of the Azores. Schöning, to whom we are so largely indebted for the best edition of Heimskringla, lays the scene of Marson's adventure at those islands, and suggests that they may at that time have covered a larger extent of territory than the present, and that they may have suffered from earthquakes and floods, adding, "It is likely, and all circumstances show, that the said land has been a piece of North America." This is a bold, though not very unreasonable hypothesis, especially as the volcanic character of the islands is well known. In 1808, a volcano rose to the height of 3,500 feet. Yet Schöning's suggestion is not needed. The fact that the islands were not inhabited when discovered by the Portuguese does not, however, settle anything against Schöning, because in the course of five hundred years, the people might either have migrated, or been swept away by pestilence. Grönland's Historiske Mindesmærker, (vol. i, p. 150), says simply, that "It is thought that he (Are Marson) ended his days in America, or at all events in one of the larger islands of the west. Some think that it was one of the Azore islands."

[224] The fact that Are Marson is said to have been baptized in Ireland the Great, does not prove that the place, wherever located, was inhabited by a colony of Irish Christians. Yet this view was urged by Professor Rafn and others, who held that Great Ireland was situated in Florida. A Shawanese tradition is given to prove that Florida was early settled by white men from over the sea. We read that in 1818, "the Shawanese were established in Ohio, whither they came from Florida, Black Hoof, then eighty-five years old, was born there, and remembered bathing in the sea. He told the Indian Agent, that the people of his tribe had a tradition, that their ancestors came over the sea, and that for a long time they kept a yearly sacrifice for their safe arrival."—Archæologia Americana, vol. i, p. 273. Yet these Indians, the supposed descendants of eminently pious Christians from Ireland, were bitterly opposed to Christianity, and had no Christian traditions. This view requires altogether too much credulity. Is it not more reasonable, especially in view of the fact that this narrative is not needed in demonstrating the pre-

Columbian discovery of America—to seek for the White-man's land in some island of the Atlantic; for if we were to allow that six, should mean eleven or twenty days sail, we should not be much better off, since there is so much difficulty in finding the white men for the land in question.

[225] It will appear from this genealogical account, that Are Marson was no obscure or mythological character. In 981 he was one of the principal men of Iceland, and is highly spoken of. Yet his connection with Ireland the Great, though undoubtedly real, hardly proves, what may nevertheless be true—a pre-Scandinavian discovery of America by the Irish. This, not improbable view, demands clearer proof, and will repay investigation. The other characters mentioned are equally well known. See Antiquitates Americanæ, pp. 211-12.

[226] Priest or Gode. This was the heathen priest of Iceland, whose duty was to provide the temple offerings, for which purpose a contribution was made by every farm in the vicinity. This office was also united with that of chief, judge, and advocate, and for the cases conducted by him at the Thing, he received the customary fees; yet he was obliged to depend for his support, mainly upon the products of his farm. The office was hereditary, but could be sold, assigned, or forfeited.

[227] It was west with regard to Norway, the people being accustomed to use this expression.

[228] Killed in Ireland in a battle, 1013.

[229] Literally, woman, with reference to Jörd, the Earth, one of the wives of Odin, and also mother of Thor.

[230] Funeral cups.

[231] Biörn's mother.

[232] This is a fling at Thorodd the Tribute Taker.

[233] This shows, that while Biörn killed the men in self defense, it was the opinion of the court that he did not get what he deserved.

[234] Jomsberg was the head quarters of an order of vikings or pirates, where a castle was also built by King Harold Blaatand, of Denmark. It was situated on one of the outlets of the Oder, on the coast of Pomerania. It was probably identical with Julian, founded by the Wends, and was recognized as the island of Wallin, which Adam of Bremen, in the eleventh century, described as the largest and most flourishing commercial city in Europe. Burislaus, king of the Wends, surrendered the neighboring territory into the hands of Palnatoki, a great chief of Fionia, who was pledged to his support. Accordingly he built a stronghold here, and organized a band of pirates, commonly called vikings, though it must be observed, that while every viking was a pirate, every pirate was not a viking. Only those pirates of princely blood, were properly called vikings, or sea-kings. The Jomsvikings

were distinguished for their rare courage, and for the fearlessness with which they faced death. They were governed by strict laws, and hedged about by exact requirements, and were also, it is said, pledged to celibacy. Jomsberg was destroyed about the year 1175, by Waldemar the Great, of Denmark, aided by the princes of Germany and the king of Barbarossa. Those of the pirates who survived, escaped to a place near the mouth of the Elbe, where a few years after, they were annihilated by the Danes, who in the reign of Canute VI, completely destroyed their stronghold. Accounts of their achievements may be found in the Saga of King Olaf Tryggvesson, in vol. i, of Laing's Heimskringla. The Icelanders sometimes joined the Norway pirates, as was the case with Biörn, but they did not fit out pirate ships. Palnatoki died in the year 993.

[235] Styrbiörn, son of King Olaf, ruled Sweden in connection with Eric, called the Victorious. Styrbiörn's ambition, to which was added the crime of murder, led to his disgrace. He joined the vikings, adding sixty ships to their force. He was killed, as stated, in 984, in a battle with his uncle near Upsula.

[236] Dasent says in describing the coast: "Now we near the stupendous crags of Hofdabrekka, Headbrink, where the mountains almost stride into the main."

[237] Referring to the dead man's blood.

[238] In Iceland the women are accustomed to bring travelers dry clothes.

[239] All of these verses are extremely obscure and elliptical, though far more intelligible to the modern mind than the compositions which belonged to a still older period. All the chief men of Iceland practiced the composition of verse. Chaucer makes his Parson apologize for his inability to imitate the practice.

[240] See the Saga of Burnt Nial.

[241] These sledges were used in drawing hay, as the roads were then, as now, too poor for carts.

[242] This is the only paragraph which applies directly to the subject in hand. The following narrative will bring Biörn to notice again.

[243] Few persons will infer much from this; nothing is easier than to find resemblances in language.

[244] The language indicates that they were riding horseback, though it is not conclusive. And at the period referred to, there were no horses in America, they having been introduced by the Spaniards, after the discovery by Columbus. At least, such is the common opinion.

[245] This is found in Annales Islandorum Regii, which gives the history of Iceland from the beginning down to 1307. Also in Annales Flateyensis,

and in Annales Reseniini. Eric was appointed bishop of Greenland, but performed no duties after his consecration, and eventually resigned that see, in order to undertake the mission to Vinland. He is also spoken of in two works, as going to Vinland with the title of Bishop of Greenland, a title which he had several years before his actual consecration.

[246] The manuscript is deficient here.

[247] The Feather Islands are mentioned in the Lögmanns Annall, or, Annals of the Governors of Iceland, and Annales Skalholtini, or Annals of the Bishopric of Skalholt, written in the middle of the fourteenth century, long before Columbus went to Iceland. Beamish suggests that these are the Penguin and Bacaloa Islands.

[248] "The notices of Nyja land and Duneyjar, would seem to refer to a re-discovery of some parts of the eastern coast of America, which had been previously visited by earlier voyagers. The original appellation of Nyja land, or Nyjafundu-land, would have naturally led to the modern English name of Newfoundland, given by Cabot, to whose knowledge the discovery would [might?] have come through the medium of the commercial intercourse between England and Iceland in the fifteenth century."—Beamish.

[249] See the Decline of Greenland, in Introduction.

[250] Markland (Woodland) was Nova Scotia, as we know from the description of Leif and others. These vessels doubtless went to get timber. All these accounts show that the Western ocean was generally navigated in the middle of the fourteenth century.

[251] In the face of this and a multitude of similar statements, Mr. Bancroft endeavors to make his readers believe that the locality of Vinland was uncertain. He might, with equal propriety, tell us that the location of Massachusetts itself was uncertain, because, according to the original grant, it extended to the Pacific ocean.

[252] See note 1, p. 81.

[253] This is a blunder. The writer must have been more of a geographer than historian. See the Saga of Leif, p. 36.

[254] The part inclosed in brackets is an interpolation of a recent date, and without any authority.

[255] Not to be confounded with, the place of the same name at Cape Cod.

[256] This is another passage upon which Bancroft depends, to prove that the locality of Vinland was unknown, when in the Sagas the position is minutely described, the situation being as well known as that of Greenland.

# The Sagas by Andrew Lang

"The general reader," says a frank critic, "hates the very name of a Saga." The general reader, in that case, is to be pitied, and, if possible, converted. But, just as Pascal admits that the sceptic can only become religious by living as if he were religious—by stupefying himself, as Pascal plainly puts it, with holy water—so it is to be feared that there is but a single way of winning over the general reader to the Sagas. Preaching and example, as in this brief essay, will not avail with him. He must take Pascal's advice, and live for an hour or two as if he were a lover of Sagas. He must, in brief, give that old literature a fair chance. He has now his opportunity: Mr. William Morris and Mr. Eirikr Magnusson are publishing a series of cheap translations—cheap only in coin of the realm—a Saga Library. If a general reader tries the first tale in the first volume, story of "Howard the Halt,"—if he tries it honestly, and still can make no way with it, then let him take comfort in the doctrine of Invincible Ignorance. Let him go back to his favourite literature of gossiping reminiscence, or of realistic novels. We have all, probably, a drop of the Northmen's blood in us, but in that general reader the blood is dormant.

What is a Saga? It is neither quite a piece of history nor wholly a romance. It is a very old story of things and adventures that really happened, but happened so long ago, and in times so superstitious, that marvels and miracles found their way into the legend. The best Sagas are those of Iceland, and those, in translations, are the finest reading that the natural man can desire. If you want true pictures of life and character, which are always the same at bottom, or true pictures of manners, which are always changing, and of strange customs and lost beliefs, in the Sagas they are to be found. Or if you like tales of enterprise, of fighting by land and sea, fighting with men and beasts, with storms and ghosts and fiends, the Sagas are full of this entertainment.

The stories of which we are speaking were first told in Iceland, perhaps from 950 to 1100 B.C. When Norway and Sweden were still heathen, a thousand years ago, they were possessed by families of noble birth, owning no master, and often at war with each other, when the men were not sailing the seas, to rob and kill in Scotland, England, France, Italy, and away east as far as Constantinople, or farther. Though they were wild sea robbers and warriors, they were sturdy farmers, great shipbuilders; every man of them, however wealthy, could be his own carpenter, smith, shipwright, and ploughman. They forged their own good short swords, hammered their own armour, ploughed their own fields. In short, they lived like Odysseus, the hero of Homer, and were equally skilled in the arts of war and peace. They were mighty lawyers, too, and had a most curious and minute system of laws on all subjects—land, marriage, murder, trade, and so forth. These laws were not written, though the people had a kind of letters called runes. But they did not use them much for documents, but merely for carving a name on a sword-blade, or a tombstone, or on great gold rings such as they wore on their arms. Thus the laws existed in the memory and judgment of the oldest and wisest and most righteous men of the country. The most important was the law of murder. If one man slew another, he was not tried by a jury, but any relation of the dead killed him "at sight," wherever he found him. Even in an Earl's hall, Kari struck the head off one of his friend Njal's Burners, and the head bounded on the board, among the trenchers of meat and the cups of mead or ale. But it was possible, if the relations of a slain man consented, for the slayer to pay his price—every man was valued at so much—and then revenge was not taken. But, as a rule, one revenge called for another. Say Hrut slew Hrap, then Atli slew Hrut, and Gisli slew Atli, and Kari slew Gisli, and so on till perhaps two whole families were extinct and there was peace. The gods were not offended by manslaughter openly done, but were angry with treachery, cowardice, meanness, theft, perjury, and every kind of shabbiness.

This was the state of affairs in Norway when a king arose, Harold Fair-Hair, who tried to bring all these proud people under him, and to make them pay taxes and live more regularly and quietly. They revolted at this, and when they were too weak to defy the king they set sail and fled to Iceland. There in the lonely north, between the snow and fire, the hot-water springs, the volcano of Hecla, the great rivers full of salmon that rush down such falls as Golden Foot, there they lived their old-fashioned life, cruising as pirates and merchants, taking foreign service at Mickle Garth, or in England or Egypt, filling the world with the sound of their swords and the sky with the smoke of their burnings. For they feared neither God nor man nor ghost, and were no less cruel than brave; the best of soldiers, laughing at death and torture, like the Zulus, who are a kind of black Vikings of Africa. On some of them "Bersark's gang" would fall—that is, they would become in a way mad, slaying all and sundry, biting their shields, and possessed with a furious strength beyond that of men, which left them as weak as children when it passed away. These Bersarks were outlaws, all men's enemies, and to kill them was reckoned a great adventure, and a good deed. The women were worthy of the men—bold, quarrelsome, revengeful. Some were loyal, like Bergthora, who foresaw how all her sons and her husband were to be burned; but who would not leave them, and perished in the burning without a cry. Some were as brave as Howard's wife, who enabled her husband, old and childless, to overthrow the wealthy bully, the slayer of his only son. Some were treacherous, as Halgerda the Fair. Three husbands she had, and was the death of every man of them. Her last lord was Gunnar of Lithend, the bravest and most peaceful of men. Once she did a mean thing, and he slapped her face. She never forgave him. At last enemies besieged him in his house. The doors were locked—all was quiet within. One of the enemies climbed up to a window slit, and Gunnar thrust him through with his lance. "Is Gunnar at home?" said the besiegers. "I know not—but his lance is," said the wounded man, and died with that last jest on his lips. For long Gunnar kept them at bay with his arrows, but at last one of them cut the arrow string. "Twist me a string with thy hair," he said to his wife, Halgerda, whose yellow hair was very long and beautiful. "Is it a matter of thy life or death?" she asked. "Ay," he said. "Then I remember that blow thou gavest me, and I will see thy death." So Gunnar died, overcome by numbers, and they killed Samr, his hound, but not before Samr had killed a man.

So they lived always with sword or axe in hand—so they lived, and fought, and died.

Then Christianity was brought to them from Norway by Thangbrand, and if any man said he did not believe a word of it, Thangbrand had the schoolboy argument, "Will you fight?" So they fought a duel on a holm or island, that nobody might interfere—holm-gang they called it—and Thangbrand usually killed his man. In Norway, Saint Olaf did the like, killing and torturing those who held by the old gods—Thor, Odin, and Freya, and the rest. So, partly by force and partly because they were somewhat tired of bloodshed, horsefights, and the rest, they received the word of the white Christ and were baptised, and lived by written law, and did not avenge themselves by their own hands.

They were Christians now, but they did not forget the old times, the old feuds and fightings and Bersarks, and dealings with ghosts, and with dead bodies that arose and wrought horrible things, haunting houses and strangling men. The Icelandic ghosts were able-bodied, well "materialised," and Grettir and Olaf Howard's son fought them with strength of arm and edge of steel. True stories of the ancient days were told at the fireside in the endless winter nights by story tellers or Scalds. It was thought a sin for any one to alter these old stories, but as generations passed more and more wonderful matters came into the legend. It was believed that the dead Gunnar, the famed archer, sang within his cairn or "Howe," the mound wherein he was buried, and his famous bill or cutting spear was said to have been made by magic, and to sing in the night before the wounding of men and the waking of war. People were thought to be "second-sighted"—that is, to have prophetic vision. The night when Njal's house was burned his wife saw all the meat on the table "one gore of blood," just as in Homer the prophet Theoclymenus beheld blood falling in gouts from the walls, before the slaying of the Wooers. The Valkyries, the Choosers of the slain, and the Norns who wove the fates of men at a ghastly loom were seen by living eyes. In the graves where treasures were hoarded the Barrowwights dwelt, ghosts that were sentinels over the gold: witchwives changed themselves into wolves and other monstrous animals, and for many weeks the heroes Signy and Sinfjotli ran wild in the guise of wolves.

These and many other marvels crept into the Sagas, and made the listeners feel a shudder of cold beside the great fire that burned in the centre of the skali or hall where the chief sat, giving meat and drink to all who came, where the women span and the Saga man told the tales of long ago. Finally, at the end of the middle ages, these Sagas were written down in Icelandic, and in Latin occasionally, and many of them have been translated into English.

Unluckily, these translations have hitherto been expensive to buy, and were not always to be had easily. For the wise world, which reads newspapers all day and half the night, does not care much for books, still less for good books, least of all for old books. You can make no money out of reading Sagas: they have nothing to say about stocks and shares, nor about Prime Ministers and politics. Nor will they amuse a man, if nothing amuses him but accounts of races and murders, or gossip about Mrs. Nokes's new novel, Mrs. Stokes's new dresses, or Lady Jones's diamonds. The Sagas only tell how brave men—of our own blood very likely—lived, and loved, and fought, and voyaged, and died, before there was much reading or writing, when they sailed without steam, travelled without railways, and warred hand-to-hand, not with hidden dynamite and sunk torpedoes. But, for stories of gallant life and honest purpose, the Sagas are among the best in the world.

Of Sagas in English one of the best is the "Volsunga," the story of the Niflungs and Volsungs. This book, thanks to Mr. William Morris, can be bought for a shilling. It is a strange tale in which gods have their parts, the tale of that oldest Treasure Hunt, the Hunt for the gold of the dwarf Andvari. This was guarded by the serpent, Fafnir, who had once been a man, and who was killed by the hero Sigurd. But Andvari had cursed the gold, because his enemies robbed him of it to the very last ring, and had no pity. Then the brave Sigurd was involved in the evil luck. He it was who rode through the fire, and woke the fair enchanted Brynhild, the Shield-maiden. And she loved him, and he her, with all their hearts, always to the death. But by ill fate she was married to another man, Sigurd's chief friend, and Sigurd to another woman. And the women fell to jealousy and quarrelling as women will, and they dragged the friends into the feud, and one manslaying after another befell, till that great murder of men in the Hall of Atli, the King. The curse came on one and all of them—a curse of blood, and of evil loves, and of witchwork destroying good and bad, all fearless, and all fallen in one red ruin.

The "Volsunga Saga" has this unique and unparalleled interest, that it gives the spectacle of the highest epic genius, struggling out of savagery into complete and free and conscious humanity. It is a mark of the savage intellect not to discriminate abruptly between man and the lower animals. In the tales of the lower peoples, the characters are just as often beasts as men and women. Now, in the earlier and wilder parts of the "Volsunga Saga," otters and dragons play human parts. Signy and his son, and the mother of their enemy, put on the skins of wolves, become wolves, and pass through hideous adventures. The story reeks with blood, and ravins with lust of blood. But when Sigurd arrives at full years of manhood, the barbarism yields place, the Saga becomes human and conscious.

These legends deal little with love. But in the "Volsunga Saga" the permanent interest is the true and deathless love of Sigurd and Brynhild: their separation by magic arts, the revival of their passion too late, the man's resigned and heroic acquiescence, the fiercer passion of the woman, who will neither bear her fate nor accept her bliss at the price of honour and her plighted word.

The situation, the nodus, is neither ancient merely nor modern merely, but of all time. Sigurd, having at last discovered the net in which he was trapped, was content to make the best of marriage and of friendship. Brynhild was not. "The hearts of women are the hearts of wolves," says the ancient Sanskrit commentary on the Rig Veda. But the she-wolf's heart broke, like a woman's, when she had caused Sigurd's slaying. Both man and woman face life, as they conceive it, with eyes perfectly clear.

The magic and the supernatural wiles are accidental, the human heart is essential and eternal. There is no scene like this in the epics of Greece. This is a passion that Homer did not dwell upon. In the Iliad and Odyssey the repentance of Helen is facile; she takes life easily. Clytemnestra is not brought on the stage to speak for herself. In this respect the epic of the North, without the charm and the delightfulness of the Southern epic, excels it; in this and in a certain bare veracity, but in nothing else. We cannot put the Germanic legend on the level of the Greek, for variety, for many-sided wisdom, for changing beauty of a thousand colours. But in this one passion of love the "Volsunga Saga" excels the Iliad.

The Greek and the Northern stories are alike in one thing. Fate is all-powerful over gods and men. Odin cannot save Balder; nor Thetis, Achilles; nor Zeus, Sarpedon. But in the Sagas fate is more constantly present to the mind. Much is thought of being "lucky," or "unlucky." Howard's "good luck" is to be read in his face by the wise, even when, to the common gaze, he seems a half-paralytic dotard, dying of grief and age.

Fate and evil luck dog the heroes of the Sagas. They seldom "end well," as people say,—unless, when a brave man lies down to die on the bed he has strewn of the bodies of his foes, you call that ending well. So died Grettir the Strong. Even from a boy he was strong and passionate, short of temper, quick of stroke, but loyal, brave, and always unlucky. His worst luck began after he slew Glam. This Glam was a wicked heathen herdsman, who would not fast on Christmas Eve. So on the hills his dead body was found, swollen as great as an ox, and as blue as death.

What killed him they did not know. But he haunted the farmhouse, riding the roof, kicking the sides with his heels, killing cattle and destroying all things. Then Grettir came that way, and he slept in the hall. At night the dead Glam came in, and Grettir arose, and to it they went, struggling and dashing the furniture to bits. Glam even dragged Grettir to the door, that he might slay him under the sky, and for all his force Grettir yielded ground. Then on the very threshold he suddenly gave way when Glam was pulling hardest, and they fell, Glam undermost. Then Grettir drew the short sword, "Kari's loom," that he had taken from a haunted grave, and stabbed the dead thing that had lived again. But, as Glam lay a-dying in the second death, the moon fell on his awful eyes, and Grettir saw the horror of them, and from that hour he could not endure to be in the dark, and he never dared to go alone. This was his death, for he had an evil companion who betrayed him to his enemies; but when they set on Grettir, though he was tired and sick of a wound, many died with him. No man died like Grettir the Strong, nor slew so many in his death.

Besides those Sagas, there is the best of all, but the longest, "Njala" (pronounced "Nyoula"), the story of Burnt Njal. That is too long to sketch here, but it tells how, through the hard hearts and jealousy of women, ruin came at last on the gentle Gunnar, and the reckless Skarphedin of the axe, "The Ogress of War," and how Njal, the wisest, the most peaceful, the most righteous of men, was burned with all his house, and how that evil deed was avenged on the Burners of Kari.

The site of Njal's house is yet to be seen, after these nine hundred years, and the little glen where Kari hid when he leaped through the smoke and the flame that made his sword-blade blue. Yes, the very black sand that Bergthora and her maids threw on the fire lies there yet, and remnants of the whey they cast on the flames, when water failed them. They were still there beneath the earth when an English traveller dug up some of the ground last year, and it is said that an American gentleman found a gold ring in the house of Njal. The story of him and of his brave sons, and of his slaves, and of his kindred, and of Queens and Kings of Norway, and of the coming of the white Christ, are all in the "Njala." That and the other Sagas would bear being shortened for general readers; once they were all that the people had by way of books, and they liked them long. But, shortened or not, they are brave books for men, for the world is a place of battle still, and life is war. These old heroes knew it, and did not shirk it, but fought it out, and left honourable names and a glory that widens year by year. For the story of Njal and Gunnar and Skarphedin was told by Captain Speedy to the guards of Theodore, King of Abyssinia. They liked it well; and with queer altered names and changes of the tale, that Saga will be told in Abyssinia, and thence carried all through Africa where white men have never wandered. So wide, so long-enduring a renown could be given by a nameless Sagaman.

Printed in Poland
by Amazon Fulfillment
Poland Sp. z o.o., Wrocław